THE
WRONG
FAMILY

BOOKS BY ELLERY KANE

The House Sitter

The Good Wife

ROCKWELL AND DECKER SERIES

Watch Her Vanish

Her Perfect Bones

One Child Alive

DOCTORS OF DARKNESS SERIES

Daddy Darkest

The Hanging Tree

The First Cut

Shadows Among Us

Lucky Girl (A Dose of Darkness Novella)

LEGACY SERIES

Legacy

Prophecy

Revelation

THE WRONG FAMILY

ELLERY KANE

bookouture

Published by Bookouture in 2023

An imprint of Storyfire Ltd.
Carmelite House
50 Victoria Embankment
London EC4Y 0DZ

www.bookouture.com

Copyright © Ellery Kane, 2023

Ellery Kane has asserted her right to be identified as the author of this work.

All rights reserved. No part of this publication may be reproduced, stored in any retrieval system, or transmitted, in any form or by any means, electronic, mechanical, photocopying, recording or otherwise, without the prior written permission of the publishers.

ISBN: 978-1-83790-493-8
eBook ISBN: 978-1-83790-492-1

This book is a work of fiction. Names, characters, businesses, organizations, places and events other than those clearly in the public domain, are either the product of the author's imagination or are used fictitiously. Any resemblance to actual persons, living or dead, events or locales is entirely coincidental.

For Gar
My partner in crime

"It is a wise father that knows his own child."

- WILLIAM SHAKESPEARE

PROLOGUE

I crouch in the dirt behind a massive tree trunk and wipe the sweat from my forehead. My heart beats like a fist in slow, hard punches against my rib cage. The only discernible sound, the labored hiss of my breathing.

The fire explodes into the darkness, coloring the sky with a fierce orange glow. It spreads quickly. Unchecked, it will raze everything in its path. Horror-stricken, I turn away. If I can't see it, it isn't real. *It isn't real.* I whisper it under my breath to comfort myself, like a frightened child clinging to a favorite toy after a nightmare.

But the longer I stay here, the more real it becomes, until the suffocating heat blankets my skin, and my eyes tear up from the smoke. The crackling, the licking and devouring. The fire makes the noises of a vicious beast consuming the bones of its prey. I can't pretend anymore. This is happening.

I should run away while I have a chance. But my guilt pins me here. My legs feel heavy beneath me, as rooted as the trees. I only make it a few steps before I'm forced to look back into the blazing heart of the fire.

From deep within it, I hear a scream of sheer terror that slices right through me. It divides my life in an excruciating instant, severing the before from the after.

What have I done?

EMAIL

To: Hallie Sherman <hsherman94@pacbell.com>

From: Family Ties DNA Testing and Ancestry Service <familyties@familyties.biz>

Subject: You have a new DNA relative!

Date: May 17, 2022

Dear Hallie,

We are pleased to inform you that our ancestry team has identified a first-degree paternal match for your DNA sample. The details of your match are ready to review at the secure link below. Upon reviewing your match, you may choose to accept or decline an introduction. Your security is our utmost priority. Your personal medical information will never be shared, and your identity will not be revealed unless you accept an introduction.

VIEW MY MATCH

At Family Ties, we believe that knowledge is power. How you choose to use that knowledge is up to you. We wish you the best of luck in exploring what makes you uniquely... *you*!

Sincerely,

The Family Ties Team

ONE

Hallie pretends it's just a normal Wednesday. She attends free yoga at the park at 9 a.m., followed by a stroll through midtown Sacramento to the Old Soul Café, where she orders her usual: two hibiscus mint teas and two blackberry scones, the small luxuries she can barely afford on a waitress's salary. She keeps one for herself and gives the other to Ernie, the homeless vet who parks his wheelchair outside the café and panhandles for change. But it's not a normal Wednesday. Far from it.

He's late. He should've been here ten minutes ago. *Twenty-eight years and ten minutes*, to be honest. But she knows he may not come at all. It would be childish to think otherwise, and she's not a child anymore. The anticipation of disappointment tightens her chest. It's a familiar pain, like the way the scar on her right leg aches just before a storm. Some wounds never heal, no matter how much time passes.

Every time the front door swings open, her eyes flick up, and her heart skips a beat. She sips her tea a little too fast, burning the back of her throat, and glances at her watch. The hunky barista, who always scribbles a smiley face on her to-go cup, watches her with curiosity from behind the counter, but she takes care to avoid his eyes. She doesn't want to encourage his approach. Usually, she takes her order to go. She never sits, never lingers. Never meets a friend for a bite. That would require actually having a friend, and Hallie's never been good at making them. As a kid, her mom had shuttled her from one ramshackle apartment to the next—one school to the next—until finally they'd ended up living in the back of their station wagon in the mall's parking lot. It's hard to invite a friend over when you're sleeping on the rumble seat of a 1990 Mercury Grand Marquis.

"Can I get you anything else?" The barista materializes at the table, blocking her view of the sidewalk with his wide grin and black apron.

Hallie cranes her neck to look around him, certain that the door has opened again. She shakes her head fast and hopes he'll take the hint. She can't afford a distraction. She needs all her focus to get through this. *If* it happens, and especially if it doesn't. She's played out both scenarios, uncertain which possibility terrifies her more.

"Alright. It's just that you don't usually stick around." When the barista rocks on his heels, she catches sight of the doorway.

Hallie knows she should say something. Smile, at least. It's the polite thing to do. But she can't look away from the man approaching the table. He's nothing like she expected. Different from her mother in every way. He moves with purpose. He's a gilded arrow gliding toward her. Tall and sturdy. The way a father should be.

"Are you Hallie?" He sounds exactly like he did on the

phone yesterday. His voice as warm and soothing as an old blanket.

Hers comes out in a squeak. "Robert Thompson?"

When she meets his eyes, the same blue as hers, she's surprised to find them wet with tears. He nods and holds out his hand. The barista scurries away, perhaps sensing that he's stumbled into the most important moment of her life.

She never imagined she would be rendered speechless. That her tongue would just lie there in her mouth, thick and useless. Nor that she couldn't trust her legs, yet she feels like a newborn fawn, wobbly and unsure of herself. When she lets him grab hold of her hand, he doesn't let go.

"It's so nice to meet you, Hallie." He takes a long, admiring look that makes her self-conscious of her ratty sweatshirt and scuffed sneakers. "I still can't quite believe I have a daughter." After a moment, he adds, "Another daughter, I mean. Natalie will be thrilled to get to know you. She always wanted a sister."

"I'm sure she's lovely." Hallie had already spent an hour or more scrolling through Natalie's Instagram page, studying every flawless photo. A twenty-two-year-old food influencer, she exudes the kind of bubbly effervescence that has always eluded Hallie. "And it's nice to meet you too. *Finally.*"

They share an awkward laugh at that. Her father has no idea how hard she's worked to find him, writing letters to every variation of Robert Thompson in the Pacific Northwest between the ages of forty-five and sixty. *Dear Mr. Thompson, I'm looking for my father. The only information I have about him is his name, which you share. I've completed DNA testing through the Family Ties company. Would you consider doing the same?* She's collected the replies like found pennies, hoping for a stroke of luck. But that's all over now. Miraculously, her father is standing in front of her.

Her father! There's so much she wants to know about him—this person who made her and then left her—it stuns her into silence.

"Well..." he begins, just as faltering as her.

"Do you have any other children?" she finally manages to ask, though she already knows the answer. Natalie had posted several candid shots with her younger brother, a rugged outdoorsy type with sandy blond hair that always looked perfectly windblown. The whole family came straight from the pages of an L.L. Bean catalog, sporty and fresh-faced.

"A son, Logan, who just turned twenty-one. He's the typical baby of the family, still finding his way. And what about you? Does your mother know you're here?" Robert scans the tables behind her, as if he's expecting to find Elizabeth Sherman.

Hallie's eyes begin to well. She knew the subject would come up eventually, but had hoped it wouldn't be so soon, before they've even sat down. "She died in a car accident when I was nine."

It sounds so simple, so inconsequential. It's not the right time to tell him the rest. The car drifting across the center line. Blinding lights. Swerve. Screech. Blackness. When Hallie awakened in a hospital bed, her entire world—and her right tibia—had been shattered. Her mother, gone forever without a goodbye. Though Hallie's bone had healed in five months, it had taken years to get her metaphorical legs beneath her again.

Robert's jaw goes slack. The lines in his forehead

deepen. "I'm so sorry to hear that. That must've been horrible for you. And after?"

Hallie can guess what he's getting at. He's wondering just how terribly it all turned out for her. How guilty he should feel. "I didn't have any close relatives. So it was foster care and group homes for me. A lot of them. I've been on my own ever since."

"I wish I had known. We could've taken you in."

"*You didn't know?*" Her knees weaken, and she drops back into her seat. Her mother had cursed Robert Thompson's name so many times; Hallie had always assumed he'd known. But Robert seems sincere, and she has no reason to doubt him. It's a salve, this realization. He didn't choose to set her adrift. It makes her wonder what else she's gotten wrong about the man in front of her.

"I had no clue. Lizzie never told me we had a baby." He pulls out a chair and joins Hallie at the table, where her tea has turned lukewarm.

She stares off for a beat, trying to regain her composure. She doesn't want to start crying like a lunatic. "I can't believe Mom let anybody call her Lizzie. She always said that nickname reminded her of the girl who killed her parents. The one who gave her mother forty whacks."

"And her father forty-one, if I remember correctly." Robert has a nice laugh, kind and jolly. But it fades as fast as a photograph in the sun. "I'd like to tell you that sounds like something she would say, but I'm afraid I didn't know your mother very well."

That makes two of us, Hallie thinks. Nine years is hardly enough to get to know the woman who birthed you. And most of what she does know, she's tried to forget. It hurts too much. Besides, nothing can be done about it anyway. No use crying over spilt milk. "So, how did the two of you meet?"

"Well, to be honest, my memory's a little spotty. I'm not proud to say I did my share of tom-catting as a young man. But we must've been introduced at the bar in Midtown where I worked part-time. Did she ever talk about me?"

Her mouth suddenly dry, Hallie gulps her tea. She closes her eyes, but it's no use. She pictures her mother on that last day. Hollowed out and desperate. It's the version she remembers best. The few happy memories have since flitted away like butterflies. The more tightly she clings to them, the further they slip from her reach. "Only a little. But then, we didn't have much time together."

Robert pats Hallie's hand. It feels strange to be comforted by him—by anyone—and she nearly recoils at his touch.

"I feel like I've let you down. I should've been there," he says.

"But how could you if you didn't even know I existed? Not until my letter."

"*Your letter?*" He puzzles for a bit, rubbing his chin. Hallie notices the little cleft in it, just like hers. Their blue eyes, too, are a match.

"You know, the 'I might be your long-lost daughter' letter. I sent them to every Robert Thompson I could find in the area, with my return address and email. I assumed that's why you did the DNA test."

"Wow." His eyes widen, and she wonders just how crazy she must seem. "I never got your letter. And I had no clue about your search until a few days ago when I opened the email from Family Ties telling me I had a match. A daughter! Shelly—that's my wife—she convinced me to do the DNA test last month. She thought it would be fun for both of us to learn more about our family tree."

Hallie marvels at her sudden dumb luck. Her letter, lost. And yet she still found her needle in the haystack. The singular Robert Thompson who shares half her chromosomes. "Little did she know there were a few extra branches. Was she upset?" Hallie asks.

From the photos on Natalie's Instagram, Hallie can't imagine Shelly angry. She's the kind of put-together woman for whom mothering comes naturally. Natalie had posted a shot of the two of them on Mother's Day, lying side by side on lounge chairs, sipping fruity drinks and looking more like sisters than mother and daughter. Usually, Hallie spent Mother's Day like every other day, trying *not* to think about her mother and failing miserably. Thinking of her only ever made Hallie impossibly sad.

"She was definitely surprised. After twenty-six years together, she probably thought she knew everything about me. You were born in, what, ninety-three? Ninety-four?"

"Ninety-four. I turned twenty-eight a week ago."

"Well, in that case, happy birthday." His smile catches her off guard with its authenticity. "Anyway, Shelly and I met in ninety-six. Believe it or not, we got stuck on a ski lift at Northstar. Two hours later, we went on our first date at the lodge. Six weeks after that we were married. I suppose it's true what they say: when you know, you know."

"And you and my mom... why did you break up?"

Robert's knee bobs anxiously beneath the table. "I'm embarrassed to say I don't recall why we stopped seeing each other or when. If I'm being honest, I didn't even remember your mother's last name until you told me. By the time I met Shelly, I'd moved to San Francisco and settled down quite a bit. The first few years of my twenties are a shameful blur."

"It's okay." Hallie's soul dies a little. "It was a long time ago."

"You're being kind, but it's not okay. I wish I could go back and change it. I treated your mother poorly. That I'm sure about. And I have a lot of regrets about the way I behaved." Those regrets linger on his face, casting a shadow, until they disappear in an instant. He sits up, excited. "I have an idea. It might be too much to ask, but I'd love to get to know you better. To do right by your mother, even though she's no longer with us. What would you say about spending a couple of weeks at the lake with the family?"

"The lake?" Hallie pretends to be curious, but she knows exactly which lake. In Natalie's last Instagram post—red bikini, paddleboard, designer sunglasses—she'd tagged her location, along with handy links to purchase every product with her special discount code. A little more digging had revealed the Thompson family home, a stone's throw from Lake Tahoe. Thanks to the Internet, Hallie learned its worth. A cool 2.5 million.

"Incline Village at Lake Tahoe. We relocated there years ago. My wife and I own a restaurant on the waterfront. The kids help out too. It's picturesque, relaxing. You'd love it."

Hallie has no doubt that she would. Growing up in foster care, she'd never had a real summer vacation. She'd never even seen the ocean. Her mother had promised once to take her to Baker Beach in San Francisco, but then they'd run out of money for gas. They were always running out of money, and Hallie had known better than to ask again. But she and Robert are virtual strangers. This is all moving so fast. Maybe too fast.

"Won't it be awkward though?" She gives voice to her hesitation. "I don't want to impose on your family time."

"I know we just met, but you *are* family. And everyone is dying to meet you." Robert gestures to the counter behind him, to the waiting barista. "Think it over while I grab myself a drink. No pressure."

But Hallie hears the sharp edge of hope in his voice. She knows it well, knows how deep it cuts. She feels it too. The hope of what might be. Of a future with her father in it. A missing piece to her puzzle.

As she waits for Robert to return, her cell buzzes against the table. She glances at the screen, her stomach knotting with dread.

You're late again. Three months past due. Consider this your eviction notice.

Hallie jumps when Robert sinks into the seat next to her, coffee cup in hand. She turns her phone face down on the table, pretending again. Pretending that it's a normal Wednesday and she hasn't just met her absentee father and been kicked out of her dumpy apartment within the same hour.

"Are you sure your wife and kids won't mind a random houseguest?" she asks. "I don't want to cause any problems."

Robert runs a hand through his sleek gray locks and offers a reassuring smile. It's no wonder her mother fell for him. He's handsome, kind, and generous. "Hallie, you're no guest. You're a Thompson. It's no trouble at all."

TWO

Usually, Hallie takes the long way home from the café, stopping to share a laugh and some loose change with Ernie. But today she hurries straight to the diner to beg Maxine for extra shifts. Somehow, some way, she's got to come up with the two grand she owes in rent or risk being homeless. *Again.* It's not like she can move in with the Thompsons permanently and, anyway, Robert will probably change his mind about the visit once he has time to mull it over. She refuses to get her hopes up. Still, Robert's warm smile tugs at her heartstrings, promising more than just a place to stay, but a place to belong.

"You know I wish I could help you, Hallie." Maxine barely glances up from her desk in the back office. Though she doesn't look at all like a woman who wishes she could help, Hallie knows better. Maxine is just like the diner's famous French dinner rolls—crunchy on the outside, buttery soft within. "After last night's little performance, you're lucky I didn't sack you altogether."

"That guy was a jerk. You said it yourself."

"But not to his face. And certainly not while dumping a root beer float in his lap. He's a paying customer."

"I told you it was an accident." Hallie pokes out her lip, playing for sympathy. "And he deserved it. He made pig noises at Darla behind her back."

"Darla can fend for herself, dear. She wasn't born yesterday."

Hallie shakes her head. Thin-skinned girls like Darla don't last at the diner. "She's barely eighteen, Maxi. And he made her cry. Besides, what kind of idiot expects the A La Mode Diner to have vegan, low-cal yogurt? And what kind of pompous ass demands it?"

"You have to learn when to let it go. You can't fight every battle."

"Can I at least come by tonight after the dinner rush and wash dishes? I really need to earn a few extra bucks."

Lifting her rheumy blue eyes, Maxine lets out an exasperated breath. "Alright. But just remember, the customer is king around here. We're old-fashioned that way. I won't be able to let it slide next time."

Hallie reaches across the desk, giving Maxine's bony arm a squeeze. Then, she hightails it out of there. Best to quit while she's ahead.

Hallie tromps up the two flights of concrete steps to the ramshackle studio apartment she can't afford and collects a stack of mail from the rusted box marked 2B. The door sticks, as usual, until she gives it a forceful kick. It bangs open, worsening the eggshell crack in the stucco. The place should be condemned: there's a strange gray spot on the ceiling above the sofa bed that's grown larger in the past year; the hot water always goes out before she's rinsed the shampoo from her hair; and the toilet won't flush without at least sixty seconds of handle-jiggling. But it's four walls and a roof over her head, and it's all hers. Well, at least until her good-for-nothing landlord kicks her out.

Hallie tosses the mail onto the coffee table and opens the fridge, letting the cold air kiss her skin. It's a small but precious gift since the A/C unit heaved its last death rattle two weeks ago. Taking her time, she surveys the pathetic contents. It's mostly empty except for a few takeout containers from the diner and a slice of leftover birthday cake. The kind of chef Hallie wishes she could be would have fresh veggies in the crisper and a crunchy loaf of sourdough in the breadbox. That chef would've finished culinary school and accepted her dream job at El Mar, the only Sacramento restaurant with a Michelin star. Instead, she gave up when her financial aid ran out and took a job bussing tables and answering to assholes. With a sigh, Hallie slides the cake toward her, inhaling its sugary sweetness. After the day she's had—and it's not even noon yet—she deserves a treat.

Her birthday had come and gone nearly unnoticed. Only the girls at work knew, and only because Maxine had told them. She'd gathered the staff in the kitchen after the dinner rush and summoned Darla from the walk-in. When Darla emerged holding the cake and bursting with song, Hallie wanted to run out right then and never come back. But they couldn't have known that her birthday wasn't a day to be celebrated, especially this one. Now, she'd officially outlived her mother by one year. On her walk home that night, she'd spotted the email from Family Ties, unopened at the top of her inbox like a perfectly wrapped present. A gift from the universe.

Hallie stuffs a forkful of cake in her mouth and opens her closet, thinking of Robert's offer. Of the sprawling cabin in Lake Tahoe. Of sunlight dancing on the water. Of fresh air and clear skies. She sections off her A La Mode uniforms, the black slacks and powder-pink button-downs with her name stitched beneath two cherries on the lapel. What's left isn't much to look at. A designer navy blazer she found in a thrift store. A few pilling sweaters. A couple of slinky dresses that don't fit her anymore. What would she pack anyway? She doesn't even own a swimsuit. And what would she pack it in? Her duffel bag smells like sweat and has a rip in the side—only one step up from the plastic trash bags she and her mom had lugged around.

Tapping her cell, Hallie brings the screen to life and opens Natalie's Instagram to scroll through her photos. This girl—this *perfect* girl—is her sister. *Half*-sister, but still. Hallie holds up her nicest dress in the full-length mirror on the closet door. There's a small rip in the hem she didn't notice before, and her brown hair looks dull and stringy in the shine of Natalie's golden locks. She'll never fit in with the Thompsons. She feels thirteen again, showing up for the first day of school in too-short blue jeans from the Goodwill bin and sneakers that pinched her toes so tight she had blisters by lunchtime.

Plate of cake in hand, she flops onto the sofa and takes another comforting bite. She flips through the stack of unopened envelopes. Past due, past due. Final notice. It seems most of her life has been spent with a wolf breathing down her door. Never having enough. After her mother injured her back at work and her disability benefits ran out, they'd careened straight down to the depths of dirt poor. A hole so deep it had been hard to climb up from, especially with her mother weighing them down with her pill addiction.

At least she can happily discard the *return to sender* Robert Thompson letter at the bottom of the pile of mail. Now that she's found the real deal, she's done with the merry-go-round of rejection and disappointment. A trip to Lake Tahoe shimmers like a mirage on the horizon. A father who cares awaits her there, in a beautiful home with the comforts she longs for. A family too. The family she's always wanted. She needs this more than she cares to admit.

Hallie lies back and stares up at the gray spot, beads of sweat already forming beneath her hair. She refuses to look at the wooden box on her bookshelf, though it holds the answer to her troubles. A strand of South Sea pearls. The only possession of value her mother didn't pawn, worth enough to buy herself a wardrobe deserving of the Thompsons. But she won't go there yet. She'll figure something out, like always.

Darla unloads a handful of dirty dishes and screws up her face at Hallie. "You got an invite to Lake Tahoe? Are you kidding me? What are you still doing here?"

"Maxine told you?" At the start of her shift, Hallie had mentioned the invitation to Maxine, one of the few people she'd told about her letter-writing campaign and the unexpected email from Family Ties. Maxine had been uncharacteristically optimistic, encouraging Hallie to give her dad a chance.

"Don't answer a question with a question." Smacking on a wad of bubble gum, Darla leans against the industrial sink, forcing Hallie to meet her doe eyes. "Seriously, girl. I know you live for scrubbing the mac 'n' cheese pan, but this is your dad we're talking about. Your dad in *Lake Tahoe*. It's literally one of the most beautiful places on earth."

"But it's two whole weeks. And I hardly know him. I mean, he seems nice, but what if the rest of the family doesn't want me there? What if I'm not what they're expecting?"

Hallie doesn't need to explain. As a runaway from Los Angeles, she knows Darla gets it. The way she can never trust the ground beneath her feet to be solid.

Darla collects the order for booth five, stopping to cock her head at Hallie. "I'm sure they're just as nervous as you. No family is perfect."

A dizzying carousel of flawless social media images spins round in Hallie's brain. Darla clearly hasn't met the Thompsons. "I know."

"Besides, they're gonna love you. You deserve this, Hallie."

The door swings shut behind her, giving Hallie no chance to protest. Maybe Darla's right, and this stroke of luck really is her birthday present from the universe. Now, if only her fairy godmother would show up to fit her in a ballgown and glass slippers.

"Welcome back, Mr. Sumner."

Elbow-deep in grimy dishwater, Hallie hears Maxine's voice from just outside the kitchen door. She lets her hands rest, listening hard. The scouring pad floats to the top, bobbing on the surface like a stopper.

"I'm delighted you decided to take me up on my offer. A meal on the house. Now, where would you like to—"

"You said you're the manager of this dump, right?"

Hallie bristles as she pulls her hands from the water. Still dripping, she peers through the round window in the kitchen door. Last night's irate customer—Mr. Vegan, Low Cal—glares down his hook nose at white-haired Maxine. Hallie sees Darla skulk into an empty booth.

Maxine takes a step back and ducks behind the register before she answers him. "Yes, I am the manager."

"Well, maybe you can help me. My shirt was ruined last night, and your employee is responsible. I expect to be reimbursed from her paycheck." He holds up a slip of paper, jabbing his finger against it. "Three hundred and fifty dollars. That's what it cost to replace at Neiman's."

"I'm sorry, Mr. Sumner. But the waitress insisted it was an accident. We can't reimburse you for your shirt. I'd be happy to offer you our best booth though."

"Best booth? *Ha.* I'm lucky I didn't get food poisoning at this shithole." A red flush creeps up the man's neck and stains his face. His grip tightens on the receipt in his hand, and Hallie half expects it to burst into flames. "You will pay me for my shirt. I'm the best goddamned lawyer in Sacramento. I can put this whole place out of business."

In the shadow of an ogre like him, tough-as-nails Maxine looks as small as a bird. But she doesn't drop her eyes, even as they glisten with fear.

Hallie can't hold it in another second. Nobody threatens her boss. Hell, Maxine's been like a mother to her, even when Hallie didn't deserve it. She bursts out, aiming her cellphone like a weapon.

"Don't worry, Maxi. I've got your back. His little tirade is going viral." She waves the screen at him, taunting him like a matador in the arena. Too late, she realizes she didn't press record. And where would she post it anyway? While everybody else seems content to broadcast a play-by-play of their lives, Hallie's always felt safer being the anonymous lurker.

She's no influencer like Natalie. She'd never even signed up for Facebook.

"Like hell it is." Outraged, he spins back toward Maxine, spitting as he yells, "I can't believe you didn't fire her."

"The only one getting fired today is you," Hallie bluffs. "Wait till your boss sees this."

"Give me that thing."

When the man swipes a paw at her, Hallie retreats toward the kitchen, baiting him. She tucks her cell away and waits just inside the door, ignoring the rueful shake of the prep cook's head. She can't stop now. Some things just need doing.

"I said, give me—"

The door flies open, and Hallie upends a pot full of gray dishwater. The man's face contorts in shock as the lukewarm water runs down his bald head and soaks his shirt. He flicks a glob of food from his cheek and lets out a frustrated growl.

Wide-eyed and speechless, Maxine rushes in behind him. Hallie realizes she's gone too far. She knows Maxine's look. The disappointed-mom face. It's not the first time she's crossed the line without thinking. A part of her feels stuck at age nine, orphaned and sitting in the social worker's office waiting for the rest of her life to be decided. That's what happens to kids like her, kids in the system. You grow up fast and not at all.

"I'm calling the police." The man shakes out his hands, sending a spray of water onto Hallie's uniform, and retrieves his cell from his drenched shirt pocket. "You're going to jail."

"I'm sorry, Maxi."

"You're apologizing to *her*? I'm the one wearing this filth." He scowls as he stabs at the screen, each jab of his finger more insistent. "It's dead. Now you owe me an iPhone too."

Hallie swallows a bitter lump and passes the man a towel from the counter. He blots at his shirt while she helps him remove several clumps of soggy noodles from his midsection. At least she can try to smooth things over for Maxine.

"Stick it in a bag of rice," she offers. "I'm sure it will be—"

His glare stops her short. She jumps back from the heat of it.

"You will pay for all of this."

Hallie knows the type. Another reason she's never been cut out for customer service. Entitled jerks like him only remind her of the unfairness of life.

Maxine appears beside her and guides her toward the back door, stopping to whisper, "You should leave in case the cops show up."

"Am I fired?"

"I don't have a choice, Hallie. I'm trying to run a business. Besides, you'll be off for two weeks anyway, right?"

Hallie shrugs, as she bites the inside of her cheek to ward off the tears. "It's okay. I understand. I just couldn't stand by and watch him treat you like that. I wasn't thinking straight."

"We'll miss you around here. *I'll* miss you." Maxine gives her shoulder a tender squeeze. "I'll put your last paycheck in the mail."

Hallie nods, though she already knows she may not be there to receive it.

"Take care of yourself, dear."

The door shuts behind Hallie with a final thud, leaving her in the dimly lit alleyway. It smells rotten, especially in the summer, with the asphalt still warm from the heat of the day. But she sucks in a breath anyway, her chest still feeling fluttery from the danger of getting caught.

When she's a few blocks away, she pauses under the glow of the streetlights and reaches into her pocket. She opens the wallet she pilfered, its expensive brown leather made smooth by time. A wad of hundred-dollar bills, a slick black credit card, and a driver's license greets her. She reads the name printed on both. *Andrew Sumner.* Then, she tucks it out of sight and keeps walking in the direction of her apartment.

She hopes Robert won't change his mind about his offer now. Because she can't stay here in Sacramento and, more than ever, she needs a soft place to fall.

Unable to wait until she gets home, she pecks out a few lines to her father and presses send.

THREE

With the window down and the wind whipping through her hair, Hallie feels free. The A La Mode Diner and her rundown apartment in Sacramento are two hours behind her. All she can see is sky and pines and mountaintops, and the sliver of highway snaking up ahead. Robert had made it possible to escape the shambles of her life, if only for two weeks. He'd even insisted on paying for her ride, seeing as Hallie had sold her beater of a Bronco a couple of years ago to help pay for culinary school. She usually liked walking. It gave her time to think, and after a mile or so, the throb beneath her scar focused her. But she couldn't very well walk to Lake Tahoe.

"It won't be long now," the driver tells her, pointing at a sign that reads *Kings Beach*.

Hallie ignores the nosedive of her stomach, turning her attention to her cellphone resting on the seat beside her. She taps out a text to Robert, as he'd requested, attaching a blurry image of the road sign. When it comes to photos, she's no

Natalie. Up until now, her life hasn't exactly been Insta-worthy.

Almost there.

We can't wait to see you!

He writes back right away, which only makes her more nervous. The Thompsons are all there. Waiting. For her. The momentousness of it threatens to overwhelm her. She imagines what her mother would say about it. She certainly wouldn't be happy. But that's exactly how Hallie feels. Happy. Hopeful. At the prospect of building a real relationship with her father. What happens after that she can't say yet, but surely it will be better than the trainwreck she's left behind her.

As the sedan ambles up Lakeshore Drive, Hallie gazes out the window in disbelief. Most of the lakefront homes are hidden behind towering redwoods and elaborate gates. Every so often, she catches a glimpse of sky-blue water that takes her breath away.

"Billionaire's Row," the driver proclaims. "Did you know that Howard Hughes used to live here? Now, it's mostly tech billionaires. Can't blame 'em though. That view is priceless."

Hallie nods, feeling completely out of place. Out of her body, really. As if she's watching herself from a great height. A down-on-her-luck waitress traveling to meet her long-lost father in the middle of a mountain paradise. Could it be that fate has finally tossed her a bone?

The driver taps his brakes and curses under his breath, snapping Hallie back to reality. A deer stops directly in their path. It raises its head and considers them with large, watchful eyes before it darts into the brush and disappears just as quickly.

"Glad it wasn't a bear," the driver says, as he inches the car forward, his head on a swivel.

"A bear?"

He laughs at her, leaving Hallie to wonder if she's in over her head. She's no outdoorswoman. The closest she's been to a bear is the Sacramento Zoo. It's one of her few happy memories of her mother, and it comes back with startling clarity. Her hand, still sticky with ice cream, clinging to her mother's outside the elephant enclosure. Hallie had shouted with glee when the baby had submerged its trunk in the wading pool and sent a spray of water toward them. Twenty years have passed, but she can still hear the rare music of her mother's bright laughter.

The driver makes a left turn and continues up Eagle's Point Drive, past the *DEAD-END* sign, to the address Robert provided. At the end of the street, Hallie sees it. A long banner strung between two massive tree trunks, with gold letters proclaiming, *WELCOME HALLIE!* Her eyes rest there for a moment, disbelieving, then to the classic log cabin nestled at the boundary of a long stone driveway. Several vehicles are parked side by side, including a muddy pick-up truck that Hallie imagines must belong to Robert. It screams dad-mobile.

Hallie remains in the backseat while the driver unloads her suitcases. Handling it with care, he sets them side by side. It was silly to spend so much for a designer logo, but looking at her bag in the shadow of the Thompson home gives her a small bit of comfort. This is the kind of suitcase that belongs in a place like this. For once, she won't look like an outsider.

And no one has to know that inside them is everything she owns.

As Hallie opens the car door, Robert ambles down the sidewalk, his grin stretched as wide as his arms. His approach, sure and steady. Behind him, the rest of the Thompson clan—Shelly, Natalie, Logan—awaits her.

Is Robert expecting a hug? Unsure, Hallie tucks her hands into the pockets of her dress and shifts shyly from one foot to the other. The idea of embracing her father seems so foreign to her that she just stands there, paralyzed by uncertainty.

"You made it." He settles for a handshake.

Before Hallie can work out what to do next, Shelly envelops her in a tight hug. Her lilac perfume smells luxurious. "It's lovely to meet you, Hallie. Welcome to our home. Robert tells me it's your first time here in beautiful Lake Tahoe."

Hallie nods, still tongue-tied. She can't stop staring at the house. It's somehow both majestic and cozy. With a massive picture window that lets in the sunlight, a sweeping roof where the snow would settle in the winter, and a wraparound upper deck for stargazing, it's the home of her dreams. It sits at the center of a manicured lawn insulated by a thicket of sugar pines. Though they'd passed other houses on the way, she can't see them from here. It's only this house, this family. Her.

"Thank you for having me," she says, finally. "Your home is..."

While Hallie mulls over the right word to capture her awe, Natalie homes in on her, beaming.

"I love your hair. And that dress is amazing on you. Those pearls!" She juts out a hand toward Hallie's neck, fondling the pearls that once belonged to Elizabeth Sherman. In the other, she holds her cellphone.

Natalie appears exactly as Hallie expected. Shiny blonde locks, teeth like a white picket fence. As carefully curated as one of her Instagram photographs. Hallie wilts next to her, managing to feel plain in the fabulous Kate Spade sundress she'd bought for the occasion.

"Call me Nat."

"Yeah." Logan snickers, pushing Natalie aside, and offers his hand to Hallie. It's a contrast to his sister's, calloused and strong. "Gnat. G-N-A-T. I keep trying to swat her."

"Shut up, Logan. You're not as funny as you think you are."

"And you're not as cool as your followers think you are."

With a stern shake of his head, Robert steps between them. But his glowering reminds Hallie of a passing storm cloud. All bluster. She imagines he's the kind of dad who lets his kids get away with anything. "Knock it off. You're being rude to our guest."

"Both of you, in timeout." Shelly laughs at her joke.

Her face reminds Hallie a little of her mother's—dewy skin and big, brown eyes—before everything went to hell. In her mother's last days, she turned into a skeleton. Gray skin like a canvas stretched on bone. Eyes flat as old pennies.

"Aren't you glad you didn't grow up with these two troublemakers?" Shelly continues.

Hallie smiles through the sting of it. Even when Natalie and Logan exchange a look that leaves her feeling left out, she watches the whole scene with envy. This is what her life would've been like. Sibling rivalries, inside jokes. Always having enough.

"Hardly grown up, if you ask me," Robert counters.

"Twenty-one and twenty-two, but they still act like teenagers. Maybe you can talk some sense into them."

Hallie remains neutral, reaching for her suitcase before anyone asks her to weigh in on the matter of her half-siblings' immaturity.

But Robert—*her father*, she supposes she should think of him as—intervenes. "Not a chance. You go on ahead. Let Shelly and Nat get you situated. Logan and I will carry your luggage."

Natalie seizes her by the arm. Pulling her in close, she snaps one, two, three selfies. "Gorgeous," she pronounces, taking stock herself before showing Hallie the pics. "My followers are going to love you. What a story!"

Hallie grits her teeth. "Um... I... I'm kind of a private person."

"Don't be silly. You look fab in these."

Fab? Not quite. But she's glad she spent extra for the upscale makeup. Not the cheap drugstore kind she usually wears. "It's not that. I just don't do social media."

While Natalie studies her curiously, as if she'd just sprouted wings, Logan barks out a laugh. "A Luddite like me, huh? Nat won't know what to do with you. She only speaks *influencer*."

"C'mon, Hallie. I'll show you to the guest room." Shelly waves her inside, through the entryway, and up a winding hardwood staircase to the second floor. "It has a wonderful view of the backyard and the grove of sugar pines behind the house."

When she reaches the landing, Hallie stops. She sucks in a sharp breath at the cathedral ceiling with its log trusses. Uncertain where to look first, she settles on the room's centerpiece, a floor-to-ceiling stone hearth and fireplace bookended by two leather armchairs. "This place must be magical in the winter."

Shelly nods wistfully.

"Until you have to dig out from beneath six feet of snow." Natalie grabs a seat at the bar in the open kitchen, spinning absent-mindedly on a stool. She barely lifts her eyes from her screen as she speaks. Hallie hopes she hasn't posted those photos.

"Don't listen to her. Her brother does all the snow-shoveling."

Hallie believes it. Those perfectly manicured hands have never seen manual labor. Hallie checks her fingernails, surprised to find the tangerine polish intact. That gel manicure had been worth it. In fact, it all had been worth it—the clothes, the luggage, the accessories—even though she'd had to set her moral compass back a few years by pickpocketing Andrew Sumner. But that seemed a meager price to pay for blending in seamlessly with a well-to-do family like the Thompsons.

"Your room is this way," Shelly says, meandering through the living room, past the formal dining table, and down the hallway, where the walls are lined with Thompson family photographs. The professional kind. Not the few out-of-focus snapshots Hallie's mom had taken with a disposable camera. Hallie had lost them all anyway, somewhere between the first and second group homes. With the last pieces of her past scattered, she'd floated untethered, not belonging to anyone but herself. Until now.

Hallie stops, gazing at the striking portrait at the end of the hall. Its ornate gold frame catches the sunlight. "That's a beautiful painting of the four of you."

"Robert commissioned it from a local artist shortly after

we moved here. We let her hang her work in the restaurant sometimes so she offered to paint a family portrait. It turned out beautifully, but sitting for it nearly drove me and Robert crazy. Logan and Nat were thirteen and fourteen at the time, so you can imagine the bickering."

Hallie widens her eyes. "How long did it take?"

"At least a month. And I'm making it sound like a chore. But the truth is, it had its moments. We'd just lost Robert's father so it gave us a chance to be together as a family. Those chances are priceless, which is why we're so glad to have you here." Shelly dabs a delicate finger beneath her eye. "Listen to me, going on and on. I know you want to get settled in your room."

Sneaking a last look at the painting, Hallie waits while Shelly turns the brass knob. The luscious hardwood doesn't stick a bit. As smoothly as a gloved hand, the door glides open, beckoning Hallie into her temporary home.

Her knees weaken at the sight of the four-poster bed. The fluffy pillows. Maybe she'll actually wake up without a crick in her neck. On the bedside table another family photograph reminds her of the Thompsons' perfection. From their matching white smiles to their color-coordinated outfits, every detail is accounted for.

"And you have access to the back deck." Shelly points to the double doors that lead outside to the sloping lawn and the thicket of trees beyond.

"I don't know what to say. This is amazing." Hallie sits on the edge of the bed, glancing at her reflection. She hardly recognizes herself with the chic, layered haircut and chestnut highlights she'd splurged on. Though she still can't quite believe she's here, the sight of her astonished face in the mirror seems confirmation enough.

"Just be sure to lock up before bed," says Shelly. "We don't want any uninvited guests." Noticing Hallie's concern, she explains, "Black bears. They've been known to open a door or two. But don't worry, there's bear spray in the closet."

Hallie's jaw drops. "Okay, that part scares me a little."

"We saw one the first night we moved into this house. That was eight years ago now. The big guy must've smelled the pizza box we tossed into the trash. Rob and I woke up to a racket outside. All we saw was the bear's hind legs sticking out of the bin. The next day, we bought bear-proof trash cans."

"I'll be on the lookout," says Hallie. It's exciting, this exotic, new place she's found herself in. It might as well be the moon.

"I'll leave you to it, then," Shelly says. "After you get settled, come downstairs for an early dinner. We're grilling out on the deck. I hope you like burgers."

"Of course. I can help out, if you like." Then, without a thought, she adds, "I'm a chef."

"How wonderful. And you were able to get away from the restaurant? Rob and I haven't gone on a trip in years, and we're only open for dinner five nights a week. Of course, we took tonight off for your arrival, but it's been a long time since we've had a proper vacation."

"Actually, I'm between jobs at the moment. But I used to work at El Mar."

It's out of her mouth before she can stop it. And then, she can't take it back. Because it's been too long since someone looked at her that way. Like she mattered. She'd always reinvented herself for every new foster placement—mathlete, prima ballerina, poet—by taking the path of least resistance. Becoming the girl they'd wanted her to be, hoping to find a place where she fit. This time feels different. She could be the chef she should've been. If she'd grown up with a real family, no doubt she would be.

"That's impressive. I hope you can give us some tips. We'd love to be the first Michelin-starred restaurant in Incline Village."

Hallie catches herself in the mirror again, puts a hand to her neck. Her mother's pearls, smooth beneath her fingers. "It would be my pleasure."

"Hallie, this is delicious." Robert takes another bite of the watermelon and cucumber salad she'd whipped up in the Thompsons' designer kitchen. Until that afternoon, she'd never held a Wüsthof knife, never chopped veggies on a fancy maple cutting board. Her apartment didn't even have a dishwasher. "You're so talented. And I can't believe you worked at El Mar! Shelly and I had dinner there once, for our twentieth anniversary. It was the best meal we've ever had. The service, the ambience, the cuisine. All of it, truly memorable."

Hallie smiles demurely, chewing the last of her burger and dabbing at the corner of her mouth. The setting sun warms her skin like a spotlight. She hopes she's not sweating. "It was a great place to work. I trained under Juan Antonio Feliz."

Finally, Natalie pries her gaze from her cellphone. "Is he as hot in person as he is on *The Gourmet Games*?"

"Hotter. He certainly made it difficult to concentrate on the food. It's lucky I didn't burn the romesco." Hallie laughs. It's not a total lie, since Juan Antonio taught a guest tutorial on sauces at her culinary school. And she had spent the time it took to peel a garlic clove admiring his chiseled jaw line. "He's nice too."

"Don't encourage her," Logan says. "Nat thinks she's going to be his next wife."

Slyly, Natalie lifts one shoulder. "Well, Natalie Feliz does have a ring to it. Don't you think?"

Four sets of Thompson eyes turn to Hallie, expectant. It all feels so strange and a little dangerous. Hallie never considered the Thompsons would draw her into their family quibbles, pulling her like a rope in a tug-of-war. She ducks from the attention, hiding behind her glass of iced tea, until Shelly changes the subject.

"So, how'd you get into cooking, Hallie?"

Foster home number two, Hallie thinks. *You won't ever go hungry if you help with dinner.* Though Hallie had never witnessed her mother so much as boil water, she blurts out, "My mom was a whiz in the kitchen. She always knew how to make something out of nothing."

"I remember that," Robert says.

His earnest look catches Hallie off guard, but she does her best to hold it together. She can reinvent herself here. Be anyone she wants to be. But in the end, she's still Hallie Sherman, desperate for any scrap about her mother. No matter how insignificant. No matter how unlike the mother she'd known.

"*You do?*" she asks.

"Just now, when you mentioned it, it jogged a memory. I think she baked an apple pie for me once. *Delicious.* Do you still have her recipes?"

Hallie taps her head. "Only up here."

"You should come down to the restaurant tomorrow. I'll

introduce you to Nick, our executive chef. Maybe we could put something of yours on the menu."

"Give her a break, Dad." Natalie grabs Hallie again, possessively. She seems intent on securing her as an ally, a co-conspirator, and Hallie desperately wants to be wanted. "Believe it or not, some people actually like to relax on vacation. Not be held prisoner, sweating in a stuffy kitchen."

Logan rolls his eyes. "You're one to talk, Miss Nat's Nibbles. You just don't want her to meet Nick."

"Nat's Nibbles?" Hallie asks, feigning ignorance of her sister's burgeoning business.

"All-natural skinny desserts. I sell them locally, mostly online and by word of mouth. But I'm hoping to expand nationwide soon." With a few clicks, Natalie scrolls through a seemingly endless reel of her sweet treats. Her red lipstick pout and shiny blonde hair backdrop every photo.

"That's Nick," she tells Hallie, holding up another snapshot.

Hallie looks more closely at this one. She hasn't seen it before. Hasn't seen *him* before either.

"He taught me everything I know about baking."

Logan scoffs. "You mean he does your baking for you."

"That's amazing," Hallie tells Natalie, ignoring Logan's jab. "And actually, Robert, I'd love to help out. I want to be useful while I'm here and, of course, I want to spend as much time with you as possible. I feel so lucky to have found you and your wonderful family."

Robert raises his glass and the rest of the Thompsons follow. Finally, Hallie joins in. Robert was right. She's a Thompson now too.

"We're the lucky ones," he says.

FOUR

Hallie wakes to the unmistakable sounds of anger, and for a heartbeat she forgets that she's not in Sacramento. That she's not a little kid anymore, frozen in her bed, listening to her dope-sick mother tear through the motel room in search of the pills she swears she didn't use yet. *Did you flush them? Did you?*

A door beneath her slams, rattling the windows, and she bolts upright.

The darkness of the room unsettles her. Every shadow takes on a sinister new life. The black mirror becomes a portal to another world. Her sundress, discarded on the chair, a figure lying in wait. But Hallie gets up anyway, tossing aside the lush down comforter, and follows the noise to the double doors that lead to the deck outside.

She inches one open, slowly, softly, and strains to hear. The conversation from below travels easily in the silence.

"Way to go, Nat. Now you really pissed Dad off. He'll never let me skip out on bussing tables tomorrow. So much for camping at Goose Meadow." The voice belongs to Logan.

"Oh, he'll get over it. I'm not wrong, you know. I can't believe he invited her here. *Now*. What was he thinking?"

"Well... she is our sister."

"Half-sister. And so what? We share DNA. She's got Dad's chin. But we don't know her. We don't know why she's popped up now or what she knows about us. What if she finds out about—"

The hard snap of a twig interrupts them. Hallie draws a sharp breath between her teeth and peers out beyond the deck to where the tree line begins. A vast canvas of black on black, she sees nothing. She hears nothing. It's too quiet. The woods that struck her as peaceful in the dappled twilight now seem threatening.

"What was that?" Natalie asks.

"Probably a raccoon. Don't be a baby."

Another violent snap, and Hallie's heart hammers.

"No way that's a raccoon. It sounds bigger. Like a..."

Bear, Hallie thinks. But Natalie never finishes.

Instead, the beam of a flashlight appears from the lower deck, aimed toward the forest. Hallie follows it as it skims the underbrush. It dances across the leaves and up into the branches. With a click, the forest goes dark again. Hallie waits, staring into the inky black spaces between the trees. The night stares back at her.

"Told ya. I don't see anything," Logan says. "It must have got a whiff of you and took off."

As her siblings bicker, a shiver zips up Hallie's spine at the thought of someone, something, just out of sight. Watching. But she's afraid to risk the light of the bedside lamp. She wouldn't want Natalie and Logan to know she'd overheard them. So, she staggers in the dark, opens the closet door and drops to her knees, searching for the bear spray. She hadn't noticed it when she hung her clothing.

Shoving aside her things and a few heavy jackets, she frantically claws her way through a stack of quilts and shoeboxes, gasping when a piece of the wall seems to fall open. She gropes blindly until she grips something cold. Hard. Its shape unmistakable, though she's never held one before.

She jerks her hand away and back-pedals toward the bed, clumsily knocking her hip against the nightstand. The framed photograph nearly topples to the floor, but Hallie manages to catch it. Relieved, she clutches it against her chest before setting it upright and taking refuge under the covers. Still, she can't get those four smiling faces out of her head.

Two questions cycle through her brain until she falls asleep. *What is it that the Thompsons are hiding? And why do they need a gun?*

FIVE

The sun's first light seeps in through the double doors, casting the guest bedroom in a soft, rosy hue. Hallie looks to the ceiling, half-expecting to see that damned gray spot. Instead, she's greeted by exposed beams and off-white paint. She turns her head to the closet. It's exactly as she left it—the doors open and blankets strewn across the floor. The smooth black barrel of the gun is visible from her vantage point, half-hidden inside the open wall panel. And there, undeniable, on the top shelf, a red can of Counter Assault Bear Deterrent.

Hallie swings her feet off the bed and pads toward the closet. With sudden urgency, she returns the gun to its secret compartment, reassembles the pile of blankets and shoe-boxes, and tugs the door shut. It feels safer with it buried and out of sight. Maybe she's being silly. With bears on the prowl, it's probably standard practice to keep a gun in the house. But even city girl Hallie knows it's a handgun, not a shotgun, the kind of weapon used to hunt wild animals.

With the rest of the house asleep, Hallie takes her time getting ready. She runs the shower scalding hot for as long as she can stand it and wraps herself in the softest towel she's ever felt. She dresses in the outfit she laid out for herself last night. An olive-green jumpsuit and brown sandals from the trendiest boutique in Midtown. Her pearls, of course. Then, she braids her hair and applies a touch of makeup. Satisfied that her look is worthy of her sister's Instagram, Hallie opens the door and follows muted sounds of conversation down the hallway. Before reaching the kitchen, she stops and presses herself to the wall, listening to the hushed voices of Shelly and Robert.

"I'm sure she'll be fine, Rob. It's probably a jealousy thing. You know how she gets."

"Yeah, that's Nat. Our little green-eyed monster. I thought it was the right thing to do, especially since the poor girl practically raised herself. Maybe Nat's got a point though. It's not the best timing."

"Actually, I think it's perfect timing. It'll help keep our mind off—"

Logan emerges at the top of the landing, interrupting his parents. Mumbling something like *good morning*, he runs a hand through his bedhead and shuffles into the kitchen. Hallie follows, not wanting to risk getting caught eavesdropping. Her eyes widen as the fancy breakfast spread on the bar comes into view—fresh fruit, pastries, boiled eggs sliced in two. It's a far cry from her usual bowl of plain oatmeal. Already, Logan's plate is half-full, one croissant hanging dangerously close to the edge and another half-stuffed in his mouth.

"This is amazing." Hallie tries not to sound like a kid at Christmas and resists the urge to load her plate. It still bubbles up on occasion, the fear of not having enough. Too many times, she'd gone hungry. The grocery money wasted on her mother's pills. Years later, the older girls at the group home bullied her for her lunch. She knows how it feels to make a meal out of bread and ketchup, to fall asleep with an empty pit in her stomach.

Shelly brightens at the sight of her, and Hallie matches her smile. It's impossible not to feel welcome with Shelly pulling out a stool for her.

"We wanted your first morning here to be special. How did you sleep?" Shelly asks.

The argument. The snapping twig. The gun. "Like a log."

"Well, I'm glad to hear it. It can be a big adjustment for some people. Especially when you're used to city living. When we first moved here, the quiet made me nervous."

"Where did you live before?"

"San Francisco, then—"

Robert coughs, takes a sip of orange juice, and coughs again. Hallie waits for Shelly to continue, but she pops a grape in her mouth instead. Then, another.

"*Mom.* Seriously?" Hands on hips, Natalie narrows her eyes at the ample offerings. She carefully selects a small apple, a perfect match for her bright red crop top. "You know I'm cutting carbs right now. I want to be bikini ready for the anniversary cookout."

She glances Hallie up and down. "You're lucky to be skinny as a rail. I'd trade my curves any day for long legs like yours. Unfortunately, I got Dad's chunky gene."

"More for me," Logan counters, snatching his third croissant from the tray. To Hallie, he adds, "On the first weekend of summer, Cerulean sponsors a cookout on the lake. Nat here thinks it's a swimsuit competition."

"I care about my health and fitness. Is that so wrong?"

"I doubt something called the Overnight Skinny Detox is the epitome of health food."

"Says the human garbage disposal."

Hallie laughs at them both. Then, she takes a luxurious bite from a chocolate chip muffin and studies her new family. She suddenly realizes how lonely she's been, and for years too. It's not so bad waking up in a full house, bickering siblings included. Besides, their battling makes her feel included, despite what she'd overheard last night.

"Are you still planning on coming to the restaurant today?" Robert asks her. "You can help prep. Maybe work as a floater during dinner service. I can give you a ride if you'd like."

"I'd love to help. But I don't want to trouble you for a ride. It's so beautiful here. I think I'll walk."

Natalie takes a small bite of the apple and leaves the rest on her plate. "I'll join you. There's nothing like the fresh air off the lake first thing in the morning."

"What?" Logan pulls a face. "You hate to walk. You always complain that it makes you sweat. And messes up your hair and your makeup and your—"

"Well, for your information," Natalie begins, wrapping an arm around Hallie's shoulders, "I want to show my sister around, so I'll make an exception. Maybe we'll even go for a hike on our off day."

"Don't be surprised if she melts," Logan tells Hallie, before he snags the remainder of his sister's apple and takes a monstrous bite.

Ten minutes later, Hallie follows Natalie down the winding path toward the lake. Despite Logan's warning, the air feels crisp, and Hallie can't look away from the clear blue water, visible now between the trees. Its calm surface shimmers in the morning light, inviting her to gaze all the way to the horizon, to the majestic outline of the mountains.

When Natalie stops abruptly and sets her hands on her hips, Hallie nearly bumps into her. Natalie turns to her, eyes narrowed. "Alright, cut the act. Who are you and what do you want with my family?"

Hallie starts to mount a protest. Guilt sloshes in her stomach, making her wish she'd left that muffin untouched. She *has* lied, after all, but not about the important things. She has the email from Family Ties to prove it. And Robert had asked *her* here, not the other way around. She has just as much right to him, to a family, as Natalie.

A burst of laughter startles her back into the moment. "Oh, my gosh. Your face! I should've filmed that. It would've totally gone viral."

Hallie manages a smile, but inside she's wobbling. As if she's just stepped off a rollercoaster with a death drop. "Ha. Ha. Very funny."

They keep walking, side by side, until they reach the main road, a stone's throw from the lake. After they pass a sign for Ski Beach, Natalie points along the shoreline, to an elegant building attached to a pier that extends into the water. "Look. You can see the restaurant from here."

"That's Cerulean?" Hallie stares, dumbfounded. The pictures online were a poor imitation, like a child's drawing of a castle. Standing here, with the sunlight glinting off the bay windows, Hallie can't wait to be inside.

"Striking, isn't it? There's outdoor seating on the pier too. It's magical at night." Natalie links her arm in Hallie's, tugging her along. "And wait till you taste the food. Nick is a genius."

Hallie nods, but she still can't shake her sister's accusation. "Are you really okay with me being here?"

"Jeez. I was kidding." Natalie gives her a playful shoulder bump. "There is one thing I'm curious about though."

"Yeah?"

"What did your mom tell you about Dad? She must've said something."

"Other than his name, not much. Don't tell him that though. I don't want him to feel worse than he already does."

"Your mother must've really hated him then."

Hallie bites her tongue and waits for Natalie to continue.

"Mom always says that Dad was a manwhore until she straightened him out. I guess she was right."

"Your mom called your dad a *manwhore*?"

Natalie's cackle frightens a pair of gulls. Hallie watches as they take to the sky and land on the pier adjacent to the restaurant. "Alright. That's not exactly how she put it. But that's what she meant. What made you try to find him after all this time?"

"Truthfully, I've been looking for years. Like I told your dad, I searched online and started writing letters to every Robert Thompson I could find in the Northwest who fell into the right age bracket. I thought that's why your dad did the DNA test, but it turns out he never got my letter. It must've been lost in mail. So, I guess it was fate."

Natalie stops, regarding Hallie with wide eyes. "Every Robert Thompson? How is that even possible. It sounds..."

"Crazy?" Hallie suggests, walking ahead. The entrance to Cerulean comes into view. Its sign, made entirely of beach shells, captivates her.

"Well, yes. But also a lot of effort and for someone your

mom hardly mentioned. I have to force myself to scribble out a few thank-you notes every Christmas."

"It's important to understand where you come from. Who you come from. To know you belong. Don't you think?" Hallie doubts Natalie can imagine what it's like belonging to no one and nothing. To wake up in the middle of the night in a strange place and be utterly alone. "Besides, it only took one hundred and twenty-one letters."

Natalie's speechlessness only lasts a moment. "And you're not angry?"

"Angry?"

"Yeah. No offense, but I'd be raging if my biological father let me grow up in foster care."

"Your dad said he didn't know about me. How can I be upset if he had no clue I existed?" Hallie walks up the steps and onto the wooden deck that leads to the restaurant's front doors. She can see straight through to the water. It's so blue, so tranquil, she keeps her focus on it. "And, anyway, I think I turned out alright, unless you count the murders."

"The what?"

That deep voice can't have come from Natalie. Hallie spots him then, in the reflection. The handsome face from Natalie's Instagram, framed in thick brown curls. But when she turns to greet him, the warmth in his eyes is unexpected. Heat spreads to her cheeks.

"Oh, uh, sorry. I was just joking."

"I certainly hope so."

Hallie cuts her eyes to her sister, who's already got one arm draped around Nick's svelte shoulders. "Gotcha, Nat. Now we're even."

Natalie smiles sweetly, then gives Nick a squeeze that feels more like a staked claim than a sign of affection. "Nick, meet my sister, Hallie Sherman." She cocks her head, her smile turning to a sour smirk. "Or is it *Thompson* now?"

The question is a kick to the shins. It catches Hallie off guard with its sneaky insinuation. Or is she being too sensitive? She stands there, watching as Natalie saunters past her and into the restaurant. Nick, at least, holds the door for her.

"Did I do something wrong?" Hallie wonders out loud.

"With Nat, there're no such thing as getting even. She's always one step ahead."

For Natalie, *one step ahead* means abandoning Hallie in the kitchen for dinner prep, with a sharp knife and a bowl of potatoes, while she plates and photographs a tray of vegan chocolate chip cookies. A powder pink placard pronounces them *Nat's Nibbles* though Hallie watched Nick pull them from the oven himself.

"Aren't they gorgeous? This one really brings out the warmth in my complexion, doesn't it?"

Is she talking about a cookie? Hallie wonders. But she smiles, nods, and cubes another potato, content with the bustle of the kitchen, the savory smells. The easy-on-the-eyes chef stirring a pan of garlic cream sauce.

"Nick? I was talking to *you*."

"I'm sure they're all equally perfect, Nat. You know my cookies are damn photogenic."

With a huff, Natalie pushes through the swinging door and vanishes into the dining room.

"Is she okay?" Hallie asks.

Nick lifts one shoulder. He doesn't look up from the stove, delivering his answer to the saucepan. "That's just Nat being Nat. Give her five minutes, and she'll be back."

"To take more photos?"

"That's a given."

A few of the prep cooks chuckle, and Hallie staves off a wave of guilt. She wants Natalie to like her.

"Are you two—"

Nick slices his hand through the air, cutting her question off at the knees. "Nope."

"Then, you're—"

"Just friends. I'm woefully single." Nick turns to her and gathers a handful of potatoes, depositing them onto a full-size baking sheet. "You of all people should know. A chef's relationships are doomed. The long hours. The stress."

"The constant smell of garlic in your hair," she adds.

"Exactly." He slides the tray into the oven. Even with his back to her, she can tell he's smiling. "So, El Mar, huh? I applied for a job there once."

Hallie keeps chopping. She will not slice a finger. She will not bleed on this man's countertop. Not when she's lying right to his face. But she has to keep up her fib, since Natalie had wasted no time telling Nick about her sister's work history with heartthrob Juan Antonio.

"Fancy place. They wanted someone with more experience. A culinary arts degree. Preferably a Le Cordon Bleu graduate."

When Nick's cell dings, interrupting him, Hallie quietly releases a breath. As he studies the screen, his face darkens. He looks tired, Hallie realizes. Tired and worried.

"Watch the sauce," he tells her. "I have to make a call."

He slips out the back door, already whispering into the phone, and Hallie's eyes follow him a beat too long. She cries out when the knife's blade sinks into the tip of her thumb. The sight of the blood—a bright red river—drags the memory to the surface again. *Blinding lights. Swerve. Screech. Blackness.* She steadies herself against the counter.

Robert rushes from the dining room to the kitchen doorway with Natalie behind him. "What happened?" he asks.

She's not sure how to answer, so she just holds out her wounded finger. Natalie regards it with abject disgust. But Robert comes closer; his brow furrows.

"Let me have a look." The way he tends to her, gently wrapping her hand in a dishcloth, puzzles her yet again. Her father certainly doesn't seem like the heartless monster her mother warned her about.

LETTER

Bob Thompson c/o Suzette Thompson
16 Amador Place
Carson City, NV

Hallie Sherman
135 Highland Terrace
Box 2B
Sacramento, CA

Dear Hallie,

I received your lovely letter in the mail yesterday. I can't imagine what it must be like to have to search for your father among strangers. I'm sorry to inform you that this Robert Thompson is not the one you're looking for. My husband and I were married before you were born and had many wonderful years together. Sadly, he passed away last February. I wish you the best of luck with your search!

Warm regards,

Suzette

SIX

With the last dinner order—two house salads, one lobster ravioli, one Dover sole—plated and on its way to the table, Robert claps a hand onto Hallie's shoulder. "Thanks for the help tonight. I don't know what we would've done without you. Short-staffed on our busiest night this week. And you, working with an injured hand."

"I'm sure you would've managed just fine."

"Oh, c'mon. You're being modest. It's not every day we have a Michelin-starred chef in our midst."

"Just to be clear, I was only a sous chef. All the credit went to Juan Antonio."

Robert chuckles. "Well, no matter. You certainly know your way around the kitchen."

Hallie's famished. Her feet ache. Her leg too. The cut on her thumb won't stop throbbing. Yet, she basks in the warm glow of her father's praise, even with the little voice in her head calling her a traitor. For as long as Hallie can remember, her mother had made one thing clear: no matter what went wrong for the two of them—flat tire, eviction notice, nosy social workers—blame lay squarely at the feet of one man. Robert Thompson. The sorry SOB who'd left them high and dry. *He didn't deserve us. But if I ever see him again, I'll make him pay.* How many times had she heard that?

"You okay? Am I laying it on too thick?" Robert sounds worried. "Shelly told me not to smother you."

She finds herself elated that he cares what she thinks of him. Eager to reassure her father, Hallie shakes her head. Then, she spots Nick watching, sizing her up. If only he knew she poses no threat to him. That her work at the diner had been small potatoes compared to the rush of a busy restaurant. "Of course not. It's just that you already have a world-class chef. Have you tasted Nick's truffle risotto? It's to die for."

Now, she's the one laying it on. It seems to do the trick because Nick's cheeks flush, and he drops his eyes back to the counter, busying himself with clean-up. She joins in and puts a few bowls in the industrial-sized sink for washing.

"Don't I know it? Actually, I'd love to see the two of you combine your talents and come up with a few new items for the summer menu. It could use a refresh. We can debut some of the items at the anniversary cookout."

To keep her heart from bursting, Hallie gloves up and sticks her hands in the hot water, scrubbing alongside one of the other cooks. It's familiar, the dirty work. That's what she's always done best. "Nick doesn't need me. I'm sure he has—"

"I'd love to hear your ideas," Nick interjects.

"You would?" Hallie risks a glance at him, hoping he's not just saying it for Robert's benefit.

He smiles back at her. "Of course. I could use the help. And I can't resist a good collaboration."

"Like Sonny and Cher?"

"I was thinking more Ben and Jerry."

"I can work with that." She tugs off a glove and extends her hand toward him, surprised at the sureness in his grip. "After all, Chunky Monkey was a creation of sheer genius."

Satisfied with their show of agreement, Robert heads toward the doorway and the bustle of the front of the house. "Then, it's settled," he says, looking over his shoulder. "Finally, one of my kids embraces the family business. Hallie, you have no idea how happy you've made me."

One by one, the staff dwindle until only she and Nick remain in the kitchen. Though Robert offered her a ride back to the house, Hallie declined, hoping to talk to Nick about their plans for the menu. Already, she's started to get excited. A sure recipe for disappointment.

Since Robert and Shelly left, Nick has been quiet, head down in his work, dolloping cookie batter onto several massive sheets. But like the calm before the storm, he radiates tension, and Hallie fears that the cooperative atmosphere from earlier has shifted.

"Are those for Natalie?" Hallie asks as Nick slides the last tray into the oven.

He doesn't answer. A blatant cold shoulder in the pin-drop silence of the empty kitchen.

"You shouldn't let her take all the credit. Not when you're the one doing the work."

His biting laugh confuses her and foretells her worst fears. In the span of one dinner service, once-friendly Nick has changed his mind about her. She winces at the clatter when he drops the mixing bowl into the empty sink, scouring her brain for any shred of evidence of what she's done wrong.

"Sorry, I overstepped. It's not my place to say anything. It's just that, it bothers me that she's—"

"Lying?" He spins around, leveling her with the intensity of his glare. It reminds her of the first week of culinary school. Three of her classmates had fled the kitchen crying. She hadn't figured him for one of *those* chefs, the kind who hurls insults like Ginsu knives and require an extra place setting for their massive egos. "Like you? You never worked at El Mar."

Hallie wishes she could disappear. Instead, she manages a half-hearted protest. "Of course I did. What are you talking about?"

"The little things. Any trained chef knows you don't flip a steak with a fork. It lets all the juices out. Your food is good, but your technique screams amateur."

She's suddenly too tired to put up a fight, too frustrated with herself. She should've known he would see right through her. "Please don't tell Robert. Give me a chance to prove myself. I do have *some* experience."

"Let me guess. Applebee's? Olive Garden?"

Tears spring to her eyes. "The A La Mode Diner, if you must know. I'm a waitress, but Maxine lets me fill in for the lead cook sometimes. And I attended a semester of culinary school. I'm a fast learner, I swear."

He shakes his head with obvious annoyance, but his voice softens at the sight of her dabbing her eyes with her shirt sleeve. "You better be."

When he tosses her a wet scrub brush and points to the bowl, Hallie follows protocol, wanting to show him she's not completely incompetent. She scrapes the bowl into the garbage disposal before dropping it into the wash sink.

"Don't worry," he says. "I won't tell Robert."

Hallie attacks the stainless steel, taking out her frustration with herself. Sticking a fork into a tender cut of Kobe beef. How could she be so stupid? *"Really? Why?"*

Nick takes the bowl from her and dunks it into the rinsing sink. "Did you see how happy he was? He's over the moon about you helping out. I owe him a lot. He's been good to me."

"And that's why you let Natalie take the credit for the cookies?"

He shrugs and sets the bowl onto the rack to dry. "It's a small price to pay. You're not the only one who wants to work in a Michelin-starred restaurant one day."

"Thank you, Nick. I won't let you down."

The corner of his mouth turns up and Hallie finds herself smiling too, until he gestures to the row of black plastic bags sitting near the exit sign. "Did anyone show you where to take the garbage?"

SEVEN

It's just before midnight by the time Hallie lugs the last of the trash bags to the dumpster bay adjacent to the restaurant and manages to hoist it in, carefully securing the bear latch Nick had warned her about. Her arms dangle at her sides like wet noodles, as exhausted as the rest of her. She needs a hot shower, stat. Though Nick let her sample the first batch of his sugar-free snickerdoodles, still warm from the oven, the monk-fruit sweetener has done nothing to boost her energy.

Taking in a breath of cool lake air, Hallie peers into the trees that grow along the shoreline. The longer she looks, the more the darkness reveals, like the thin dirt path that winds between them. Grateful for the hooded sweatshirt Nick lent her—she'd been surprised by the cold summer nights—she tucks her hands inside the front pocket and turns toward the restaurant, eager to head back to her temporary home.

A sudden movement in her periphery stops her. Her whole body stiffens. A slim figure waits at the edge of the woods. Head down, hood up, Hallie can't make out his face. Uneasy, she hurries for the back door, her heart scampering ahead of her. When she reaches it, she lets out a small gasp. It's closed, shut tight. Locked. The stone she'd used to prop it open sits in the grass, mocking her from several feet away.

Minus the prowling black bears, Hallie doesn't scare easily. Not even in the big city, with its smog, traffic, and criminals desperate for a dollar. So she's surprised to feel the grip of fear on her neck in little Incline Village, with its immaculate streets and the single movie theater she spotted on the car ride through town.

She pounds on the door with her fist, then braces herself, uncertain whether she should turn and face the mysterious stranger or take off running.

When the back door swings open, Hallie yips like she's been bitten.

"Lock yourself out?" Nick doesn't try to conceal his amusement.

"I thought you'd left, and I—I saw someone." Breathless, she glances over her shoulder at the bone white tree trunks and the black space between them. The man is gone.

"Probably just some kid trying to scare you. On the weekend nights, they sneak out here to drink at The Grotto."

"The what?"

Nick points down the winding dirt path. "We call it The Grotto. It's just an outdoor space where the restaurant hosts parties and special events. There's even a firepit for roasting marshmallows. I'll show you in the morning."

"I thought the restaurant was closed on Mondays."

"And I thought *you* had a summer menu to plan and a long-lost dad to impress."

Hallie laughs, but she can't shake her unease. Before she follows Nick inside, she takes one last look back. Seeing nothing, she shivers anyway.

. . .

Hallie finds the house key beneath the hide-a-spare rock, exactly where Natalie showed her that morning. She fumbles with the lock, her nerves still humming. Nick had taken her only partway to the house, stopping at the far end of Eagle's Point. As they drove, his phone had buzzed repeatedly from the console. His eyes darted to it each time, as if he might find a bomb attached. After she'd waved goodbye and Nick's muddy jeep disappeared from view, she started jogging. The house had beckoned to her. The warm, rosy glow, her sanctuary.

Finally, the key slides in and the door opens. It's dark in the foyer, but the lights are on upstairs. Hallie pads up the hardwood steps, surprised to find Shelly waiting with a half-empty bottle of wine, her bare feet propped up on the coffee table. She's still wearing the one-shoulder red dress she'd donned for her hostess duties, but her bun has come loose, and her blonde hair spills onto the cushions behind her.

"You're up late," says Hallie.

Shelly pats the sofa cushion next to her and pours a glass for Hallie, dribbling a little on the dark wood. "Oops," she says, blotting clumsily at the spot with a napkin. "It's your first night at the restaurant. I couldn't let you come home to a sleeping house."

"You didn't have to wait up. I'm sure you're exhausted." Hallie takes the glass, grateful for a distraction from red-eyed Shelly, who reeks of alcohol.

"It takes me a while to wind down, especially on the weekends. Rob's always out like a light the moment his head hits the pillow. But me, I'm a worrywart."

Hallie sits at the edge of the cushion and takes a cautious

sip, overthinking her next move. This carefulness, this watchfulness, feels familiar to her, having been her constant companion for the first nine years of her life. *Don't wake Mommy while she's sleeping. Don't give Mommy a headache. Don't look in the nightstand drawer. Mommy keeps her special medicine there.*

"Robert says that you were a big help tonight. That you stepped right in, like you'd been there all along. It's nice seeing him excited. Nat and Logan could take it or leave it, as far as the restaurant's concerned."

"I don't know about that. Cerulean is a huge success. They must be so proud. Meanwhile, I'm probably just getting in Nick's way."

"Did he make you take out the garbage?"

Hallie frowns. "Yes."

"Did you get locked outside?"

"*Yes!* So, he was the one who kicked the rock away?"

Shelly laughs, hiccups, and laughs again. "That's as good a Nick Morelli welcome as you can get. I see he let you borrow his favorite sweatshirt. Nat would have a conniption fit if she saw that."

Hallie finally lets herself relax, leaning back against the sofa with a tired smile. "Let me guess. Did Nick pay off the creepy stranger too? I'll bet he told one of the kitchen staff to lurk in the woods and scare me. I should've known."

The blood drains from Shelly's cheeks and she appears to sober up fast. The urgency in her expression snaps Hallie to attention. Mouth, shut. Spine, straight as a board. "What stranger? What did he look like?"

"Um..."

"Did he say anything to you? Threaten you?"

Hallie can't think of the right words. She can't think of

any words. Not with Shelly's fingers digging into her upper arms, shaking her like a rag doll. Even through the bulk of Nick's sweatshirt, Shelly's nails hurt.

"*Mom?* What's going on in here?" Logan appears at the top of the staircase in his pajamas.

Hallie frees herself from Shelly's panicked grip, retreating to the edge of the sofa.

"It's nothing. Go back to bed."

Logan waits for Hallie to say otherwise, while Shelly's eyes plead with her. She knows what's expected. What's required to cover up for a mother on the verge. She has experience with that sort of thing.

"Everything's fine. We were just talking."

In the silence that follows, Hallie watches his skepticism wane. He mumbles goodnight and his footsteps fade down the steps.

"It's been a long day for all of us," Hallie offers. "I think I'll go to bed now."

"I'm sorry. I don't know what came over me, drinking so much tonight. We've all been under a lot of stress lately and—"

"You don't need to explain. It's already forgotten."

"Thank you, dear. That's awfully kind of you." Shelly takes the glasses to the sink and recorks the bottle. "Could I ask one favor? Please don't mention that stranger to Robert. He'll only blow it out of proportion, and he's already had a warning from his doctor about his blood pressure."

"Of course." Hallie ducks out of the living room, with a sheepish wave, and hurries to the guest bedroom, shutting the door behind her. She pulls the sweatshirt over her head and examines the moon-shaped red marks on her arms in the light of the bedside lamp. The scratches look angry, raw, desperate. No different from Shelly's expression when she'd made them.

Hallie thinks of the faceless stranger in the woods. Then, of the strangers sleeping here. In this house. With her.

Propelled by a sudden urgency, she lunges at the door and locks herself inside.

LETTER

Robbie Thompson
Crescent Bay State Prison
Fog Harbor, CA

Hallie Sherman
135 Highland Terrace
Box 2B
Sacramento, CA

Hi Hallie,

You won't believe how excited I was to get your letter. It made my day... hell, it made my *year*. I don't get too many letters these days, especially since my mom passed away. She was the only one who cared to visit me anymore. The rest of my family can't be bothered, not with a crime like mine. First degree murder, three counts. You see, I'm twenty-five years into a life-term. That's right. They'll be carting me out of here in a pine box. Back door parole is what they call it. So, am I your daddy? For your sake, I hope not.

But if you want to be my pen pal, I sure could use a friend.

Robbie

Inmate Number 88AB7

EIGHT

Hallie beats Nick to the restaurant on Monday morning, walking alone with the sunrise. She hardly slept. It turns out a four-poster bed and two fluffy down pillows have no sway against the power of her imagination. All night, she dreamed of running through the woods chasing a hooded figure. When she finally caught up to him, her lungs burning with the effort, and spun him around by the arm, it ended the usual way. *Blinding lights. Swerve. Screech. Blackness.* And then she woke up, tangled in the sweat-soaked sheets. At first light, she penned a note to the Thompsons, slipped out the door, and headed to Cerulean. In only a day, the restaurant had become her safe place.

Instead of waiting on the front deck, she skirts along the side of the building toward the dumpster bay, uneasy at the prospect of seeing the stranger from last night. In the dappled light of day, the dirt path doesn't look so foreboding, and she finds herself following its winding curves into the sugar pines in search of The Grotto.

The path widens, opening into a grassy clearing

buttressed by massive stones, like the ones that dot the blue waters of Lake Tahoe. On the night of her arrival, Logan had recounted his first thrilling jump from Bonsai Rock, which Hallie imagines resembles these behemoths. Antique black lanterns hang by thick rope from the trees, and three massive oak picnic tables rest side by side, waiting to be filled. But Hallie's eyes go elsewhere. To the beat-up red bike resting against the rockface and the nearby heap of threadbare blankets. The human shape underneath them. A few feet away from the ad hoc camp, Hallie locates the firepit, where a pile of charred wood rests inside a stone enclosure.

She steps closer. "Hello?" And closer still, until she smells the musty odor wafting from the makeshift bed. She leans down, half-convinced she's stumbled upon a dead man. With her foot, she nudges the lump.

It moves, groans. Not dead then.

"Are you alright?"

An ice-cold hand shoots out and seizes her wrist. It's strong. Stronger than hers. Still, with a firm pull, she manages to wrestle her arm from its grasp. She stumbles back, fully prepared to bolt.

"Wait. Don't go." A muffled male voice sounds from under the tattered covers. "I'm cold. And hungry."

"Who are you?" Hallie considers pulling the blanket away to reveal the face beneath. Maybe it's better not to see. "Was it you? Last night outside the restaurant?"

"Hungry," the voice repeats.

Though he frightened her at first, his pleas tug at her heart. It reminds her of the first day she dropped a few quarters in Ernie's cup. *Looking for a home*, his handmade sign had read. She could relate.

"Okay, okay. I'll try to bring you something later. But I

can't make any promises." Hallie retreats a few steps down the dirt trail before she turns around. "And I want to see your face."

The man shifts, burying himself in the warmth of the covers, and Hallie wonders how long he's been here and why. Who he was before he became a man without a place in the world. Already, she regrets speaking to him at all. Her problems have always been more than enough to deal with. But, now, she can't forget him.

Hallie finds Nick seated at a table on the deck overlooking the water, with a notepad in his lap. She follows his gaze across the smooth surface of the lake to the other side, where the mountaintops kiss the sky. Despite her nagging worries, the view leaves her awestruck. It makes her feel small, but not in the usual, invisible way. She could grow accustomed to standing in the shadow of this kind of beauty. It's impossible to look away, despite Nick and his chocolate brown eyes competing for her attention.

Nick, however, seems distracted. He checks his cellphone, then slides it back into his pocket. Moments later, he checks it again.

"So, you're a wise guy, huh? You thought it would be funny to lock me out last night."

A lazy grin stretches across his face. "Shelly told you."

"I won't reveal my sources, but fair warning, you should watch your back or I might toss a few habaneros in your red sauce."

"You wouldn't dare," he teases.

"And I'm keeping your sweatshirt." She shrugs one shoulder, trying to seem mysterious, but nearly trips on the chair he's pulled out for her. At least she's managed to hold his attention.

"Aren't we going inside?" she asks, even as she takes a seat.

"I figured we'd let the view inspire us first. Unless you'd rather stare at a stainless-steel countertop."

"This works." From here, Hallie can read the handwriting on his notepad. *Summer Menu.* Beneath it, a large blank space she can't wait to fill. If only she could focus. Her mind keeps flitting like a bothersome insect from one thought to the next. The view. The gun. The peculiar stranger. Shelly's nails digging into her arm in a panic. What exactly has she gotten herself into?

"I found The Grotto." She sticks a pin in a single squirming notion. "You didn't tell me how beautiful it is back there."

"I figured you'd like it. Wait till you see it all lit up. During the summer, Robert hosts a staff dinner out there at least once a month on our off days. And there's a big get-together before the anniversary cookout."

"How long have you known the Thompsons?" Maybe Nick can help her make sense of her new family. Or at least provide a handsome distraction from her apprehension.

"About eight years, I guess. Time flies."

Hallie leans her ear toward him and raises her eyebrows with expectation, making Nick laugh.

"Alright, I'll tell you the Nick Morelli origin story. But only if you agree to tell me yours."

"That's sort of why I'm here, I suppose. To find out where I came from." She hopes he won't press her for more. There're a lot of dark pages—whole chapters, really—in her story. Chapters she hasn't shared with anyone. "I never imagined Robert would be so generous to invite me into his home."

"I'm not surprised. Robert would give you the shirt off his back. He could see I was going through a rough time when I started as a busboy at the restaurant. He took me under his wing, helped me work my way up the food chain. He even paid for me to go to culinary school. When the last guy left for some fancy hotel in South Lake Tahoe, he promoted me from sous chef. Like I told you last night, I owe him a lot."

"He paid for your tuition?" While Hallie had slaved in the diner, struggling to make ends meet, Nick had taken the tuition money that could've been hers. But she couldn't blame him. She couldn't blame her father either. Sometimes, the worst part of being alone in the world was not having anyone to blame.

"Well, between you and me, he intended for Natalie to go, but she bailed at the last minute. Said her creativity would be stifled in the classroom." Nick's derisive tone tells Hallie that he shares her outrage. "I think she was hoping that he'd gift her the money to expand her fitness business. That was after the makeup line and before the cookie company."

Nick chuckles at Hallie's astonishment.

"And Logan wasn't too happy about it either. He wanted to use the money to buy a bunch of gear for a wilderness venture. Instead, Robert gave the whole staff the chance to earn the money at the anniversary cookout contest. And I won."

"What was the winning dish? It was the risotto, wasn't it?"

"You said yourself that it's to die for."

She rolls her eyes, but she's enjoying the banter. It's been a while since she felt free to flirt, not weighed down by worry and responsibility. She reminds herself to be careful. She knows where flirting can lead, especially with hawk-eyed Natalie already staking her claim.

"What's *your* winning dish then?" He passes her the notepad and pen. "Go on. Wow me."

Hallie feels the warmth in her cheeks. "I can't make anything that fancy. But once I baked a seafood lasagna at the diner. Darla said the cream sauce was the best thing she's ever put in her mouth."

He gives an ironic laugh. "Somehow, I don't doubt that. A cream sauce won't work for a summer menu though. It's too heavy."

"What about lobster grilled cheese? Is it too lowbrow?"

"Are you kidding?" He taps the paper. "Write it down."

Tentatively, Hallie pens the item at the top, wondering if he'll scratch through it later. Now that she's told him the truth about her lack of experience, she can't help but see herself as a pretender. A little girl playing dress-up in her mother's kitchen.

"Can I ask you a question?" She plows ahead, not allowing him a chance to stop her. "Do you think Robert's really happy to have me here? Or was it a pity invitation?"

"Honestly, he seems thrilled. The day he got that email from Family Ties, he announced it to the entire staff. If you ask me, I think he's had it up to here with Nat and Logan. He loves them to death, but they don't share the same passion for the restaurant. You know how it can be with family businesses. It's created some tension over the years."

Hallie doesn't say that she would give anything to know what that's like. To have someone who cares enough to be disappointed in you. "Is that why he's been stressed?"

"How do you mean?"

"Shelly mentioned he's been on edge lately."

Nick's cellphone dings, drawing his attention again. He stares at it for a beat, the deepening crease in his forehead and the clench of his jaw giving him away.

"Is everything okay?" she asks.

Before he answers, Natalie disturbs the peaceful morning. "Are you two seriously working on a day off?"

"I wouldn't call it working. We were just talking about—"

Nick clears his throat, cutting Hallie short. She takes the hint and turns the notepad face down, though she can't imagine why her lobster grilled cheese should be a secret.

"I knew Nick was a workaholic, but you too, Hallie? Don't you want to have a little fun? Explore Lake Tahoe? Get to know your amazing sister?"

That doesn't leave her much choice. "What do you have in mind?"

"A hike to the Galena Creek Falls. It's beginner friendly, and there are like a million wildflowers, if you're into that sort of thing."

"That sounds..." She gives Nick a wary glance. "Fun."

Natalie squeals, pulling her to her feet. "You're invited too, Nick. We'll run home and change and meet Logan at the trailhead."

"I don't know." Nick consults his cellphone again. "I need to make a shopping list for the week and do a deep clean of the restaurant freezer."

Natalie pouts for a moment before trying once more. Hallie can tell she's used to getting her way. "Pretty please. You know Logan's hopeless with directions."

"I thought he was an outdoorsman," Hallie says.

"*Thinks* he's an outdoorsman. There's a big difference." Natalie shares a laugh with Nick. "The last time he went camping, he got his leg caught in a bear trap. The trip before that, he got sick from drinking creek water. He's kind of a disaster."

Hallie grimaces, then turns to Nick, echoing Natalie's pleas. A disaster is the last thing she needs right now before she's even gotten to know her new family.

"Alright. But only because I don't want to have to rescue you later." He looks them both up and down, eyeing Natalie's wedge sandals. "And please, for the love of God, put on appropriate footwear this time."

"I'll have you know those boots were designer. And totally adorable."

"Yeah. Not so much after the heel broke and I had to carry you."

"The photos were priceless though. That brand gave me a sponsorship. So, I'd say it was a win-win. Hashtag *boot addict*."

Hallie listens to their teasing, annoyed by the twinge of jealousy pricking at her insides. Nick would never be interested in her anyway, especially now that he knows she's a liar. Besides, he's a head chef with a head chef's salary at the most popular restaurant in town. They're from two different worlds.

As Hallie trails after Natalie, a sudden rush of guilt threatens to bowl her over. She imagines the homeless stranger, waiting for her, shivering in the chilly dawn beneath those rag-tag blankets. She let him down.

"Give me one minute," she tells Natalie, before she jogs down the path toward The Grotto. She stops short in the clearing and slows her approach. The blankets, gone. The man and his bike too.

Hallie approaches the dead campfire and pokes at the cinders with a stick. She can't tell how long it's been there. In the kindling, atop a few charred fish bones, she spots the curling edges of a photograph that she plucks from the ashes. The image melted, destroyed, save for one face. Younger and thinner, it's still utterly undeniable. That man is Robert Thompson.

NINE

Hallie plants her borrowed hiking poles into the earth and trudges behind Nick. Up ahead of them, Logan and his oversized backpack lead the way, weaving through the trees, compass in hand. Hallie peeks at her watch, not wanting to let on how tired she feels. Or how her right leg has begun to throb. She's accustomed to yoga in the park, not a fifteen percent incline with the sun blazing down on her. Natalie had promised an easy two hours to the falls, but at the trailhead, Logan announced a change of plans. A little-known, steeper route that would lead them across the creek to a waterfall, newly formed after the heavy snowfall that winter. At least she'd thought to buy hiking boots on her shopping spree. These top-of-the-line Merrells are saving her from looking like a total amateur.

Nick slows his pace and waits for her. "Are you alright?"

From somewhere behind her, Natalie groans dramatically.

"That depends," Hallie answers. "Are we close?"

"It's not much farther." Logan stops to take a swig from

his water bottle. He wipes his face, looking more gleeful than exhausted. "Isn't it great? There's not another living soul out here. I'll bet we're the first ones to hike this route this summer."

"And that's a good thing?" Natalie asks. "Isn't this the same trail where those hikers were attacked a few years ago?"

"Attacked?" Hallie's voice cracks.

"Don't listen to her," Nick says. "I heard they were tourists. They probably got spooked by a squirrel."

But Hallie has to agree with her sister. The emptiness of the trail unnerves her, especially with the remnants of that burned photograph lingering in the back of her mind and at the bottom of her pocket. What kind of person burns a family photo? An angry one, she decides.

"There's the bridge," Logan announces. "It won't be long now."

When Hallie spots the footbridge, her stomach somersaults. A bridge should be made of steel and concrete, not rope and wooden planks. A bridge shouldn't sway in the wind. As she makes her way up the steep embankment, her mouth dries at the sight of the churning water just below her feet, deeper and faster than she'd expected.

"Is he serious?" she asks. "I thought it was a creek. That's a raging river."

Natalie finally catches up. "You don't have to do it. You can wait for us here." She dabs on lip gloss from her pocket and straightens her hair, in selfie-mode, before snapping a photo of herself in front of the bridge. Somehow, she manages to glow while Hallie's T-shirt sticks to her back, no doubt drenched with sweat.

Hallie looks back at the trail and surrounding forest. The mid-afternoon sun spotlights the trees nearest them but leaves the rest in shadow. Anything could be hiding just out of view. Anything or *anyone*. Thank goodness she'd thought to bring the bear spray in her backpack. Still, the sound of a twig snapping in the underbrush gives her a chill. "I'll try."

Logan pauses halfway across the bridge to wave them on. "The view is totally worth it. You won't regret it."

"I've heard that before."

Despite Nick's uncertainty, Hallie watches him take the first shaky step across the suspension bridge. It swings under the weight of the two men.

"Go ahead," she tells Natalie.

Her sister traverses the bridge as effortlessly as the catwalk.

Inhaling deeply, Hallie focuses on the other side. On Natalie, already snapping another photo. On Logan, munching on a bag of trail mix. On Nick, waiting for her, with a stupid boyish grin that makes her brave.

Still, the planks wobble under her feet. She can taste the mist of the roiling water on her lips. The rope, thick as it is, tightens in her grip, as if it could snap at any moment. She counts her steps, each one careful, and lets Nick take her hand, guiding her off the bridge and down the slope of the embankment to the valley below. Natalie stops to pick a yellow wildflower, tucking the stem behind her ear for another photo op.

After surviving the bridge, the last half-mile passes quickly with Hallie and Nick discussing the winter's record snowfall, which had left the restaurant without power for three days. The Sacramento winters are too mild for snow, and Hallie finds herself dreaming of a white Christmas in the Thompsons' cozy cabin. Of any Christmas that she doesn't feel compelled to work to snag the holiday overtime.

When she hears the whisper of the falls, Hallie stops chatting. Like a salve to her soul, its soothing sound grows louder. They follow it through a break in the trees.

Gossamer-like water cascades down a sheer cliff face and into a pool that leads back to the pebbled creek bed. The fairytale beauty of it takes Hallie's breath away. Even Natalie rests her phone for a moment.

"I had my doubts, man." Nick claps Logan on the back. "But this is cool."

"Told ya I'd find it," he says, eyeballing his sister. "And we're all still in one piece."

"*Whatever.* The trip is only half over. Don't get cocky now, loser."

Hallie marvels at her siblings, at how differently from her they turned out. She expected to see more of herself in them. To find more in common than a pair of blue eyes. In the age-old debate, score one for nurture. "Does your dad hike a lot?" Hallie asks.

"You mean *your* dad?" Logan chuckles at his joke. But thinking of Robert as hers gives her an unfamiliar sort of comfort. "He used to. He was a real adventurer back in the day. Rock climbing, white-water rafting, deep-sea fishing, he did it all. Remember that trip to Zion, Nat? When we all went hiking in the Narrows? Dad insisted we keep going, even after the rain started and..."

Ignoring her brother, Natalie shoots an arm around Hallie and ropes her into an impromptu photoshoot. Grimacing at the unflattering shot, Hallie cleans a smudge of dirt from her cheek and tucks a stray lock of hair behind her ear. "Don't post that," she begs, already fearing the worst with yesterday's snapshots. That any one of Natalie's followers might recognize her from the diner... or somewhere else. From the past she'd put miles behind her. Unlikely but not impossible.

Natalie taps her screen. "Too late. Don't worry. You look authentic. Like a *Survivor* contestant. No one would ever accuse you of photoshopping."

"Well, thank God for that. I can't think of anything worse."

Though Nick and Logan laugh, Hallie immediately regrets her tone. She should be grateful to her siblings for bringing her here, for opening their home to her. For sharing their father. But Natalie irks her. She's too oblivious to her good fortune.

"So, what happened in the Narrows?" Nick asks. "That place is on my bucket list."

Hallie makes a mental note to Google it later. Her bucket list has always been remarkably short. *Find my father*. In recent years, she'd added, *Become a chef*. Cooking for others gave her a feeling of belonging, even if no one had ever saved her a seat at the table. She wonders if Robert's memory of her mother is accurate. Had Elizabeth Sherman really been a cook? The thought that her mother had given her more than a strand of pearls and an abundance of bad memories leaves Hallie unusually hopeful. But then, Robert had admitted to the gaps in his recollection. He probably had her confused with some other normal Elizabeth.

"Oh, nothing happened." Natalie waves her hand dismissively. "It stormed. The water level started rising. Mom freaked out, so we climbed to higher ground. No biggie."

"You climbing anything seems pretty major." Nick grins over his shoulder, as he reclines on a rock in front of the falls.

While Natalie snaps a few more photos of the falls and

herself—*mostly herself*—Logan adds, "We had help. An adventurer, same as Dad and me."

The way his sister scoffs as he puffs out his chest leaves Hallie feeling sorry for him. The poor guy just wants to be like his dad.

"We should probably head back," Natalie says. "Given your track record, we're bound to get lost."

She leads the way, with Nick following close behind. Logan hangs back, shoulders slumped, still gazing at the falls. Hallie joins him there for one last look and to snag a small heart-shaped pebble that she tucks in the pocket of her jeans next to the remains of the photograph.

"Thanks for taking us here. For what it's worth, I think being a wilderness guide is in your blood. Don't let your sister get you down."

"She's right though. I'll never be enough for him."

Hallie doesn't need to ask who he means. "I doubt that. Your dad seems so proud of both of you." An ache fills her chest, raw and bone-deep, for what might have been. "I wish I had that."

"It's not all it's cracked up to be." Muttering to himself, Logan takes off. He leaves her a few steps behind, and she strains to hear him over the sound of the waterfall, only managing to make out a few words. "You don't... about... yet."

Hallie stands there, weighted by her confusion, until she hears a rustling in the trees behind her. Glimpses a flash of movement too fast to register. Feels a pair of unseen eyes upon her. When Nick calls to her from the trail, she propels herself forward with her hiking poles. Convinced they're not alone out here, she quickly catches up to the group.

The rumble of the creek grows more thunderous with each step. But its roaring is no match for Logan's outburst.

Fists clenched, he shouts in anger. She looks past him, searching for the footbridge.

"Are we in the wrong spot?" Natalie asks, echoing Hallie's thoughts.

Logan shakes his head and points down at the stakes that once secured the rope and planks. "The bridge is gone."

In disbelief, Nick marches past the two of them and joins Logan near the drop-off of the embankment. The way he gazes down at the creek makes Hallie's heart race. She wants to stay here in this spot, safe from the raging water, but Natalie drags her forward until they reach the edge. She leans over, peering into the swirling rapids, and gasps. The bridge swings like a pendulum from the other side, jostled by the current.

Hallie takes a step back, reeling. In the soft dirt near the stakes, she spots boot prints. "Are those your tracks?" she asks Logan.

"Nope." He kicks at the stake, where the end of the thick rope lies, severed. "It's been cut. Someone cut the goddamn ropes."

"*What?*" Natalie looks around, as if she's expecting a camera crew to step from behind the redwoods and tell her it's all a joke. When reality sets in, her mouth drops open. Her skin turns ghost-white. "What kind of psycho would do that? Are you sure it wasn't washed away by the river?"

"That's a thick rope to cut through," Nick adds, obviously skeptical.

"Not if you have a serrated blade. It's made for a job like this." Logan drops to one knee and holds the split piece in his hand. "Anyway, I think the most important question is how are we going to get back?"

"I don't know, little brother. You're the master outdoorsman."

Hallie swallows her fear. She can do this. She can be useful. "Isn't there another place we can cross?"

No one answers, and her question hangs there for a moment, seemingly as useless as the bridge itself. She certainly doesn't want to wait here any longer with a psycho, as Natalie put it, wielding a knife, leering at them from the brush.

"We have my hiking poles," she tries again. "Can't we use those to help us?"

"You're right," Nick says. "Let's not panic. We'll hike downstream a bit, where the river widens. It'll be safer to make an attempt there."

"This is crazy." Disgusted, Logan drops the sliced end of the rope and trudges off after Nick. "I can't catch a break."

Hallie knows exactly how that feels. She leans down to study the rope, still determined to talk herself out of Logan's theory. The rope, cut? Surely not. But it's knotted tightly to the stake and doesn't give when she tugs on it. As much as it unnerves her to admit it, she can't deny the clean slice through the thick fibers or the tracks in the earth. The current didn't do this. An animal neither. At least not the kind on four legs. She hurries after the rest of them without looking back.

TEN

Knee deep in the frigid water, Hallie struggles to keep her balance. It swirls around her, leaving a fine mist on her skin, and the pebbles on the creek bed shift every time she tries to spear the bottom. In the ice cold, her scar starts to ache, reminding her that, no matter how far she travels, the past is never far away. Nick holds tight to her other hand, as they coordinate their steps—slow and measured—to the other bank.

From behind her, Hallie hears her sister huffing. Out of anger or fear, it's impossible to tell. But Hallie knows she's not happy. Not with Logan. Not with Nick. And certainly not with her. After they'd finally found a spot low enough for crossing, Nick had paired off with Hallie to make the risky trek. Natalie's pouting made no sense to Hallie or to her brother, who let her know, in the most annoying voice he could muster, exactly how she was acting. *Like a spoiled brat.*

Nick plants one boot on solid ground, then the other. Effortlessly, he pulls Hallie up behind him. She stumbles, grabbing on to his forearms before she manages to find her footing. By the time she steadies herself, her siblings have almost reached the shore, with Natalie clinging to the other hiking pole, teeth chattering. Without warning, she tosses the pole onto the bank and lunges toward safety. Her feet slide from beneath her, and she lands hard, her lower half submerged in the water.

"What the hell, Nat?" Logan hauls her up and shoves her forward. Soaked and shivering, she stomps off, heading up the embankment alone.

"I'll check on her." Hallie follows her to the path, trailing her wet footprints.

Natalie doesn't stop when Hallie calls to her; anger seems to quicken her pace to an arm-pumping march. She may not know where she's going, but she'll get there fast and first.

With no choice, Hallie gives up. "Is she mad at *me*?"

"She's probably embarrassed that she bit it in front of Nick." Logan heaves a weary sigh. "Just let her go. It's the best thing to do. Give her time to cool down."

Sure enough, an hour later, Natalie waits for them at the trailhead. Her wet clothes swapped for a set of dry ones. When Hallie smiles at her, she turns her head, pretending not to notice, and mutters, "About time you made it. I've been waiting on you slackers forever."

"We should probably call the park service and let them know about the bridge," Nick says.

"Already done. I tagged them on Instagram." Natalie holds up her cell for proof. "And I updated my review from last year. *One star.* I could've drowned."

"The park service has reviews?" Nick wonders.

A smirk toys at the end of Logan's mouth. "Hell, I'm still stuck on the first part. The park service has Instagram?"

Practically growling, Natalie stamps off toward the car. It's going to be a long drive back to the house. Hallie would rather stay here, sneaking peeks at Nick's bare chest, as he tugs a clean T-shirt over his head. But she knows better than to be caught looking.

"Wait up." As she jogs, her boots squish against her wet feet, and she's certain her nose is a little sunburned, but she feels accomplished. City girl Hallie can hardly believe she crossed a running river.

Her good feelings vanish when Natalie stops abruptly and hisses, "Did you do this?"

"Do what?"

"Sabotage the bridge."

Stunned, Hallie can only stare at her, open-mouthed.

"Well?"

"Of course not. I was with you all the whole time."

"Maybe you paid someone to do it for you."

The more she ponders Natalie's allegation, the more ridiculous it seems. "Why would I do that?"

"You tell me." Natalie raises her eyebrows, casting a pointed gaze straight at Nick. Thankfully, he's already shut himself inside Logan's vehicle. *Smart*, Hallie thinks, cursing herself. She should've gone with Logan too, avoided this altogether.

"This is about *Nick*? You think I paid someone to sabotage the bridge so that I could *what*, hold his hand? Are you messing with me again?" she asks.

"Does it look like I am?"

Hallie hesitates. She'd been so skilled at reading her mother, divining her moods by the sound of her breath, the heaviness of her footfalls. But girls her own age always proved trickier. "I honestly can't tell. I just met you, remember." Just then Nick waves at them in her periphery, but she keeps her eyes glued to her sister. "Look, I'm not interested in him. He's all yours."

"Please, don't placate me. Every single female within a fifty-mile radius is interested in Nick. I post a photo of him, and my socials blow up. My engagement doubles. I heard about your ploy to spend more time with him. That you convinced Dad to let you work on the summer menu. Did you know that *I* wanted to do that?"

"I had no clue. You can help us."

"Nick doesn't want me to help. He says I have no culinary experience. *Ha.* No experience. I created Nat's Nibbles from scratch. I started with two followers. *Two!* And one was Mom." Natalie opens the driver's side door.

Suddenly, Hallie fears she's about to be left. "Let me talk to him. I'm sure—"

"I don't need your pity. Just don't get any bright ideas about winning over Dad, 'kay?"

The realization hits Hallie like a brick to the face. This isn't about Nick. It's about Robert. "It's not a competition, Nat."

"Lucky for you. Because I never lose."

Natalie skips the Thompson family dinner, complaining of a sun-induced headache, and Logan decides to spend his off-night barbecuing with friends. Hallie wonders if he's only trying to save face in front of his father, who seemed downright disbelieving that the rope bridge had been sabotaged. It's a relief to have Shelly and Robert to herself, even with Shelly's strange outburst last night, without their bickering children at the table. Though she supposes after the awkward car ride home she now qualifies as one of them. She'd always wanted to be an older sister. But the six-year gap between her and Natalie feels more like twenty.

After polishing off Shelly's spaghetti and meatballs, the three of them sit at the hand-carved table, drinking coffee and sharing stories. The way Hallie always dreamed it would be in a real family. Not like the families who'd been paid by the state to put a roof over her head.

Robert tells her about his first restaurant in Oakland. A self-described disaster, it closed after one year. His last restaurant, at a winery in Napa, sank amid too much competition. "You live and learn," he says. "Failure is just a pit stop on the way to success."

It's the sort of trite dad-advice Hallie cherishes, if only because she's never heard it until now. She could listen to him all night.

Shelly asks about her life in Sacramento, with Hallie expertly ducking and dodging the questions she can't answer. Giving enough to satisfy Shelly's curiosity. Hallie admits she doesn't have a boyfriend. Omits that she never has. It's hard to get close to people, waiting for them to leave you. To hurt you. To send you on your way. Hallie learned early to never unpack her suitcase. She admits she's searching for a new job. Omits the unfortunate incident with the pot of dishwater.

"With your experience at El Mar, I'm sure some lucky restaurateur will snap you up in a heartbeat," Robert says. "If you'd like, I can help you with your résumé. You can list me as reference."

Hallie hopes her smile reads as grateful but noncommittal. A quick change of subject is in order. "Should I help you clear the table?"

Shelly nods and finishes the last sip of her coffee. Hallie expertly pretends she didn't see her pour a splash of bourbon into the cup before she served them. This part comes easy to Hallie. The looking the other way. If she's honest with herself, Shelly scares her a little. Beneath the hairspray and makeup, she seems slightly unhinged. Not unlike Hallie's mother.

When Robert retreats into the living room to watch the evening news, Hallie joins Shelly at the sink. It's the only thing to do, the polite thing, even if she's uneasy. Hallie handles the dishes with care, like precious heirlooms, drying each one and returning it to its place in the cabinet. The task absorbs them both, and they fall into a predictable dance. Wash and dry. Wash and dry.

Shelly runs a plate beneath the water and holds it out to Hallie, dripping. "I've been meaning to ask you, did you happen to notice a framed picture on your nightstand?"

Startled by the strange question and its sudden intrusion into their quiet rhythm, Hallie nearly drops the dish. Heart in her throat, she manages a strangled, "I think so." She pauses for a moment to gather herself. "Do you mean the photo of the four of you?"

"That's the one. At the beach with matching white shirts and sunburns." Shelly chuckles and keeps washing, her hand making slow, gentle circles inside the serving bowl.

But Hallie feels accused. She glances toward the sofa for a lifeline, and finds Robert dozing. On her own again, then. Always on her own.

"Why?"

"It's missing."

"What do you mean?"

"I went into your room to straighten up this afternoon

and found the frame face down on the nightstand. When I turned it over, that's when I realized. Natalie said you probably took it."

"She did?" Hallie racks her brain, trying to remember the morning. Surely, she would've noticed an empty frame. But then, it had still been dark when she'd left. She thinks of the photograph she pulled from the ashes at The Grotto and secreted in the pocket of her jeans. Could it be the same one? She averts her eyes to hide her unease.

"Well, it was in your room, dear."

That she can't argue against, and her shrug seems a weak protest. "I don't know what happened to it. But I promise, I had nothing to do with it."

"Don't worry. I'm sure it will turn up." Shelly finishes scrubbing the bowl and passes it to her. "I think that's the last of it."

"Alright." But as Hallie watches the sink drain, she can't shake the feeling that something strange is going on here. That she's not the only one keeping secrets.

EMAIL

To: Hallie Sherman <hsherman94@pacbell.com>

From: Bob Thompson <justanotherbob@quickmail.net>

Subject: Your letter

Dear Ms. Sherman,

Sadly, I am not the man you are looking for. Is it strange to say that I wish I was? Growing up, I never knew my father. He was killed in combat in Vietnam in 1957. I was two years old at the time, so I met him only through photographs and stories that were often too painful for my mother to tell. She missed him terribly. I always dreamed of being a dad myself, but my wife and I struggled for years to have a child of our own. I was diagnosed with immunological infertility, which simply means that my body doesn't want me to be a father. Not by the usual route, anyway. We adopted our son, Benji, the year you were born. He's been the joy of our lives. I can only imagine that your father will feel the same when you finally find him.

Good luck!

Bob

ELEVEN

Hallie lies in bed, eyes wide open. At least two hours have passed since Shelly questioned her about the missing photograph. Since she'd excused herself to the guest bedroom and slipped her hand into the pocket of her hiking pants, finding only the heart-shaped pebble. Even after she'd turned the pants inside out and shaken them vigorously. The photo was simply gone, leaving her to stare at the ceiling in a state of uneasy confusion. What has she gotten herself into?

Between Natalie and Logan's whisperings, Shelly's panic about the stranger, finding the gun in her room, and the now-missing burnt photo, Hallie's convinced there are secrets to be unearthed. There always are. Foster care taught her that. A kid nobody wanted could snoop without being noticed, could uncover the little lies hidden behind every white picket fence. Affairs, bankruptcies, addictions. It felt therapeutic to find the evidence of imperfection. She wasn't the only one whose life had taken a wrong turn. And if she's truly a part of this family now, she deserves to know exactly what the Thompsons are keeping from her.

When the voices from the television have long been quiet, Hallie slides from beneath the covers, satisfied she won't be interrupted. She moves quickly through the room, with the finesse of a cat burglar, uncertain what she might find. She peers into the dusty shadows beneath the bed, peeps into every drawer, and examines the empty photo frame sitting on her nightstand. Despite her dread, she even moves aside the quilts and shoeboxes in the closet to take another look behind the secret panel, but she doesn't dare touch the gun.

After she's exhausted all possible hiding places in her room, she cracks open the door and pads out into the hallway in her bare feet. A moonbeam streams through the row of windows, shining a spotlight on the painting of the Thompson family. With no one to watch her, Hallie examines it more closely. Robert and Shelly loom in the background, their bright smiles eerie in the soft light. Younger versions of Natalie and Logan take up the foreground. Both of them, an amalgam of their parents. Robert's eyes. Shelly's nose. She covers them with her hand and imagines herself in the painting instead.

An owl's sudden hoot makes her jump and she scampers like a mouse down the hall. The large hutch in the corner of the living room draws her in. Like most of the house, it's adorned with family photos, each one more endearing than the last. The top shelf displays the oldest memories. A wedding photo, circa 1997, with Shelly's beauty hidden behind a massive bouquet of roses and poofy sleeves. Another of the happy couple on the dance floor, wilted and red-faced, eyes only for one another. Toddler-age Natalie with chocolate cake smeared across her face and Logan swaddled in his father's arms. There are firsts too. Steps, birthdays, days of school. More recent photos of the foursome are expertly curated, but Hallie finds herself drawn to the messiness of real life.

With careful precision, she opens the cabinets at the bottom of the hutch and picks through a few photo albums. Each spine is neatly marked with the year in bold, black handwriting. She counts eight in total, one for every year that the Thompsons have lived in Lake Tahoe. Strangely, Hallie finds no baby books among them. In the earliest album, Natalie celebrates her fourteenth birthday on the back patio. It makes Hallie feel better to see her sister's awkward phase up close. The braces, the pimples, the too-short bangs. She commits it to memory, then moves on.

She opens the kitchen drawers, scans the pantry. She even investigates the freezer, remembering the time she discovered a stack of money in a container of vanilla ice cream at foster home number three—the woman who claimed to not have enough money to buy Hallie school supplies. By then, Hallie didn't think twice about pocketing a hundred-dollar bill or using it to buy a pair of designer jeans. But the Thompsons' ice cream is legit, and she's starting to lose faith in her instincts. Maybe the Thompsons really are the perfect foursome, and it's only her warped imagination searching for the fly in the ointment.

Hallie remembers a small desk in the recess at the bottom of the staircase. It's a risk, since Natalie and Logan sleep down the hallway, but she finds herself descending the steps toward it. Expelling a breath, she guides the single drawer outward. It sticks a bit on a thick stack of papers, and a few fall to the floor. Hallie ignores them for now, flipping through what remains. Most of the documents appear to be related to Cerulean. A liquor license. A rental agreement. The hand-drawn plans for The Grotto. Dissatisfied, she stuffs them back inside and turns her attention to the piece of mail, addressed to Robert Thompson, that's landed at her feet. URGENT is stamped in bright red letters across the envelope.

Red for stop.

Red for danger.

There's no choice but to look closer. The return address reads: *The Law Firm of McKinley and Sparrow*. It's postmarked two weeks ago. Robert's voice echoes in her head. *Maybe Nat's got a point though. It's not the best timing.*

Taking a wary survey of her surroundings, Hallie opens the envelope and unfolds the contents, skimming the page.

...contacting you on behalf of our client, Jordan Markum... in conjunction with the settlement agreement you reached... dissolution of your partnership in Last Glass restaurant... Napa... a final payment of two million dollars... if we do not hear from you... pursue the matter in court...

The sudden interruption of a rumbling engine in the driveway sets her heart racing. Before she can return the envelope to the drawer, her bare foot sticks to a loose sheet of paper that had also fallen in her hasty search. Hallie hurries to read the handwritten scrawl.

WATCH YOUR BACK. YOUR FAMILY WILL PAY.

With no time to process this, she stuffs everything back into the desk and darts to the window, careful to stay out of sight. Key in hand, Logan stumbles up the porch steps toward the front door. He must be drunk. Drunk and driving.

Hallie hurries up the stairs and waits, listening for the

turn of the key in the lock. She counts to ten before approaching the landing.

"You're out late."

Logan's head jerks up, eyes wide and bloodshot. Seeing her there, he laughs a little too loudly, then whispers, "I thought you were Mom or worse. *Him.*"

"I couldn't sleep. Your mom was right. It's too quiet."

Rather than retreating down the hall toward his bedroom, Logan wobbles up the stairs, holding a finger to his lips. "Keep your voice down. I don't want the third degree." But the more he rambles, the louder he becomes. "Logan, you're not taking your future seriously. Logan, you need to grow up. Logan, you're such a disappointment to your mother and me."

"Well, drinking and driving is pretty stupid." Hallie pulls out a stool at the counter, hoping he'll join her there. Loose lips and all. "Does your dad actually say that stuff to you?"

"Not in so many words." With a groan, Logan sways and drops onto the sofa instead, out of her line of sight. "But it's obvious."

"So, what does he want you to do? Go to college? Move out?"

"Something like that."

"Why haven't you?" Hallie speaks the question that's been nagging at her since her arrival. "Don't you want a place of your own? I'm sure your parents would understand if you don't want to work at the restaurant."

His bitter laugh cuts right through her. "It's not that simple."

"It's not?"

"Mom and Dad want us to grow up. But at the same time, they don't. They want to keep us trapped in their little bubble forever. Where nothing bad can happen again. That's why Dad wants us at the restaurant, where he can keep an eye on us. That's why he pays Nick extra to bake Nat's stupid cookies."

"*Again?*" Hallie asks.

"Hunh?"

"You said, where nothing bad can happen *again*."

"I did?" Logan sits up fast, his head poking over the back of the sofa, like a turtle emerging from its shell. "I had way too much tequila. I think I'm gonna be sick."

He makes a run for the guest bathroom, leaving Hallie alone in the kitchen. She watches the minutes pass on the microwave clock until he emerges, looking worse for wear.

"Want some coffee?" she asks.

"Nah. But thanks for offering. I better go to bed before Mom wakes up." He shuffles over to the landing, then pauses, glancing back over his shoulder at her. "You won't tell anybody about this, will you?"

Hallie isn't sure if he means the puking or the drunk driving or the saying too much. But she can keep a secret. "Of course not. What are big sisters for?"

After helping Logan down the stairs to his room, Hallie hurries back to hers, softly closing herself inside. The plush guestroom doesn't feel as safe as it once did. Her nerves buzzing, she buries herself under the covers with her cellphone and types *Last Glass, Napa* into the search bar. Frowning, she scrolls through the first page of results, then the second and the third. Nothing. She can't find a single mention of the restaurant. It's like it never existed at all.

TWELVE

The next morning, Hallie wakes before dawn. She turns to one side, then the other, unable to quiet her worried mind. The events of the last few days play back on an endless loop, ending on a hard stop at the desk in the recess. *Your family will pay.* Though Hallie understands she's not a Thompson in name, the threat still resonates, vibrating like a tuning fork at the back of her brain.

Unable to lie still any longer, she decides to head to Cerulean. Before leaving, she fills a bag with a few items from the closet and the back of the Thompsons' pantry, remembering the promise she'd made yesterday morning.

When Hallie reaches the restaurant, it's still dark, but the vague hint of twilight blurs the horizon. Using the flashlight on her cellphone to illuminate the path, she walks toward The Grotto with her offerings.

She only looks straight ahead, afraid to cast her tiny beam into the thicket of the trees and the inky shadows between them. She hums to herself to drown out the other noises. The shuffling, rustling, snapping of God-knows-what. *A bear?*

She won't let herself think it, though it's not the worst animal she can imagine, slinking through the forest alongside her, waiting on two feet for the time to strike.

Before she reaches the clearing, she detects the faint smell of woodsmoke. The orange glow of the fire leads her to the man's makeshift camp, where she finds him concealed beneath the same tattered coverings. She nudges him with her foot and drops the bag beside him.

"I brought you some food and a warm quilt. I can get you some other supplies too, if you need them."

Slowly, the blankets part, revealing a man's tired face. A young man. Younger than she'd guessed. He ducks away from the glow of her flashlight, shielding his eyes beneath one hand.

"Too bright."

"Sorry." But Hallie suspects it's more than that. Perhaps he is trying to stay hidden as well.

One arm snakes out and takes hold of the bag, then quickly burrows out of her view again.

"What's your name?" she asks.

"You can call me Jay. Yours?"

"Hallie. My... uh... dad owns the restaurant on the water." The word *dad* clunks out, both strange and revelatory coming from her mouth. "How long have you been staying out here?"

"I dunno. A month or two, I guess. I haven't seen you before the other night though."

"So that *was* you?"

Jay's sheepish nod shames Hallie for calling him creepy. "I didn't mean to scare you. The staff usually clears out by then, and I go through the dumpster. You'd be surprised how much good food they throw out. Some nights, I eat like a king. I do have to watch out for the bears though. They don't like to share."

Hallie stiffens, but Jay merely shrugs, unfazed. "The big lugs are just hungry, same as me. I only wish I could fish as well as they can. Have you ever tried to catch a trout with your bare hands?"

She puzzles. "Uh..."

"Exactly."

"Do the Thompsons know about you? They're not bad people. I'm sure they'd want to help."

The dry rasp that comes from his throat leaves her wondering how long it's been since he laughed. "You can't tell them about me. Incline Village isn't the place to be homeless. I'm a nuisance. They would call the cops and complain. Or worse. Then, I'd probably get sent back."

"Back where?"

"Prison. I'd rather take my chances with the bears." He blinks up at her from the cocoon of blankets. "And before you ask, *no*, I don't want to talk about it. And, *yes*, I'm happy out here. I like the freedom of living off the land. It's the people who make life difficult."

"Fair enough." Slowly, she steps away from him, out of his reach. Prison could mean a lot of things, none of them good. But who is she to judge? "I should probably head inside. I'm meeting the chef and we're—"

"Are you afraid of me?" He emerges from the blankets, revealing his scraggly beard and untamed mane. A dirty sweatshirt hangs from his thin frame. His hands, too, are soiled, and he tugs at the sleeves to cover what looks like the tail end of a scar on the inside of his wrist.

Hallie gapes blatantly. "Should I be?"

"Most people are." Jay extends his hand toward her, testing her it seems.

She thinks of Ernie, the way passersby ogle his leg, amputated at the knee. Of her mother too, who'd been just as maimed on the inside. Before answering him, she takes his hand in hers. "Well, I'm not most people."

No matter what she'd told Jay, Hallie's hands tremble as she unlocks the side door of the restaurant with the key Nick had loaned her in case she arrived before him. She flips on every light and the small portable radio, not wanting to be alone. It isn't Jay's untamed appearance that frightens her but the pain reverberating in his voice. Pain like that turns to poison, wilting everything it touches.

Thankfully, she and Nick had agreed to meet this morning, but not until eight, which means that she'll be on her own for at least an hour. To distract herself, Hallie gets busy in the kitchen, tossing a couple of garlic cloves into a pan to sauté. Then, she cuts lobster claw and knuckles into bite-size pieces, careful to avoid another sliced finger, and adds them to the crab already in the pan. With any luck, she'll be able to present Nick with the perfect lobster grilled cheese to sample for the summer menu. She plans to mix up the ingredients, try a few different cheeses, until she finds the most delectable combination. The one that will make her appear to be more than what she is. A lowly diner waitress. *Ex*-diner waitress.

As the bread cooks in the skillet, she layers on slices of Havarti and Gouda. Her mouth starts to water, which she takes as a promising sign. She spoons the seafood mixture onto the bread and plates the sandwich, pleased with the even grill marks. At least it looks tasty.

Mid test-bite, the side door swings open. Hallie grips the fork tighter in her hand, intent on using it as a weapon. But it's only Robert, and she feels silly.

He gives her a wave, seemingly unsurprised to see her there, and doesn't seem to have noticed her momentary panic. "That smells delicious."

"I wasn't expecting Nick till eight," she says, explaining herself anyway. "I didn't realize you'd be here this morning."

"May I?" Robert points to her creation, lifting half of the sandwich to his mouth before she answers. He chews, nods, moans.

Hallie takes a delicate bite from the other half. "Needs more garlic."

"Tastes pretty darn flawless to me."

She won't ever tire of hearing him sing her praises, even if he's just shining her on. That's what a dad is for, right? Shameless cheerleading. "Do you always come in on your off days?" she asks.

"When you own a restaurant, there are no off days, hon. No vacations. It's not that different than having a child. You love it. You do your best to make it successful. And you worry all the time."

Hallie thinks of her late-night talk with Logan, as she fires up another pan for round two, adding a pinch more garlic this time. Unlike her brother, she relishes Robert's attention. She's yet to find a flaw in the man, despite her mother's legacy of bitterness. "But Cerulean is doing great, isn't it?"

"We're okay. In the restaurant world, the margins are so small, you're often just one bad week away from going under. It's so competitive. You do what you have to, to stay afloat.

Sometimes, it's dog eat dog. I've made a few enemies over the years."

"Enemies?" Hallie can only wonder which one of his enemies had scrawled that note. "That sounds stressful."

Robert steps in to help her, dropping in the mixture of crab and lobster while she stirs. Though she's always preferred to work alone, she finds that she doesn't mind him standing by her side at the stove. "It can be. But I wouldn't have it any other way. Especially now you're here. I'm glad to give you a place to showcase your talent. It's the least I can do."

"So, how did you get into the restaurant business?"

"Well, ironically enough, I followed in my father's footsteps. Would you like to hear the story?"

Robert only needs Hallie's eager nod, and he's off. Voice booming, hands gesturing like a famous orator. No wonder he spends most of his time in the front of house, mingling with customers. Hallie feels like a little girl, sitting at her father's feet for story time.

"In 1963, my dad, Wallace Thompson, worked as a cook in the army. He saved up enough money to buy a condemned building in Little Italy in San Francisco after his discharge. He had a dream of opening an authentic Italian restaurant. Of course, he didn't have an ounce of Italian blood in him, so the place flopped. But then he met my mother, Cecilia, and fell in love with her meatballs. They reopened a year later, filling the menu with her recipes, and the C&W Café was born. My brother and I bussed tables there until my mom got sick and my dad shut the place down."

Hallie waits for him to continue, but he keeps quiet, watching while she flips the sandwich to grill the other side.

"Did your dad ever try again?"

"He couldn't. Not with a broken heart. After my mom died, I promised him I would keep their legacy alive. Ever since then, I've been nose to the grindstone. When I met your mom, I was saving my bartending tips to buy my first space."

"Your father must be proud of all you've accomplished."

"He would've been proud of me no matter what. But he never had a chance to see all this. He died before we moved to Lake Tahoe."

"I'm so sorry."

"It's alright." He studies her for a moment. "You remind me of him, you know. Resilient, determined. He worked for everything he got. But he was a horrible cook. My mother wouldn't trust him to boil water."

"You take after him then?" She pokes a teasing elbow into his ribs, then offers him dibs on her second attempt.

"Exactly. I've never had the knack for it. I've got expert-level taste buds though." He takes the cheesiest bite right from the center, pronouncing it even better than the first. "Elevated comfort food. It's perfect for the menu. I'm sure Nick will agree."

Robert smiles warmly at her, and she wonders again how her mom could've been so wrong about him. Hallie can't imagine him turning his back on his child.

"Those pearls are lovely. Too lovely to wear in a busy kitchen." He leans in to examine them closer. "Were they your mother's?"

"Yes. Do you remember them?"

When his face drops, Hallie feels bad for asking. He'd already told her he didn't remember much about Elizabeth. Why did she have to push the issue?

"No. I'm sorry. I don't. I only assumed they belonged to her since you've been wearing them so often."

"My mom would be thrilled to see me in them. She wore them almost every day." The pearls feel familiar beneath her fingers, but she fights the sudden urge to tear them from her neck. The past can be so suffocating. "Honestly, as a kid, I hated them. I've never told anyone that before."

"You hated her necklace? Why?"

Her cheeks get hot. Her mouth, dry. But she wants to say it out loud, even if it's a poor approximation of the truth. An outright lie, really. "I thought you gave it to her before you left us."

"Did she tell you that?"

Hallie shakes her head. She feels so small, like a little girl tugging at his jacket. "I didn't want to think about how else she would've gotten it. We never had nice things. Looking back, I'm surprised she never pawned it. She sold everything else at least once. Our television set. Her mother's gold earrings. My clarinet. Sometimes, she'd buy things back and sell them again at another pawn shop."

"I didn't realize that Lizzie had financial trouble. I wish I could've helped out."

"That's what happens when you spend most of your money on pills." Before Hallie can pull it together, the tears leak out. The kind that burn her throat and make her feel as if she's underwater. Her mother never took her crying seriously, and the foster and group homes had no time for her tears. So, she learned to save them for the nighttime, sobbing into her pillow.

But Robert opens his arms to her. "Oh, honey."

Enveloped in his sturdy embrace, Hallie finds herself

strangely comforted. Though he's still very much a stranger, her body seems to know he's hard-wired to protect her.

"If only I'd known. If only..." Robert snuffles. "A father should provide for his children. He should be there. Is there anything I can do to make it up to you? Anything at all? Just say the word."

Natalie appears over Robert's shoulder, standing in the main door, hand on her hip. It's obvious she's heard her father's groveling. "What's going on?"

Hallie frees herself from his arms, straightens her spine, wipes her face. "Nothing."

"Just chopping onions, Nat." Her father expels a breath and dabs at his cheeks. "It's a surprise to see *you* here so early."

"I'm here every morning, Dad. You never notice how hard I work. Who else is going to process the online orders for Nat's Nibbles?" She flips her hair over her shoulder and saunters toward the counter, scowling at the grilled cheese as she passes. "That's like a day's worth of calories. Mom and I think the summer menu should be more health conscious."

"People don't come to Cerulean for health food, Nat. They come for decadence. And Hallie's sandwich fits the bill."

"Well, it's not an either-or. My cookies are decadent. *Look.*" She holds out her cellphone. "Jenna Star says so."

"Who's Jenna Star?" Hallie can't resist stirring the pot. Especially after Logan's revelation last night that Robert pays Nick to keep Nat's Nibbles flush with his delicious cookies.

Natalie lets out a huff of sheer frustration. "Seriously? She's only the most famous fitness influencer in the world, and she lives right here in Incline Village. She called my fat-free coconut macaroons *yumscious*. So there."

Moments later, a frantic Nick bursts through the side door with apologies for running late—"sorry, I overslept"—and Hallie tries to warn him about the Nat-train headed his way. But he mistakes her raised brows and wide eyes for disbelief.

"No, really. I did."

"Nick, do you think we should be serving food that clogs our patrons' arteries? That elevates their blood sugar? That—"

"That sandwich smells amazing." Nick gestures to what's left of Hallie's lobster grilled cheese. When he grabs a bite, Hallie notices his hands shaking.

"Whatever." Which Hallie already understands is as close as Natalie comes to conceding defeat. She smacks a sheet of paper against the counter. "Two more rush orders for four dozen vegan chocolate chip for that customer in Kings Beach. I'll be back this afternoon to pick them up."

Even if he is getting paid for his troubles, Hallie wishes Nick would stand up for himself, but he only nods. His attention is focused on the hem of his gray polo. He quickly tucks it into the waistband of his jeans, but not before Hallie notices the dark red stain there.

Blood. She tries not to think it.

"This is definitely going on the new menu," Nick says.

Her head spinning, Hallie forces a smile.

Robert eases toward the back office, oblivious. "I'll leave you experts to the menu planning then. I've got some paperwork to drown in. You know where to find me if you need a taste test."

"Yes, we do." Hallie watches him go, then turns back to Nick, only to find him looking right at her. She drops her gaze and takes a breath.

"Did you get in alright?" he asks.

She nods, placing the restaurant key in his palm without meeting his eyes. At least his hands aren't blood-spattered.

"You okay?" he asks.

"Fine. You?"

"Never been better."

LETTER

Father Robert Thompson
Holy Trinity Parish
3 Prayer Circle
Richmond, CA

Hallie Sherman
135 Highland Terrace
Box 2B
Sacramento, CA

    Dear Ms. Sherman,

    I am disheartened to hear that you grew up without your father. How difficult that must've been! And how brave of you to look for him now, standing ready to forgive his absence from your life. Sadly, I must inform you that I am not your father. I was ordained as a Catholic priest two years prior to your birth, and as such, had taken a vow of celibacy which I have never broken. I will keep you and your father in my daily prayers. No matter the outcome of your search, take comfort in Psalm 68:5, which reminds us, "Father of the fatherless and protector of widows is God in his holy habitation."

If the Almighty Father is willing, I am certain you will find what you are seeking.

Yours in prayer,

Father Bob

THIRTEEN

Forty-five minutes into planning the summer menu, Hallie catches Nick glancing at his cell again. Sighing, he runs a hand through his hair, sending his chestnut curls askew.

"Hey, I hate to do this, but I've gotta run."

"*What?* We only just started. You got here late. And then, you spent thirty minutes prepping Nat's cookies." Hallie can't hide her disappointment. After her fruitless Internet search for Last Glass, she'd passed the rest of her sleepless night brainstorming ideas for the menu. Bacon-wrapped black cod. Grouper tacos with summer slaw. Fresh lobster spring rolls. She'd never have another chance like this. Nick didn't get it. He couldn't. He'd never know how much she'd overcome to get here. How many dreams she'd let go like lost balloons, floating out of sight. "I really wanted you to try my sriracha shrimp skewers. I think they'll pair well with the peach salad you suggested."

Nick's eyes flit to the door. His jaw clenches. "They will. But, I can't. Not right now."

"What about the cookies?"

"They're cooling in the back. She packages them herself."

Knowing full well she's being childish, Hallie scoffs at him anyway. "That's a surprise."

"I can meet you later. Maybe after lunch?"

"I promised Logan I'd kayak with him this afternoon." She hates lying to Nick, but he's the one acting shady. The one monitoring his phone. The one with blood on the hem of his shirt. Robert entrusted him with the restaurant, paid his way through culinary school. Hallie bristles at the thought of him taking advantage of her father's kindness. He's uncovered her secret. What is *he* hiding?

"Kayaking? With Logan? Good luck. And don't forget your life vest."

Hallie waits until Nick disappears out the side door. Then, she springs into action, finding her father hunched over his desk in the small office with a stack of bills and a calculator in his hand. The cloud of worry lifts from his face when he spots her in the doorway.

"Would you mind if I borrowed your truck? Nick stepped out for a bit, and I'd like to swing by the drug store to pick up a few toiletries."

"Of course. Whatever you need. Just be careful on the roads." After a brief rummage through his drawer, he tosses her the key. "Do you have enough money to cover it? I know you're between jobs at the moment. But I could offer you an advance on this week's work, if you need it."

"That's not necessary. You don't have to pay me a salary. I'm happy to help out." Hallie thinks of her mother's wooden heirloom box. Of the few remaining bills hidden inside. She still has enough to get by for now. "I'll be back in thirty minutes."

Hallie fires up the truck and follows Nick at a safe distance, tapping on the brakes every time she gets too close. It's easy to be spotted on the two-lane roads through Incline Village, so she waits for a garbage truck to pull in between them and provide her with cover. Still, she holds her breath, hoping Nick won't recognize Robert's beast of a pickup stalking him.

She exhales when he turns off the main road and leaves the grandeur of the gated homes in his rearview. The smoothly paved asphalt turns rutted, the carefully manicured grounds of Lakeshore Drive giving way to unkempt plots. The further he drives, the more familiar it feels to Hallie, though she's not yet ventured far from the Thompsons' neighborhood. The houses that line the road look similar to the ones she grew up in. Plain. Unassuming. Like the modest four walls that contained a family that belonged to her... temporarily. Until the rubber met the road, and she and her trash bag of belongings had been shipped off to the next house. Rinse and repeat. They hadn't all been bad, her foster homes, but they'd all been fleeting.

A half mile ahead, Nick pulls into a small shopping center. Hallie slows and drives past, planning to circle back. She turns around in the nearest dirt driveway, catching a glimpse of the house at the end. The peeling paint. The roof in desperate need of a repair before the winter snowfall. Only a couple of miles from the pristine views of the lake, it's another world out here. A thin line between the haves and the have-nots. It pains her to imagine what it must be like for these regular folks to live in the shadows of such wasteful opulence.

By the time Hallie reaches the lot, idling near the entrance, Nick is moving with purpose toward a stucco building adjacent to a thrift shop. The sign above the door reads: LOW COST EMERGENCY CLINIC, AFFORDABLE PRESCRIPTIONS. He vanishes inside.

Hallie finds a spot with a clear view of the door and hunkers down, waiting. With the sun warming her through the window and the radio softly humming, her eyelids grow heavy. She catches herself drifting off—*swerve, screech*—and she startles awake, blinking back the flash-bang image of her mother, bleeding from a gash on her forehead. The sheer white of her bone poking out of her skin.

The clinic door swings open, and Hallie gasps.

It's her mother, straight from the grave. Gray-faced and rail-thin, holding tight to a white paper bag. Inside it, the devil pills. That's how Hallie had thought of them. Because they turned Elizabeth Sherman into someone else. Someone dark and needful. Someone unfit to be anybody's mother. It had taken less than a year for her mom to morph from a chronic pain patient to a doctor shopper to a full-blown addict.

Hallie squeezes her eyes shut, breathes in and out. Looks again.

Not her mother, then, but some other lost soul, with the same hollow eyes.

Hallie shouldn't be here. She *can't* be here. She'll start seeing her mother in every downtrodden face, the way she had for months after the accident. Every time it happened, she felt relieved, then disappointed, then ashamed. Besides, it's been nearly thirty minutes, and she doesn't want Robert to worry.

She forces herself to concentrate on her clumsy hands as she texts Nick.

Kayaking didn't pan out. Will be at the restaurant... if ur still free.

By the time he replies, she's speeding back to Cerulean, eager to leave the clinic and its ghosts behind her.

Heading 2 farmers market in Truckee 4 fresh veg. Won't be back till late.

Hallie spends the next three hours in the restaurant kitchen, deflecting her thoughts with aromas and spices and sizzling saucepans, and perfecting her contributions to the summer menu. After plating the finished dishes, she snaps a quick photo on her cell and summons Robert from the office for a taste test. He samples the last dish, then dabs his mouth with a napkin and shakes his head in disbelief.

"Wow, Hallie. You've outdone yourself."

"You think?"

"Absolutely." He winks at her, and her heart swells. "You're really giving Nick a run for his money. I have a feeling this year's anniversary cookout will be our best yet. You know, you're allowed to submit an entry for the cooking contest. The best summer dish you can whip up in less than fifteen minutes as judged by Norma Todd, a local food critic. The winner takes home a cool T-shirt."

"A T-shirt?"

"Oh, did I forget to mention the cash prize? Five thousand dollars *and* a cool T-shirt."

Hallie pretends to be unbothered. But five thousand bucks would go a long way. At the very least, she could put a deposit down on a new place. She wouldn't have to couch surf between Maxine and Darla, waking early every morning to start the coffee maker and stack her blanket and pillow. Anything to feel like less of a burden.

"So, are you in?" he asks. "It would be incredible to see a Thompson win the grand prize."

A part of Hallie resists his claim to her. She's a Sherman, even if her mother let her down in all the ways that counted. But it feels good to be wanted, especially after all the years of believing she hadn't been. "I'm in."

"Be sure to fill out the online registration as soon as possible. We limit the field to ten competitors. And thank you. You have no idea how happy you've made me." Still beaming at her, he points to the leftovers. "Box those leftovers up for me. I'll take them home later for a midnight snack."

Hallie floats across the Saltillo tile, scrubbing the dishes and sanitizing the countertops. All the worries of the morning scatter like birds, leaving her mind blank as the clear blue sky above the lake. When the steel sparkles, she tosses the dishcloth in the laundry bin and tells Robert she's walking home. *Home.* The word is a touchstone, a comfort. A prayer. Even Natalie's sudden appearance in the side doorway can't drag her back to earth.

"Where are my cookies?"

"Nick left them in the back. They're ready for packaging." Hallie attempts her most sisterly smile, before adding, "Would you like me to help you before I head out?"

"It's a one-woman job."

Natalie pushes past and heads to the pastry room without a word to Robert. Relieved to be free of her, Hallie steps into the sunshine, anticipating a leisurely walk along the lakeshore to gaze out at the boats dotting the horizon. But her sister's scream of pure rage grabs her by the ankles and yanks her back inside.

Hallie rushes over, only to stop and stare at the counter. Robert, too, pulls up short behind her. The smell of chocolate is overwhelming. The three trays sit empty. Broken cookies cover the floor.

Natalie stomps toward her, accidentally crushing another cookie beneath the sole of her sandal. She lets out a primal grunt. "What did you do to my cookies? The entire order is ruined."

"I didn't touch them. I haven't been back here all day."

"Let's not blame Hallie. There must be a logical explanation."

Robert tries to soothe his daughter, wrapping an arm around her shoulder, but she shakes him off, indignant.

"A logical explanation? Dad, those cookies are destroyed. And look at my cute pink bags." Natalie holds up a few of the bags featuring her logo, now with a scalloped slash right through the center of them that reminds Hallie of the sabotaged rope bridge. Logan had mentioned a serrated blade.

"This wasn't an accident," Natalie says. "Someone did this on purpose."

Sensing an incoming accusation, Hallie shrinks back, hiding behind their father.

"And I'm betting it was *her*. Who else could've done this? Who else would've wanted to?"

"Okay, honey. Slow down and think. You know how

busy we get on Tuesdays with food and wine deliveries. We had a repairman in earlier to take a look at the sink in the back, and the tables have already started to arrive for the cookout next week. Some clumsy soul probably bumped the trays, knocked them over, and didn't want to tell anybody." He softens his voice. "I mean, can you blame them?"

"The bags too?" Natalie wails. "Did they accidentally fall on a bread knife?"

Robert sighs but Hallie stays quiet, not daring to admit that her sister has a point.

When Natalie turns on the waterworks, Robert does what comes naturally to him. He gives in, cocooning her in a bear hug. "Why don't you call your client and apologize? Let them know their cookies might be late, but you'll throw in an extra batch. I'll even make them with you if you'd like."

"Thanks, Dad. Nick will fix it. He always does."

Hallie fights the urge to give Natalie a tongue lashing but thinks better of it. She always dreamed it would be fun to have a sister. Now, she's sharing a house with an enemy. For a brief moment, she wonders if Natalie sabotaged the scene herself. It's preferable to the alternative, an unknown figure slipping in unseen to stir up trouble. First, the bridge, now this. *Your family will pay.*

"I'm sorry about your cookies," Hallie says. "And the bags. Don't bother Nick. I'll stay."

"Well, it *is* the least you could do." She pulls out of Robert's embrace and eyes Hallie with suspicion. "Assuming you can follow a basic recipe."

"There's a joke here," Robert offers, tucking Natalie back beneath his arm and roping Hallie in with the other. "Something like, that's the way the cookie crumbles."

Hallie finds herself groaning in chorus. At least they agree about Robert's dad jokes then.

"I don't expect them to be half as good as Nick's," Natalie assures her. In case there was any doubt that she'd been forgiven. "Just as long as they're edible."

"Don't worry. Hallie's mother baked a mean apple pie. Dessert runs in her blood."

The one stray fact Robert recalls about her mother still baffles Hallie, and the contradiction makes her chest ache. The Elizabeth Sherman she'd known had baked Hallie's birthday cakes from the store-bought mixes and brought takeout to the potluck dinners at the office where she worked as a secretary. *When* she worked. In the three years before the accident, her mom had scraped by, spending her welfare checks before she'd cashed them. But what if her mother had been different before Hallie was born? What if Hallie had been the catalyst, the worm in the apple, that turned her mother rotten? And what if she did the same to her father without meaning to?

"I'll do my best," Hallie says, already knowing her best won't be nearly good enough.

After Natalie exits the side door with a dramatic hair toss, Robert turns to her, frowning. "Could someone have snuck in here?"

"It's possible. The table delivery guy propped the back door for a while. And the cuts on those bags didn't seem like an accident."

"I agree. But I didn't want to send Nat into hysterics. She's already a bit sensitive about your being here. I never expected she'd be so jealous."

Hallie nods, choosing her next words carefully. "Do you think we're in danger?"

"Danger?" She's caught him off guard.

"You know, from your enemies?"

"That was just an expression, hon. I didn't mean to worry you." Robert gives a mirthless chuckle. "Besides, if my worst enemies are only smashing cookies, I'm doing something right."

FOURTEEN

Raucous laughter travels through the Thompsons' front door, reaching Hallie on the other side. She studies her reflection in the window, wiping an errant smudge of flour from her forehead. There's not much she can do about the chocolate chip stains on her shirt. But at least Natalie will see proof of her efforts. Maybe that will win her over, or at least remove the target from her back.

Optimistic, Hallie tries the door—*locked*—before retrieving the spare and letting herself inside. Someday soon, she hopes Robert will give her a key of her own. Something tangible to confirm that she belongs here. That she's not just a guest, a temporary visitor.

Following the cheerful noises, she heads up the stairs to find the entire family in the kitchen, sitting at the bar. Robert and Shelly are unpacking several large take-out bags. A born performer, Natalie gestures wildly as she tells a story, and Logan laughs along with her. Neither seems troubled by the events of the last two days. The sabotaged suspension bridge, the broken cookies. All of it, nearly invisible in this picture of domesticity.

Hallie pauses on the landing, quiet as an intruder, and suddenly wishes she could turn around. As much as she wants to be a part of it, of this family, it scares her too. She senses the tension beneath the surface, like a shark lurking underwater. But it's too late for an escape. Logan spots her and lets out a joyful whoop.

"You made it just in time to settle a debate."

"Oh?" Hallie accepts a glass of red wine from Shelly and pulls up a barstool. Cautiously, she sits, surprised Natalie hasn't launched an inquisition into the fate of her precious cookies. After three failed batches, Hallie realized her mistake had been trusting her sister to send her the correct recipe. Once she'd made the adjustment—1/2 cup of coconut oil, not 1/4 cup—her last attempt had been pure perfection.

"Juan Antonio Feliz's ceviche versus Nick Morelli's truffle risotto." After laying out the options, Natalie watches her closely. Blue eyes boring like lasers, she can feel the heat.

"You're so lucky to have tried them both," Logan says.

"She wishes," Natalie mutters, just loud enough for Hallie to hear.

Buying time, Hallie takes a sip of her wine and pretends to contemplate her answer. Inside, she's gone into full panic mode. Relief washes over her when Robert speaks.

"It's like comparing apples to oranges, don't you think? The delicacy of a ceviche and the hardiness of a risotto. Both winners in their own right."

"Absolutely." Hallie doesn't care if she sounds like a brown-noser. She's grateful for her dad's lifeline. It's given her time to think. "I can't imagine choosing between them."

"But if you *had* to," Natalie insists, taking a casual bite from her plate. "Who would win the cookout? Hypothetically speaking, of course." She pauses before adding, "Unless you'd be willing to call Juan Antonio and ask him to enter the contest this summer. I mean, you were like his protégée and all, right? It would be great for business."

"Let's not pressure Hallie." Robert comes to her rescue again, and she fights the urge to duck behind his broad shoulders, to let him take the bullets meant for her. She knows it will only make it worse. She'd dealt with girls like Natalie in foster care. Standing up for herself was the only way.

"Protégée might be a slight exaggeration. I haven't spoken to him in a while." True, though she could count on two hands the number of words she'd said to him. *How do you recommend fixing a broken sauce?* Eight, then. "And I'm not even sure how to get in touch with him anymore. Besides, I'm planning on entering the contest. Why would I invite more competition?"

"Smart gal." Robert flashes her a pleased smile and spoons a dollop of potato salad onto his plate. "Now, enough restaurant talk. Let's eat."

While Hallie prepares her plate, she launches one more shot over the bow. After all, the best defense is a good offense. "Your cookies turned out great, by the way, Natalie. I just made a small tweak to your recipe."

After dinner, Hallie sits on the bed and removes her mother's string of pearls. The beads are warm in her palm and coiled like a snake. Once, there had been a tiny tag affixed to the clasp. *For Grandma, with love.* Not her grandmother, of course, but someone's. Hunched over a cane, the elderly woman had emerged from the grocery store into a dimly lit parking lot, with a single plastic bag wrapped around her frail wrist. Those were the dark days, the desperate days, when her mother had no qualms about taking what she wanted. At least she told Hallie to cover her eyes. Naturally, Hallie had peeked through her fingers anyway, watching the woman freeze in terror. Her mother had returned with the pearls and a story. *Your good for nothing father made me do it. He might as well have taken these himself.*

Hallie carts the strand to her precious wooden box and drops them inside. She decides to keep the pearls locked away. They feel marked, haunted. She doesn't know why she's held on to them for so long. Looking down at them, resting atop the remaining crisp bills she'd pilfered, she fears she's not so different from her mother after all, and the thought disturbs her.

"Hallie?" From the other side of the door, Shelly's slurred voice beckons her. She waits there, dressed for bed with a robe wrapped around her and fuzzy slippers on her unsteady feet. That's what happens after four glasses of wine. Hallie had counted. "Can I talk to you for a sec?"

"Of course." She steps aside to allow Shelly a wide berth. The earthy scent of Bordeaux trails her, heady as a cheap perfume. "Come in."

Shelly drops onto the edge of the bed, her eyes drifting around the room and settling on the nightstand. Even when she's tipsy, Hallie can't read her.

"Did I do something wrong?"

"You said that you didn't take that photo."

"I didn't." Hallie prepares to stand her ground, though the empty frame mocks her.

"What's this then?" Shelly reaches into the pocket of her robe.

It takes Hallie exactly one frantic heartbeat to recognize what Shelly pulls out. It's the charred photograph remnant she rescued. The knot in her stomach tightens. "That's the photo? I found it in a burn pit at The Grotto."

"It was in your pants pocket."

"How did you—" Hallie stops herself. She's already in enough trouble without accusing Shelly of poking around in her things. In foster care, she'd grown used to adults snooping for contraband, kids stealing her stuff. She'd gotten smarter, sneakier. Is she losing her edge?

"Nat's the one who discovered it," Shelly says, anticipating her question. "She picked up the pants from the laundry room, thinking they were hers."

"I didn't leave them in the laundry room." After searching the pockets for the photograph last night, Hallie had set the heart-shaped pebble on the nightstand and stuffed the pants into the laundry bag in the closet.

"Maybe I picked them up by mistake." Shelly shrugs, but her eyes are intense. And a little red around the rims as if she's been crying. She twists the curled edges of the photo with such force, Hallie wonders it doesn't rip in two. "Why didn't you mention finding it? You knew we were looking for it."

"Honestly, I didn't even know which photo you had in mind. There's not much left to identify. And I wasn't sure who put it there." Hallie dials back the frustration in her voice. "I didn't want to upset anyone."

"Then, what were you going to do with it?"

Unsure how to placate her stepmother, Hallie searches for a reply. "Keep it, I suppose. I know it sounds weird, but I couldn't bring myself to toss it. It's the first photo of my dad I've ever had."

Shelly winces but her sympathy does little to deter her attack. "Well, Nat seems to think you burned it. That you're secretly angry with Robert for abandoning you. And at her and her brother for having the life you didn't. She doesn't trust you, Hallie. She told me what happened with the cookies and her slashed Nibbles bags."

"I didn't—"

"I'm not saying I believe her. She can be envious at times. But since you've got here, things keep happening. Strange things."

Hallie can't argue with that. At least she's not the only one who sees it. "I'm not an angry person. Really, I'm not. I only want to be a part of a family. Of *your* family." But Hallie hears her mother's voice again, speaking the familiar words. The ones her mother wrote on her soul, even as Hallie quietly railed against them. *Your father didn't want you. He doesn't. He never will.*

Shelly leaves the ruined photo on the bed, though it feels less like an offering and more like an accusation. "Goodnight, Hallie."

When the door clicks into place, Hallie hurries to retrieve the wooden box. She tucks it at the bottom of the closet, inside a shoebox, and covers it with the stack of blankets. She won't let down her guard again.

EMAIL

To: Hallie Sherman <hsherman94@pacbell.com>

From: Robbie Thompson <rumbarobbie@dance-mail.com>

Subject: Hello from Las Vegas

Hi Hallie,

My partner, Nelson, received your letter and shared it with me on our last video call. I am currently performing in the *Dance, Dance, Dance!* show at the Mirage in Las Vegas. As you may have already inferred, I'm not your father. I came out to my parents—very traditional upper-crust Los Angelians—in the summer of my fifth-grade year, after I auditioned for the role of the Sugar Plum Fairy in *The Nutcracker*. Thankfully, they've not only accepted me, they've embraced me. In fact, my father walked in the Pride Parade with me last year in San Francisco. Imagine that! I can only hope your father turns out to be half as cool as mine. When you find him, I've got front row tickets to the show for both of you.

Keep dancing!

Robbie

FIFTEEN

Robert summons Hallie before dawn with a soft knock on her door. Her eyes burn when she rubs them awake. It feels like she spent the night staring into the sun. The ruined photograph had haunted her from the nightstand until she'd buried it in the drawer.

"I'm sorry to wake you so early," he whispers. "But if you're up for it, I'd like to take you to a special place to watch the sunrise. Just you and me."

You and me. Hallie's head bobs eagerly at the prospect. At least her father hasn't taken Natalie's side. Not yet anyway. She wonders if Shelly told him about the photo. Probably not since she hadn't wanted to worry him.

In ten minutes, they're out the door with two travel mugs of hot coffee, a pair of binoculars, and a flashlight. They make the short drive in companionable silence, with Hallie peering out her window and into the dark woods, half-expecting a bear to lumber out and cross the road in front of them. The only animal sighting so far, a pair of deer nibbling at the grass at the edge of the tree cover. At the first sign of the truck's high beams, they dart away, their white tails vanishing like bobbing ghosts.

Robert announces their arrival, exits the truck, and leads her into the predawn stillness. She tucks her hands into the front pocket of Nick's hooded sweatshirt, a futile defense against the chilly air that bites at her skin, and follows the beam of Robert's light. But the hike is a steady uphill climb, and before long, she's breathing hard and shedding layers. She ties the sweatshirt around her waist and dabs at the sheen on her forehead.

"We made it." Robert directs the flashlight onto a wooden bench near the overlook.

Hallie gladly rests her tired legs and watches a sliver of sun breach the horizon, casting the lake in hues of red, orange, and gold. "What is this place?"

"It's the Stateline Fire Lookout, the best panoramic view of the North Shore." She follows his finger across the water. "You've got Crystal Bay on the Nevada side and Kings Beach on the California side. The Sierra Nevadas. There's not much you can't spot from here."

"It's amazing. I've never seen anything so beautiful."

Robert directs her attention to a section of tree-covered peaks. "Your grandfather, Wallace, was born in a cabin in those mountains in the middle of a record snowstorm. Highway 50 was impassable for six weeks, and the snow was so high that you could walk in and out of the upstairs windows."

Hallie giggles at the thought. She settles in, relishing again her father's storytelling.

"Wallace's mother, my grandmother, went into labor early, and he was breech. To hear him tell it, it was touch and go for a while. Like most folks, they didn't have a phone line in the cabin, so Grandpa had to ski into town to find the doctor. By the time the two of them made it back, Wallace was already crying so loud, Grandpa heard him from the road. Turns out, he'd righted himself. He told us that story every time we ventured out into nature. He'd always joke that he'd been born with an inherent sense of direction. And any Thompson worth his salt shared the same genes."

Poor Logan. No wonder he'd pronounced himself a disappointment. "That's an incredible story. Your dad sounds like quite a character."

"That's putting it mildly." Robert chuckles. "You two would've gotten along like peas in a pod. He admired anybody who went after a dream."

Despite her guilt about lying to the Thompsons, a wide smile stretches Hallie's cheeks. Each time Robert applauds her, she feels like she's won a contest. His praise is addictive. One hit just isn't enough. Hallie understands the roots of Natalie's envy.

"Logan and Natalie haven't mentioned their grandfather. Did they know him well?"

Robert doesn't answer—not at first—but in the silence Hallie hears the muted snuffle of his tears. Not wanting to embarrass him, she keeps her eyes straight ahead on the spot where lake meets sky. The colors are so intense, the horizon looks as if it's on fire.

"It's hard for them to talk about," Robert says, finally. "For me too. The way he died, it was painful for all of us. After he passed, I thought it would help to move the family out here, to the place he grew up. The place he loved. I hoped it would make him a little less gone. I imagine it's something like what you went through losing your mother."

Blinding lights. Swerve. Screech. Blackness. "I still dream about it sometimes," she hears herself admit. She doesn't talk about it either. Not with anyone. Not ever. For the first few years after, grief doubled her over, burning like a shard stuck between her ribs. Now, it's just a dull ache, pressing on her chest. Some days, she forgets entirely. Other days, it's heavy as a boulder.

"Do you want to tell me about it? No pressure, but maybe... well, sometimes talking helps. Or at least that's what they say."

"It was my fault," Hallie blurts out. As if she's been waiting nineteen years to say it. "And don't tell me it wasn't."

Robert holds up his hands in surrender. "Wasn't gonna. To tell you the truth, I blame myself for my father's death too."

"You do?"

The sharp nod of his head in her periphery makes her feel less alone.

"I do," he says, turning to her with a sad smile. "And now *you* don't tell me it wasn't."

Sunlight streaks across the lake. The wind blows a strand of hair across her face. Time slows, then speeds up again. The same way it did that night. "My mom shouldn't have been driving. She'd had too many pills. But I'd made the school play, and it was opening night. I just wanted to be a normal kid with a normal mother, who would sit in the front row clapping and cheering and embarrassing me. I begged her to come. It was only a stupid chorus part. I didn't have any lines. Still, I was desperate to have her there, and she was too stoned to know better. Mom started dozing and then..."

Hallie stops herself before she goes too far, says too much. "The car went off the road, and we ran head on into a tree. I don't remember much after that. Just bits and pieces."

Robert exhales. In a way, Hallie takes pleasure in his

shock. She wants him to understand how much she struggled. How much it took to get here.

"Were you hurt?" he asks.

She extends her right leg. "An open fracture of the tibia. When I came out of surgery, I asked for my mom. I was so worried that they'd arrest her for being high on pills. I never considered there could be a worse outcome. That she didn't make it."

"No kid should have to go through that. Especially not alone. I suppose you were lucky to survive at all."

Lucky. Hallie ponders the word for a moment. It doesn't suit her. She's always been anything but. "After a few days in the hospital, one of the responding officers came to visit me. He told me my seatbelt saved my life. Mom didn't like to wear hers. *It hurt*, she said. Everything hurt."

"So, she was sick? In pain? That's why she took pills?"

Hallie wishes she had an easy answer. It boiled down to the age-old chicken or the egg dilemma. The OxyContin or the pain, which came first? And what sort of pain was it? The bang-your-knee kind or the heartache?

"It's hard to say. She spent a lot of days in bed, complaining that her whole body hurt. It started when she injured her back at work, picking up a box of office supplies. The pills helped at first. Until they didn't. Then she just needed more and more to function, and after a while, she stopped functioning altogether."

Robert takes her hand and gives it a squeeze. "You are one brave gal. And determined too, writing all those letters looking for me. Your mother would be incredibly proud of you."

It's good to hear it, even though Hallie knows better. If Elizabeth Sherman saw her here, watching the sunrise with the man who ruined their lives, she would call her a traitor. She would tell her it was a bad omen that this Robert Thompson's letter got lost in the mail. She would never, ever forgive Hallie.

As they walk back to the truck, she tips back her head to marvel at the cloudless blue sky. Somehow, her steps feel lighter. Her head, less cluttered. Even if she hadn't told him the worst part. The way her mom's arm had jutted out, right before impact, to protect her. That instinct, still sharp, no matter how the pills had dulled the rest of her. Elizabeth Sherman's last thought had been of Hallie and that stuck between her ribs like a hot knife.

Robert pulls up short, as if he's just remembered something.

"You know, Mark Twain wrote a story about the lookout. Ironically, it was one of my dad's favorites."

"I don't doubt it. Anyone would be inspired by that view."

"Actually, Twain nearly destroyed it. He and his brother built a fire to heat their dinner, and it escaped the pit. Set the whole damn place ablaze, including their lean-to. They could only watch from the overlook, helpless, while it raged across the mountains. Life is so fragile."

Hallie needs no reminding of that. But Robert isn't talking to her anyway. Not really. He gazes off, lost in his own world.

"You never said how your father died."

His reply rasps from his throat like a dry wind. "Fire."

SIXTEEN

The morning quickly fades to afternoon, with Hallie busy at Cerulean helping Nick and the team prep for dinner service. The kitchen hums along in its fast but steady rhythm. It's safe, predictable, and consistent, the aspects of cooking Hallie finds the most appealing. She can foresee what will happen when she adds flour to the sauce or sprinkles a dash of salt into the soup. She can measure more carefully, stir faster, control the outcome. People, on the other hand, don't follow a recipe, often behaving in strange ways she can't anticipate, no matter how she tries. Like Natalie rolling in midday to casually retrieve the rush order cookies she'd been tied in knots about yesterday. At least she'd muttered a begrudging *thank you.*

Halfway through dinner service, Robert pokes his head in. "Hallie, would you mind bussing a few tables? We're slammed out there. A couple of our regular staff didn't show. Logan came in to help out, but between you and me, he's hopeless. He's got no sense of urgency and two left feet."

"As long as the boss gives me the okay." Hallie nods at a

harried Nick. "It's a madhouse back here too. I've been helping him expedite."

"I can manage," Nick answers, without breaking concentration. He cleans a bit of stray sauce from the edge of a plate before placing it beneath the warmer.

She takes a tray and follows Robert through the doors and into the crowded dining room. Nearly every table is occupied, and a line snakes from the front door to the hostess stand, where Shelly greets the patrons with a warm, lipsticked smile. When a guest summons Robert to their table, calling him by his first name, he leaves Hallie to fend for herself amid the din—an amalgam of chatter, clinked glasses, and dropped silverware. Hallie prefers the busy kitchen, where she knows her role. Where she can keep her head down. Out here in the fancy dining room, she flops around like a fish out of water until another busser directs her to a table in need of cleaning. She stacks the dishes onto the tray and carries them into the back. That part, at least, is old hat for a diner waitress like herself. After retrieving a new set of linens, Hallie stares at the table, uncertain. The A La Mode Diner had never seen a white tablecloth or a salad fork. The most expensive item on the menu was the $22 prime rib and baked potato. She hopes Robert doesn't see her, looking like an imposter. Surely, all the chefs at Michelin-starred El Mar could do every job in the restaurant passably.

"Need a hand?" Logan asks.

"Is it that obvious?"

"No. But it's harder than it looks. The centerfold of the cloth goes right in the middle of the table. Otherwise, Dad will pitch a fit." With that vote of confidence, he starts toward the back, telling her, "I'll grab the place settings."

Hallie nods. How hard can it be? It's a tablecloth, not molecular gastronomy. She swaps the linen, taking care to follow Logan's instructions. Pleased with herself, she steps back to admire her work. Not bad for her first time.

Logan approaches the table with his hands full, just as a boisterous guest belts out a roar of a laugh. Hallie studies the man's bald head, finding something unnervingly familiar about the shape of it. When she realizes, she nearly gasps.

What is Andrew Sumner doing here, a hundred and twenty miles from Sacramento and a world away from the A La Mode, where she'd left him wallet-less and covered in dishwater?

The scene unfolds in slow motion, Hallie powerless to stop it. Logan's foot meets a chair leg, sending the place settings into the air. Logan isn't nearly as aerodynamic, landing with a thud in the middle of the dining room.

The room stills. Heads turn, forks poised mid-bite. Hallie knows she should rush to help her brother. Instead, she flees, never lifting her eyes from the floor. She hardly breathes, as she waits just outside the kitchen for Andrew to stand up and point his finger at her. To tell everyone within earshot about her little stunt at the diner. To call her a thief. Then the Thompsons will know what she's been hiding, every sordid bit of it. She'll end up on a bus back to Sacramento, or worse, in jail. No, she's not lucky. Never has been. This sort of disaster always happens to her. Like the time she and her foster sister shoplifted a tin of Christmas cookies. Hallie had been the one caught with the crumbs in her bed and shipped off to a group home the following day.

"Thanks for nothing." Logan brushes past her, his face still alarmingly red.

"I'm sorry. I..." She glances back at Andrew. He's telling

a story, seemingly oblivious to her presence. At least for now. "Everybody was looking, and—"

"Yeah, at *me*. The perpetual screw-up." His shoulders slump. "At least help me finish the table."

Hallie avoids eye contact, wishing she could disappear. She *can't* go out there. It will mean the end of all this, and she'll be utterly alone again. By the time she prepares to stammer out an excuse, she realizes Logan's attention has landed elsewhere, on his mother at the hostess stand. Shelly is holding her hands up in defense as a dark-haired man in a business suit jabs his finger at her like a weapon.

"Damn it, Jordan," mutters Logan.

Jordan. Robert's partner in Last Glass had that name. Hallie remembers it from the law firm's letter she found.

Her brother takes off toward the entrance. Robert, too, hurries from across the restaurant. And slowly, surely, the other diners are starting to notice the commotion. Hallie shrinks away to watch the exchange from the safety of a dark corner. She can't risk being seen by Andrew Sumner. If she puts herself in the middle of the action, she may as well tap him on the shoulder and say hi.

Though she can't hear her father over the noise of the restaurant, his lips are easy to read. *Get out. Now. Leave my family alone.* Every word sharp as a dagger.

Jordan stands his ground, puffing out his chest, and Hallie decides her hunch is correct. They know each other. It's escalated too quickly for a disagreement between strangers.

Shelly pulls at Robert, but he seems not to notice her there, even as she grows more insistent. She gestures wildly to the crowded restaurant, tugs at his arm again. He pushes her away with a sudden flourish that leaves Hallie stunned.

Angry Robert scares her, giving her a stark reminder of how little she knows him.

The stalemate can't last. Jordan drives forward, leaving only a fist of space between them. His nostrils flare, and his hands clench at his sides, ready to strike. Shelly dissolves into tears, cowering by the wall. As Hallie predicted, nearly every diner's head begins to turn toward the scene, Andrew's included. An eerie quiet descends over the dining room.

Logan bravely pushes himself between the two men. In the hush, his voice rings clear. "Get out, Jordan. Or I'll call the police."

Jordan retreats toward the door and pulls the handle so hard that Hallie jumps back at the sheer aggression of his movement. Then, he stops, turns. "You're going to pay one way or the other, Thompson. And I'll make damn sure everyone knows what kind of man you really are."

Hallie doesn't dare breathe as she watches Jordan open his mouth, no doubt prepared to unleash her father's secrets. But Logan strikes first, landing a solid punch to Jordan's jaw. The man wobbles backward, stumbling out the door. Logan, too, staggers back, then doubles over, grabbing his fist.

"What's going on?" Nick appears behind her, sounding concerned. "Should I call the police?"

The question reverberates through Hallie like a strong wind. She can only think about hiding herself from Andrew Sumner, protecting herself and her secrets. If she doesn't, who will?

"I don't know." It's all she can manage before disappearing into the kitchen.

SEVENTEEN

Hallie wipes down the counters once more, taking comfort in the routine. With Nick's permission, the rest of the crew left early. Still on edge, Hallie isn't ready to go. She doesn't want to answer any questions about why she left Logan to fend for himself after his trip and fall. Or why she spent the rest of the evening holed up back here, avoiding the cops and her new family in equal measure.

"What a night, huh?" Hallie tests the waters with Nick, hoping he'd been too distracted to notice her strange behavior. He'd returned to the kitchen looking unusually flustered and delivered the news. *The police are here. Robert says to close up early.*

"That's an understatement." He leans against the counter. His sigh puts her at ease. "Did you recognize that guy?"

Hallie realizes which guy he means. The mysterious Jordan. Still, she pictures Andrew Sumner, dishwater dripping down his face. It figures a wealthy prick like him would frequent a place like Incline Village. Though her prior

Google search had planted him squarely in the Richmond Grove neighborhood of Sacramento, with her luck, she'd overlooked his second home on Billionaire's Row. "No. You?"

"Not at first. But I overheard Robert talking. His name is Jordan Markum. He's kind of a big deal in the restaurant world, especially in the Bay Area." Nick shrugs. "At least Logan didn't get arrested. The sheriff is one of our best customers. Sometimes it pays to have connections."

"*Sometimes?*" Hallie laughs, finally letting herself relax. Despite his reticence, Nick has a way of disarming her, and she cautions herself to guard against it. It's better not to get too close. Tonight was a good reminder of how easily all this could disappear. How quickly she could be out on her ass. Broke and alone. Right back where she started.

"Want a ride back to the Thompsons' place?" Nick asks. "I think the cops told Robert to drive Logan home."

"Only if it's not too much trouble. Do you live nearby?"

"On my salary?" Nick snorts. "Not everybody in Incline Village can afford a mansion on Lakeshore Drive. You'd be surprised how many folks around here can barely make ends meet, much less have money left over to entertain a houseguest for the summer."

Hallie winces. This is why she has no friends. She can't stand the whiplash. "It was just a question. I didn't mean anything by it."

"That came out wrong. I'm sorry." He puts a hand behind his neck, kneading the tension. "It's been a rough couple of days. I shouldn't take it out on you."

She aims a pointed glance at the counter, where he'd placed his cellphone. It's been noticeably silent tonight. "You have been pretty busy lately. I'm surprised that thing's not Velcroed to your hand."

His face instantly brightens, making Hallie reconsider. Maybe he isn't like everyone else, jerking the rug from underneath her at a moment's notice.

"Well, I *am* the executive chef at the most popular restaurant in Incline."

"You'll get no argument from me on that one, boss."

"Good. Then, you can take those out while I lock up." Smirking, he points to the bags of trash by the side door and laughs out loud when Hallie salutes him.

She supposes she had it coming. But she's never minded the grunt work. Besides, she needs to see Jay again to ask him about the burned photograph she found in the firepit.

"I'll meet you at the jeep," she calls over her shoulder, as she slings the bags out the door. She wishes she'd remembered to fix a plate for Jay. The idea of him dumpster diving makes her cringe.

After tossing the bags, she hurries down the trail that's become familiar to her now. The sun has only just dipped below the horizon, leaving remnants of light between the trees. It seems a lifetime ago that she saw it rise with her father at her side. She'd felt so close to him then. Now, the old doubts have crept in. The questions, the judgments. The feelings that once belonged to her mother are hers now, a part of her intangible inheritance. What if she's been wrong to trust Robert? To trust the Thompsons?

Hallie reaches The Grotto and scans the ground for signs of Jay. No fire in the rudimentary pit. No mound of blankets. But she spots his red bicycle hidden in the trees. When the breeze picks up, the antique lanterns begin to sway. She fights off a chill at the sound of the creaking branches.

"Jay," she dares to whisper. "Are you out here?" She sits atop one of the oak tables, still warm from the sun, and waits, knowing she can't stay long. Nick will be looking for her. "The police are gone, if that's what you're worried about."

A soft stirring draws her attention. Jay appears from the grove of sugar pines. He lingers at the edge, his face cast in shadow by his hoodie. He reminds her of the skittish deer from the morning. "Did you tell them about me?"

"No. I didn't tell anyone. I promised I wouldn't."

"So, what were they doing here then?"

Fearing she'll spook him, Hallie doesn't dare move. "My brother punched a man in the face."

"He *what?*" Like a sudden gust of wind, the strength of his voice surprises Hallie. "Why?"

"I'm not really sure. But he was defending our dad so..." A strange thought occurs to her. "Do you know Logan?"

"*Who?*"

"I just thought, the way you reacted, that maybe you knew him. Not that I know him well either. I only met him a few days ago, but he's not the type to go around punching people. It surprised me. It surprised *everyone.*"

"Who'd he punch?"

"Some restaurant bigwig named Jordan Markum. He knocked him right out the door when the guy threatened Robert." Hallie tells herself to stop rambling, but Jay doesn't protest. He stands rigid, with his hands stuffed into his front pocket, leaving her no choice but to continue. "Though I suppose, when you have a real family, it makes sense. To protect them, no matter what. I wish I'd had somebody to fight for."

Jay looks pained. "It doesn't always turn out that way. Some animals abandon their young. Did you know that most pandas have twins? The mothers choose one to love and leave the other."

Hallie frowns at him, disturbed by the strange and tragic fact he just spouted.

"It's just something I read at the library. I spend a lot of time there these days. Free air conditioning, internet access, and a clean bathroom. Can't beat it."

She wants to press him for more. But she's running out of time to ask about the photograph. "I found a burned photo in the firepit on Monday. A family photo of the Thompsons. Do you know how it got there?"

"I burn whatever I find," he answers with a shrug. "I'm resourceful. Life in a six by eight box will do that to you. Give me a cup of ramen and a bottle of ketchup and I'll make you a gourmet meal."

"But where did the photo come from? Did someone give it to you? Have you seen anyone sneaking around back here? Somebody broke in and vandalized my sister's cookies too."

From the path, the crunch of footsteps on gravel signals an approach. She squints into the murk, as the sound grows louder. "Hallie! You back there?"

"Coming," she calls, hoping to slow Nick down. "Be there in a minute."

When she turns back to the spot where Jay stood, still hopeful for an answer, he's been swallowed by the dark. Only his boot prints in the dirt remain.

Hallie lies in bed wide awake, replaying her conversation with her father on repeat. She'd arrived home to find all four Thompsons in the living room, huddled together like a football team. *Just an unhappy customer*, Robert had told her, looking her dead in the eyes she'd inherited from him. *Nothing to worry about.* Her father has lied to her. Natalie hates her. Shelly doesn't trust her. And though she can't prove it, she suspects that even Nick is hiding something.

Hallie pulls the covers up, then kicks them off. Flips her pillow. Turns this way and that. Still, she can't ignore the nagging in her head. A part of her wonders whether it was a mistake to come here at all. Maybe she should pack her designer suitcase and run like hell. At least she knows what to expect from her old life in Sacramento. Another crappy apartment she can't afford. Another job she doesn't want. She makes a mental list of the last few years. Culinary school dropout. Pizza delivery girl. Nanny. Motel housekeeper. Dog walker. Gas station cashier. Sad to say, but waitress at the A La Mode was the closest she'd been to her dreams. And still, she'd been about as close as the distance between the earth and the center of the Milky Way.

When she hears the hushed voices of her siblings on the back deck below, she slips out of bed and skulks toward the double doors, edging one open a fraction.

"I can't believe you punched him."

"What was I supposed to do? Let him blab about everything in front of the whole goddamn restaurant?"

"I just didn't think you had it in you, little brother."

"Gee, thanks for the vote of confidence."

"No, *really*. I'm impressed. Dad was too." Natalie lowers her voice, forcing Hallie to open the door wider. She holds her breath, straining to hear. Even then, she can't quite catch it all.

"How do we... she's not in... it? Like... spy or..."

"For Jordan or...?"

Hallie knows it's a risk when she steps one foot onto the upper deck. Her entire body clenches at the creaking of the wooden planks. But her siblings go on, oblivious.

"I *know* she stole that photo. She probably burned it too. And my cookies. The rope bridge. Maybe he told her to do it all. He must be miserable. Who knows what he'll do to mess with us?"

"What would Jordan want with our family photo?"

Natalie's exasperated sigh comes out with the force of a strong wind. "Not Jordan, dummy."

A wispy cloud stretches across the moon. Hallie waits for Logan to speak.

The sudden ringing of her cellphone blasts through the quiet evening with the delicacy of a sledgehammer. Below her, she hears the scrape of a deck chair.

"What's that ringing?" Natalie asks. "Is that a phone?"

Cursing under her breath, Hallie ducks back inside without closing the door. She dives for the phone, silencing it with a tap, and buries herself beneath the comforter.

Inside her inky cave, she peers at the screen. One missed call from Maxine Mintz. Even before she presses play on the fifteen-second voicemail, her stomach takes a nosedive.

"Hiya, Hallie. It's Maxine. I thought you should know that your well-to-do vegan friend has been sniffing around the diner. He reported you to the police. What were you thinking? I'm not sure where you are now, but it's probably best you stay gone."

Hallie stays under her blanket fort, letting the subtle horror of her situation sink in. Someone is out to get the Thompsons. Her siblings don't trust her. And now, there's no running back to Sacramento with her tail between her legs. Hallie has to face facts. She's trapped.

EMAIL

To: Hallie Sherman <hsherman94@pacbell.com>

From: Janet Thompson <janet.thompson57@quickmail.net>

Subject: How dare you?

Ms. Sherman,

You should be ashamed of yourself. Your letter was most unwelcome and brought up many unpleasant feelings for me and my son, Robert. When he was only sixteen years old, Robert was paralyzed from the neck down in a car accident. His life has never been the same. He has never married, has no children, and requires daily nursing care. It's been incredibly painful for him to watch his friends live full lives—with jobs, travel, marriage, and families—while he remains caught like a fly in amber, unable to progress. Since receiving your letter, Robert has been very depressed. I don't expect you to understand our predicament, but I implore you to carefully consider the consequences of your actions before you harm another innocent Robert Thompson with your silly little letter.

Please do not contact my son again.

Janet

EIGHTEEN

Hallie startles awake at the sound of angry voices, uncertain how long she's been sleeping. She's still buried beneath the comforter with her cellphone tucked in her hand, the battery nearly dead.

"I can't believe that asshole. He's taken it too far now. I'm calling the cops."

"We don't know it's him."

"Like hell we don't. First, he leaves that nasty note in our mailbox. Then, he comes into the restaurant last night, intimidating you. Threatening me and my family. Now, he's stooped to vandalism. Hell, maybe he was the one who sabotaged Nat's cookie order."

Unable to ignore Robert and Shelly's argument, Hallie slings off the covers. The clock on the nightstand reads 5 a.m. She pads down the hallway, barefoot, still rubbing her eyes and finds them in the kitchen in a standoff. Logan and Natalie arrive at the landing together, looking equally bewildered. Hallie takes a smidgen of pleasure in the circles under

Natalie's eyes, the pimple cream dotted on her forehead. Her hair sticking up, haphazard, not unlike her brother's.

"What happened?" Natalie asks.

"Someone slashed your father's truck tires."

"Not *someone*, Shelly. Don't sugarcoat it."

"Who then?"

Hallie clears her throat to announce her presence. "Am I interrupting?"

Natalie wastes no time putting her in her place. She prances her socked feet across the living room and puts on an air of pretend politeness. "Yes, this is a family matter. Would you give us some privacy, please?"

Wounded, Hallie shrinks back toward her room, when she hears Robert's voice. "C'mon. Hallie *is* family. There's no reason she can't hear this. In fact, I want her to hear it. She needs to know what he's capable of. As far as I'm concerned, we're all in danger."

"You've known her for less than a week, Dad." Natalie flicks her eyes to Hallie, dismissing her with a single glance. "Besides, if you were so comfortable telling her everything, then why did you lie to her last night? Why haven't you told her about—"

"*Nat.* Enough." Shelly holds up her hand, palm out. Her eyes are wide and wild. She looks as if she's trying to stop a train.

"I didn't want you to worry," Robert addresses Hallie. "I had no idea he would take it this far."

"Who?" Hallie plays dumb. "The angry customer?"

"He wasn't *just* an angry customer. His name is Jordan Markum. He's my former business partner. We owned a restaurant together, and he blamed me when it went south. He claims that I owe him a lot of money. It's been an ongoing issue, but a few days before you arrived, it reached a boiling point. His lawyers sent a letter. Then, a creepy note showed up in our mailbox. A threatening note."

Unsure how to reply, Hallie says nothing. It's safer that way.

Robert adds, "Remember the place I told you about in Napa? The one we couldn't get off the ground."

"You told her about Last Glass?"

Hallie turns to find Logan gaping at his father. Natalie takes up so much air in the room that she'd nearly forgotten about him.

"I can't believe you told her," he says again.

Hallie tries to make herself small, the way she'd learned to do as a child. So small, she won't be noticed. Though no one questions her, her body reacts as if she's on display. Her cheeks warm, stomach twists. It's the old feeling that she's done something wrong. That she's to blame for everything.

"I told her that the restaurant business is fickle. That you have to work for every scrap of success. And you certainly can't freeload your way to the top."

"*Really?* You're gonna make this about me? I've told you a million times, I'm not like you. I'm not like Grandpa Wallace. I don't want to take over the restaurant. I don't even want to work there."

Robert throws up his hands, then starts pacing like a caged tiger. He stabs at the screen of his cellphone, finally putting it to his ear.

"Why don't we all have a seat and calm down?" Shelly looks panicked. "The police will be here soon."

Natalie and Logan close ranks, shutting everyone out of their hushed conversation.

Fleeing to the picture window and the expanse of pastel

sky beyond it, Hallie lingers for a moment, then opens the door that leads to the upper deck in the front of the house. She leans over the railing to inspect the truck in the glow of early morning. From here, she can see the flattened tires on the front and rear driver's side. Imagining the violent slash in the rubber, she rubs the sudden goosebumps from her arms, uncertain whether she's frightened or cold or both.

The police arrive within ten minutes—no lights, no sirens, just a white SUV marked *Washoe County Sheriff*. Hallie had spent the entire wait on the deck, shivering in a wooden Adirondack chair as the sky turned a pinky orange. She felt better out there. Not like a broken-winged bird locked in a gilded cage.

"They're here," she says, though she doubts anyone hears her. Natalie had shut the door wordlessly, leaving Hallie alone outside.

She watches the two uniformed officers approach the front door and knock. She would rather not speak to them. To be asked questions she doesn't want to answer about where she's come from and why. But Robert motions her inside, giving her no choice in the matter. He's only been her father for a week and she doesn't want to disappoint him. She's duty-bound.

Robert greets both officers by their first names—Sheldon and Jimmy—with a handshake and a *how's the family* and an apology for bothering them so early in the morning. Hallie doubts they mind at all, since she can't imagine they see much crime in tiny Incline Village. A criminal mischief call might just be the highlight of their month.

"It's no problem, Mr. Thompson." Sheldon, the older of

the two men, removes a pocket notepad and glances up at her father with expectation. The younger officer, Jimmy, lets his eyes wander the room, landing on Hallie, then flicking away again. With his doughy cheeks, spiky red hair, and freckles, he looks more like a kid playing cops and robbers than an actual police officer.

"What seems to be the trouble?" Sheldon asks.

"Well, around 4:45 this morning, I thought I heard a noise out front. I figured it might be a bear trying to get into the bins again, so I came out here and took a look from the deck. That's when I noticed something wasn't right with the truck. I went outside to investigate and found all four tires slashed. I have a feeling I know who did it."

"Rob, we don't know for sure. Let's not spread rumors," said Shelly.

"Speak for yourself, hon. I *do* know." Frowning, Robert turns back to the officers, and Shelly returns to her perch on the armrest. Hallie doubts she'll open her mouth again. "I assume you heard about the trouble at the restaurant," Robert says.

"We sure did. Garcia and Millhoff took the call. It sounded like a dispute over a past business dealing, correct?"

"I wouldn't put it that nicely. Jordan came to Cerulean asking for trouble. He was looking to pick a fight. He outright threatened me. I'm glad this kiddo was there to step in." Robert clasps an arm around Logan's shoulders in a gesture that looks equal parts possessive and proud. "Who knows what would've happened?"

Jimmy grunts his agreement. "My big brother is in town visiting from Sacramento, and he was at the restaurant for dinner with some friends. He saw the whole thing go down."

"I'm sorry he had to witness that. Tell him to come back anytime. The next meal is on us."

Hallie takes a sudden interest in the nameplate pinned to the younger officer's lapel. Her throat constricts as she reads the name. Then, disbelieving, she reads it again. The room closes in. Hoping to suck up a breath of fresh air, she inches toward the door she's left open.

"And who's this lovely lady?" Sheldon nods in her direction, pinning her into place like an insect on a display board.

She pastes on a polite smile and accepts her fate. There is no escape now, only survival.

Even Robert's good-natured chuckle sounds foreboding. "It's a crazy story. This is my daughter Hallie. Believe it or not, we just met last Wednesday. You'll have to come dine with us on your off night. She's quite the chef."

Her blood whooshes through her ears. She watches Sheldon's mouth move, hears nothing but her panicked thoughts. Natalie watches her, hawk-like, from the corner of the room, somehow seeming to sense her fear. Even Logan appears impatient with their father's gushing. Meanwhile, Hallie wishes she could scrabble away like a field mouse and hide under the floorboards.

When her senses return to her, Robert is nodding. "Absolutely, Sheldon. That's exactly why I called tonight. This is really getting out of hand."

"Well, let's have a look."

Robert leads Sheldon back down the stairs and out the front door while Jimmy stays behind, to Hallie's dismay.

"Would you like a drink?" Shelly asks. "I can brew some coffee."

"That won't be necessary." Jimmy plucks his notepad from his pocket and flips the front cover open to the first page. It looks brand new. "Did you four hear anything suspicious?"

"Nothing." Hallie answers first, wanting to be done with it. She hopes that no one else hears the tightness in her breath. "I only woke up when Robert and Shelly started arguing."

The instant it's out of her mouth, she wants to take it back. More so, when Shelly looks at her with a mixture of betrayal and surprise. But she finds that she can't shut herself up.

"What I meant is, I heard a commotion in the kitchen. Not really arguing, but loud talking. Like raised voices and—"

Natalie interrupts, silencing Hallie with the sharpest of tones. "I think what Hallie means to say is that Mom and Dad were obviously upset about the truck and afraid of what might happen next. Weird things have been happening lately. It's got us all on edge."

"That's exactly what I meant," Hallie parrots. She sounds pathetic. But Jimmy seems to buy it.

"Weird things?" he asks, tapping his notepad, his pen poised, ready to solve the caper. "Like what?"

Natalie cuts her eyes at Hallie as she explains the suspicious happenings on their hike and at the restaurant. She even mentions the missing photograph, burned in the firepit. Jimmy scribbles it all down with beginner's enthusiasm. He's clearly never worked the beat in a big city like Sacramento, where the cops would surely laugh in your face if you reported the crime of ruined cookies.

"Anybody else who might've done something like this? Disgruntled customers? Exes? Enemies?"

"No," Shelly answers first and firmly. And suddenly she's

willing to indict the man she'd been defending all night. "It must be Jordan. There is absolutely no one else it could be."

After the Washoe County Sheriff's vehicle disappears from sight, Hallie doesn't run. She doesn't hurry. She makes up an excuse about needing to use the bathroom and calmly places one foot in front of the other until she reaches the guest bedroom. Only when the door has been shut and locked behind her does she move with urgency toward her cellphone. Her thumbs fly across the screen's keyboard, typing two names into the search engine. She already knows, but she needs confirmation. She needs to see it for herself.

She scans the results on the people-finder page first, panic fluttering like a wild thing in her chest. Then, she finds the article. A recent obituary for a woman named Mary Sumner—survived by her two sons, an officer of the law and an attorney—and the thing in her chest has her heart in its claws, squeezing.

Tiny Incline Village suddenly feels a lot smaller. Jimmy and Andrew Sumner are brothers.

NINETEEN

Hallie stays in her room until Shelly calls her for breakfast, cycling through the litany of worst-case scenarios. Public humiliation. Rejection. Jail. She stands in front of the mirror and pictures herself in an orange jumpsuit. She supposes that at least she'd have three meals a day and a bed to sleep in. Once, her mother had been arrested for shoplifting in the dollar store and carted away while Hallie watched, helpless, from the back of the station wagon. Usually, Hallie tries to suppress that particular memory, because it was the loneliest weekend of her life, waiting for her mom to return. She'd been so afraid of being found out that she drove the car herself, clumsily parking it around the corner in a spot by the underpass. After that unfortunate incident, Hallie's mother changed tactics. Pickpockets rarely got caught.

When Shelly summons her, she decides right then. She can't go to Cerulean. Not today. Not after the offer Robert had made to Jimmy. *Tell him to come back anytime. The next meal is on us.* Her safe space feels like minefield.

"I don't feel so good," she says to the closed door. She tucks herself into the covers in case Shelly peeks inside.

"Oh, goodness," Shelly says through the door. "Is there something I can do?"

Shelly's genuine concern makes Hallie feel even worse. Her stomach flip-flops. Maybe she really *is* ill. "It's probably just a stomach bug. I'll stay here and sleep it off."

"Alright. I'll let Rob know. He already had the truck towed to the nearest tire shop. Should I tell Nick you won't be there to help with the dinner service?"

Another stab of guilt, right to the flank. She pushes through it. "It's probably best that I don't go in. I don't want anyone else to get sick."

Shelly opens the door a smidge and gives her a pitying smile. "Are you sure I can't get you anything? Peppermint tea? Antacid medication?"

Hallie's never been properly mothered before, so she doesn't know how to respond to her kindness. She shakes her head, lowers her eyes. "I'm sorry I told that cop you and Robert were arguing. I hope it didn't cause any trouble. I just blurted it out without thinking."

"You were telling the truth as you saw it, dear. Don't be sorry for that." Shelly gives a dismissive wave of her hand. "Besides, we've known Jimmy since he moved out here from Sacramento with his wife. He's at the bar at least once a week with his buddies. He's harmless."

Hallie tries to quash the nervous laugh that bubbles up inside her, threatening to spill out. "Are Nat and Logan still around?"

"Nat's at the restaurant dropping off the Nibbles orders, and Logan went for a run. I'll be heading out too, in a bit. You'll have the whole place to yourself."

"I'm planning to spend the day right here." Hallie tugs the blanket up to her chin and pretends to settle in. "It's been a whirlwind of a week. I think it's all catching up to me."

Shelly makes a sympathetic noise. "Get some rest. And keep the front door locked."

"You don't think Jordan will come back, do you?"

"If you'd asked me yesterday whether he would show up at the restaurant and confront me like that, I wouldn't have believed it. He was always a little short-tempered but..." She shakes her head. "Obviously, we didn't know him as well as we thought."

"Are there any other suspects?"

"Not that I've heard. Rob's convinced it's him. Apparently, Sheldon said the knife marks were unique. *Serrated.* And Rob kept going on about the cuts to Natalie's Nibbles bags being similar. Suddenly, he seems to think all these incidents are connected. That they're all Jordan's doing."

"The suspension bridge too?"

"Rob certainly believes so." She pauses, her lips pursed tight with worry. "Better safe than sorry, I suppose."

Hallie imagines a dark figure creeping through the woods with a blade. Gloved hands stabbing and slicing through rubber. A glint of teeth in the moonlight. A satisfied smile. "I'll be careful."

Hallie listens to the fading rumble of Shelly's sedan before she flings off the covers and approaches the window. She tugs her hair into a ponytail and pulls on sweats and a T-shirt before opening the door and calling for her siblings. No answer. Satisfied that every member of the Thompson clan has taken their leave, she shuts the door behind her, more certain than ever that her newfound family is hiding a secret. A secret that's put them all in danger.

First stop, the master bedroom.

As Hallie anticipated, the door is locked. Steadying her hands with a breath, she slips two bobby pins from her hair. She straightens one and bends the other to create the lever. A simple lock like this one should pose no real obstacle. It's just finding the right spot, maneuvering the pins until she hears the magic *click*. Even now, she gets the little thrill she had the very first time she'd picked a lock. It was at foster home number four, where the baddest bad girl had nudged her awake at midnight and led her to the locked liquor cabinet, two paperclips in tow. Hallie had spat out the swig of vodka, unimpressed. But the zip up her spine on being able to open the lock, that stuck with her. The freedom it gave her. She could go where she wanted, no matter who didn't want her there.

The door creaks open to reveal a luxurious four-poster bed canopied beneath a cathedral ceiling. Hanging from the center beam, a deer antler chandelier. It's no trouble telling which side of the bed is Shelly's. On the nightstand, an empty wine glass rests atop a dog-eared Harlequin paperback. Robert's side is bare save for a box of tissues and a pair of reading glasses. Though she spots one leg of a claw-footed tub that makes her groan with envy, Hallie doesn't bother with the master bathroom. Instead, she enters the walk-in closet and comes face to face with a lock she can't pick with bobby pins. She should have known Robert and Shelly would keep their skeletons locked up tight in the kind of safe you could only open with a fingerprint. Annoyed, she locks the door from the inside and pulls it shut behind her, frustrated with the time she's wasted.

When she reaches the recess with the small desk where she found the threatening note and the letter from Jordan Markum's attorney, she takes a right and heads down the long hallway. Looped around the knob of Natalie's door is a pastel pink do-not-disturb hanger. She knocks and presses her ear to the wood, just to be safe.

After making quick work of the locked door, Hallie shakes her head at the state of Natalie's bedroom. Her unmade bed, the least of it. She navigates around a mountainous pile of clothing, sidesteps a grimy makeup bag, and dodges a Snickers wrapper and two empty packages of Oreo cookies. So much for carb-counting. The far right corner of the bedroom has been marked as holy ground. There, Hallie can actually see the carpet. There, a laptop sits idle with a screensaver of Natalie blowing a kiss to the camera. There, a rechargeable ring light guides the way to a Nat's Nibbles logo on the wall and a small box of body tape on the nightstand. *Enhances cleavage*, the container reads. There, on this island amid the chaos, Natalie influences. Hallie wonders what her followers would think of the unglamorous reality.

She snoops around in the drawers, finds more chocolate. Looks under the bed, wonders if Natalie has ever used a vacuum. Finally, she makes her way to the walk-in closet, pulls open the door, and takes in an audible breath at the stack of unopened boxes from brands she recognizes but could never afford. Hallie's disdain grows with every pair of shoes she counts. Most of them appear brand new. Her entire sixth-grade year she wore the same pair of thrift store sneakers every day. And before her recent acquisitions, she'd deemed her heels from Target fancy.

To spite her sister, she dons the most expensive-looking pair of black leather boots with spiky heels sharp enough to kill a man and checks herself in the mirror. With shoes like that, she could've been a head chef by now, probably in an exciting city like Los Angeles or San Francisco, schmoozing with big names like Juan Antonio at industry parties. Of course, she would've had to learn to walk in the damn things first.

Still stamping around in Natalie's boots, Hallie peruses the upper shelf of the closet, where she spots a letter box that seems promising. She boosts herself on a stepstool and tugs the box down, bringing a poof of dust with it. Inside, Natalie keeps her girlhood treasures—ticket stubs and silly photos and a Prom Queen sash from Incline High School. Hallie tosses it all back in as she staves off another wave of indignation at the unfairness of it all. Suddenly, she wants to be anywhere but in this room, having her nose rubbed in the life that might've been hers.

When she affixes the lid to the top of the box, it sticks a little, resisting her pressure. Heaving a sigh, she pulls it off again to reorganize its contents. She identifies the culprit as the bent edge of an envelope, postmarked this year, with an unusual return address: California Youth Correctional Facility. She knows the place all too well. It's prison... for kids. You can stay until you're twenty-five, provided you weren't tried as an adult.

Slipping her finger beneath the flap, she slides open the envelope to reveal the handmade greeting card inside. It's intended to be funny, with a silly drawing on the front: a building ablaze, bright orange flames shooting from the windows. On the brick façade, a sign reads: *Ace Trick Candles*. A group of cartoon firefighters is rushing to the scene, one exclaiming, *I've never seen such a stubborn fire.*

Intrigued by the skill of the artist, Hallie reads the

message inside. *I haven't forgotten. I won't ever. Happy birthday. See you soon!*

She turns it over, examines the envelope again. No name or signature. *How odd.* But she can't mull it over for long. Not with Logan's bedroom left to search.

She strips off Natalie's boots and returns the left to the shoe rack. She tucks the right beneath her arm. Then, with a grunt of pleasure, she breaks the heel just enough so that it still appears intact and sets it beside the other. A little mischief never hurt anyone. Besides, Natalie never deserved these shoes.

Hallie finds Logan's door unlocked. Compared to his sister's room, it's military-level neat and not nearly as interesting. Bed, made. Floor, visible. Clothing, expertly folded and stacked in the drawers. The framed photographs carefully arranged on the walls—surfing, mountain climbing, kayaking—reflect both Logan's passion for the outdoors and his insecurities. All the photos are stock, with trite captions beneath them like, *Smooth seas never made a skilled sailor* and *You can only climb as high as you can dream.* Half his wardrobe looks like it came straight from Bear Grylls' closet. The poor guy even owns a book called *Kayaking for Dummies*. No doubt gifted to him by his sister, it rests in a place of honor on the nightstand beside his Garmin tactical watch.

Though Hallie doubts she'll uncover any state secrets in here, she completes the requisite rounds. Drawers. Closet. Mattress. Even the floor beneath the bed appears spotless. She wanders to the bookshelf, inspecting it for clues, but she only finds... *books*. Mostly of the travel and adventure variety.

Her eyes settle on the top shelf, where a small gold statue

of a bear draws her attention. She picks it up, surprised to find it's not a statue at all but a trophy. On the bear's outstretched paw, an engraved FIRST PLACE. Near the bottom of the square stand, she reads: *Two Man Survival Competition: Adolescent Boys Division.* It's dated nine years ago, just before the Thompsons moved to Lake Tahoe. Logan would've been twelve or thirteen.

Hallie's ears prick at the hint of a sound. She returns the trophy to its dust-free home without delay and slips out of the bedroom.

The knock at the front door comes only a moment later. Her heart starts firing, but she keeps her cool, taking her time to walk to the entryway. She straightens herself and rises to her tiptoes to peer out the sidelights before opening the door.

"Nick? What are you doing here?" Hallie hates herself for sounding so giddy. She makes a mental note to take her voice down an octave.

"Well, Shelly told me that you weren't feeling well, and I needed a break. So I thought I'd bring you..." His voice trails off, uncertain, as he hands over a paper bag. "I'm realizing now that you might not even like chicken noodle soup. And you'd probably rather be sleeping right now." Nick sizes her up from head to toe. At least she'd put on a bit of lip gloss. "Oh God, did I wake you?"

She shakes her head, holding tight to the bag. It's warm on the bottom, and a flavorful aroma reaches her nose. Her mouth starts to water, but she dials back her excitement. She's supposed to be sick. "This is so thoughtful of you. I'm glad you came. I was already getting so bored that I started to miss veg prep. I thought I'd dice a few onions for fun."

His laugh sounds different outside of the kitchen.

Lighter, freer. But his ever-present cellphone peeks out of his jeans pocket, waiting patiently to summon him.

"Do you want to come in for a sec?"

"Sure. If you're feeling up to it." He follows Hallie inside and up the stairs. "So, Robert said there was some drama this morning. Slashed tires?"

"Yeah. Pretty unoriginal."

Hallie sets the paper bag on the kitchen counter and takes a seat on one of the barstools while Nick makes his way around the other side. He retrieves two bowls from the cabinet and two spoons and a ladle from the drawer with the absent-mindedness of someone who knows his way around this particular kitchen.

"He thinks Jordan Markum is responsible," she says. "For all of it. The rope bridge too. And Natalie's damaged cookies."

"*Really?*" Nick grimaces as he doles out her portion of the soup and slides the bowl toward her. "Seems a bit far-fetched. A restaurateur like him playing childish pranks."

Hallie doesn't want to say too much. Her loyalties lie with the Thompsons now, no matter how imperfect her family might be. Still, she can't help but ask, "Did you know that the Thompsons owned a restaurant in Napa?"

Nick ponders her question. "Yeah. Robert was devastated when it failed. But he's tight-lipped about it."

She nods, blows on a steaming spoonful of broth, and waits for him to say more. As a waitress, she'd quickly picked up on the way her customers filled the silence. She'd only need give them a nod or a murmur, and they would talk her ear off. Divorces, affairs, births, and deaths. She'd heard it all, whether she wanted to or not.

"Just between you and me, there was a rumor about it

years ago. That the place burned to the ground. I overheard a couple of the kitchen staff talking and told them to mind their own business. That's what *I* do. Keep my head down and focus on the cooking. The rest is all bullshit."

Not wanting to seem too eager, Hallie doesn't push it. Besides, she agrees in theory. But she is a part of this family now, and she doesn't like being kept in the dark. Especially when she feels like an unwitting target. She sips the first spoonful. "Wow. This is the best soup I've ever tasted. And I'm not just saying that because you're my temporary boss."

Nick tries a sip himself and beams. "It's my mom's recipe with a few tweaks. Leeks instead of onions. A dash of thyme and a splash of dry white wine."

"Does your mother live here in Incline Village?"

Hallie regrets the question because of the way Nick's face changes. A subtle darkening, like a cloud passing over the sun. He murmurs a yes.

"Well, I'd love to meet her sometime. She must be proud of all that you've accomplished at the restaurant."

"I suppose. Though she would've preferred I followed in my father's footsteps."

"What did he do? Doctor, lawyer, congressman?"

Nick rewards her with another warm laugh. "*Handyman.* The Morellis are a simple people. Before he died, my dad always said that there's nothing like getting your hands dirty. Putting in a hard day's work for your paycheck."

"I like simple." She cocks her head at him and holds up her partially healed finger, still bandaged from its run-in with her careless knife. "But chefs get their hands plenty dirty, thank you very much."

"It's a different kind of dirt, apparently. Not dirty enough."

Hallie smiles though it's a sad sentiment that reminds her of Logan. The constant striving to be good enough. The never quite reaching that summit of high parental expectation. She supposes it's the one good thing about losing her mother early. She didn't have enough time to disappoint her. It worries her too. The more time she spends with Robert, the more he'll get to know her. With all the lies she's told, it can't end well.

"You know how you said that kids hang out at The Grotto sometimes. Do they ever light a fire in the pit?" she asks.

Nick stops eating, sets his spoon down. The hard set of his jaw scares her a little. "Why? Did you see a fire back there?"

"Uh..."

"Because you need to tell me if you did. It's fire season around here, and the trees can turn this place into a tinderbox. I'm serious, Hallie. You have no idea how fast a fire can get out of control. How deadly it can be."

She raises her hands in surrender. "I didn't see anything. I just..." In an instant, she decides to tell him. But not everything. She'll feel terrible if Jay gets arrested for loitering or, worse, sent back to prison. "I found one of the Thompsons' family photos burned up in the pit. Natalie told Shelly I put it there. And, obviously, I didn't. But the photo was framed and had gone missing from my room, so..."

"That's strange."

"Do you think Natalie might've done it on purpose? To make me look bad? I get the feeling she hates me. And I can't really blame her. Until now, she's been Daddy's little girl. Daddy's *only* girl. Then, I show up and steal her thunder."

"That seems extreme, even for Nat. But she can be ruthless when she wants something. Or some*one*." Nick's eyes flick up to hers. "I don't think it's only Robert that she's worried about you winning over."

Nick leans in the doorway, one shoulder against the frame. He's been leaving for the last ten minutes, but they can't stop talking. About the summer menu. The anniversary cookout. Their shared love of coriander seed. It's kept Hallie's mind off Andrew Sumner. The slashed tires. The idea that Jordan could be lurking in the sugar pines waiting to make his revenge upon the newest member of the Thompson clan. *Your family will pay.*

"Are you sure it's alright if I take the night off?"

"Technically, you're the owner's daughter, not my employee. You can do whatever you want."

The truth in his words jolts Hallie. She's never been lucky like that. Never been able to do whatever she wants. It makes her feel guilty to be taking advantage. But not guilty enough to ignore her worry about being spotted by Sumner. "It's nearly the weekend though. The place is bound to be slammed."

"We'll manage." He gives her arm a tender squeeze that she enjoys more than she should. "Feel better."

Finally, he steps out onto the porch, waving before he departs.

Armed with her new knowledge, Hallie runs up the stairs to her bedroom, where she returns to her cellphone and tries a new search. *Fire Last Glass Napa.* Predictably, the first few pages only turn up the most recent fires in the Napa region, and there are quite a few. But as she scrolls through page after page, fire after fire with no results, her suspicion grows. Maxine had once told her that, years ago, after a rash of food poisoning at A La Mode, she'd been approached by a company that would actively bury any negative online press. Maxine couldn't afford the hefty fee so those damning reviews were still out there. Like cockroaches, they'd live forever, crawling to the surface anytime they were summoned. Could Robert have paid to bury the news about Last Glass?

Hallie loses focus at page twenty. Her eyes glaze over, and she nearly misses the headline: *Cause of Diablo Fire Remains Under Investigation.*

> The devastating Diablo Fire that consumed 75,000 acres of vegetation in the Napa Valley, destroyed over three hundred structures, and resulted in the deaths of two people is under investigation, according to CAL FIRE spokesperson Jenna Li. The fire reportedly originated at the Toast of Napa winery, home to the newly opened Last Glass restaurant. Due to the high winds and drought conditions, the blaze took over three weeks to fully contain, which officials say has hampered the investigation into its causes. "We expect to determine a cause in the next few weeks," Li said. "But, at this point, we cannot rule out any cause, accidental or intentional."

Hallie stares at the article for a long time. Rereading the last line again and again, she can only wonder what else her new family is hiding.

EMAIL

To: Hallie Sherman <hsherman94@pacbell.com>

From: Bobby Thompson <bobalicious@orion.net>

Subject: Hey baby girl...

Attachment: Bobpic1.jpg, Bobpic2.jpg, Bobpic3.jpg

I looked you up online. U R Hot! Would love to be UR "daddy." Check out my sexy pics.

;-) Bobby

TWENTY

The following morning, Hallie tells herself to suck it up. She can't avoid the restaurant forever, and she certainly doesn't want to let Nick down or to disappoint Robert. She'll be in the kitchen anyway, where not even Andrew Sumner can spot her. Besides, holed up in the house, she can't stop thinking. About the thick woods that surround the place. About the distance to the nearest neighbor. About the way no one would hear her scream.

Hallie packs a few extra bagels from the bag on the counter and reassures Shelly that she's feeling much better, though the churning in her gut intensifies as she nears the restaurant. As if the Sumners will be out front, waiting for her—one with handcuffs, the other pointing the finger of blame. Dark blots on an otherwise clear, blue sky.

Hallie notices Robert's truck out front, with four brand new tires. Nick's jeep is parked nearby. She makes her way around the back, feeling herself drawn to The Grotto despite her misgivings.

There's no sign of Jay in the usual spots. The firepit is

clean and cold. But when she turns to go, she hears a whisper from the trees, calling her name. Then, the sound of rustling in the underbrush. She follows the noises through the thicket of sugar pines until she finds Jay with his bicycle. Just beyond his camp, the trees part and reveal the water's edge. It's a magical place where forest meets water meets sky.

"For you." She passes him the bagels she snagged, concerned to see that he's still wearing the same clothes.

Immediately, he digs in, taking a wolfish bite from the wholewheat sesame nobody wanted. She tries not to stare, but finds she can't look away. As he chews, he glances up at her self-consciously.

"You disappeared the other night." She directs her eyes to the water instead. "I wanted to talk more, and you ran away."

"I told you. I'm not going back. There's nothing like losing your freedom."

Hallie doesn't want to dwell on that. "But why would they send you back to prison? You're not hurting anyone."

"I just got off parole. I don't have a stable address or a job. And it's damn near impossible to get one without the other." Jay takes another bite. This one, a bit more restrained.

"I know."

"*You* know?"

His laugh rubs Hallie the wrong way. Her hackles rise, the same way they had at her first group home, when nobody believed a girl like her could have had it rough. As if her life had to show up on her face. As if her wide smile and blue eyes could shield her from pain. As if she couldn't be both pretty and astoundingly unlucky.

"I thought you said your dad owned the place. What would you know about being broke and homeless?"

She doesn't need to defend herself, but she's gone so long feeling unseen. It's not enough that Robert feels guilty. She wants somebody else to acknowledge the depth of her suffering. Even if it's just Jay, the vagrant parolee. Maybe *especially* Jay. He would sympathize with her. Ernie always had.

"It's complicated. I've only just met my dad. When I was nine, I lost my mom in a car accident and grew up in the foster system. Before that, we moved a lot. Sometimes, we didn't have food to eat. We slept in our car. If we hadn't owned the station wagon outright, we would've been living in the street. So, I understand you a lot better than you might think."

Jay quietly finishes the first bagel and starts on a second. His silence leaves Hallie exposed, convinced that she's overshared. Apparently, he doesn't feel the need to reciprocate.

"I'm sorry I misjudged you," he says, finally, after polishing off all three bagels. "Most folks around here don't get it. Hell, I was spoiled too until I got locked up. In there, it doesn't matter if you're rich or poor. Everybody wears the same jumpsuit and eats the same slop. It'll humble you real quick."

"Have you reached out to your family since you got out?"

"Here and there."

"And? Surely, they'd want to help you. They wouldn't like you living out here."

"They don't know where I'm living right now. I prefer it that way. They made it crystal clear that they don't give a shit about me. Do you know how many letters I got? How many visits? Zero. The day I stopped being perfect, I stopped being a part of the family. So screw them. I don't need their help."

Jay doesn't flinch as he says this. Still, Hallie knows it must hurt. Her heart has callused over too, but lately, she's been feeling more than just resentment and malaise. Beneath her thickened skin is a pinprick of hope that scares her.

"It's none of my business, but I think you should give them a chance. They might surprise you. Take my dad, for instance. My mom always told me that I was better off without him. That he didn't want me. But he's been nothing but kind and generous. He invited me to stay at his home. He let me work in the restaurant, doing what I love. He even took me to his favorite lookout spot. It makes me think my mom got it all wrong."

Jay sighs and hangs his head, his shaggy hair falling over his face like a curtain. "Maybe she did. But you said you only just met him, right? I'm twenty-five years old. At this point, there's not much I don't know about my parents. The only surprises have turned out to be bad ones."

"I hope the bagels were a good surprise, at least." Hallie realizes there will be no convincing him. "I was thinking, maybe I could ask Robert about getting you a job. The restaurant is always busy, and they could use another dishwasher. You could probably work your way up to—"

"I'm not your charity case." He looks up now, his eyes more gray than blue in the shade of the sugar pines. Like two stones set upon her.

"I know. But you said you were jobless and broke, and I think Robert will—"

"I said no. Just stay out of it." Jay slings his backpack over his shoulder and reaches for his bicycle. "Thanks for the bagels. I'll get out of your way."

Reluctantly, Hallie backs a few steps up the path, watching and waiting for Jay to change his mind. She sees a bit of herself in him, the bit that's always expecting the worst.

"Uh, Hallie?" Here it comes. He's about to reconsider. "Stop moving."

"What do you mean?"

He lowers his bag to the ground. His body, rigid as a tree trunk. "Stop. Moving."

Hallie hears the siren's blare of a warning in his voice. The crunch of twigs at her back. The hoarse breathing, not hers. As the hairs on her neck rise, Jay motions her toward him. *Slowly*, he mouths. *Slowly*.

She follows his instructions, taking one calculated step, then another. Her stomach clenches with a primal kind of fear. The fear of not knowing. She turns her head ever so slightly, and gasps. Her blood drains from her.

A bear ambles in her direction, snuffling at the ground. It pauses, lifting its snout into the air. A scream rises in Hallie's throat, but she clamps a hand over her mouth. She squeezes her eyes shut. She tries not to think about what she saw—its massive paws, ending in long, black talons. Or what she didn't—the sharp teeth, designed for ripping and tearing the flesh of its prey. *Her*.

"Go on, bear." Jay waves his arms, tentatively at first. Then, wider, making an arc behind him. "Get out of here."

Hallie wishes she could be that calm. Talking to the bear, like it's no big deal. *Excuse me, Mr. Bear, but would you please run along before I die of a heart attack.*

As Jay continues his ursine cajoling, Hallie risks another glance, then wishes she hadn't. The bear moves closer, standing on its hind legs to take another audible whiff of lake air.

"You're just a curious gal, aren't you? There's nothing to see here. Nothing to eat. You best get a move on."

Hallie's natural instinct to run fires through her muscles,

but she doesn't obey its will. She knows better than that. Run and the bear will give chase. Surely, it can already sense her terror.

"That's right. Keep going! And don't come back."

Hallie checks over her shoulder, in time to watch the bear's massive backside disappear between the trees. She staggers toward Jay, her wobbly legs barely keeping her upright. "You seriously saved my life," she says. "Are you some kind of bear whisperer?"

Jay shrugs, nonchalant, and she can only assume it's not the first time he's crossed paths with a bear. "She was just checking things out. She wasn't gonna hurt you."

"How do you know?"

"Because she didn't."

TWENTY-ONE

Hallie hasn't thought of Andrew Sumner in hours. Or Jordan Markum, for that matter. She hasn't wondered about the burned photograph or the slashed tires or her sister's jealous tirades. The only plus side of a bear encounter: she has been thoroughly distracted. So distracted, that she's nearly burned two orders of Nick's risotto.

Robert and Nick had laughed while she recounted the entire episode—sans Jay, of course. She certainly couldn't get him in trouble now that she owes him her life. She can relate to him too. She knows what it is like to feel utterly alone, to have no one to depend on but herself. Natalie, who'd shown up to help out with the weekend crowd, remained skeptical of Hallie's story all afternoon and into the dinner service, voicing her doubt every chance she got.

"I still don't get it." Natalie, assigned to the lowly salad station, arranges a small plate of romaine lettuce. "You scared the bear away all by yourself?"

"After your mom mentioned it on my first night, I Googled it. 'What to do if you encounter a bear.' You definitely don't run, since black bears can travel up to thirty miles per hour, just a hair slower than the grizzly, and their bite is strong enough to crush an iron skillet." Hallie hadn't learned those facts from the Internet but from outdoorsman Jay, who'd given her a mini lesson before he'd ridden away on his bike. "You have to make yourself huge and scary. It's all pretty simple, really," she continued, trying to sound blasé.

"Right. I suppose that would be simple for you." Holding a grater in one hand, Natalie attacks a hunk of Parmesan, sprinkling the casualties on top of the Caesar salad. "And it was a big bear, you said?"

"Big enough. I'm no bear expert, but when it raised up on its hind legs, it towered over me. And its paws looked as wide as a catcher's mitt."

Natalie makes a noise of disbelief, then hurls a scoop of handmade croutons onto the plate. "What were you doing in The Grotto anyway? *Smoking?*"

"Smoking? Where would you get that idea?" But then she remembers. The photo in the firepit. "It's beautiful back there. Peaceful. I went for a quick walk to clear my head before coming into the restaurant."

"Well, it's closed to visitors. And I noticed some cigarette butts near the picnic tables a few days ago. We take littering seriously around here. It's a minimum two hundred and fifty dollar fine."

Sending out an order of salmon croquettes, Nick groans. "Jeez, Nat. Give it a rest. You're like a dog with a bone."

Natalie harumphs. "Well, smoking is dangerous. And even more so during fire season. You know that."

"I wasn't smoking. And I didn't burn that picture." When Hallie spots Robert watching from the doorway, she immediately regrets her tone.

"What picture?" he asks.

"It's nothing, Dad." Natalie slits her eyes at Hallie in warning. "Hey, did you remember to bring that chocolate vodka from home? I scheduled an Instagram live tonight from the bar, showcasing my skinny chocolate martini."

"I thought your mother was supposed to bring it."

"She told me she asked you to do it."

Robert looks skyward and heaves a sigh. "I'm sorry, honey. I must've forgotten it on the counter. There was a lot going on this morning. I have to admit, I've been a bit distracted with this nonsense with Jordan."

"It's fine." Natalie waves him off and keeps her head down, preparing the next plate for her salad production line. Lettuce, Parmesan, croutons. Some chefs make their food with love. Natalie sprinkles her salads with heaping spoonfuls of rage.

"If things slow down a bit, I can run back to the house and get it," Robert offers.

"I said, *it's fine*. I'll just have to cancel the livestream. Disappoint my followers. Let down the sponsor. Hopefully, I won't lose the collaboration altogether."

Hallie can't bear to see her father's face crumple. To watch Natalie play him like a fiddle. "I'll go."

"What?" Nick jerks his head toward her in disbelief. She can't quite believe she said it herself. "That makes no sense. I need you here. There's no reason why Nat can't get her own damn vodka."

"Hey. I'm busy. On the—*how did you put it?*—'critical' salad station. Hallie's a floater. She's expendable."

"I'll be quick." Hallie reminds herself she's doing this for Robert. She wants him to understand that she's reliable. Dependable. Loyal. This will be one less worry on his mind. "I promise. You won't even know I'm gone."

Hallie zips back to the house in record time, parking Robert's truck in the driveway. The moon hangs above the house and casts the eaves in a silvery glow. She stops to take it in, remembering her arrival a week ago. How perfect it all had seemed. A perfect illusion.

The dark house unnerves her—with its vacant, all-seeing eyes—but not as much as the woods beyond it. The shadows between the trees; the delicate sounds that belong to the night. Jordan could be lurking nearby. What better way to retaliate than by targeting one of Robert's children? Hallie pushes the thought away. It's probably just leftover bear-panic, her nerves still buzzing from her chance encounter. For all she knows, those slashed tires came courtesy of a drunk teenager. The rest of it, mere coincidence.

Still, the image of a faceless stranger stalking toward the truck and plunging a knife into rubber does nothing to quell her unease. Before she works herself up into a panic, Hallie secures the spare key and lets herself inside.

She locks the door behind her and flips on the downstairs lights, relieved at the way it chases away her fears. She curses herself for being so silly.

Eager to retrieve Natalie's precious vodka and return to the restaurant, she heads up the stairs. She doesn't want Natalie to accuse her of slacking. Or worse, snooping. The more she ponders the possibility of her sister's false allegations the more paranoid she becomes. She needs to get in, get out, and get back to the busy kitchen, where no matter what mistakes she makes, there's a room full of witnesses. With Natalie, it feels impossible to win a battle of she-said, she-said.

The bottle of vodka sits smack in the middle of the countertop, where Robert had left it. Hallie grabs it and turns to go, already imagining herself returning as the hero in her father's eyes. But then, her feet grind to a halt.

Something imperceptible draws her attention to the hallway that leads to the guest bedroom. An urge grips her, leading her down the corridor, past the bathroom toward her door. It'll only take a moment to check, to confirm that everything remains as she'd left it.

Hallie's eyes flit across the walls. The family photos, dimly lit by the moonlight. Everything looks different in the dark. Smiles become sinister. The clutch of an arm around a shoulder becomes suffocating, predatory. She should've turned on all the lights.

When her gaze fixes on the painting of the Thompson family, she doesn't scream, though her fear bubbles up unbidden, demanding release. She simply stares. Her feet grow roots. Nights ago, she'd stood in that same spot, covering the faces of Natalie and Logan, and picturing herself in their place. Now, their faces are gone. A wide gash ripped through the canvas, through Robert's likeness as well.

Hallie blinks several times to be sure it's not a trick of the light. She desperately wants it be. But each time she opens her eyes, the wound reappears in the painting as proof that someone has been here. Could Jordan have done this? Why now, eight years after the fire? This seems more personal than an unpaid debt.

Patting her pocket, Hallie's stomach sinks. In her haste, she'd left her cell on the truck's console. She moves toward the guest bedroom door, remembering the gun in the closet. The knob feels warm to the touch. Though she knows it's illogical, that alone convinces her that someone has been—*is still?*—inside her room.

Mustering her courage, Hallie takes a breath and flings it open. Empty. The realization floods her with relief, and she hurries to the closet. Tosses the blankets aside. Her box with her mother's pearls and the last of her cash remains safe in the shoebox. But her stomach curdles with dread, as she tugs at the wall panel.

She lets out a cry of despair and scratches her hands against the empty compartment, as if she can conjure what's missing. Someone has been inside the house. Inside her room. And now that someone is armed with a gun.

Hallie runs back to Robert's truck, trying to ignore the tornado of worries spinning through her head, leaving clutter in their wake. She should call the police. That's how a reasonable person would react. But a reasonable person wouldn't have done what she's done. For her, summoning the police would be a colossal mistake. She can't bring Andrew Sumner or his cop brother anywhere near her orbit.

Instead, she steadies her hands on the wheel. She breathes in, breathes out. After five deep inhales, she finds her eyes in the rearview. She looks calmer than she feels. Without further delay, she pilots the truck down the driveway and back to Cerulean.

Vodka bottle in hand, she enters the kitchen through the side door and finds no sign of Natalie at her designated station. Nick glances up at her. With a defeated shrug, he points her toward Robert's office. She finds Natalie at the desk, barefoot in a black sheath dress, applying lipstick in a portable makeup mirror. On the floor next to her, the infamous boots.

Hallie forces a smile and raises the bottle. "Your chocolate vodka has arrived."

"It's about time." Natalie doesn't break contact with her reflection. Hallie wonders if she's tried on the boots yet. "What took you so long?"

"Ducks."

"Excuse me?"

"On the drive back, there was a brood of ducks crossing the road. It held up traffic. You wouldn't expect me to run over a duckling, would you?"

"First, it's a bear. Now, ducklings." Natalie blots her lips on a tissue, leaving a blood-red imprint. "Who are you, Bindi Irwin? Don't be so dramatic."

With a wave of her hand, Natalie dismisses Hallie, and reaches in the desk drawer for a roll of clear packaging tape. "I don't have time for this. I'm going live from the bar in five minutes, and the heel of my Jimmy Choo boot is broken. So unless you're a cobbler, I can't be bothered. My followers are waiting."

Hallie ducks out of the office, eager to get back to work and push the scarred painting and the missing gun out of her mind. As she reties an apron behind her waist, Robert pokes his head in from the dining room. *Dad*, she thinks, for the first time. That alone is a salve. A dad is a fixer. A pillar of strength. A dad can make anything better.

"Did you find it?" he asks.

"Exactly where you said it'd be."

He gives her an enthusiastic thumbs up that may as well be a blue ribbon pinned to her chest. It doesn't even matter that Natalie is a spoiled snot who couldn't care less. More concerned about fixing the heel of her designer shoe than saying thank you. Hallie doesn't regret snapping it, not one bit.

"You remembered to lock up?"

"Of course."

"You're a lifesaver, Hallie. What would we do without you?"

Her cheeks warm at his very public praise. Though she shrugs to downplay the compliment, it's too late. From behind her, Natalie storms through the kitchen with one heel maimed and the bottle of vodka in a death grip.

After the last of the diners leave the restaurant, Hallie offers to stay late to assist Nick with cleanup. Better to avoid the house entirely for as long as she can. She doesn't want to be there when Robert and Shelly arrive home, ascend the staircase, and lay eyes on their precious painting. She would much rather be here, tackling the unpleasant task of scraping leftover food into the disposal.

"So, what's the real story with the bear?" Nick asks, as he scours the stove clean.

"What do you mean?"

He stops scrubbing and gives her a pointed look. "I was fifteen years old when my mom and I moved to Lake Tahoe. That summer, the first time I saw a black bear, I screamed so loud my mom thought I'd been stabbed by a madman. She ran out of the house just in time to watch the bear run off with a watermelon rind from the neighbor's trashcan."

"Well, I didn't say I wasn't scared. I was terrified. But I stayed calm, just like I read online." Hallie shrugs, gives him a sly grin. "Some people handle stress better than others."

"I know your secret."

Her stomach somersaults but she doesn't let on. "Oh, really?"

"Bear spray," he deadpans.

"A lady never tells."

While they finish tidying the kitchen, Hallie ignores the vibration of her cellphone inside her pocket. Certain it's Robert, she decides to wait to answer. She wants to be alone when she feigns ignorance about the painting. Lately, Nick's presence has made it even harder to lie.

After she lugs several trash bags out to the dumpster, she slips into the shadows at the edge of the woods to check her phone. Three missed calls from her father. She dials him back, telling herself to play it cool. Still, the moment he answers, she turns into a terrified teenager late for curfew and spews the longest sentence of her life.

"I'm so sorry but I was busy cleaning with Nick and I didn't see you calling until right now and I checked my phone and now I'm freaking out thinking that something is wrong. *Is it?*"

"Uh..." In his long pause, she lives a thousand lives, imagining what he'll say next. Maybe she should've called the police. "Shelly and I decided to pop over to the casino at the Grand Lodge. I'm not sure what Logan and Nat have going on tonight, but I didn't want you to worry if we weren't home when you arrived."

"Oh." That's all she can come up with. She used to be good at this. But lying to your foster parent isn't the same as fibbing to the real deal.

"We'll be home after midnight, so don't wait up."

Hallie mumbles a goodbye and ends the call before she says something really stupid. Then, she heads back through the propped side door, her mind already made up. She can't go back to the Thompsons' house. Not yet.

"Hey," she says to Nick, after taking out the last load of trash. "Wanna come to the casino with me? After fending off that bear... and Nat, I'm feeling lucky."

Nick consults his watch, then his phone. "It's a couple minutes' walk. I'll meet you there in twenty minutes. I've got to make a call first."

LETTER

R.J. Thompson
2555 Green Leaf Rd
Portland, OR

Hallie Sherman
135 Highland Terrace
Box 2B
Sacramento, CA

Dear Hallie,

You are correct. I share a first and last name with your father, but my mother gave me the nickname R.J. (my middle name is James) in kindergarten, and it stuck. She didn't want me to be one of a million Bobs, I suppose. The year you were conceived, 1993, was a rough one for me. I spent the better part of it in rehab, kicking my cocaine habit. I'm sad to say it took a few more stints before it stuck, but I've been clean and sober for twenty years now. We do have one heartache in common though. During my addiction, I fathered a child, a little boy named Sam. His mom and I couldn't get it together, and we lost our chance to be his parents. The termination of my parental rights was my rock bottom. I've always held out hope that Sam might come looking for me one day, but I'd never thought about submitting my DNA to Family Ties. Maybe your letter was meant to find me after all. I can only hope Sam is looking for me with as much determination as you're looking for your Robert Thompson.

Good luck!

R.J.

TWENTY-TWO

Hallie despises the casino. The way it glitters with its false promises. The palpable scent of desperation that reminds her of her mother on her worst days. She prefers to leave nothing to chance. To make her own luck, though she's never had much of it. But tonight the onslaught to her senses—bright lights and clinking coins—is a welcome distraction. At least Nick seems to be enjoying himself. True to his word, he'd shown up in twenty minutes, and his first pull on the penny slots had yielded a fifty-dollar payday, which he'd generously split with Hallie.

"I should probably quit while I'm ahead," he says.

"Where's the fun in that?" Though she'd already collected her portion of the winnings. With her cash running out, she can't afford to have fun. She's already worried Nat will try to pin the slashed painting on her. Then, she'll be on a bus to anywhere but here. And buses aren't free.

Nick cocks his head and pulls the lever once more, watching the reels spin. Another fifty-dollar winner. "You must be my good luck charm."

She smiles despite her unease. "Have you ever heard of probability? Random number generation? I don't want to burst your bubble, but—"

The reel spins round again, proving Hallie wrong.

"Alright, maybe I *am* your good luck charm." They share a laugh that makes it easy to forget the reason she'd come here in the first place.

"I'm surprised we haven't run into Robert yet." Nick reads her mind. "He usually plays poker at the high roller table."

Hallie follows his gaze to the room in the corner. Then, she scans the periphery of the casino. No sign of Robert or Shelly. She considers calling him back. Isn't that what a good daughter would do? But she doesn't want to overstep. After all, he's a grown man, and she invited herself here.

Her cellphone vibrates in reply, reminding her that she can't avoid the inevitable forever. "Hello?"

"Thank God you answered. Have you seen Dad?" Logan sounds more panicked than he had at the river, staring out at a bridge to nowhere.

Instantly, she knows he's seen it.

"He called about an hour ago and told me that he and Shelly were going to the Grand Lodge and that I shouldn't wait up."

"The casino?"

"That's what he said. But I haven't seen them here."

"You're at the casino?" Logan's pitch goes up an octave. Hallie can't imagine him ever winning a survival contest. Don't bears smell fear? She'll have to ask Jay.

"Yeah, I thought it would be fun. Nick is with me. What's wrong?"

Hearing his name, Nick stops playing the slots. He turns to her, his brow furrowed.

"Remember that family painting Mom told you about?" Logan asks. "The one hanging on the wall by your room."

"Uh-huh." She braces for it.

"It's completely destroyed. Just like the tires and the rope bridge. *Slashed.* With the same type of blade." Having said it, he gulps in a breath. "Jordan must've done it."

"*What?* That's crazy. Are you by yourself?"

"Yeah. I called Nat. She's on the way here. But I'm freaking out, Hallie. What if something happened to Dad? What if Jordan hurt him?"

Hallie had never considered the possibility. Tires are one thing. But hurting Robert is something else entirely. She remembers Jordan's face, teeth bared in anger, and the missing gun. Her mouth dries, and she struggles to swallow. "Do you really think he would do that? Over a failed restaurant?"

Nick rises to his feet, already taking his keys from his pocket. He must hear the urgency in her voice because he gestures for her to follow.

"Dad owes him a ton of money. And we don't have it. There was a fire at Last Glass, and Dad spent the insurance money on the move to Tahoe and the Cerulean build. There's nothing left, and Jordan's run out of patience." She hears the rhythmic thump of Logan pacing on the hardwood, but she doesn't dare interrupt. He's spewing family secrets left and right. "I shouldn't be telling you all this. Dad paid some media firm to bury the story online. But there's nobody I can talk to anymore. We lost so much more than the restaurant in that fire. We lost..."

When he doesn't continue, Hallie whispers a guess. "Grandpa Wallace?"

Logan makes a noise of agreement, confirming her suspicions. Before she can press him any further, Natalie gasps in the background. "Oh my God."

"I'll be there as soon as I can," Hallie tells Logan. She follows Nick out the front doors of the hotel and into the parking lot.

"Is that Hallie?" Natalie makes her name sound like an accusation. "Did you leave the door unlocked when you left? You probably let the guy in!" She's shouting now, her allegations traveling to Hallie's ear with the zing of an electric shock.

"I didn't realize you came home," Logan says to Hallie.

"It was just for a couple of minutes during dinner service. Nat left something behind. To be honest, I only went to the kitchen."

Nick taps her shoulder and opens the passenger door for her. *C'mon*, he mouths.

So much for her plan of avoidance. She has no choice but to get in. "Keep trying Dad. Nick and I are on the way."

As Nick speeds down the two-lane road toward the Thompsons' house, Hallie wonders if she made a mistake. In not calling the cops. In not telling the truth about herself. In coming here to live in a house with virtual strangers. In not letting go of this whole fantasy notion of the perfect father, the perfect family. Now, she's caught in the middle, with guilt squeezing her from all sides.

"You okay?" Nick asks.

She shrugs, helpless. "Ever since I arrived, it's been one thing after another."

"It's not your fault."

Those brown eyes are so earnest that she wants to believe him. But there's no denying her past. All the *failed* placements—the social worker's term that seemed to apply to her personally. She was the common denominator. She *was* the failure. Every time she's tried for normal, life reminds her that she's not.

Hallie sighs. "Then why do I feel like I've just been dealt a dead man's hand of eights and aces?"

TWENTY-THREE

Hallie approaches the house like a walk to the guillotine. At least Nick agreed to come inside with her. There's no sign of Robert and Shelly—no one to referee—and from outside the door, she already hears her siblings going toe to toe.

"I told you it was a mistake for Dad to invite her here."

"C'mon, Nat. You sound crazy. You really think *she* destroyed the painting?"

"She had means. She had opportunity. She's certainly got motive. I mean, the worst of the gash is right across *my* face. What if she's working with him?"

"You said that you told her to come back here. To get your stupid vodka."

"What are you saying? That I set her up?"

As Nick closes the door behind them, Natalie's voice reaches a crescendo. The firm thud silences her, leaving her judgments to echo in the pin drop. Hallie wishes she could turn and run away. Maybe it would have been better to risk coming face to face with Officer Sumner again. But she's made her bed. She can't blame anyone but herself.

Hallie waits for Nick at the top of the stairs, knowing she needs an ally. When she finds Natalie still huffing, she realizes that too is a colossal mistake.

"I didn't realize you were with Nick."

"We were just blowing off a little steam at the casino after cleaning up." Hallie decides to pretend she didn't hear Natalie throwing her under the bus. Instead, she leans her head to the side, peering around her sister. "So, where's the painting?"

"Logan took it down. It was upsetting me."

"You said it was slashed?" Nick wisely directs his question to Logan, who replies with a solemn nod. "Is anything else destroyed or missing?"

Hallie busies herself, scanning the surroundings. She tries not to think about the gun. Naturally, it's all she *can* think about.

"Everything seems alright otherwise. The front door was locked when I got home." Logan looks down at his T-shirt and sweats. "I changed out of my busboy uniform, and my room seemed fine."

"What about the extra key?" Hallie asks. "I'm sure I returned it."

"I checked. Still under the hide-a-spare, where you said you left it."

Relieved that Logan doesn't share his sister's suspicions, Hallie releases an audible breath.

"Were you able to reach Dad?" she asks Logan.

"Still trying." Frustrated, he jabs at his phone screen. "It's going straight to voicemail. So is Mom's."

"Maybe we should call the police," Nick suggests. "If you think that guy from the restaurant did this, there's no telling what else he might do."

Again, the gun floats up to the surface of her mind, like a body rising from the depths. She nods her agreement, her finger poised to dial.

"It's him!" Logan shouts.

Headlight beams blare through the window, and Hallie hurries to look out at the driveway. Robert shuts the engine and exits the truck with Shelly close behind him. Both oblivious to the panic above them.

Logan wastes no time. He throws open the door to the upper deck and yells down to his father. "Where were you? I've been calling you for thirty minutes."

Robert's smile disappears; he gapes up at them. "We went straight to the casino after work. My phone died. I figured you kids would be in bed by now. What's going on?"

Before Logan can answer, Robert hustles toward the front door. Hallie waits in the window, watching Shelly. Though she's still clad in the black pants and silk blouse she wore to the restaurant, her shirt is untucked and sweat-stained. Tendrils of her hair have come loose from the bun at the nape of her neck.

Shelly must sense her gaze because she lifts her face. Hallie raises her hand in greeting, all the while taking in her splotchy cheeks. Her red-rimmed eyes. Embarrassed for her, Hallie turns away and flees inside.

With the damaged painting splayed on the coffee table, its injuries are obvious. Fatal. Worse than Hallie realized. Though Shelly's likeness hasn't been sliced liked Robert's, her eyes are poked clean through. A dozen smaller gashes dot the background. Beneath the light, Hallie clocks the distinctive edges of the cuts. Serrated, like little teeth taking a bite. Shelly whimpered when she first saw it and settled onto the sofa between her children. Still weeping, she floats from room to room now, searching for any other damaged or missing items. Next stop, the guest bedroom.

Shelly pauses outside the door and calls to her. "Do you mind, Hallie? I only want to be sure everything is in order."

"Of course. Go ahead."

She sniffles and disappears inside.

Nick joins Hallie, shaking his head at the disturbing display. "Are you sure you don't want to call the police, Rob? This doesn't seem like the kind of thing that you should ignore, especially with the anniversary cookout coming up. It's like he's building up to something."

"I agree. The guy's a real sicko. But I doubt he's coming back tonight."

"What's stopping him? You don't have cameras. You don't even have an alarm system. With all due respect, it's not safe."

Hallie wants to chime in. It certainly doesn't feel safe. Not in the middle of the night, with the trees surrounding the house like enemy soldiers. She's coming around to Robert's side now, wondering what else Jordan's done. Cut the rope bridge? Smashed Natalie's cookies? Harmless pranks that suddenly don't seem so harmless.

"Thanks for your concern, Nick, but we've got it handled." Robert moves toward the stairs with expectation, politely ushering Nick out of the house. "It's late, and I'm sure you need to get home. We'll all get some sleep. Tomorrow, I'll talk to the police and put in a call to a security company about getting an alarm system installed."

Nick gives Hallie's arm a squeeze, says his goodbyes to the others. She watches him disappear down the staircase. Hears the door shut behind him. She turns to them, then. *Her* family. Yet, she's never felt less a Thompson and more a suspect. Natalie's eyes bore through her like a drill, targeting all her soft, hidden places.

"Are you sure you didn't see anything suspicious when you came home earlier?" she asks Hallie again. "Think hard. The smallest detail could be important."

Hallie keeps her head down. She won't look at the defiled painting. She won't let her worries about the gun show on her face. If she mentions any of it, there will be questions. Questions she doesn't want to answer. Why was she snooping through the closet? Why didn't she call Robert right away? What does she have to hide?

"I wish I had seen something. But I knew you needed me to be quick. I was in and out. I grabbed the vodka. I didn't even turn on the lights."

"Wasn't it dark though? I'm surprised you didn't bump into a bear."

"Very funny. But I—"

Robert clears his throat, stepping in front of Hallie. "That's enough interrogation, Nat. Hallie has no reason to lie. Now, more than ever, we need to stick together."

Pouting, Natalie retreats down the stairs but not before cutting Hallie with a sharp glare. Pale-faced, Shelly returns to the living room. Her eyes flick to Hallie and away again. She says nothing about the state of the guest bedroom, wringing her hands with worry instead.

"Was everything accounted for?" Hallie dares to ask.

Shelly replies with a curt nod that leaves Hallie dumbfounded. She can only assume Shelly didn't check the wall panel. Perhaps she didn't even know the gun was there in the first place. Somehow, that only makes Hallie more frightened. She searches the eyes of her family, wondering who is lying.

"Well, at least we're all safe," Robert says. "That's the most important thing. More important than a silly painting."

"Really, Robert?" Shelly sounds wounded. "*Silly?*"

"I'm so sorry," Hallie tells her. "I should've paid better attention."

Robert wraps an arm around her. "You were trying to help out your sister. You've done absolutely nothing wrong."

Hallie nods and rests her head against his sturdy shoulder, wishing with all her might that was true.

Still feeling shaky, Hallie changes into her pajamas and retrieves her half of Nick's casino winnings from her jeans pocket. She takes the crisp bills to the closet, intending to deposit them in her wooden box for safe-keeping. With the money in her stash, she hopes to have enough to buy Robert a small token of her appreciation. A necktie. A bottle of wine. A box of cigars. A dad gift. But what sort of present do you get the father you just met? With the money you stole from another man's wallet, no less.

Dropping to her knees, Hallie takes the shoebox in her lap and lifts the lid.

She clasps a hand to her mouth and peers into the empty box. Frantic, she tells herself it's a mistake. The wooden box was here mere hours ago, her pearls and cash inside it. She must've grabbed the wrong one. Box by box, she opens them all in a frenzy, discarding them in a pile behind her.

By the time she reaches the last shoebox, she already knows what awaits her. Her tears flow freely. Her stomach clenches into a fist. Her pearls are gone. The money too. Now, she's convinced Jordan Markum isn't the only villain who's stepped foot in this house.

TWENTY-FOUR

By the morning, the defiled family portrait has been removed from the coffee table. The white pillar candles that were shoved aside to make room for it have returned to their stations. Even the picture hook that hung on the now bare wall is gone, leaving only a small hole to be patched. The Thompson family, too, seems to have returned to normal, with Shelly serving them a pancake breakfast on the deck before they leave for their respective destinations: Natalie, to her room to process a new batch of Nibbles orders; Logan, to the running trail alongside the lake; and Robert and Hallie to Cerulean to get a head start on preparations for the cookout, which is less than a week away.

"We have a lot of deliveries for the festivities arriving today." Robert speaks to the windshield, but it's a welcome relief to hear his voice after his unusual silence at breakfast. "I'll need your help unloading and organizing."

"Of course." Hallie tries to sound enthused. Rested. Though she'd spent the night under the covers, jumping at every creak of the floorboards, and reading about Jordan

Markum, the hotshot restaurateur behind several of San Francisco's best eateries. She even found a photograph of him and Chef Juan Antonio Feliz at a charity banquet at the Fairmont. In his black bowtie and shiny wingtips, she couldn't picture Jordan wielding a knife. But she knows appearances can be deceiving. Her mother's doe eyes and unassuming smile had taken nearly every pain doctor in Sacramento for a ride.

"I assume you've decided on your dish for the contest."

"The lobster grilled cheese. I've already completed the online registration with my list of ingredients."

"Excellent."

Hallie glances over at her father, trying to get a read on him. Surely, he won't keep up this charade.

As if on cue, he gives her a closed-mouth smile and turns up the AM radio to listen to the local forecast. "Sounds like it's going to be a perfect weekend for the cookout."

Still perplexed, she murmurs her agreement.

"With school out for summer, it's sure to be quite a crowd. Gets bigger and better every year. I can't wait for you to see it for yourself."

As the truck comes to a stop in front of the restaurant, Hallie blurts out, "Are you planning on talking to the police?"

"Of course. Not to worry." Robert pats her hand. "I didn't want to bring it up at the house. Shelly worries too much. Officer Sumner is meeting me here."

"Oh. Great."

"He may want to speak to you as well, since you were the only one at the house yesterday evening."

Hallie stuffs her panic. "Sure."

"Logan told me that you and Nick went to the casino

looking for us. We must've just missed you when we snuck out the back to the beach to take in the stars. Shelly loves that view at night. Says there's nothing like it. That it makes her problems seem so small. After the week we've had, she needed a night off and so did I. But I'm sorry we weren't reachable. I feel awful about it. Please don't mention it to the police. It'll only upset Shelly that much more."

"You don't need to explain. With everything that's happened, I can only imagine what you and Shelly are going through." He looks so pleased with her that she doesn't stop there. "As far as the cops go, I'm happy to help. Whatever you need."

"That's my girl."

My girl. Those two words from her father make it all worth it.

Hallie isn't going to wait around for Officer Sumner to turn a casual conversation into an interrogation. Which is exactly what will happen the moment he realizes the truth about her. Surely, his brother has mentioned the name of the woman who stole his wallet. Then, she'll be the one leaving in handcuffs. The thought of it conjures memories best left for dead.

With Nick procuring the propane tanks for the cookout and Robert organizing the bar, Hallie finds herself alone in the kitchen with the food deliveries. The perfect scenario for her plan. As she checks the freshness of the salmon, she peers out the small window, awaiting Officer Sumner's arrival. The moment she spots his uniform, his lawman's saunter, she grabs one of the fish for authenticity and exits the side door. After stopping at the dumpster to toss the fish inside, she hurries down the dirt path toward The

Grotto, knowing she can hide out there until it's safe to return.

Though she's certain Officer Sumner didn't spot her, she finds herself glancing over her shoulder and thinking back to her missing pearls. It feels as if an invisible presence lurks behind her, drops out of sight each time her eyes dart in its direction. By the time she reaches the clearing, she's all worked up and breathless. It's too open here. She's too exposed.

Instead of sitting at the picnic tables, she heads deeper into the sugar pines toward the site of Jay's last camp. She moves with purpose, hoping her heavy steps and clapping hands will scare off any ursine visitors. Provided she doesn't get eaten, she can pass the next thirty minutes on the hidden section of beach metaphorically sinking her worries under the serene surface of the lake.

She realizes too late that she should've brought provisions for Jay. The guy saved her life, for God's sake. She'd been too focused on herself and her troubles. Like the Midtown jerks who passed by Ernie's wheelchair without a second glance. Sometimes, he joked about it—*I'm the Invisible Man*—but she knew it hurt.

Her heart drops when she sees Jay sleeping on the beach, using his backpack as a pillow and a baseball cap as a sunshade. Slowly, she turns away. She holds out hope he hasn't noticed her.

"Where are you going?" He turns the cap backward to reveal his eyes, which must've been open all along.

"I didn't want to bother you. I was just..." Hallie throws up her hands. "Running away."

"Well then, welcome to Run Away Beach." He sits up and spreads his arms wide, gesturing to the small patch of sand around him and the blue water that laps near his bare feet. "It's the perfect spot to hide out. The trees shield you from the boaters and the bears protect you from the nosy hikers."

"Don't say the b-word, please."

Laughing, Jay pats the spot next to him. "Noted." He seems less burdened today, and she curses herself again for coming empty-handed. "So, what are you running from?"

Hallie drops into the sand, burying her hands in its warmth. She picks up two fistfuls and watches the grains slip between her fingers. "I imagined it would be different, having a family. I always envied the kids at school who got to go back to a *real* home with people who wanted them there. Brothers and sisters who were more like built-in best friends, and parents like the ones on the TV sitcoms. I thought I'd outgrown my idealism, but now I'm not so sure."

"So, the honeymoon's over then, with the uh... Thompsons, was it?"

"I wouldn't say that. Robert has been so supportive of me. But his daughter, Natalie, hates me, and his wife doesn't trust me. It makes me wonder how much longer Robert will put up with me. It's bigger than that though. It's like taking a bite of the reddest, shiniest apple in the batch, only to find a worm inside."

Jay roots around in his backpack and produces an apple, holding it up to her with a wink. At least he has *that*; he won't be starved. After humming a little tune of suspense, he sinks his teeth into its flesh. "No worms."

"Phew." She pretends to wipe her brow. "You know what I mean though."

"They've got problems. Is that what you're saying?"

Hallie nods and lies back on the sand. It's easier to talk

this way, spilling her guts to the cloudless sky rather than a virtual stranger. "Someone broke into the house and cut up their family portrait. There's been other things too. Robert's tires got slashed with a similar knife. Someone left a threatening note in their mailbox."

"Damn." Jay takes another large bite. "That's twisted."

"Yeah. Really twisted. My dad wants me to talk to this police officer about it. That's why I'm hiding out back here. I don't like cops."

"Me neither. Obviously." He pauses for a moment, then cuts his eyes at her. "Are you a *suspect*?"

Hallie hates that word. It takes her back to places long buried. Places that should stay that way forever. "To Natalie, I am. She blames me for everything. I'm sure she'll tell everyone who will listen that I destroyed the painting out of jealousy."

"Did you?" Jay asks.

"No. But I was the last one at the house, so it's easy for her to point the finger. Thank goodness my dad is on my side. He knows I didn't do it. I would never."

"Of course you wouldn't."

Though Jay can't possibly know what she's capable of, Hallie feels grateful to him for voicing his support. For letting her go on about her problems when he's the one struggling. "Remember that guy my brother punched the other night? Robert thinks he's the one who slashed the portrait... and the tires. I guess he's got an axe to grind."

Jay finishes the last of his apple, core and all. "Doesn't everybody?"

Hallie thinks of all the nights she lay awake, fantasies of revenge playing on a loop in her brain. Like a movie she'd seen so many times she'd memorized the dialogue. Revenge on her mother for turning into an addict. Revenge on her father for abandoning her. Revenge on all those foster families for not caring enough. But her mother was dead and until ten days ago, her father was a stranger. Long ago, she'd decided to grind her axe against the world itself. To balance the scales. To take what belonged to her even if it meant leaving someone else without.

She nods at Jay. "I suppose you're right."

TWENTY-FIVE

By the time Hallie returns to the restaurant, Officer Sumner and his patrol car have gone. It doesn't bring the wave of relief she'd expected, especially when Robert pokes his head out of his office. The wrinkle in his forehead deepens.

"Is everything okay?" he asks. "Where'd you run off to? Officer Sumner wanted to get a statement."

"I'm really sorry." Hallie continues sorting through the supplies, afraid that if she meets his eyes, she'll confess everything. "One of the salmon was spoiled. I tossed it in the dumpster, but I couldn't get that rotten smell out of my nose. I took a break to breathe in some lake air. I hope that's okay."

"Gianelli's sent me a rotten fish? Are you kidding?"

Hallie hadn't bargained on this. She stays quiet and still, hoping not to encourage him.

"It's the third time this year."

"The rest were fine. Perfectly fresh."

"I want to see that fish. 'Ocean to table,' my ass."

"You want me to dig it out of the bin?" Hallie's panicked heart starts to race.

"Damn right, I do. I want to take that fish to Gianelli himself and slap his smug face with it. Do you know he had the nerve to raise his prices last month?"

The side door opens and Nick appears, huffing. Hallie dares to hope he can settle Robert down or at least point his frustration in another direction.

"We've got a problem," Nick says.

Robert casts his eyes skyward and lets out a bear of a sigh. "Good Lord. What else can go wrong?"

"I think there's a homeless man living in The Grotto."

"What?" Hallie blurts out, trying to cover her alarm with surprise.

"On the way back, I saw a guy cutting through the woods on a red bike. He had a pack with him. Hallie, you said yourself that you found some burned debris in the firepit."

"You did?" Robert asks.

Hallie can only shrug.

"We should probably put up a No Trespassing sign like we did last summer. The last thing we need is a bunch of folks camping out back there."

Robert appears skeptical. But at least he's forgotten about the salmon. "Homeless? In Incline? That's unlikely. It's probably some spoiled kid like Logan, pretending to rough it for a night."

"C'mon, Rob. You know better than that. Not everybody around here lives like you and Shelly. What about your dishwashers and your busboys? Your prep cooks? Miguel, the local who landscapes your yard?" Nick's voice builds to an uncomfortable volume. One that Hallie's never heard from him before. "What about *me*?"

An awkward silence hangs over the kitchen until Nick joins Hallie at the counter. He starts sorting through the produce arrivals, handling each box as if it's offended him personally.

Robert stands there, looking but not seeing. His face, shell-shocked. "I don't appreciate your tone or your insinuations," he says, finally. "I know we've had to make some cuts in recent years, but I've done my best. I've always been more than generous with you."

With a stranglehold on a head of broccoli, Nick nods. "And we both know why that—"

"Why don't we put a pin in this conversation for now? I've got enough to worry about at home. Not to mention the anniversary cookout. I'll have one of the staff put up the No Trespassing sign as you suggested." Robert retreats to his office, giving the door a firm pull behind him.

"He never closes his door," Hallie whispers. "And you never yell."

"Oh, you're an expert now? You've been here, what? One week?"

"What is with you today?"

"You didn't exactly have my back with Robert. You could've chimed in about the firepit." What he doesn't say is that she owes him one. Which she does. He's kept her secret safe, exactly like he'd promised. But she owes Jay too. She owes him her life.

"After last night, I didn't want to worry him. He's going through a lot right now."

"Yeah, well..." Nick finally relinquishes his grip on the broccoli. After chucking it in, he carts the entire box toward the walk-in fridge. "He's not the only one with problems, Hallie. And neither are you."

. . .

A successful restaurant kitchen demands communication. Even culinary-school dropout Hallie knows that. But Nick's been barking out the orders tonight, more drill sergeant than head chef, and she knows she's partly to blame. For that reason, she didn't argue when he relegated her to the salad station. The place where chefs go to die. She'd simply nodded and gone to work, adding her special touch to every Cobb, Caesar, and caprese.

After plating the most recent order—one Cobb, hold the bacon—she takes a look around the harried kitchen and lets the energy of the place bubble through her. The pure shot of adrenaline instantly improves her mood. It's the only reason she'd lasted so long at A La Mode. She belongs in kitchens. These are her people.

Hallie finds Nick toggling down the line of sous chefs and offering his feedback. He tastes the red sauce, frowns, tastes it again. Hallie suspects it needs a dash of salt, but she knows better than to speak up now.

When she sneaks another peek a moment later, Nick's cellphone rings. He drags it out of his pants pocket and glances at the screen. Cursing, he slams the saucepan against the counter, sending a spray of red sauce into the air and onto his chef's coat.

The buzz of the kitchen stops. Hallie gapes. Everyone does. Even Nick seems shocked at himself.

"What are you all looking at?" he asks. "Keep working."

Hallie leaves her station to find Nick still staring at his screen. "What's wrong?"

Pushing past her without a word, Nick rushes away into the dining room. Hallie watches through the small window as he approaches Robert. Though she can't make out his words, he's more animated than she's ever seen him. Her father points back to the kitchen. Nick shakes his head, obviously frustrated. Another finger stab, more emphatic this time. She reads her father's lips. *Hallie.*

When Robert turns toward the kitchen, Hallie retreats to the salad station. The rest of the staff follow her lead, keeping their eyes down and their hands busy.

Robert bursts through the door and heads in her direction. In an instant, her brain starts firing off excuses, lies, and alibis to answer the perpetual question: What has she done wrong now? Thanks to Elizabeth Sherman and the child welfare system, she's hardwired that way. But to be honest with herself, she *has* done wrong. A lot of it.

"I need to speak to you." His hand on her elbow, her father guides her to the corner of the kitchen. Nick lingers nearby, his eyes darting between her and his phone screen.

"Is everything okay?"

"Nick has to leave the restaurant."

"What?" When several staff swivel their heads, she lowers her voice. "In the middle of dinner service?"

"I realize it's not optimal. But he's had a family emergency. I need you to take over."

"Me?" One syllable seems all she can manage.

"Yes, you. There's no one else who can do it. With your experience at El Mar, it should be a piece of cake."

She grits her teeth and glances at Nick, only to find him looking back at her. "What does Nick think?"

"Nick's opinion doesn't matter."

"But he's the executive chef. Of course his opinion matters. I don't want to do it if he's not on board. Let one of the sous chefs take over. That's the *fair* thing to do." After the word leaves her mouth, she tastes its bitterness. This could be her big break. This is her chance to put her thumb on the scales. To take back the future that's been stolen from her.

"I told him you couldn't do it." Nick directs a pointed glance at her. "That you wouldn't want anyone to think you were getting special treatment because of your relationship with the family."

Hallie stiffens. Because she knows what he really means. She's not capable. She's a culinary-school dropout, a diner waitress. A wannabe.

"That's ridiculous," Robert assures her. "No one will think that. If they do, they can take it up with me. The decision is yours, Hallie."

She doesn't hesitate. "I'll do it."

TWENTY-SIX

After the final order comes in two hours later, Hallie finally allows herself a moment. She's done it. Coordinated a dinner service as head chef. Sure, there were a few bobbles. One overcooked steak, an under-salted creamed spinach. A steaming bowl of cioppino dropped by one of the sous chefs. Those mishaps aside, her first night in Nick's borrowed chef's coat went better than she could've imagined. Almost as if she really *had* studied under Juan Antonio at El Mar.

On cue, Robert pokes his head in from the front of the house and beams at her. She feels giddy. Like a little girl with a red balloon.

"Can you come out here for a sec?" he asks.

Her balloon popped, her stomach drops to her knees. She flashes back to Wednesday night. To the white tablecloth. To Logan's mishap. To Andrew Sumner's bald head, shining in the soft candlelight. "Out there?"

"Just for a moment. Don't worry, I won't keep you long."

She searches for an excuse but comes up empty. Her

mind suddenly thick with white noise, she leaves her post and marches zombie-like toward her father.

As Robert pushes through the door into the dining room, she feels a slight sense of relief. It's Saturday night. Busy, loud. Even if Andrew Sumner is here, it's unlikely he'll ever spot her. Still, she scans the tables anyway, searching for the stranger whose face she'd know anywhere.

"So, what did you need?" Her voice disappears in the din.

Two glasses of champagne await them at the bar. Holding one high, Robert offers her the other. When she hesitates, he motions for her to join him. Seeing no other option, she takes the glass.

"Could I have everyone's attention?" In an instant, he commands it. That's her father. The kind of man who demands the eyes of the room set upon him. Upon her too, unfortunately. "I want to thank you all for coming out tonight. Since Cerulean opened its doors, all of you have welcomed us into your wonderful community. As you may already know, this Friday marks the anniversary of our grand opening, and I usually save the speeches for the cookout, knowing that most of you will be too drunk and too full not to indulge an old man. But, in the last couple of weeks, my life has turned upside down in a good way. In the best way. I simply couldn't wait to share the news with all of you. You know my wife, Shelly, and my children, Logan and Natalie."

Shelly waves from the hostess stand, covering any surprise with a bright smile.

"I want to introduce you to Hallie Sherman, my other daughter. She's visiting us from Sacramento. Tonight, when I needed a reliable head chef, Hallie stepped in like a pro and ran an entire dinner service. Hallie received her training at one of the best restaurants in California, and it's an honor to have her here at Cerulean as a supremely talented chef and, most importantly, as my daughter. Everyone, please raise a glass to Hallie!"

Hallie's heart threatens to burst. She should be scanning the room, searching for signs of Andrew Sumner. But she can only stand there, speechless, imagining the bright red rash of embarrassment that's creeping up her neck. Her eyes glaze with tears; her throat swells.

"Speech! Speech!" a familiar voice shouts from across the restaurant. Natalie grins wickedly before tossing back her glass of champagne.

"No, no. I can't."

Robert doesn't seem to hear her. Wrapping his arm around her, he pins her into place. There's no escape now so she finds a friendly face, fixing her gaze on the sophisticated silver-haired woman at the bar who offers a kind smile and a gentle nod. A smile that says she understands the discomfort of the spotlight. A nod that reminds her the only way out is through.

"I don't know what to say. I'm overwhelmed by the kindness that Robert and his family have shown me. Before I came to Incline Village, I had no family. My mother died when I was a girl. I always had the dream of finding my father, and I never stopped looking. Fortunately, technology allowed us to make a DNA match through Family Ties and here I am. I'm so grateful to be here. It's the Thompsons who we should be toasting tonight." Hallie lifts her glass. "To Robert and Shelly!"

Her vision still blurry, she tries to slink back to the kitchen amid the applause. She plans to flee out the side door and let the cold night air snap her back into her body.

"That was some toast Dad gave you." Logan intercepts her escape route. Even with a tray of dirty dishes balanced in one hand, he doesn't appear to be in a hurry.

"I'm still a bit overwhelmed." She takes another step, hoping he'll take the hint.

"I hear ya. I'd drop dead of shock if he ever said anything like that about me. I swear, he'd rather have you and Nick as his only children."

Though Logan follows it up with a chuckle, it doesn't assuage Hallie's guilt. Guilt that worsens when Natalie approaches, arm-in-arm with the woman from the bar.

"Hallie, this is Julie Danbury. She writes for the local paper, *The Daily Incline*."

Hallie wants to run in the other direction. Instead, she extends her hand. Robert reappears at her side, playing the role of proud father to them both, listening intently while Natalie drones on.

"I told her a bit of your story. How you wrote to all those Robert Thompsons. She thought it was fascinating and wondered if you'd be willing to sit down for an interview. With Dad, of course. It could be great publicity for the restaurant."

So that genial smile hadn't been born from empathy but journalistic curiosity. In other words, nosiness. The urge to flee grows so strong that Hallie grinds her teeth.

"I'm not sure if that's such a good—"

"It's a great idea!" Robert interjects. "Think of the exposure for Cerulean. For your career. That kind of publicity could attract the right people, the right opportunity. That is, if we don't manage to convince you to stick around forever."

Hallie feels herself torn right down the middle. She doesn't know whether to laugh or cry or scream. Her father's words speak to the damaged place inside her. He wants her *here* with *him*. At the same time, she can't agree to an interview, can't have a reporter poking around in her business and unearthing the bones of her past. Even if Robert could forgive her lie about El Mar, everyone has their limits. She feels certain she's travelled far past them.

"Sure." The picture of amiability, Hallie forces the corners of her mouth up. "Maybe we could sit down later in the week, assuming I'm not too busy. I want to focus my energy on winning the cooking contest. That would be the ultimate show of gratitude to my newfound family."

Thankfully, Ms. Danbury seems used to being put off. She slips her business card into Hallie's hand. "Think about it, dear. A sweet story like yours and Rob's could go viral. And you know what they say. Going viral will change your life."

A dark cloud passes across Robert's face, so quickly Hallie wonders if she'd imagined it. But then, he grips on to her elbow, steering her in the direction of the kitchen.

"We'll think about it," he calls over his shoulder.

Inside the safety of the kitchen, her father shakes his head. "I don't know about you, but unlike my other daughter, I have no interest in *going viral*."

His mocking air quotes make Hallie giggle. That and the relief. They're on the same page after all. "In my experience," she says, "the only thing a virus gets you is pneumonia."

LETTER

Sergeant Robert Thompson
Military Police Brigade
Unit 49 Box 870
APO AP 92055

Hallie Sherman
135 Highland Terrace
Box 2B
Sacramento, CA

Dear Ms. Sherman,

Thank you for your heartfelt correspondence. Unfortunately, I cannot be of assistance to you, as I was stationed overseas in Germany during the time frame you referenced. However, your letter has weighed heavily on me for several weeks, and I found it necessary to reply. As a member of the military police for the last twenty-one years, I must pose several questions to you regarding your search. First, what leads you to believe that your father wants to be found? Second, if your father failed to provide for you when you needed him most, why on earth would you want to find him now? Lastly, I would urge you to take caution in the personal details you share with any potential matches. It's a dangerous world, especially for a young, vulnerable woman like yourself.

Take care,

Sgt. Thompson

TWENTY-SEVEN

On Sunday morning, Hallie intends to avoid breakfast. After Robert's over-the-top toast last night, she feels undeserving and awkward. Out of place. She cracks her bedroom door and listens to the Thompsons' dance, their morning rituals, starting with Natalie's update of her follower count and the order totals for Nat's Nibbles. Shelly's nervous puttering around the kitchen. Logan's endless ribbing of his sister. The steps are predictable and executed to perfection. Hallie will only get in the way. She knows too much now. Too much to ignore the unsaid, the electric charge that crackles between them all like the air before a thunderstorm. But when she tries to sneak past them, Shelly insists she eat something before leaving for the restaurant.

Hallie stuffs a bagel in her mouth, chomping the biggest piece she can manage. In four bites, she'll be out of here. Or choking to death on a pumpernickel. An escape, either way.

"Any word from the police?" Logan asks.

Hallie stops chewing, surprised at the deviation from the usual superficially choreographed routine.

Logan continues. "Did they arrest Jordan yet?"

Shelly fidgets with the carton of cream cheese, moving it from one side of the counter to the other, then offering Natalie a dollop. Her lip curled in disgust, Natalie shakes her head.

"Robert spoke with an officer yesterday morning. They're looking into it. Until then, let's be diligent." Shelly glances in Hallie's direction. "I made you a copy of the house key. We won't be using the hide-a-spare anymore for obvious reasons."

Hallie slips the key into her pocket, pretending it's not the first time she's been trusted with the key to a family home. Once they'd discovered her sticky fingers, not one of her foster parents had dared offer her unrestricted access to their prized possessions. Despite her self-doubt, the Thompsons' faith in her gives her a little thrill.

"Rob also mentioned that there might be a vagrant living in the woods behind the restaurant. With all that's gone on around here lately, I worry that whoever it is might be working with Mr. Markum or even spying on us. If you see anyone sneaking around back there, let me know immediately. Please don't trouble Rob."

"Of course."

Robert soon emerges from the master bedroom, gives Shelly a quick peck on the cheek, and rounds to the other side of the counter, where he claps a hand against Hallie's shoulder. "Why don't you ride with me this morning?"

Hallie gulps down the fourth and final bite of pumpernickel and follows her father.

Instead of taking her to the restaurant, Robert continues onto the highway, driving for a few miles in silence before he turns onto the access road for Sand Harbor Beach. He parks the truck, opens his door, and motions for her to join him. It's still too early for the beachgoers, the kayakers, the screaming kids in brightly colored swim trunks. For better or worse, they have the entire beach to themselves.

Hallie trails Robert down to the water's edge. It's so clear she can see the sandy bottom. Out a bit further, an outcropping of smooth gray rocks protrudes from the turquoise surface. Robert points to the tallest among them. "Believe it or not, I jumped from the top of that one once, just like Logan."

"You did?" Uncertain why Robert brought her here, Hallie measures her words. "The water looks shallow. It seems dangerous."

"The lake was deeper back then, before the drought. But you're right. It was dangerous. I didn't care. Anything outdoors was fair game to me. Give me a rock, I'd scale it. A tree, I'd climb it. A river, I'd swim it. I had no fear."

"Then Logan was telling the truth about you being an adventurer."

"Is that what he called it?"

Hallie nods. "He and Nat mentioned a trip to the Narrows in Mount Zion. Something about a storm and a stranger who helped you all to safety. I get the feeling you're the reason Logan wants to conquer the outdoors."

Robert's expression remains as flat as the lake's surface as he reaches down and selects two rocks. He places one in Hallie's hand and sidearms the other, both of them watching as it skips expertly over the water. "That's the problem with Logan. Always tagging along after somebody, he's never been his own man. He's got to find his identity—the way you have—not steal it from someone else. The outdoors just isn't his thing."

The rock warms in Hallie's palm. She doesn't know the first thing about skipping a stone. The only time she's ever thrown one, the jackass kid at foster home number one needed three stitches above his left eye. On the plus side, he'd never called her a loser again.

"Just sidearm it." Her father demonstrates with a flick of his wrist.

But she only squeezes the stone tighter, worried she'll disappoint him. This must be how Logan feels.

"But didn't he win a trophy or something?" Hallie hopes her noncommittal tone will stop Robert from wondering how she acquired that particular detail. She should just keep her big mouth shut, but Logan's predicament tugs at her heart. The way he lives for the scraps of his dad's approval. The way Natalie rubs his face in his failures. Why can't Robert cut him some slack?

"Hmm... I don't remember a trophy. Did he tell you that?" When Hallie doesn't immediately answer, he adds, "Logan exaggerates sometimes. I think it makes him feel better. Frankly, I'm surprised he didn't portray himself as the hero on that trip through the Narrows."

Hallie whips the stone toward the lake. It makes a splash and disappears beneath the surface, sending ripples all the way back to the shore.

"Not a bad first effort." Her father plucks another from the ground and offers it to her. "Try again."

She throws harder this time with the same result, and he picks up a third rock. Surely, her father didn't bring her here to skip stones. Confused, she frowns at him.

"Is there something you need to tell me?" he asks.

"Um... I'm not very good at this, for one thing." Her

throw doesn't even reach the water. The rock sends up a spray of wet sand when it hits the beach.

"Oh, never mind that. I always bring the kids out here to talk. The stones are incidental."

Hallie tries not to overreact. But all she can do is count the lies she's told. Who's to say which one he's caught her in? "Talk?" her voice squeaks out. "About last night? The toast you gave me? Shelly wasn't upset that you shared all that, was she?"

"No, she's glad I did. We're both so proud of you. You've done so much with so little. It's a good lesson for the other two."

While her ego swells with false pride, the ugly truth of her situation weighs heavy in her gut, dragging her back down to earth. "Is it about the man that Nick saw in The Grotto? Or the damage to the painting?"

Robert heaves a weary sigh, and she worries that he sees right through her. That he's grown tired of her games. She lets her shoulders slump.

"I hope I'm not a bad luck charm."

"We certainly have had a string of it lately, but you're not to blame, Hallie. You're the one bit of good news I've had in a long while."

Bolstered by his answer, she replies, "If I've done something wrong, just tell me."

"I heard that Logan spilled the beans about a piece of Thompson family history."

Hallie suspects his vagueness is intentional. He's feeling her out to see how much she knows. "Oh. *That.* He was worried about you and Shelly the other night, when he couldn't reach you. I didn't understand why this Markum guy would have it in for you. It was my fault for being nosy. He didn't really say much."

"Did he tell you about the fire at Last Glass?"

It takes effort to swallow, so Hallie only nods.

"Then, he said more than he should have. Not because I don't trust you. *I do.* But I'd rather not revisit the worst time of my life. You can understand that, right?"

Boy, does she ever. She's wished entire years of her life away. Like mismatched socks, she'd stuffed them into the darkest, dankest corners until she'd nearly forgotten their existence. "Yeah, I totally get it. The therapist I saw as a kid warned me that I couldn't outrun my past. The very next morning, my foster mom found me doing sprints in the backyard."

"I think I need better running shoes." Robert gives her a sad smile. "If the police ask you what you know about Jordan Markum, it's best to tell them nothing. Don't mention Last Glass. Let me handle it. I don't want you to get mixed up in our mess."

"But I *don't* know anything about Jordan. Only that he's your hothead former business partner."

"Good. That's the right answer. The less you know, the better."

"That makes sense." But it doesn't. Not really. Determined to win her father over, Hallie selects a small stone, worn smooth by the water. She takes a few practice flicks of the wrist. "I realize that it's hard to talk about, and if I'm out of line, let me know. But there is one question that's been on my mind about the family... and the fire. What really happened to Grandpa Wallace?"

Hallie pitches the rock toward the shimmering lake. It

skips once, twice, before it settles beneath the surface. Though it's such a small feat, her heart leaps.

"Not bad, kiddo. Not bad at all." Robert gazes out, watching the ripples until the water calms again. Then, almost to himself, he says, "Dad wasn't supposed to be at the restaurant. Nobody was. But the next day was Natalie's birthday and, typical Nat, she'd demanded a chocolate cake. So, he decided to take the kids down to the Last Glass to make one from scratch. God knows what possessed him, since he couldn't bake a lick. When the fire broke out, they all ran. Nat said Grandpa was right behind her. We're not exactly sure why he went back in."

Looking at the regret that stains her father's face, Hallie finds herself on the verge of tears. "Did they ever figure out what caused the fire?"

"That's two questions." He nudges her with his elbow. "Only kidding. Apparently, it was a kitchen fire that burned out of control. Oil spilled on the gas cooktop. But like I told you at the lookout, I've spent a lot of time blaming myself."

"It wasn't your fault. Just like it wasn't mine that our car went off the road." She searches for another skipping stone to place in her father's hand. Anything to make him smile again, though her innate need to please him unnerves her. It's been so long since she wanted a parent's approval. "Show me again how it's done, Dad."

TWENTY-EIGHT

As Robert makes the turn into the Cerulean parking lot, Hallie spots Nick on the outer deck with his notebook.

"Is he okay?" she asks her father. "After last night, I mean. The family emergency."

Robert waves his hand dismissively. "He better be. Unless he wants a demotion."

"You don't mean that."

Shutting the engine, he turns to her. His expression, grave. "My executive chef needs to be as reliable as clockwork. I can't have someone cutting out mid-dinner service and leaving us all in the lurch. Between you and me, Nick's been off lately. I think this gig might be too much for him, especially now that Nat's cookie business has taken off. I'm wondering if she should hire him full time and let you take the reins here. You've got more fine dining experience, that's for sure."

Suddenly, the truck's cab closes in. It's too small and too hot. She opens the door, eager to escape.

"Oh, I don't know about that. Nick's been your head chef for a while now. He's a big part of your success."

She *likes* Nick. She likes him a lot. The thought of stealing his job out from under him makes her stomach ache. Because that's a rotten way of getting what she wants. And because he holds the power to break her. He knows her secret... or one of them, at least. Surely, if Robert threatens his livelihood, Nick will happily throw her under the bus.

"You're right. He has been invaluable to Cerulean. But he has to recognize his role. No one is irreplaceable. Not even Nick."

Hallie tries to stay calm. A spider caught in her own web, struggling will just make it worse. Still, it seems necessary to mount another protest. "His food is delicious. He's talented, determined, and loyal."

"So are you, Hallie. Don't forget that."

"I won't." She forces herself to meet his eyes. "You should talk to him first. If he's been distracted, I'm sure he has a good reason."

"That's good counsel. I think I will."

Horrified, she can only watch as Robert covers the ground between the parking lot and the deck. He doesn't look back.

Hallie retreats into the restaurant, taking refuge in the kitchen, where she sets a timer and starts to assemble the ingredients for a practice run through her contest dish. With her valuables gone God knows where, she needs to win. She needs the money. Mostly, she needs to create something right now to feel in control again. As the pan heats on the stove, her heartbeat slows to a normal rhythm. But her relief gets jerked out from beneath her. Gone, just as fast as it came.

Natalie emerges from the pastry room. She manages to look effortlessly chic in a white shirtdress, even while lugging a large box overflowing with packages of Nat's Nibbles. She balances it against the counter to make a show of it.

"Wow. That's a big order." Hallie widens her eyes, hoping to play to her sister's ego. It might be an impossible task, but she's determined to win her over for Robert's sake. At the very least, to work her way down from the top of Natalie's hit list.

"It's the fourth one this month from the wife of a tech CEO. And before you ask, I really can't say who. Maintaining my client's privacy and all." After a dramatic pause, during which Hallie makes the expected impressed face, Natalie gives her a once-over. "You're missing something."

"Um..." Her skin warms under her sister's scrutiny.

"I know. You haven't been wearing your pearls. Come to think of it, you didn't have them on yesterday either."

Hallie puts a hand to her neck, tracing the ghost of them. In her mind's eye, the empty shoebox looms like an empty grave. "Actually, the clasp broke a few days ago. I'll have to take them to a jeweler when I get back to Sacramento."

"But that necklace is totally Insta-worthy, a real statement piece. I'm sure Dad knows someone local. I'll ask him." It's suspicious how nice she's being. It can't last. "Speaking of, where is Dad?"

"Outside. Talking to Nick about last night." Hallie holds open the side door for Natalie. It's the sisterly thing to do. Not to mention, she wants her gone as soon as possible. Instead of walking through it, Natalie shakes her head in judgment and drops the box onto the counter.

"Oh. Well, good for you."

"What do you mean?"

"C'mon. We both know this is what you wanted."

Hallie feigns ignorance. It's that or wallop her perfect blonde head with the pan. "I have no idea what they're discussing. Frankly, it's none of my business or yours."

Natalie rolls her eyes—her go-to move—and Hallie realizes that she's dealing with a petulant twenty-two-year-old who never graduated from adolescence. There's no winning. "You're right. Cerulean is not *your* business. But you sure seem intent on making it yours. Ever since you arrived, you've been trying to push Nick out to take over as executive chef. You want to push me and Logan out too, so you can be the favorite child. But you'll learn. As long as you do exactly what Dad wants, he'll keep you on his pedestal. The minute you stop toeing the line, he'll lose interest. When Dad loses interest, he'll forget you exist. He's done it before."

"Is that why you hate me?"

"I don't hate you. I pity you. You have no idea what Logan and I have been through. If you want all this..." She gestures behind her to the empty dining room. "...it's yours. Just don't come crying to me when the bill comes due."

Shell-shocked, Hallie looks on while Natalie attempts to make a dramatic exit. Holding the cumbersome box with one arm, she grapples with the door handle until she finally relents. "A little help here, please."

It would be so easy to tell her where to stick it. It would feel so good. But Hallie knows that will get her nowhere. She steels herself, the way she had so many times with her mother. Addicts can be ruthless, even to their children. *Especially* to their children.

When Hallie opens the door, she finds Nick on the other side, appearing equally stunned.

"I warned you, Nick." With a strained grunt, Natalie collects her box of cookies and brushes past them, letting the door smack shut behind her.

Nick ignores Nat's hostility, as Hallie retreats to the stove, the pan hot as hellfire by now. Her fifteen-minute timer, ticking relentlessly. After tossing in the butter, she flicks her eyes up, trying to read Nick's face.

"So, I heard you made quite the splash last night."

"Robert told you?" Of course he had. She'd all but encouraged him to do it. Without waiting for an answer, she asks, "What did he say?"

"That he's disappointed in me for leaving during service. That I need to remember my place." Nick drops a handful of garlic cloves into *her* pan. It's only a pan, but she feels territorial. She moves in closer, forcing him to step back. "I also got an interesting text from Natalie this morning. She seems to think that I'm on the way out. That you're next in line for the Cerulean throne."

"That's crazy."

"Yeah, it is." Nick lowers the heat on *her* pan. She turns it back up. "We both know you were in over your head last night. You're not a head chef. You're not a chef at all."

"But I pulled it off. You said yourself that my food is good." She swats Nick's hand away from her bowl of pre-cut lobster tail and stirs the sauté. "It's not like I asked for this. I even defended you to Robert. But you abandoned the restaurant in the middle of service. You're always distracted, looking at your cellphone, running out to God knows where. What did you expect to happen?"

Lightning fast, Nick swipes the bowl before she can grab

it. Then, he has the nerve to smirk at her. "I'm not distracted."

"Well, you're sneaking around. You're lying. I saw you that day at the clinic, when you told me you went to the farmers' market."

"Did you follow me?"

Hallie uses the moment of surprise to reclaim the bowl. She drops *her* lobster into *her* pan and readies another skillet to grill the bread. "I wanted to know what you were hiding. I was protecting Robert. What about the day you were late? You had blood on your shirt."

Nick steals the loaf of sourdough from the counter, holding it hostage behind his back. "You were protecting Robert from me? That's rich. As far as I can tell, you're the one who's lying here."

"Thanks for throwing it back in my face. I admitted as much to you. You promised you wouldn't tell him. It would only hurt him."

"And now, it's hurting *me*. If I told your dad what I know—"

Hallie makes a desperate lunge for the bread. When Nick jumps out of her reach, he bumps his hip against the stove, sending her pan and its contents to the floor. Embarrassed, they gawk at each other. The timer dings, a fateful toll.

"What's going on in here?" Robert demands from the doorway. His sternness spooks her, but it's also a reassurance. Someone cares enough to scold her, to demand more of her.

"It's my fault." Hallie gestures to the mess, willing her father to unhear Nick's unfinished threat. "It was an accident."

Dishtowel in hand, Nick drops to one knee. He offers his

explanation to the sacrificial chunks of lobster. "No, it was *my* fault. We were goofing around. I was just teasing Hallie about her lobster recipe."

"As we discussed, you need to be focused on tonight's dinner service and the cookout this weekend. On getting back to the Nick I promoted. Not flirting with my daughter. Understood?" Then, he turns his attention to a red-faced Hallie. "Don't let him become a distraction."

After Robert disappears into his office, Hallie joins the clean-up. "Thank you," she whispers. "For not telling him."

"I'm not a tattletale, but he's going to find out anyway. It'll be better if it comes from you." Nick cuts a vicious side-eye in her direction. "And for the record, I wasn't flirting."

"Noted."

TWENTY-NINE

An uneasy truce settles between Hallie and Nick. She doesn't mention his unexplained departure during dinner service the day prior and he doesn't call her a bald-faced liar. He doesn't punish her by relegating her to the lowly salad station. Likewise, she doesn't call him out on his frequent cellphone checks. *Father knows best*, as they say. She needs to stay focused. It helps that the restaurant stays busy all night, with a constant stream of orders.

After the last of the staff clears out and Robert locks up the office, Nick turns to her with a peace offering. "Do you want to fire your grilled cheese again? I know you wanted to practice before the contest. Fifteen minutes goes by quick. I was being a jerk before, getting in your way."

"It's okay. I'm exhausted. I'm overthinking it anyway. I've made that sandwich a thousand times. I don't need to practice. If you ask me, it's my prize to lose."

"Alright, then."

Hallie feels guilty when he doesn't come back with a snappy retort. She's grown accustomed to his sharp wit, and his lack of a comeback leaves her cold. "Aren't you going to ask me to take out the trash, Chef?"

"I'm not sure you can handle it. You said you're exhausted. I don't want to push you too hard." The corner of his mouth hints at a smile. "When I beat you, I want to beat you at your best."

Giving in, Hallie laughs, and so does Nick. A weight lifts from her chest, at least for the moment. He doesn't hate her. "For what it's worth, I really did defend you to Robert. I told him you must have a good reason for flaking out. I didn't know he was going to confront you right then and there."

"Flaking out, huh?" He cocks his head at her. "Do you have time for a drive?"

"What about the garbage?"

"We'll come back for it." Nick holds the door open for her. "Don't worry, you've still got trash duty."

"Is this the part where you take me into the forest to hack me into pieces and bury my body?" Still, she walks through the doorway, her eyes immediately drawn to the newly erected sign at the entrance to the trail. *NO TRESPASSING—VIOLATORS WILL BE PROSECUTED*. She hopes Jay hadn't been caught off guard. Or worse, *caught*.

"I would never bury your body." Nick looks at her in earnest. "I'd just let the bears take care of it."

"How thoughtful of you."

"Hey, they've gotta eat too."

Hallie squints into the absolute darkness, her eyes fatigued from the long day. Beyond the headlights of Nick's jeep, the deserted road bleeds black. An endless inky well. They've long since passed Incline's center, the single stoplight that marks the intersection of several strip malls. That lone movie theater, the Mecca of entertainment.

"We're almost there."

In the quiet of the cab, with only the rumble of the asphalt beneath the tires, Nick's voice startles her. Night drives always make her anxious, for obvious reasons. It's easy to feel alone out here. Like the only person marooned on a distant planet. And even easier to imagine the car drifting off the shoulder, pulled like a magnet toward the stoic line of ancient tree trunks. Any one of them massive enough to end her. *Blinding lights. Swerve. Screech. Blackness.*

She shakes off a shiver at the memory. "And where is 'there' exactly?"

"I told you I'll explain when we arrive."

Hallie grimaces. "Alright, Ted Bundy."

She doesn't mean it, of course. Not entirely. But she still wonders about Nick's strange behavior—the blood, the clinic, the way his eyes seem tethered to his cellphone screen. So, she'd sent Robert a message, letting him know that she and Nick would finish up trash duty when they returned from an errand. If she disappears tonight, at least she's left a trail of breadcrumbs.

The ticking of Nick's blinker sounds like a countdown. He checks for oncoming traffic, though they haven't passed another vehicle in miles, and turns onto a gravel road. When he flicks on his bright lights, a small cabin appears in the distance. The porch steps droop under the weight of past snowfalls, and the red door could use a fresh coat of paint. But the yard appears neat and clean, a stark contrast to the wild, witchy woods beyond the fence line.

"This is my place," Nick says. "It's a far cry from the Thompsons' mansion, but it's home."

"It's cozy."

"It used to be nicer. Since it's been so busy at the restaurant, I haven't been able to keep up with the repairs."

A flash of movement in the single lit window draws Hallie's eyes. "Do you live alone?"

"Not exactly. That's why I—"

A wisp of a woman flings open the front door. She stands in the threshold, her flowing white nightgown whipping around her legs. One arm extends toward them, her finger pointed at Hallie; the other rests at her side, wrapped in a bandage and sling. Hallie stares, open-mouthed.

Through the window, Hallie hears her wailing. "It was you. *You!* You took my Albert."

"Who's Albert?" It's the first question that pops out of her mouth.

"My dad. He died eight years ago. She forgets that he's gone. Sometimes, she thinks I'm him." Nick cuts the engine and sits there with his head in his hands, elbows braced against the steering wheel.

Like a fire that's burned itself out, the woman suddenly tires. She lowers herself to the ground and hugs her knees, rocking back and forth.

"That's your mother?" Hallie sees the resemblance in the thick gray curls that frame the woman's face, the Roman nose they share. She sometimes forgets she's not the only one with family trouble. "She's the reason you've been so distracted."

"I'm sorry. I should've warned you. I thought she'd be asleep by now."

"It's okay." Though Hallie hadn't expected this, it makes sense. How many times had she been late to school, taking care of her mother? How many days had she found it impossible to concentrate, worrying about her? "What's wrong with her?"

"She had a stroke a few years back and developed dementia. When my father's savings ran out, we couldn't afford assisted living or in-home care, and I couldn't bear to put her in a nursing home. She's been living with me for a year now, and she's a handful." Nick gestures to her bandaged arm. "The blood you saw... she put her fist through the bathroom mirror. She thought someone was spying on her through it. She wanders too. It's a constant worry that Adult Protective Services will start snooping around and tell me I can't take care of her, which wouldn't be far from the truth. Luckily, I've got cameras inside and out that I can monitor from my phone and I call her at least ten times a day to check in. *That's* why I'm distracted."

Stunned, Hallie waits in the jeep while Nick tends to his mother, helping her to her feet and into the house. Another light comes on and Nick waves to her through the window, beckoning her inside. It's silly to admit that she's afraid, but Mrs. Morelli's vacant eyes remind her of her mother's. The past feels dangerously close—too close—like she's clinging to the edge of a vortex.

Reluctantly, she leaves the safety of the jeep. It's the polite thing to do since he trusted her enough to bring her to his home and to reveal the kind of secret she would keep under lock and key.

"In here." His voice leads her into the kitchen, a homey nook that seems left in time. No granite countertops or stainless-steel appliances, it calls to mind the only kitchen she and her mother had shared. Before pain pills became more essential than rent payments. As Hallie scans the room, she spots the differences. The plastic locks on the stove knobs; the Post-it note reminders; a timed medication dispenser. The all-seeing eye of a camera fixed above the doorway. The evidence of decline makes Hallie's chest ache with sadness. With guilt, too, for the way she'd jumped to conclusions.

Nick clears his throat and turns down the volume on the small vintage television that sits atop the counter. "Hallie, meet my mom, Sofia. Mom, this is my friend Hallie. She works with me at the restaurant."

Subdued now, Sofia takes a sip from the cup of milk Nick sets in front of her.

"It's nice to meet you, Mrs. Morelli." Unsure of herself, Hallie gives Sofia's hand a gentle squeeze.

"Do you know my Albert?" Sofia asks, hopefully.

As Hallie shakes her head *no*, her heart breaks a little. She glances to Nick, who nods encouragingly. "Tell me about him."

Sofia settles back in her chair and wipes a dribble of milk from her chin. "My Albert is a good egg. If you ever need a handyman, he's the best in town. He should be home any moment now if you'd like to stay for dinner."

"Hallie can't stay, Mom. It's time for bed."

Confused, Sofia's eyes dart to the stove and back to Nick. "Where's the pot of stew I made? The fresh bread I had in the basket on the counter?"

Nick sighs. "You haven't cooked in a long time. It's not safe anymore." To Hallie, he adds, "That's why I keep the fridge bare. It's hard for Mom to see fresh produce and not want to chop it and cook it. She's hurt herself before."

"Don't back-talk me, Nicky. I made stew. It's your father's favorite."

Hallie knows how to sidestep disaster. Sensing an

impending meltdown, she asks, "How do you season your stew? I always use a little Worcestershire sauce and honey."

"My Albert likes it with chili powder. The spicier the better. Even if he does regret it the next day." She smiles at the memory.

"Maybe we could make it together sometime." Hallie leans in and whispers, "Unless it's your secret recipe."

Sofia blushes, embarrassed by the attention. "It's not a secret."

"Okay, then. We have a date."

With that settled, Nick guides his mother from her chair. *Thank you*, he mouths over his shoulder, pausing to gaze at Hallie like she's some kind of saint. Then, he leads his mother down the hallway. If Nick knew the truth about Hallie, it would make him sick. She's no angel. Far from it.

As Hallie listens to their muted voices, she snoops out of habit, first taking a peek in the fridge. Empty, save for a bottle of mustard and a box of leftover pizza. Chef Nick should be ashamed of himself. But she understands his explanation. He's only trying to keep his mother safe. Then, she wanders to the counter, where she spots a loose stack of bills. The red OVERDUE stamp, familiar to her, Hallie thumbs through the pile, studying the company names.

"They're medical bills," Nick announces from the doorway.

Hallie jumps back, embarrassed that she's been caught. She tucks her prying hands into her pockets and turns her eyes to the late-night news broadcast on the muted television, looking anywhere but at him.

"I didn't mean to be nosy. But you should tell Robert. I'm sure he would want to help you and your mom. You said yourself that he—"

"He already knows, Hallie. He's known all along."

It stuns her, no less than a slap to the face. "But he said you were distracted. That you were acting differently."

"I asked him not to say anything. Until recently, I've been able to manage. But she's been getting worse, and I worry about her hurting herself. I can't blame Robert for being upset with me. Besides, he doesn't need me anymore now that he has you to take over the family business. I'm not a Thompson."

"I'm not either." But she knows how Robert thinks of her. Blood matters more than a surname. "Let me talk to him about the situation. He could at least give you a raise. That would help, right?"

"I've already asked. He's helped here and there, as much as he could. Between you and me, he can't afford it right now."

"But the restaurant is packed every night."

"Summer is our busy season. But Robert's not the best at managing money. By the time he pays himself and the rest of the family their salaries, there's not much left to go around for the staff. That's why we're down a prep cook."

Hallie doesn't argue. She knows the Thompsons owe a small fortune to Jordan Markum. She's seen the proof in the urgent letter from the law firm. In the fire in Jordan's eyes when he barged into dinner service and issued his threat. Logan had told her as much, when he'd said, *There's nothing left*.

"I'll figure something out." Nick holds up his cellphone, posing goofily in front of the screen. "Hey, maybe I can become an influencer like Nat."

Hallie stops mid-laugh and points to the face on the fuzzy TV screen. "Is that...? Turn it up."

"...are asking for the public's help tonight in locating a missing person. San Francisco native and restaurateur Jordan Markum has not been heard from since Friday, according to his family. On Sunday morning, police located his rental car in the parking lot near the Stateline Fire Overlook, a popular hiking spot with locals and tourists. Markum had been visiting the Lake Tahoe area on business and planned to return home on Saturday. Police suspect that he may have gone hiking near the overlook late Friday afternoon or evening and become lost or disoriented; however, officials have not ruled out the possibility of foul play after Markum was involved in a violent incident at Cerulean restaurant on Wednesday. Markum is a well-known figure in the Bay Area, having financed popular restaurants such as Serafina and Farmer's Table."

Her head spinning, Hallie searches for what to say. Nick seems equally bewildered. He clicks off the television, his face as blank as the screen.

"That's the guy Logan punched at the restaurant," he says. "The one Robert thinks slashed his tires and vandalized the painting."

"Among other things. Yeah. Jordan Markum. That's definitely him."

"Damn. I wonder if your dad knows yet."

Has not been heard from since Friday. Since Friday. Friday! The words play back on a vicious loop, even as Hallie shrugs, her shoulders heavy under the weight of it all. On Friday evening, her father and Shelly had been God knows where, unreachable for at least an hour. And Robert had asked her not to tell the police.

"We should probably head back." A quick change of subject seems necessary before Nick starts asking the same questions that plague her. "As long as you're sure it's okay to leave your mom."

Nick lifts his eyes to the camera. "She takes a pretty powerful sleeping pill, so she'll be out for a while."

"Alright then."

The drive to the restaurant goes on too long, and Nick stays too quiet, leaving Hallie no choice but to fill the silence. Better to ramble on than to listen to her thoughts, skittering around up there like ants. "Thank you for bringing me to your home, and for introducing me to your mom. I'm sorry you're going through all that. It means a lot that you shared it with me."

Nick briefly takes his eyes from the road and touches her forearm resting on the console. She tells herself it means nothing. That she can't afford to care too much. It's too risky.

"Well, I couldn't have you thinking I was a slacker or that you couldn't trust me."

"I don't trust most people," she admits. "For the record, I didn't think you were a slacker. A murderer, maybe, with the blood on your T-shirt. But never a slacker."

"That's the strangest compliment I've ever received."

"You're welcome," she teases, immediately scolding herself for flirting. "If you want, you can just drop me off at the restaurant. I'll take care of the trash. It's a quick walk home."

Nick bites his lip and frowns at her. "Not a chance."

"Why not?"

"First of all, I'm not an asshole. Second, it's not safe. You saw the news report. 'The possibility of foul play.' That guy's missing, and someone's obviously targeting your family."

Hallie hates hearing it spoken aloud. But she knows he's right. "Fine."

"And third..." Nick guides the jeep into the parking lot and cuts the engine. His shy smile makes her wary. It would do a number on her, if she let it. She's been swayed by a man's charms before. It ended poorly to say the least. "I like spending time with you. We've got a lot in common."

"Are you sure about that? There's plenty you don't know about me."

"Like what?" Nick asks, boldly. "Are the cops after you?"

Despite her best efforts at concealment, panic registers on her face.

Nick gestures to the rearview mirror. "Officer Sumner, incoming at your six o'clock."

Now, she really *is* panicked. "What's *he* doing here?"

"I have no idea. I locked up, right?"

Hallie's head bobs up and down. "Of course you did." Already, she's questioning her memory. She's wishing she'd gone straight home. "At least, I think you did. I'm not sure."

"I hope that guy didn't break in. You know, the homeless man."

"He wouldn't—I mean, I doubt that. What would he want anyway?" *Food*, Hallie thinks. *Shelter. Running water. The list goes on, dummy.* She's never been gladder to hear the knock against Nick's window. She prefers over-eager Sumner and his badge to Nick's discernment.

"Howdy, Nick."

Hallie sinks back in her seat.

"Mind following me down to the station?"

"Sure. What's this about?" Nick sounds casual, relaxed. The way an innocent person would.

Meanwhile, Hallie's heart hammers against her throat so mightily she's certain Officer Sumner can hear it. She doesn't dare make eye contact, but she can make out his movements in her periphery. The gun at his waist. The cuffs, too. She remembers the snap of the cold metal, the ache of her wrists against it. The shame of knowing she'd deserved to be locked away.

"Have you heard about the missing person, Jordan Markum?"

"Uh, yeah. We saw it on the news back at my house. The guy was in here on Wednesday night. He's the one who got into it with Robert's son, Logan. I don't know him personally. Haven't seen him since."

Officer Sumner makes a noncommittal sound. Hallie wishes Nick would stop talking.

"But you had a meeting with him Friday night."

"I *what*?"

"Markum's family hasn't heard from him since Friday. Your name and number was written in the planner that we found in his rental car, so naturally the Washoe County detective wants to have a word."

"I was with Hallie on Friday at the casino. They have security cameras."

She feels Sumner's eyes slither past Nick to the passenger seat. Still, she doesn't look at him.

"Is that true, ma'am?"

Her *yes* sounds like the mewl of a kitten. If she keeps up this pathetic display, she'll be the one in the hot seat. "That's right," she says, with as much fortitude as she can muster.

"Alright, we can sort it out down at the station. I'm sure it's nothing, just a mix-up. We'll have you in and out in no time."

That sounds like total BS to her, but Nick doesn't protest.

"Tonight?" she blurts. "It's nearly midnight."

Officer Sumner leans into the window then. She can't avoid him any longer. "Aren't you Robert's daughter? The chef in town from Sacramento."

For a split second, Hallie's brain shuts down. *How does he know where I'm from? That I want to be a chef?* But then she recalls Robert's over-the-top toast and the way news must travel like wildfire in a town this small. "Yes, I met you and your partner, Sheldon, the other night at the Thompsons' house."

"Oh, yeah. You're the one I was looking for yesterday. To get a statement about the vandalism at your father's home."

"I'm sorry I missed you. There was an incident with a spoiled fish. But I'm not sure what I can add. I didn't see anything. Or anybody."

It unnerves her that she can't read behind his frown or discern the meaning beneath his grunt. She hasn't been this close to getting caught in so long that the thought makes her skin crawl. Getting away with it used to be exciting.

Officer Sumner turns his attention back to Nick, then jerks his head toward the patrol car. This time his message is clear. Under the weight of expectation, Nick shifts beside her.

"Hallie and I were just finishing up at the restaurant. I'm giving her a ride home. Surely, all this can wait until the morning."

"No, sir, it can't. This investigation is our top priority. I expect to see you at the station in thirty minutes or I'll come looking for you."

Hallie follows Officer Sumner in the rearview. He retreats to the patrol car, where his partner waits for him, and gives them a friendly wave before he drives off. Hallie knows better. He's just a different kind of con man. Like the foster parents who'd made bank on her, then tossed her out like yesterday's newspaper. Like the social worker who pretended to care. The handsome group home counselor who'd smiled at her in secret, knowing how hard she would fall.

"What was that all about?" she asks Nick.

"I have no idea, but thanks for vouching for me. That guy makes me nervous." With a new urgency in his voice, he pushes the door open. "I guess we better hurry with the trash. Don't want to keep them waiting."

Nick leaves her in the truck and heads toward the restaurant. As Hallie rushes to catch up, an uneasy relief settles over her, until she remembers the twenty-minute gap between when she'd left Nick at the restaurant and when he'd shown up at the casino.

He hadn't been with her the whole night. She's right back where she started, where she's always been, wondering if there's anyone she can trust.

EMAIL

To: Hallie Sherman <hsherman94@pacbell.com>

From: Bob Thompson <bigbob@bigbobs.biz>

Subject: Maybe...

Dear Hallie,

Am I your father? Maybe. Before I opened Big Bob's Used Cars, I attended community college in Sacramento, and I was quite popular with the ladies. In fact, I even dated a woman named Elizabeth (she went by Betty), and we talked about getting married. As luck would have it, I caught her cheating with my best buddy. We broke up, and I never heard from her again. Her loss! I wouldn't put it past her to get herself knocked up and keep it a secret. Clearly, the woman was crooked as a dog's hind leg.

    Since then, I've been married and divorced a few

times. I have enough kids to field a baseball team. But I suppose there's always room for one more. I submitted my saliva sample to Family Ties like you asked. In the meantime, can I interest you in a preowned vehicle? We've got a wide inventory of quality cars, trucks, and SUVs to fit any price range. I'll guarantee you a friends and family discount... even if we're not related.

Ciao!

Bob

THIRTY

Jordan Markum is missing. The thought crashes in like a rogue wave when Hallie awakens. She drags the covers over her head, wishing that she hadn't come here to Incline Village. That she'd gotten to know her absent father the way a normal girl would. Slowly and cautiously, from a distance. Not a headfirst dive into water so deep she can't see the bottom. Her mother would've said, *I told you so.*

Hallie scans her cellphone for news on Jordan's disappearance. *Search Begins for Restaurateur Missing in Lake Tahoe.* With no new details, she scrolls to the comments, hoping to find a clue amid the chaos. She'd spent half the night tossing and turning, replaying the last few days in hopes that it would all start to make sense. That the puzzle pieces would fit into place, revealing the answers to questions she couldn't articulate. But all she has to show for her sleepless night are bloodshot eyes and a fuzzy head.

The comments offer no help. They range from the typical speculation of the armchair detective—*the wilderness is a great place to dispose of a body*—to the blatant callousness of the keyboard warrior—*what kind of moron goes hiking at night?* After examining a page's worth, she clicks out of the article and checks again for news from Nick. When he'd dropped her off last night outside the Thompsons' house, he'd promised to text, and it worries her that she hasn't heard from him. Who's taking care of Sofia? Did she wake up alone, wondering why her Nicky had disappeared?

She dials his number more than once. Each time her call goes straight to voicemail, she grows increasingly disheartened. One part of her worries; another part wonders. After all, there's plenty that Nick doesn't know about her. It stands to reason his ailing mother is just the tip of the iceberg.

The sound of another heated conversation draws Hallie toward the double doors that lead out to the deck. Outside, the sky remains dark, but the birds are awake. It won't be long until sunrise.

Hallie moves quietly, edging toward the sound of Shelly's voice. "We should help with the search. It's the right thing to do. If the national media gets ahold of this, it's only a matter of time before they dig up the whole story. We need to start to spin this in our favor."

"The cookout is only a few days away," Robert says. "There's too much to do. Besides, I'm sure search and rescue will find him. He'll turn up like that hiker who was discovered by his own dog a couple of years ago."

"Really, Rob? *A dog?* This is serious. You keep talking like that and you'll become a suspect."

Hallie holds her breath in the silence.

"A suspect in *what*, exactly? The man went for a hike and didn't come back. It happens all the time out in the wilderness. There's been no crime, as far as I can tell."

"Still, I think we should cancel the cookout."

"And take a loss on all the food we've already ordered? We're already in trouble. We can't afford that."

"Doesn't it worry you, though?" Shelly asks. "The timing of everything. The painting, the tires. The faulty bridge. The cookies. I understand why you want to blame Jordan for all of it, but how do you know—"

"Because I know. We would've heard something, if there was a problem. I told you it would be fine. Don't bring it up again."

"But I—"

The door slams below, reverberating up through the wall like a small earthquake. Hallie counts to one hundred before she leaves the bedroom. She pads into the kitchen, still bleary-eyed.

"Is everything okay?" Hallie's eyes skirt across Shelly's tired face, bare of makeup. She takes stock of the worry lines, the dark circles. Robert hasn't fared much better. His usually clean-shaven face wears a day's worth of stubble. "I heard voices from the deck."

"Guilty," Robert says. "I hope we didn't wake you."

Hallie shakes her head, seemingly oblivious, and busies herself pouring a glass of orange juice. The tension between them is palpable, even with her back turned. "Did I hear something about canceling the anniversary cookout?"

Natalie announces herself with a sharp gasp, storming up the stairs and into the room as if she's been awake for hours. "Are you kidding? I'm going live from the lake on Friday. My followers are expecting special content. I already teased an interview and baking sesh with Nick. I can't back out now. Do you realize what that would do to Nat's Nibbles?"

"Insta-*death*," Logan deadpans from behind her. "*Like*, you mean you might have to, *like*, get a real job. *Like*."

"You're one to talk."

Shelly shakes her head. "This isn't the time."

"Yeah, Nat." Logan brushes past his sister, roughly bumping his shoulder against her. "What's your problem?"

"Quiet, both of you." With a voice as punishing as a whip, Robert silences them both. "Jordan is missing."

"*What?*" The siblings glare at each other, apparently annoyed by their brief moment of synchronicity.

Hallie sips from her glass, trying to disappear into the background. But Shelly catches her eye.

"Did you know about this, Hallie?"

"I saw the news story last night." An unwelcome flash of Officer Sumner's face comes and goes again, leaving her unsettled. "But I don't know any more than you do. Probably less," she adds, without thinking.

Shelly's frown sends Hallie scrambling. So much for blending in.

"I assumed you must have heard something since you and Robert are friendly with the police. And you have so many friends in town. I didn't mean anything by it."

"Of course you didn't," Robert assures her. "We only heard about it on the news too. Same as you. Given what happened at the restaurant on Wednesday night, I'm sure the police will stop by the house at some point."

Natalie drops a slice of wholewheat bread into the toaster. "Why do we care about him anyway? He's tried to take this family down since day one. As far as I'm concerned, good riddance."

That gets Shelly's attention. Hallie can breathe again.

"Natalie Lynn Thompson. Don't let me hear you talk like that. That man has a family who's very worried about him."

"*Who?* Some model girlfriend? I doubt she cares. She'll be on to the next by the time he turns up."

As Shelly launches into another well-deserved tirade, Hallie studies her sister. The messy bun piled atop her head, the fuzzy slippers. And, *gasp*, the tiniest pimple on her chin. She's human, alright, though she sounds cold-blooded.

Unbothered by Natalie's distastefulness, Logan glances up from his cellphone. "They're looking for volunteers to help with the search. Volunteers who have experience hiking in rough terrain."

"Absolutely not," Robert counters.

Natalie ponders for a moment, then takes a delicate bite of her toast. "It sounds dangerous. You should do it."

Logan looks only at his father. Hallie can sense his desperation. How badly he needs his approval.

"It's brave of you to want to help, son. But I don't think it's a smart move. The police might get the wrong idea."

"Well, you know what? I don't need your permission. I'm tired of waiting around for you to love me like..." Logan glances across the room at Hallie. Behind his eyes, he holds back a hurricane. "Like a father should."

Hallie grips so tight to the glass in her hand, she fears it might break.

"You shouldn't be here, Hallie. You're better off without him. All he cares about is himself. Himself and his precious restaurant. The rest of us are just collateral damage."

"You don't mean that." When Shelly reaches for Logan, he pulls away.

But Robert latches on to his wrist, seizing it like a whip. Matching jaws clenched, father and son face off at the top of the staircase. A live wire sizzles between them.

"Where do you think you're going?" Robert hisses.

It's all so familiar to Hallie, this dance. Like a caged bird, her heart flutters against her ribs. On the days that her mother had turned into an insatiable monster, with a pill-shaped hole for a mouth, she'd fled from the station wagon across the parking lot and into the safety of the Valley Fair Mall where the cold air and smell of waffle cones overwhelmed her senses. Where no one noticed her wandering the aisles of the costume jewelry store or slipping a pair of cheap gold-plated loops into her pocket. Where she felt the relief of invisibility.

"Just let him go." Her voice seems to come from far away, as if she's fallen down a well. That's how she feels. Trapped. "Please."

Her supplication breaks Robert like a spell, and he relinquishes Logan's arm. Logan flees down the stairs and out the door while Robert wilts like a weed.

"I'm sorry," he says, his eyes locked on Hallie's. His head hung low, he retreats to the master bedroom, leaving them all in stunned silence.

Ten minutes later, there's still no sign of Robert. Only the locked bedroom door and the tense silence behind it. Shelly knocks again.

"Are you okay in there, hon?" She presses her ear against the wood and wipes a tear from her cheek. With a quick exhale, she straightens herself, newly resolved. "Nat, will you swing by the restaurant and meet the guy from the brewery? Rob ordered some extra kegs for the party, and I have to stick around. The alarm company will be by later to give us an estimate."

The way Natalie groans from behind her, Hallie fully expects to find her laid out on the floor, afflicted with serious bodily injury. But no, she's upright and spreading avocado on her toast. "Logan is such a brat. *What?*" she asks, seeing her mother's reaction. "He *is*. He doesn't think of anyone but himself. I have so much to do before the cookout. I don't even know what I'm wearing yet."

"I'll do it," Hallie offers. She casts a cautious glance toward the bedroom. "As long as you're okay here."

"I think I can manage my own husband." Before the sting wears off, she adds, "I didn't mean it to come out like that. I appreciate your concern. It's just—"

"It's okay. The last few days have been stressful." Hallie back-pedals toward the staircase, planning a speedy escape. The house that had once felt so warm, so welcoming, doesn't anymore. The walls close in like a jail cell, and she's not sure whether the faces that surround her are her fellow inmates or her jailers. "I'm happy to help."

"Thank you. There's a spare set of restaurant keys in the desk in the enclave. The kegs should arrive around nine."

"Nine. Got it." Though she wants to sprint for the door, she forces herself to take one stair at a time.

"And if you see Nick," Natalie adds, "tell him we need to talk about the segment. He's been MIA since last night."

Halfway down the steps, Hallie glances up at Natalie leaning over the railing. Her sister's smirk stops her cold.

"Are you seriously going in your pajamas?"

THIRTY-ONE

The beer delivery complete, Hallie locks up the restaurant. She tucks the spare key inside her jeans pocket and hurries back to the truck with provisions, intent on speeding to her next destination. The one she's had in mind all along. A part of her had hoped Nick would be there, lounging outside on the Cerulean deck, notepad in his hand. Another part already understood he wouldn't be. She checks her cellphone again. Nothing. Not a call or a text or a smoke signal. She wonders when she started caring. When she started worrying. When she stopped protecting herself from exactly this. The last time she cared about a guy, she'd done stupid things, criminal things. She'd hurt someone.

Hallie pilots the truck through town, stopping at the lone intersection. As the light turns, a familiar red bicycle catches her eye. It's locked on a rack outside the Incline Village Library. She stares at it until a honk from behind propels her forward. Instead of driving past, she whips into the lot.

Just five minutes, she tells herself, as she jogs toward the entrance. At least she can quiet her mind about Jay. She can lay eyes on him. She can see for herself that he's alright.

Hallie finds him at the computer hub, hovering over a keyboard with the focus of a hawk. His fingers glide effortlessly across the keys, stopping only when he spots her. He waves her over, pulling his hood down to reveal his stringy hair and stubbled face. Guilt pinches at her insides when she notices how tired he looks. Still, he seems glad to see her.

"Fancy meeting you here," he says.

She takes the open seat next to him, glancing at the screen. *Welcome to your public library. Please enter your library card number to get started.*

"Just surfing the web," he explains. "Killing time."

"I'm sorry about the No Trespassing sign. I feel like it's my fault."

He shakes off her self-reproach. "Nah, I got too comfortable. Someone spotted me."

"But your secret beach, your firepit..."

"Exactly. I let my guard down. That's when you know it's time to move on."

Hallie gets it. Moving on used to be her middle name. Jobs, cheap apartments. She'd learned from her mother that nothing is built to last. That it's better to do the leaving than to be left. She understands it now more than ever, with her secrets closing in.

"So, you found a new place?"

"Not exactly. I tried to sleep on a park bench last night near Ski Beach but the cops woke me up with a flashlight in my eyes. Told me I couldn't stay there. But I got lucky this morning." His wide grin reveals a set of straight, white teeth. Straighter and whiter than Hallie expected. "Look at this," he says, rummaging through his bag.

Hallie hides her surprise at the item in his hand. She makes a show of reading the name on the bag, as if she doesn't recognize it on sight. "Nat's Nibbles?"

"These damn cookies are addictive." He opens it, offering her one, but Hallie declines. She knows exactly how they taste. "What kind of monster would throw the whole bag in the trash uneaten? It didn't even look like they'd been opened."

"You found those in the trash?"

He widens the mouth of his backpack, showing its contents. Hallie's mouth drops open.

"Yeah. Like I said, a lucky find. Usually, it's all leftovers. Pizza crusts and days-old bread. Today, I found four whole bags of deliciousness. Who knew vegan chocolate chip could be so tasty?"

"Four bags?" Hallie asks, incredulous. "Where?"

"*Sheesh.* Don't get greedy. I offered you one of mine." Jay gives her a teasing nudge. "Kidding. They were in the bin outside of those fancy new condos on Lakeshore."

"Maybe I'll check it out." Hallie laughs, though she fully intends to do just that. She tries to imagine one of Natalie's hoity-toity clients, Prada bag in one hand, dumping her wares into the garbage.

"I call dibs on anything with peanut butter."

"Understood." She lifts her eyes to the clock. "Are you going to be here all day?"

Jay cuts his eyes at the gray-haired librarian behind the desk and pulls a face. "Can't. I don't want to overstay my welcome. Janice doesn't like it when I get crumbs on the keyboard."

"Here." Hallie reaches for a pen on the desk. She tears

off a corner from the Nibbles bag and jots down her number. "Take it, in case you need anything."

"That's really nice of you." Jay folds the paper and slips it into his pocket. "You know, I'm thinking of reaching out to my family. To give it one more try."

"That's amazing. What made you change your mind?"

Jay rubs the cleft in his chin. "Well, honestly, *you*. The way you put yourself out there with the Thompsons, even when it didn't turn out exactly how you expected. I only hope they'll be as understanding as you are."

Buoyed by Jay's good news, Hallie skips toward the exit, glancing back to give Jay a wave. His face hidden beneath his hood again, he doesn't lift his eyes from the screen.

Hallie makes quick work of the next few miles, only slowing when she reaches the turnoff. From the mailbox, she sees no evidence of Sofia or Nick. No jeep on the lawn. No wild woman waiting to indict her from the porch steps. Still, she exercises caution, tapping the brake as the truck creeps up the gravel road at a snail's pace.

Unlike last night's soft moonglow, the midday sun casts a harsh spotlight on the cabin's flaws. The sagging eaves hint that the roof may not survive another winter. Neither will the porch steps that creaked under her weight last night. But the tall pines that gather at its back, like soldiers standing guard, give the place a quiet strength, not unlike the Morellis themselves.

Hallie parks the truck in the dirt driveway and cracks the window. Even here, miles from the lake, the air smells divine. A summer fragrance with lingering notes of fresh pine and barbecue. Despite her misgivings, Incline Village has grown on her. She wonders what will happen when her two weeks are up. Maybe she'll win the contest on Thursday. Maybe she'll stay.

From behind her, footsteps creep across the gravel, making a delicate crunch. But the voice bears down like a sledgehammer. "Get off my property."

Sofia appears in the side mirror, wielding a baseball bat. Her legs, swallowed up by an oversized set of outdoor boots. Her face, half-covered by her long gray hair. "I told you about coming around here, threatening me and my Albert." She raises the bat above her head. It hangs in the air, ready to strike.

"Wait!" Hallie sticks her hands out the window. "It's me. Nick's friend, Hallie. We met last night. You told me you season your stew with chili powder."

"I don't know anyone by that name." Hallie hears a trace of doubt. Sees the faintest glimmer of recognition. Though Sofia lowers the bat, she insists, "And my Nicky's gone off to college."

"Well, that explains why I haven't heard from him. I was worried about you."

"That's ridiculous. I can take care of myself." Menacing, she slaps the bat against her palm and approaches the side of the truck. With each thwack, her hand trembles.

"I see that you're more than capable. There's no doubt about that." With Sofia in full view, Hallie gestures to her peace offering, grateful that the idea had struck her. "I brought a few things from the restaurant kitchen. I was hoping you could show me your recipe. Beef stew, the way Albert likes it."

Sofia snorts. Her feet stay planted in the dirt. "Do you have potatoes?"

Hallie nods.

"What about carrots?"

"Yes."

"I'll bet you got the stewing meat, didn't you?" Sofia can't hide her disdain. Top lip curling, she bounces the fat end of the bat against the toe of her boot.

"Puh-lease. I would never make a rookie mistake like that. Any chef worth their salt knows better."

"Prove it." Lifting her chin, Sofia peers down her nose into the truck.

"Look at that marbling." Hallie proudly displays her meat selection. "I got the beef chuck."

With a brief raise of her eyebrows, Sofia stalks off toward the house, pausing at the front stoop. She leans the bat against the steps and leaves it there. "C'mon, then."

By the time Hallie makes her way inside the kitchen, Sofia has already taken off her boots, secured the cast-iron stew pot—its surface worn with use—and placed it on the counter. She putters around the kitchen table in her socks, searching, as if she's lost something essential.

"I can't find my apron," she tells Hallie, pointing to the back of the closest wooden chairs. "I left it right here." Her brown eyes dart from one corner to the other like a spooked deer.

"I'm sure it'll turn up." Hallie starts to lay out the vegetables, hopeful the sight will distract her. "Aprons are overrated anyway. Didn't your husband always say that it's good to get your hands dirty?"

Her mouth quirks. "You're right. Albert says that all the time. How did you know?"

"Nick told me." The ingredients laid out, Hallie presents them with a sweeping gesture. "What do you say I cube some potatoes?"

Hallie finds the knives hidden in a child-proof cabinet. After selecting the paring knife, she sets up Sofia at the sink with a vegetable brush. Sofia washes; Hallie peels and slices. Sofia's hands are surprisingly steady under the cold water, and she makes quick work of scrubbing the potatoes. In her element again, her whole body relaxes. Her mind, too. Hallie knows the feeling.

"You mentioned that Nick is in college." Hallie cubes the last of the potatoes and starts on the carrots. "What school did he—I mean, *does he*—go to?"

"Sonoma State." Sofia beams with delight. Before she met Robert, Hallie would've been jealous. She'd always wanted a parent to revel in her achievements, to cry at her disappointments. To feel every emotion as deeply as if it was theirs. Now, she's closer than ever to having just that. "That's right, my Nicky is a college boy. The first in our family."

"Congratulations. You must be so proud of him."

"He comes home every weekend. He's a real mama's boy. It's a blessing he stayed so close."

Hallie hides her confusion with the relentless chop of her knife. Sonoma State isn't exactly close. "Where do you live, Mrs. Morelli?"

"You don't know?" She laughs, a brief burst that lights her face, before her eyes lose their shine. "Or do you forget like I do?"

Hallie watches while Sofia combines the flour and pepper in a mixing bowl and coats the beef, one piece at a time. It's all muscle memory. She wonders what her own muscles will remember in forty years. The creativity of the kitchen; the making from scratch. Or the things she's lost, gone without. The dark deeds she's done to get by.

"I... um..." She doesn't want to lie.

"It's okay. It happens to all of us sometimes. That's what Nicky says." Sofia points outside the kitchen window. "This is Napa. Surely, you've heard of the Napa Valley. It's famous for its wine."

Hallie nods, as she adds the coated beef to the pot of oil to brown. She can't stop thinking the obvious. This isn't Napa, and Nick hadn't told her about living there.

"How long have you lived here? In Napa?"

"Quite a while. Nicky was just a little boy when Albert took the handyman position at that winery. Oh, what was it called?" She flutters her hand through the air, dismissively. "Anyway, that was the first of many. Nicky used to go to work with his dad in the summer and play cops and robbers in the wine cellar."

Sofia hums to herself, peeking over Hallie's shoulder at the stew pot. "That aroma. It's heavenly. Albert says I should go to culinary school now that Nicky's all grown up. He thinks we can afford it."

"And what do you think?"

"I'm not sure it's necessary. I've always believed there are some things you can't learn in a classroom. Cooking is in here." She taps Hallie on the chest, leaving a spot of white flour on her T-shirt. "If you've got it, you've got it. If you don't, you don't. No fancy school is going to teach me to cook from the heart."

"Amen to that." Hallie uncorks the bottle of Merlot, planning to reduce the heat and stir in a cup of wine and vinegar, and offers Sofia a swig. It's easy to forget that Nick's mother is a time traveler, lost in another place. Living in the past.

"Cheers," Sofia exclaims, tossing a splash into the hot oil without warning.

They both yelp when a sudden flame shoots up from the pan.

Sofia scuttles across the kitchen, panicked. "Fire! Fire! Fire! We need to get out now!"

"It's okay. It's okay." With a quick turn of the knob, Hallie lowers the heat, and the flame disappears.

Sofia lunges toward the front door, banging her fists against it, wide-eyed and wailing. "Albert! Hurry!"

Hallie runs over. Her attempts to calm Sofia met only with increasing panic, she grabs Sofia by the arms and tugs her from the door. "It's okay. We're safe in here."

Sofia shakes her head so hard her teeth rattle. She jabs her finger against the small window at the top of the door. "Albert! He's inside. He's burning."

When she works up the courage to peer out the smudged glass, Hallie gasps. It's not a fire. It's not Albert either. She flings open the door, and Sofia shuffles through it, collapsing against her son.

"Where have you been?" Hallie sounds more demanding than she intends. "Your mom is... *upset*."

"Yeah. I see that." Nick soothes a sobbing Sofia, peering over her head to look at Hallie. "What's going on? Why are you here?"

"I asked you first."

When he drops his eyes to his mom and back up again Hallie realizes how exhausted he looks. "Later," he says, shushing Sofia as he guides her up the steps and inside.

Hallie follows, explaining how she ended up at his cabin with a pot of half-made stew still simmering on the stove and his mother in the throes of a breakdown. "I didn't think it was a big deal. Just a small flare-up but..."

Sofia lets out another wet gasp that cleaves Hallie's heart like an axe blade. "My Albert is gone. He's gone, isn't he?"

Hallie can hardly bear watching the lost memories flood in. The time traveler returns to the here and now, only to find their world upended, a critical piece gone forever.

"Nicky? Is your father really gone?"

Nick nods. "It's been eight years, Mom."

"Eight years?" She repeats the words again and again and again, still uncertain. Like she's wrestling with the truth of it.

"I'm so sorry," Hallie mutters. She leaves them near the front door and retreats to the kitchen to shut off the burner. Drained, she slumps into a chair.

Sofia takes an audible breath from the hallway. She stands on her own now, with wobbly knees, and gazes in at Hallie. The vacant finality on her face is worse somehow than her confusion.

"I won't be able to finish the stew today, dear. My Albert died in a fire."

THIRTY-TWO

Hallie hasn't moved from the table when Nick returns to the kitchen. He joins her there, looking just as defeated.

"Is she okay?" Hallie asks.

"She will be. I told her to lie down for a while." Nick hangs his head. "By the time she wakes up, who knows where she'll be. Most days, she forgets that he's gone. It's a blessing and a curse."

"I feel terrible. I thought cooking would be a great way to distract her. To distract us both, if I'm being honest."

He lifts his eyes, finally. "It's not your fault. I know you were trying to help. There's no telling what will set her off. I appreciate you coming to check on her. I certainly didn't want to send the cops out here. Something like that can push her over the edge. Once, she chased the mailman off with a—"

Hallie feels the hint of smile coming on. "Baseball bat?"

"How did you—" Nick's jaw drops slowly, tugged by the weight of realization. Then, he smiles too. A little ray of sunshine piercing through the clouds. "Oh, shit. *Seriously?* That must've been a sight."

"I shouldn't have been surprised after last night. I suppose I didn't think it through, showing up here. But I didn't want her to be alone and I hadn't heard from you." She tries not to phrase it like an accusation.

"That's because my cellphone is in police custody."

"What? *Why?*"

Nick shrugs, but he looks worried. "Hell if I know. But I wasn't going to argue. Let them have it. There's nothing there. I don't have anything to hide."

She studies him again. Yesterday's clothes. His messy curls. The stubble shadowing his jaw. "Have you been at the station this whole time?"

"No. But between worrying about my mom and the cops, I hardly slept." Hallie makes a sympathetic face and waits for him to continue. "It turns out the Washoe County detective they mentioned was already in bed last night and had no intention of speaking with me till the morning. I think they were just messing with me. So, they took my phone and sent me home with instructions to come back first thing this morning. Which I did."

"What a bunch of jackasses." Not that she's surprised. Cops have lied to her face so many times. Just as many times, she's lied right back.

"Exactly. Small-town police, too big for their britches. They were right though. My name is written plain as day in his calendar. They said he might've been trying to poach me from Cerulean as payback to Robert."

"That sounds..." Hallie ponders for a moment.

"Far-fetched?" Nick suggests.

"I was going to say 'possible.' Apparently, there was no

love lost between those two. What better way to stick it to Robert? You have a lot to do with Cerulean's success."

"Tell that to your dad. He's ready to send me packing for some novice."

Hallie takes the hit. She deserves it. Then, she rises, steady on her feet, and makes her way back to the stove. Fires up the burner again. "Wait till you taste my stew."

Grumbling a bit, Nick joins her there. "Wait till I beat you on Thursday," he counters.

"We'll see about that."

They work side by side for a while, both of them alone with their thoughts, until the veggies are chopped and the beef is ready to simmer. Hallie places the lid on the pot and turns to Nick.

"It's probably none of my business..." Actually, she's sure it's not. He's already shared so much. "But did your dad really die in a fire or was that just—"

"The dementia talking?" He stares off for a beat without answering the question.

Hallie wonders if she's overstepped. If he's about to tell her just that.

Instead, his eyes soften. "My dad died of sepsis. It's a severe blood infection."

"I'm sorry. It's hard to know what's real." Taking a breath, she confesses, "My mom was like that too. For very different reasons. A pill addict will say anything to get what they want."

Nick shows no surprise, no judgment. Just an easy calm, as he lifts the lid to taste the broth. "Does Robert know what she was like?"

"Only what I've told him. I spared him the worst parts.

Though my mom would've hated that. She never had a good word to say about him."

"*Really?* What made you want to find him then?"

It's not the first time Hallie has asked herself exactly that. "A million reasons. At first, I wanted to confront him. All my mom ever did was blame him, so I did too. But as I got older, I realized that I saw him through her eyes. That I'd inherited the same warped view. I guess it all boils down to wanting the truth. I needed to make my own judgment. To see if we had anything in common. To find the other person that made me, *me*."

Nick lifts the spoon to his mouth. He wrinkles his nose, then laughs when she gives him a playful shove. "Not bad for a novice."

LETTER

Robert Thompson
Napa Valley Psychiatric Facility
F-Ward
Napa, CA

Hallie Sherman
Box 2B
Sacramento, CA

Dear Ms. Sherman,

I know you're not who you say you are. I'm not sure how you found me. I can only hope that my SOS signal finally reached you after all these years. I need your help. I'm a prisoner of war, held against my will for crimes against humanity. They locked me up, handcuffed me to the bed, and implanted a device in my skull. Some nights, I feel it pulsing in my brain, trying to wipe my thoughts clean so I don't remember what they've done. Other nights, I hear it blaring. It's sending out a message, telling my captors what I'm planning. I tried to dig it out, but it's too deep, and I need to save my strength for the escape. You are my last hope.

PLEASE HELP ME!

Robert

PS My mother's name was Elizabeth.

THIRTY-THREE

The heady smell of homemade stew clings to Hallie's T-shirt. As she pulls up the Thompsons' driveway, she smiles to herself, remembering the moment Sofia had emerged from the bedroom and found her and Nick at the kitchen table. "Don't forget to skim the broth," she'd said, shaking her finger at both of them. Her meltdown, totally forgotten.

Cooking always makes everything better. Cooking *and* Nick, she begrudgingly admits to herself.

While Hallie parks the truck, Logan emerges from the front door, clad in cargo pants and a long-sleeve shirt and carrying two hiking poles. His blond hair is hidden beneath a camo bucket hat. Beneath the shadow of its brim, Logan's face looks dark and determined.

"Where are you going?" Hallie speaks gingerly, not wanting to poke at his wounds.

"Back to the lookout to help with the search. The hell with Dad."

"*Back?*"

"Yeah. After Dad flipped out this morning, I drove up

there to check it out, but I didn't have my gear with me. Everybody in town is helping. *Everybody*. I'm tired of sitting on the sidelines just so he can feel like a big man bossing me around. He doesn't give me any credit."

"I think he's just worried about you. Your mom too. They don't want you to get hurt."

Logan huffs out an exasperated breath. "You've known him for less than fourteen days. He's been my dad for twenty-one years. And bossing me around for most of it. He makes a good first impression, but don't think for one minute that you really understand him."

Hallie wants to prod him for more but Shelly appears on the deck upstairs, waving her hands to grab Logan's attention. "Your father says he's coming with you. He won't take no for an answer."

Logan curses under his breath.

"Do you want company?" Seeing the answer in her brother's eyes, she adds, "I'll get my boots."

Logan sits in the backseat, with Hallie riding shotgun as the designated buffer between father and son. Though neither says a word, their silence speaks volumes. Robert pilots the truck down the familiar path to the Stateline Fire Lookout. On Hallie's first trip to the lookout with her father, only the pines had borne witness, lining the road like ancient, all-knowing gods. Now, police cars block her view of the forest on either side, and a long caravan of volunteer vehicles trails down the hillside.

After an officer directs Robert to park the truck alongside the highway, they don the rest of their gear and walk toward the search and rescue check-in station, a long fold-out table where volunteers hand out water, orange reflective vests, and maps of the area. Taped to the table, she spots a laminated poster that features Jordan's face, alongside a description. Just the facts.

> 5'10", 185 pounds, short brown hair, brown eyes. Last seen wearing a San Francisco 49ers T-shirt, black running shorts, and white sneakers.

"Running shorts? Sneakers?" Robert winces, as he reads aloud. "That's not hiking gear. It gets cold out here at night."

Hallie can't help but think of Jay, enduring the days' heat and night after night of chilly temps, with nothing but a sleeping bag to protect him from the elements. No one should live like that. At least she and her mother had the rusted roof of the station wagon over their heads.

The volunteer coordinator waves them over, and within a few minutes, they're on their way into the wooded mountainside. Hallie stays close to Robert and Logan, recognizing her limitations. All around, she hears the unanswered calls of Jordan's name, echoes that leave no doubt about how easily an entire person can disappear in the wilderness.

Slowly, they hike down toward the valley. Poking her hiking stick into piles of leaves and detritus, Hallie scans the underbrush for any signs of life and adds to the chorus of voices. Every few steps, they stop to listen for a reply. A whistle, a call, a cry for help. Then, they keep on.

Despite the reason for the search, Logan seems more intent on proving himself as an expert outdoorsman, taking the opportunity to educate Hallie on the flora and fauna of the region while simultaneously radiating heat toward their father. A current of resentment travels between them, no matter how stubbornly they insist on ignoring each other.

Once they reach the valley below the lookout, they

spread out, joining the other volunteers. Hallie stops in the shade to catch her breath and counts at least twenty orange vests within eyesight. A few have dogs with them, their wet noses pressed to the ground and working.

"Are you okay?" Robert stabs his hiking pole into the soft earth. "I know things have been a bit dramatic since you arrived. I promise there's not usually this much excitement."

"It has been a little unsettling," she admits. In truth, she'd never expected this. That the idyllic town and perfect family she'd coveted would turn out to be a mirage. That she'd feel in danger here. "Do you think someone will find Jordan?"

"I certainly hope so." He joins her beneath the sugar pine. "No matter what trouble he caused our family, I never wanted this. I'm sure we could've worked it out."

A few days ago, he'd been ready to see the guy in handcuffs. But Hallie nods. Best to keep her mouth shut.

"Should we catch up to Logan?" She points ahead to where she last saw him.

A bark and a shout from that direction set her heart off like a sonic boom. She and Robert exchange a wide-eyed look then hurry toward the sound, running as best they can over the rough terrain, hiking poles in tow. The tall grass bites at her ankles, and the muscle beneath her scar begins to throb.

As Hallie fights through the thick underbrush, she hears another yell. Near a boulder in a small clearing, a group of volunteers have formed a circle, an audible buzz surrounding the crowd. It takes Hallie too long to identify the source of the droning. By then, a fat, black fly has alighted upon her. Watching its tiny legs scuttle against her wrist, she feels sick. One of the female volunteers starts to cry softly.

"Logan?" Breathless, Robert approaches the periphery.

"Here, Dad! Hurry!"

They push their way past the line of volunteers to find Logan crouched by the rock, stoic as a soldier, with a tight grip on his walking stick. Alongside him, Hallie first spots a white sneaker, scuffed with dirt. The ankle. The shin, scraped raw. Overwhelmed, she turns away.

"It's..." Logan rasps, leaving his sentence unfinished. "He's dead."

A sheriff's deputy moves in, kneeling by Logan. His canine partner sits beside him, fixated on the body. The dog barks again, pulls forward; the flies scatter, moving like a black cloud in the trees.

"Move back." The deputy springs up and pushes his hands toward the crowd. His dog follows his lead and gives another spirited chorus of barks. "Give us some space."

Hallie flinches but doesn't budge. She isn't sure she can. Robert, too, remains firmly planted beside his son.

Logan glances up at his father. "I saw something shimmering in the brush in the sunlight, so I came over to investigate. I didn't think it was—"

Robert claps him on the shoulder. "C'mon, son. Let's get out of the way. The police will handle it from here."

Ignoring his father, Logan stays put, white-knuckling those hiking poles. Suddenly, Hallie's chest gets tight. She leans forward, allowing herself to look at the rest of the body splayed out in the grass.

Bruises and scrapes cover the exposed skin. A piece of black nylon is tangled in a broken twig, the shorts ripped at the hem. The face resembles the photograph—a warped version, bloated and bloodied. Across the forehead, a large seeping gash. Hallie's stomach turns, and still, she can't look away.

It's the right arm, bent at an unnatural angle, that

captures her attention. She follows its contortions to the hand, the clawed fingers clutched in a death grip. *It can't be what it looks like.* She must be seeing things that don't exist. She tells herself not to scream, though every panicked cell in her body demands release.

Blinding lights. Swerve. Screech. Blackness.

Hallie squeezes her eyes shut, hoping the hand will disappear. It does not. If anything, the sight of it becomes clearer, spotlighted by the unforgiving sun. Robert has noticed it too. He makes no sound, but the tense set of his jaw commands her to stay quiet.

"C'mon," Robert says again. "Let's go."

Finally, Logan finds his feet but he fixes Hallie with a hard stare. He knows. They all do.

She has no explanation. All the bad she's ever done: this is how it ends. This is how it catches up to her. With the dead body of a man she doesn't even know and nowhere to run to.

Unable to resist, she looks back once more to be certain that her eyes aren't playing tricks. That it's really Jordan lying there, with a string of pearls clenched in his lifeless hand.

THIRTY-FOUR

Hallie trails behind Robert and Logan, keeping her head down. Thoughts pinball through her mind, one after the other, so fast she can't keep up. None of it makes sense. Why would Jordan steal her pearls? Why is he holding them now, lying dead in the brush at the bottom of the mountainside? What will the cops think when they realize the pearls belong to her? How will she explain her past without looking guilty? She can't. Facts are facts.

When Robert reaches the larger group of onlookers, he stops and waits. Hallie scurries beside him and takes shelter in his sturdy confidence. It's silly, she realizes. But beside her father, she feels safe—like no harm can come to her—and she needs him to know that no matter what else she might be, no matter what else she's done, she is *not* a murderer.

She nudges his arm, whispers, "The other night, after someone slashed the portrait, something else turned up missing. I should've told you. I don't know why I didn't." Through it all, Robert's face remains a blank. Logan offers a pained, sympathetic look that makes her feel better and worse at the same time. "My mother's pearls," she squeaks out.

"Don't say another word." Robert's lips hardly move, so that his voice seems to come from nowhere. "We'll talk when we get to the truck."

Hallie nods. Surely, they'll leave then. She can hardly stand still. She needs to get away. Instead, Robert lingers, and she forces herself to watch for a while in silence. Whispered words snake through the crowd. Some she holds on to, turning and turning them like worry stones. *Dead. Head injury. Fallen. Necklace.*

A team of search and rescue volunteers descend the hillside. The police string the yellow tape between the trees, set up a garish perimeter. Finally, when the group around them begins to disperse, Robert follows suit, waving Hallie and Logan on behind him. She realizes then, he's done this for her benefit. Running away would only make her look guilty.

They form a solemn procession, marching back up the way they came. Hiking poles anchoring them to the steep slope. Their footfalls plodding in a metronomic rhythm. The push and pull of their breathing grows more ragged as they reach the top. The sirens, too, become louder, and by the time they approach the volunteer check-in station, the warm asphalt is awash with red and blue swatches.

Hallie strips off her vest and uses it to wipe the sweat from her forehead. As she gazes down the long stretch of highway, the impulse to run overwhelms her. To toss her possessions in a bag and never look back, the same unceremonious way she'd fled from foster homes four through seven. Because running had always been easier than explaining. But mostly, because running meant she'd made the choice to be the leaver, not the one being left.

Robert puts a protective arm around her shoulder and she settles like a skittish pony. If she runs now—*this time*—she'll never stop. This place—this family—represents her last chance at belonging. But the truth is, really, she has no other place to go.

Reading her thoughts, her father squeezes her closer. It should be a comfort, but it's a double-edged sword. A reminder that, for better or worse, she's not going anywhere.

"Let's head home," he says.

Hallie nods and puts one foot in front of the other.

"Were those your pearls?" Logan blurts from the backseat the instant Robert turns the key and revs the motor.

Though she'd expected the question, Hallie's heart jumps into her throat. "I don't know. I mean, they could be anyone's, right? A lot of women around here wear pearls."

But as she says it, it doesn't ring true. For all its wealth, Incline Village isn't showy. Even the sprawling lakeside mansions are tucked away behind stony gates, their lavish faces only visible from the water. Some of Cerulean's best customers come straight from the beach in tanks and flip-flops.

"When did you realize the necklace was missing?" Robert asks.

"After the cops left on Friday night." She certainly can't admit the truth. That she'd found the painting slashed. That the pearls had been there, safe in their wooden box, and disappeared after she'd returned to the restaurant. Not now. Not after her staunch denials and Natalie's suspicions. She has no choice but to dig a deeper hole.

He turns the truck onto the main road and glances in her direction. "Why didn't you say anything?"

Hallie sinks into the bucket seat, wishing she could

disappear. "I panicked. I didn't want to cause any more trouble. I knew how worried you all were about the portrait and the tires. Shelly told me how stressed you've been. You believe me, right?"

"Of course I believe you." Robert pats her arm. "You can always come to me. There's no problem too big to solve when we put our heads together."

Logan shifts behind her, tossing his hat onto the floorboard. It flops down in Hallie's periphery. "If that shoe hadn't caught my eye, who knows when they would've found him. *If* they would've. Another night out there, the animals would've scattered the body for sure."

Hallie grimaces.

"I just can't believe he's dead. Do you think the cops will want to talk to me?" asks Logan.

Robert grunts, a non-answer that doesn't satisfy his son. Hallie can't blame Logan for worrying. Half of Incline Village saw him throw that punch.

"Well?" he asks again.

"Not now, son." Robert slows to a stop at the intersection. To the right, Lake Shore Drive and home. Straight ahead, the center of town and the police station. It's clear he's weighing their options.

Hallie turns to face a disgruntled Logan. "I can't believe it either. Are you okay?"

"Not really," he mutters. "Not that anyone cares."

"I do. You're a hero for finding him. No one would say otherwise."

"Right. A hero."

With a quick breath, Robert jerks the wheel and lays on the accelerator, and the truck jolts forward. "We're going back to the house and calling the police. They're going to fingerprint those pearls, and that will lead them straight to you, Hallie. We need to get out ahead of that, but I want to do it on our terms. On our turf."

When they pull up to the house, Shelly is waiting outside on the upper deck. She must already know about Jordan. Her nervous pacing clues Hallie in. When Shelly sees the truck, she hurries inside, appearing on the front porch before Robert cuts the engine. Moments later, Natalie materializes in the doorway.

Her feet still bare, Shelly jogs toward the truck. "Is it true? They found Jordan dead?"

Robert nods and opens his arms to her.

"Logan found him," Hallie tells her.

But she's already wrapped in Robert's embrace. Natalie joins them, cellphone in hand, quietly waiting in the background. For once, she keeps her opinions to herself, though Hallie fears that will change, and soon.

Finally, Shelly pulls away and gathers herself, addressing the family. "It all seems so silly now, doesn't it?"

"Unbelievably silly," Robert replies. "We were great friends once. I can't stomach the thought that we let money come between us."

"There was more to it than that," Logan mumbles.

Shelly dismisses him with a wave of her hand. He retreats to the truck to unload their hiking poles and backpacks.

"Nothing that we couldn't have solved," Shelly says, over the noise of his frustration. She lowers her head, wipes a tear. "His sweet mother. Jordan was her only son. I can't even begin to imagine what that poor woman is—"

The last of their gear lands with a thud on the driveway. Natalie's eyes tick up from her phone to her brother.

"So, do they know what happened yet?" she asks. "What did the body look like?"

Shelly groans. "What kind of question is that?"

"I think it's a reasonable one. If Logan found him, then he would know. Was he stabbed? Shot? Beaten? Enlighten us, little brother."

No one excels at winding Logan up more than his sister. Predictably, his face reddens.

"What do you mean *if*? Of course I found him. I was the first one on the scene in a heavily wooded area. If I hadn't been paying attention, he might never have been found. From what I could tell, he had a lot of bruises and his arm was broken. It looked like a fall to me."

"An accident then?"

Robert slings two of the backpacks over his shoulder and points toward the house and the still open front. "This isn't a driveway discussion. Now, zip your lips and get inside, all of you."

As Shelly follows orders, trailing behind Robert, Natalie pouts. Then, she turns to Logan. "What was that all about?"

Logan glances at Hallie and back to his sister. "Ask her," he says.

THIRTY-FIVE

Hallie lets the hot water sting her skin. She runs it as long as she can stand, hoping it will burn hotter than the memory of Jordan's twisted limb and the pure white pearls tangled in his bloated fingers. Sufficiently scalded, she turns the dial in the other direction and immerses her head beneath the cold deluge. It's not cold enough or strong enough to drown out Natalie's voice in the hallway. Hallie feels certain Natalie intends it that way.

"I keep telling you all that we can't trust her. How can we be sure she's telling the truth about the pearls?"

"Nat, take it easy." Robert rushes to her rescue again. "Hallie hasn't done anything wrong. She'd never even met Jordan."

"So she says. What do you really know about her, Dad?"

Hallie cuts the water. Their voices go mercifully silent, but it gives her no comfort to imagine them whispering about her. She towels off, avoiding the mirror. After hearing Robert defend her, it's hard to look at herself. The knowledge of what she's done weighs heavy in the pit of her stomach. But she can't change it. The past is written in stone.

When the knock on the front door comes, it reverberates through her body like a small earthquake. Her hair still damp, she tugs on a T-shirt and jeans before forcing a quick glimpse at her face, pinked from the sun. At least she appears innocent.

From inside the bathroom, she hears them. Boots thudding up the stairs, followed by a polite exchange of voices.

"Good to see you, Jimmy. Thanks for coming on such short notice. Hallie will be out in a moment."

Of course, it would be *him*. Hallie briefly considers fleeing out the window. Instead, she opens the door and shuffles out into the living room. Thankfully, Natalie and Logan have gone to eavesdrop elsewhere. Shelly, too, has vanished.

Robert gestures toward the dining table, where a seat waits. Opposite her executioner, it may as well be electric. "Hallie, you remember Officer Sumner."

She nods stiffly. "We seem to keep running into each other."

"Indeed." Officer Sumner waits for her to take her place at the table, direct in his line of fire. When she remains standing, he continues. "So, Robert tells me that a necklace was stolen from your room on Friday night."

"I believe so. I kept it in a wooden box. After you and your partner left that evening, I noticed it missing from my room. But it's not just any necklace. It was made of South Sea pearls and it belonged to my mother."

"South Sea pearls?"

"They take longer to form, making them more valuable."

Officer Sumner scribbles a word or two on his notepad. Hallie imagines him writing *guilty*. He wouldn't be wrong.

She's guilty of so many things. But you're only guilty if you get caught. That's what her mother had told her. The wise words of an addict.

"Was there anything else missing?"

Hallie weighs her options. She can't tell them about the money that she'd pickpocketed from Andrew Sumner. But she desperately needs him to believe her, for so many reasons. Least of all that her pearls turned up in the hand of a dead man. "A gun. But it wasn't mine."

Robert's jaw clenches. Hallie hates herself for pulling the rug out from beneath him.

"Whose was it, then?"

"I'm not sure. It was in a compartment in the closet. I found it the day I arrived, when I went looking for the bear spray. I assumed it belonged to Robert or Shelly. That they kept it for protection."

"Protection. Hmm..." The way Officer Sumner says it, she may as well have accused them of using the neighbor's windows for target practice. "You didn't tell your father about the stolen gun either?"

"No, she sure as hell didn't." Robert speaks for her. "It's the first I'm hearing about it. That antique pistol belonged to my father. I've had it for years. I'm not sure how it made its way into the guest room."

An antique pistol? Hallie bites the inside of her lip to stay focused. The gun in the closet was no antique.

"I should've told them everything," she says. "About the gun, the necklace. All of it. But the Thompsons were so upset about everything that had happened. I didn't want to make it worse. Honestly, I wondered if maybe I'd lost the pearls somewhere. One time, the clasp came undone, and the necklace fell off while I was working. Luckily, a customer turned it in."

"I see." More words scrawled, as the furrow between his brows deepens. "And you believe that you saw those pearls today?"

Robert offers an encouraging nod. "It's okay. I already told Jimmy what happened. This is why we called him."

"Maybe," Hallie replies. "I can't be sure those were my pearls. I didn't get close enough to examine them."

"Could you tell, if you were able to look closely?"

"Probably. The pearl nearest the clasp has a small scratch in its surface." Hallie doesn't say how it got there. That she'd watched her mother working a pair of wire cutters to remove the small engraved *For Grandma* tag. Her mother had cursed when the tool slipped, leaving a permanent mark.

"Okay. That's helpful." For the first time, Officer Sumner smiles at her, and she lets go of the tension in her shoulders. "We'll certainly take a gander at those pearls and be in touch."

Robert takes a few steps toward the staircase, signaling the end of the conversation. "We appreciate your understanding, Jimmy. As you can imagine, we were all pretty shaken up by what we saw today, Hallie especially. I'm sure she'd like to get some rest."

Officer Sumner makes no move to follow him, directing his gaze back to Hallie. His lips, a thin, accusatory line. Like an arrow pointing straight at her. Even in the comfort of the Thompsons' living room, he manages to make her squirm.

"While I'm here, I was hoping I could ask you a few questions about your relationship with the deceased."

"What relationship?" Hallie asks. "I didn't know Jordan

Markum. I'd only seen him the one time he showed up at the restaurant looking for a fight."

"Did you know that he'd arranged to meet with Nick Morelli?"

Robert whips around and rushes back to the table. "What the hell are you talking about? A meeting with Nick?"

"Nick told me he didn't know anything about it."

"Well, we're going to find out one way or the other. It's in your best interest to tell us what you know. Was Nick working with Jordan?"

"I don't know. I only met Nick a little over a week ago."

"If you lie to us, we can't help you. You could be charged with accessory after the fact."

"I'm not lying." Hallie marvels at the steadiness of her voice. Inside, she's quivering like a leaf.

"For your sake, I hope not. But we've spoken with some of the staff at Cerulean. They describe you and Mr. Morelli as close. And you were with him last night, late. Well after the restaurant had closed."

Nick's cattail-brown eyes. His smile. She pushes it all from her mind. "We work together. It's nothing more than that."

"Alright, Jimmy. That's enough. I didn't call you out here to give my daughter the third degree. You're questioning her like she's a suspect."

Finally, Officer Sumner gets to his feet. He collects his notepad and walks away unbothered. Like he didn't just set off a bomb. "I'm only asking questions, Robert. That's my job. I always say, the innocent have nothing to hide and they definitely don't leave town."

"And *I* always say, trust in God but have your attorney on speed dial. So, if you have any more questions for Hallie or anybody else in this family, you'll need to go through him." Robert lingers at the top of the staircase. "Goodnight, Jimmy."

After the front door closes, Hallie collapses onto the sofa and stares out the picture window, amazed that the sun hasn't yet dipped below the horizon on this never-ending day.

"It'll be okay," Robert says from behind her. "We'll get through this."

"I know." But when Hallie glances over her shoulder, she realizes he's not talking to her. He's not even looking in her direction. Shell-shocked, Shelly stands on the landing, with Natalie and Logan on the step below. Their faces tell the story. They heard everything.

"I don't understand." Shelly shakes her head. "Nick and Jordan? That makes no sense."

Natalie shrugs off her mother's confusion. "He *has* been acting weird lately. He's constantly checking his phone, and he hasn't been returning my texts. He even flaked out on our last Instagram shoot."

Hallie thinks of Sofia. How tender Nick had been with her. Indignation coursing through her veins, she feels compelled to join in the argument. "Nick hasn't returned your texts because the cops took his phone. He certainly didn't hurt Jordan."

"And how can you be so sure?" Natalie counters.

"Because I was with him the night Jordan went missing. We were at the casino. Together."

"Convenient. What about when he left the restaurant in the middle of dinner service? Were you with him then?"

Hallie shakes her head. "You know I wasn't."

"Exactly. What if he was moving Jordan's body?"

"Wow, Nat. That's out there. I think you've listened to one too many crime podcasts." With a scoff, Logan pushes his sister aside and makes his way into the living room. "If we should be suspicious of anyone, it's her."

"Me?" The finger Logan points at Hallie is undeniable. "What about you? You punched the guy in the face."

"I also led the cops straight to his body. Do I even get a thanks for that? A word of recognition? Of course not. I might as well be invisible." He marches up the stairs toward his father, bumping his shoulder as he passes. "Speaking of which, where were you, Dad? Don't think you get a pass."

"Excuse me?"

"The night I found the painting. The night Jordan supposedly disappeared. You and Mom were MIA for hours. And we all know the lookout is your favorite spot."

"We told you kids where we were. *The casino.*" Shelly's eyes well, as she pleads with Logan. "Your dad's phone died, and I left mine on the charger at the restaurant. You know how forgetful I can be when..."

She drops her gaze to the floor, embarrassed.

"I get it, Mom. I know what happens when you get wasted."

"Enough. All of you." Robert throws up his hands and stalks across the living room toward the hutch. He flings opens the cabinet and reaches inside, withdrawing the damaged family portrait and jabbing at it with his finger. Shelly whimpers at the sight of him. "We need to start acting like a family. The anniversary cookout is right around the corner, and I expect us to present a united front."

Natalie narrows her eyes at Hallie. "She's not one of us."

"The hell she isn't. She's here for a vacation, and in one week, she's done more for the restaurant than either of you.

To the cops, we're all Thompsons. Right now, that means every single one of us is a suspect." Robert points at the sofa. "Sit. Now."

With the family assembled, he levels them with a look. No one moves or speaks as he walks to the master bedroom and disappears inside. Hallie sits on her hands to stop their shaking.

Moments later, Robert reappears, looking newly determined. "I have one question, and nobody's leaving this room until I get an answer. I just confirmed that my antique pistol is in the safe in our bedroom. So, I need to know one thing. Who in the hell hid a gun in the hidey-hole in the guest bedroom?"

The silence stretches between them, taut as a string. A trigger-wire, set to detonate. A miles-high tightrope over the hard, hard ground.

"It was mine."

All eyes turn to the small voice at the end of the sofa.

"It was mine," Shelly says again.

It makes no sense to Hallie. But Robert nods, inexplicably. "Because of Jordan and his threats, right, hon?"

Shelly's vacant stare seems to land on the empty space where the family painting had once hung. "I just didn't feel safe in this big house anymore. I thought the gun would be a comfort. Not that I ever planned on using it. I wouldn't even know how."

No one says a word. But Hallie suspects they're all thinking it. If they weren't safe before the gun went missing, they're certainly not safe now.

LETTER

Bobby Thompson
7 Glenn Allen Drive
Portland, Oregon

Hallie Sherman
135 Highland Terrace
Box 2B
Sacramento, CA

Dear Hallie,

I understand your predicament; however, I refuse to submit a sample of my DNA to a corporation that has no qualms about violating my privacy. Family Ties has a long history of governmental lobbying in order to secure their position as the leader in DNA technology with few safeguards to regulate their use of our genetic material. Worst of all, Family Ties cooperates with law enforcement in criminal investigations, which I consider an abhorrent infringement on my rights.

Let me present you with a purely hypothetical scenario. I committed a murder—possibly more than one—and I left behind the tiniest skin cells beneath the fingernails of my victim. I have gone undetected for many years, hiding in plain sight. If I supply my DNA to Family Ties (or if any of my relatives do so), I may as well surrender to the police, admit my guilt, and testify against myself. I'm sure you can understand my reluctance to end up behind bars.

I urge you to strongly reconsider submitting your sample unless you can be absolutely certain you will never find yourself on the wrong side of the law.

Stay safe,

Bobby Thompson

THIRTY-SIX

Hallie keeps checking the lock on the door. She'd felt more secure in her ramshackle apartment in Sacramento, with the sirens blaring outside her window all night, than sleeping in the Thompsons' sprawling cabin. It might be the proximity to her sister turned mortal enemy, the missing gun Shelly had claimed, the unshakeable unease of permeating secrets, or any of the other strange occurrences that seem to be piling up. Confident that sleep isn't on the agenda, she scrolls through the latest news about the discovery of Jordan's body. The police call his death suspicious but there's no mention of the pearls. Nobody uses the *m* word. Not yet.

Hallie wishes she could talk to Nick, her alleged co-conspirator. But his confiscated phone is probably sitting in an evidence locker, and it's for the best. Reaching out to him now would only bolster Officer Sumner's ridiculous theory. Nick wouldn't hurt Jordan, or would he? Surely he'd need more than that missing twenty minutes to make it to the lookout and back.

Hallie fluffs the pillow behind her head and tries to close

her eyes. From outside the double doors, a scratching disturbs the pin-drop quiet. She pulls the covers over her head, hoping it will go away. All of it. The scrabbling noise. The cabin. The whole damn town.

When Hallie peeks out in the direction of the sound, aiming the beam of her cellphone flashlight, a pair of yellow eyes shines back at her. The phone clatters to the floor while her heart rattles around in her chest like a snare drum.

"Damn you." She shakes her fist at the raccoon prowling across the deck, grateful Natalie can't see her now.

Hallie snakes a hand out from beneath the blanket and retrieves her phone, navigating to her sister's Instagram page where she half-expects to see her own face on a WANTED poster.

Hallie stares at the image on the screen. Not because it's salacious or shocking or even out of the ordinary. It's the normalcy of it that disturbs her. One hour ago, Natalie posted a selfie from the back deck—her skin, filter flawless—toasting herself with a glass of wine and one of her cookies. #roughday #workhardplayhard #natsnibblestotherescue

Hallie scans the sparse comment section, puzzling for a moment. Though Natalie's follower count has already eclipsed 500,000, the image has only garnered ten comments and a couple hundred likes. To be fair, she'd only just taken it, the numbers would no doubt swell soon; the reverent way Natalie spoke about her followers' admiration suggested nothing short of cult-like status. Besides, what does Hallie know about Instagram anyway?

Still, with a determined raccoon skulking outside her door and her new siblings plotting her demise, she has nothing better to do than to investigate further. She examines a handful of her sister's latest posts. A pattern emerges. So blatant, Hallie can't believe she didn't notice it before. With a quick Google search of her question, she figures out what to do next. Running Natalie's account through a social media statistic website confirms her suspicions. Two days ago, Natalie added ten thousand followers. A week ago, another five thousand. The Internet's verdict: Natalie is fake famous.

"Can you believe it? She bought her followers." Hallie presses her nose to the glass door and taps it with her finger. The raccoon freezes then darts away.

With a chuckle, she pads back to the bed. She won't sleep, but at least she knows the truth. Under this roof, she's not the only fraud.

THIRTY-SEVEN

Hallie waits inside her bedroom, reluctant to leave her safe zone. Days ago, her only worry had been defeating Nick and claiming first prize in the cooking contest. Now, she has the cops on her tail for—of all things—a crime she hasn't committed. But sooner or later, they'll find out about the ones she has. She feels hunted, with the past breathing down her neck like that bear in the woods. When it catches her... well, she won't let that happen. She can't.

From the slim opening in her door, she listens to the Thompsons as they awaken one by one and descend upon the kitchen to pillage the breakfast Shelly lays out for them. When she arrived, she envied these little scenes. Now, it's like she's stumbled across enemy lines. She waits in the trenches, uncertain when she might take a knife to the back.

"I can't reach Nick." Natalie manages to make it sound like an accusation. "Last night, an order came in for four dozen of the vegan chocolate chips. What am I going to do? He's so unreliable."

"Here's a thought," Logan says. "Make the damn things yourself. Your name is on the package."

"I'm the face. The brand. Not the talent."

"At least you admit it."

Hallie hears a short scuffle, imagining the siblings scrabbling with one another. A shove from Natalie. An elbow from Logan. She would pay to see the two of them in a cage match.

Predictably, Shelly groans. "Cool it, you two."

"I'll help you with the order," Robert says, way too graciously.

"No offense, Dad, but the last time you baked cookies, Logan used them as hockey pucks. I'll just have to cancel the order and hope for the best. It's suicide for the Nibbles brand, but oh well."

Hallie pictures her sister in a theatrical pose, a hand draped across her brow.

"That sounds a little dramatic, honey." Shelly delivers a dose of tough love. Her words made ironic by her display last night. After confessing to hiding the gun, she'd cried so fitfully that Robert had ushered her into their bedroom, where they'd remained for the rest of the evening. "With everything that's going on, your cookies are not exactly top priority."

Steeling herself for battle, Hallie emerges from her hiding place. "I can help out, if you'd like."

All four Thompson heads swivel in her direction, equally surprised by her offer.

"Why?" Natalie studies her with a mixture of confusion and disgust until Robert clears his throat. "Uh, I mean, thanks, sis. You're the best."

A knock at the door interrupts the awkward tension.

Natalie rushes to the picture window, gazing down in astonishment. "It's Nick. He has a lot of explaining to do."

As she hurries into the kitchen to primp in the microwave's reflection, Logan rolls his eyes. With a shake of his head, he turns away to butter a slice of toast. "How are we related?" he mutters.

Hallie can admit she's wondered the same.

Natalie scampers down the stairs and opens the door to take Nick to task. "Are you okay? I was so worried about you. I texted you like a million times."

"Is Hallie here?"

"Anyway, I had a big order come through for a birthday party. Obviously, I need your help. Let me grab my purse, and we can—"

"Natalie, stop."

Hallie waits for Nick to continue. Listening hard, she inches toward the staircase.

"Stop what?"

"Stop acting like you're the center of the universe. A man is dead, and the cops think I had something to do with it. So, I don't have time to bake your goddamned cookies."

"That's too bad. Hallie already said that she would help me."

Hallie peers over the landing, giving Nick a shy wave. "Wanna bake some vegan cookies with me?" she asks.

Natalie stiffens. "Well, I'm coming too. They are *my* cookies after all."

Robert appears alongside Hallie. "First, I need a word with Nick."

. . .

Natalie insists that Hallie ride with her, not Nick. Insists on Hallie photographing the two of them in Cerulean aprons in the pastry room. Insists on squeezing Nick's arm every chance she gets. But when it comes time to commence the actual work, her sister disappears into Robert's office to engage with her followers, aka goof off, leaving her two minions to mix up the batter and dollop it onto the oversized trays.

With Natalie vanished, Nick turns to Hallie with a harried whisper. "Apparently, the cops think we're partners in crime."

"They talked to you too?"

"If you consider pounding on the door at four o'clock in the morning and interrogating me at my kitchen table 'talking,' then yes. Yes, they did."

Shocked, Hallie pauses mid-dollop. "What did they say?"

"That evidence was found linking you to Jordan's death and I'd better fess up or they might have to charge me with accessory after the fact."

"That's what they said to me too." She drops the dough onto the tray and spoons another. "You don't believe them, do you?"

"Of course not." Nick slits his eyes at her. "*What?* There's something you're not saying."

"It's just... that night we went to the casino, you didn't come with me right away. You said you needed to make a call."

He releases an exasperated breath. "Really? You think I offed Jordan?"

"No. But..."

"I get it. You did tell me you had trust issues. Look, I

called my mom to check in. That's where I was. I figured you'd worked that out."

"What a mess," she says. "This is all my fault. I should've just told Robert about the pearls... and the gun. I don't know what I was thinking."

"The *what*?"

While they prepare the remaining forty-two cookies for baking, Hallie fills Nick in on Monday afternoon's circus, beginning with the search at the lookout and ending with her cross-examination by Officer Sumner.

"Robert didn't mention any of that to me. He just wanted to hear my side of the story about this supposed meeting with Jordan. At least *he* seemed to believe me."

"The cops don't?"

"It's hard to say. They certainly want me to think they don't." Nick slides the trays into the preheated ovens and sets the timer. "So, you think Jordan stole the pearls and the gun?"

"I suppose it's possible, but it seems unlikely. I have another theory."

"Which is?"

Holding a finger to her lips, Hallie grabs Nick's hand and tugs him through the kitchen and out the side door. When they're safely out of her sister's earshot, she turns to him in earnest. "Promise me you won't call me crazy. I think Natalie set us up."

"That Natalie?" He points a thumb back in the direction of the office. "Are you kidding? She's a spoiled brat, I'll give you that. But she's no mastermind."

"Did you know she's buying followers?"

Nick mulls it over, twisting his mouth, then shrugs. "It's

not exactly the crime of the century. Nothing's real on the Internet."

"Okay, okay." Hallie understands his skepticism. Natalie has a way of portraying herself as guileless, a perpetual victim. "What about Nat's Nibbles? Is that real?"

Nick frowns deeper this time. "After the hours I've put in, I sure as hell hope so."

"Have you ever actually seen an order form with a customer name and address? Gone with her to deliver the cookies?"

"A few months ago, a lady came in and picked up an order, but that was a one-off. Nat usually delivers them herself. Personal service. It's part of her brand."

"Exactly. What if I told you that an entire batch of your cookies was found in a trash can? I think her whole business is a sham to get Robert's money. He pays her a salary to work at the restaurant, and, well... you've seen how much work she actually does. She's just loafing around on his dime." Realizing that she's afraid of her own sister, Hallie lowers her voice. "If she's willing to lie to get it, there's no telling how far she'll go to keep it."

"Assuming it's true—and I'm not saying I believe it—what do you propose?"

Hallie checks her watch. In exactly two minutes, the oven timer will beep, pronouncing Nat's cookies done. "A covert mission."

THIRTY-EIGHT

Nick stays several car lengths back as Natalie navigates away from the center of town and into an upscale residential neighborhood. A large pink bag rests on her passenger seat, affixed with her custom Nat's Nibbles sticker. Hallie carried the bag to the car and placed it there herself. Inside it, four dozen Nibbles, twelve per package. Before Natalie had left the kitchen, she'd pulled Nick aside, stage-whispering for Hallie's benefit, "I don't want to name drop but you know that Olympian who won the gold medal in snowboarding last year? His girlfriend loves my vegan chocolate chips. I mean, who doesn't? It's her birthday. She's having a barbecue on the private beach behind their house."

When Natalie activates her blinker and pulls into a gated, tree-lined driveway, Nick slows to a crawl and guides the jeep onto the shoulder, waiting.

"What now?" he asks.

Hallie can only shrug. Already, she feels silly. Beyond the stone gate, the eaves of a lavish home kiss the sky. It's the sort of place Hallie could never dream of owning, a compound with a perfectly manicured entrance and a call box. She imagines a display case on the mantel that holds a gold medal or two. An expansive yard with a built-in grill and swimming pool. Hallie had been quick to brand her sister a liar, but this house belongs to someone special.

"We should go," she says. "It looks legit."

But Nick stays put. They duck down in their seats and watch Natalie drive forward and press a button to speak.

Moments later, the gate glides open and a hulk of a man appears. Ropy muscles strain the confines of his black suit, and he hides his eyes behind mirrored sunglasses. When Hallie hears the bright burst of Natalie's laughter as she passes the bag through the window, his chiseled face cracks into an unnatural smile.

"Damn." Nick raises an eyebrow. "Looks like they've got private security."

Their transaction complete, Natalie reverses course then pulls forward, her taillights disappearing over the hill.

Hallie hangs her head. "I'm sorry I wasted your time."

She feels the warmth of Nick's hand on hers. "It's okay. I don't trust her any more than you do. I only tolerate her for Robert's sake."

"Yeah, but I called her a fraud. My own sister."

"You know, she's not *really* your sister."

Doubt stirs the solid ground beneath Hallie, leaving her wobbly. "What do you mean?"

"Sure, she shares your blood, but a sister is someone who sticks up for you. Who looks out for you. Nat's more wicked stepsister material than anything."

Hallie laughs, letting go of the tightness in her chest. Relieved at Nick's understanding, she gives his hand a squeeze, and their fingers lace together so naturally she doesn't question it. For a few breathless heartbeats, she wonders if he might lean in and kiss her. If he'll know right away that the last time was the first time. That she'd sworn off men since the group home. That her heart still bears the scars. Still, she closes her eyes, ready to be broken again.

"Hey, what's he doing?"

Hallie jerks back in her seat, face flaming hot, as the security guard tears into the large pink bag and retrieves something from within it, secreting it in his jacket pocket. Then, he opens a package of cookies and devours a vegan chocolate chip in three massive chomps before walking to the curb and depositing the remaining Nibbles into the trash bin. Mouth still full and working, he disappears back behind the gate.

"Did he just throw away my cookies?" said Nick.

"Now do you believe me?"

He nods, a pained expression on his face. Without a word, Hallie opens her door and slinks up the sidewalk toward the trash can. Satisfied that no one's watching, she fishes out the pink bag by the handle and hurries back to the jeep.

"Shall I do the honors?"

Nick sighs. "Go ahead."

Hallie widens the mouth of the bag to reveal all four packages of cookies, uneaten minus the one casualty. "I don't get it. Is there something wrong with them?"

Swiping the bag from her, Nick peers inside to see for himself. He removes a cookie, takes a bite, and levels her with a look. "My cookies are delicious, thank you very much."

"Then, what just happened?"

Nick glances down again. He rummages through the bag, puzzling. "What kind of pills did your mother use?"

"Uh, Vicodin at first. Then, whatever she could get. Oxy, Percocet. You name it, she tried it. Why?"

"After my mom injured her hand, they prescribed her OxyContin too. The little blue tablets, right? That's some strong stuff. Mom got dizzy after the first dose."

Hallie remembers the first time she asked her mom about the pills. To her, they looked like Smarties, the chalky candies in the plastic wrapper that her first-grade teacher had handed out at Halloween. *Is it candy?* she'd asked, watching her mother pop three or four at a time. *It's special candy. Adult candy.* That was before her mom crushed and snorted the tablets. Long before she dissolved them in water and stuck a needle in her vein.

A truck zips by them, sling-shotting her back to the present. To Nick, with his soft curls and kind eyes. His expectations. "Where are you going with this?" she asks.

Like a magician, he pulls his hand from the bag and opens his palm to Hallie, revealing his find. "What does this look like to you?"

Blinding lights. Swerve. Screech. Blackness. She turns away from the small blue pill with its distinctive markings. She doesn't need to look any longer, any closer. Those marks are burned into her brain like a bad tattoo. "That's Oxy."

The way Nick looks at her, he'd already known the answer to his question.

"I don't think Natalie sells cookies," he says.

LETTER

Samuel Katz
Katz and Spencer Agency
1335 Hollywood Blvd
Los Angeles, CA

Hallie Sherman
135 Highland Terrace
Box 2B
Sacramento, CA

Dear Ms. Sherman,

I am writing to you on behalf of my client, Mr. Robert Thompson, who recently received your correspondence, which was forwarded by his fan mail coordinator at SFTV Studios. Though Mr. Thompson does not usually respond to unsolicited requests, your letter both touched and concerned him, and he asked me to write to you on his behalf to assure you that he is not your father and to notify you that any attempts to sell your story to the media will be met with swift legal action. As a gesture of good faith, Mr. Thompson also instructed me to include a signed photograph of himself (enclosed) following his recent Emmy win for his portrayal of patriarch Marcus Gardener in the longest running network soap opera, *The Promise of Tomorrow*.

All the best,

Sammy Katz, Agent

THIRTY-NINE

By the time Hallie and Nick return to the Thompsons' house, they've stopped going round in circles debating what to do about the little blue pill left behind in the Nat's Nibbles bag. Nick had won out, insisting he would handle it. *Let me talk to Robert*, he'd said.

Usually, Hallie preferred a stealthy approach with a gotcha moment. Like the time at the third group home when she'd found marijuana in another ward's sock drawer and yelled for the counselor, using the girl's panic to extort her for an autographed photo of Gordon Ramsay she'd shoplifted from a memorabilia store. But if Natalie could con her entire family and set Hallie and Nick up to take the fall for Jordan's death, it would be unwise to sneak up on her. In fact, it seemed a sure way to end up with that knife in her back.

Hallie pauses in the driveway, with Nick beside her, and takes stock of the cabin yet again. Though its beautiful façade remains unchanged, she no longer views it as the uncomplicated, unblemished escape of her dreams. Instead, it's a grim reminder of real life. Thorny and tangled and impossible to run away from. The harder she'd try to escape, the tighter those vines would wrap themselves around her ankles.

Nick gives her a nudge and smile that says they're in this together. She follows him inside.

Canned music and stoic voices from the television travel down the stairs, stopping Hallie cold on the first step.

"...with special coverage of the suspicious death of restaurateur Jordan Markum, who had been visiting luxurious Incline Village on business. Today, authorities announced that Markum's death is being investigated as a homicide, coinciding with the coroner's report, which identified blunt force trauma as the manner of death. According to a spokesperson for the Washoe County Sheriff's Department, the time of death could not be precisely estimated due to the body's exposure to the elements, but is believed to have occurred at least thirty-six hours prior to the discovery of Markum's remains..."

Hallie grimaces at Nick as they make their way up to the living room. Robert paces behind the sofa, muttering to himself while the news update cuts to footage from yesterday's search. Shelly brings a wine glass to her lips. The bottle rests on the coffee table, already half-empty. Oblivious, Natalie swivels in a barstool, tapping away at the screen of her cellphone. Only Logan registers their arrival.

"What took you so long?" he asks. "Nat's been back for hours."

Nick shrugs. "Just some clean-up and last-minute cookout prep."

Natalie perks up and flashes her cell at them, grinning from ear to ear. "I already got feedback from the client. She loved my cookies. One of her friends even booked me for a

Fourth of July party. Four dozen vegan chocolate chip again. Four on the Fourth? Get it?"

"We got it." Nick takes a seat at the bar, leaving one stool empty for Hallie on his other side.

Grateful for the buffer, she slides in beside him. "What's with the news update?"

Like a contestant in a drinking game, Shelly takes another swig, as Robert explains. "Apparently, Jordan was murdered."

"Bludgeoned with a boulder," Natalie chimes in, unbothered by her graphic description. "The gal at the corner store said they found a bloody rock in the woods near the lookout parking lot. She overheard one of the cops mention that they found useable prints." Then, she leans around Nick to fire a bullet in Hallie's direction. "I hope you've got a good alibi."

"BS," Logan interjects. "Everybody knows you can't get prints from a rock."

Predictably, Natalie's fingers fly across the tiny keyboard of her cell. "Actually, that's not true, according to Google. It's challenging, not impossible. But nice try, Sherlock. I'm surprised they didn't fingerprint Hallie already. Unless her prints are already in the system."

Robert sucks a breath in through his teeth. "Cut it out, Nat. We talked about this. You agreed to—"

"No, Dad. I didn't agree to anything. It's not my fault you can't see through her. She probably offed the guy to impress you. And if we're being honest, aren't you and Mom sort of relieved that Jordan's dead? All your deep dark secrets went with him... well, almost all of them."

Leaving her wine glass on the counter, Shelly flees down the stairs and out the front door.

"I'll deal with you later," Robert tells Natalie, before he runs after his wife.

"Damn, Nat. Way to piss off Dad."

"You know I'm right though. They've been keeping secrets for way too long."

"What about yours?" Hallie mutters, unable to stop herself. Even with the knife block within Natalie's reach. "We saw you today."

"That's cryptic. I know you saw me. I saw you too. We were together at the restaurant. Duh."

Nick whips his head toward Hallie, shocked at her sudden veer off course. Though he may be stunned, he doesn't miss a beat. "We saw you with the cookies, after you left Cerulean," he says.

"Like, you followed me?"

"I'm glad we did. Otherwise, we would have never found this." He reaches into his pocket and reveals the small blue tablet.

Natalie barely glances at it, but Logan pinches it between his fingers, holding it under a pendant light for inspection.

"What is it?" he asks.

Hallie fields his question like an expert on the witness stand. She's been training her whole life for the answer. "It's a pain pill called OxyContin. An opioid. It's highly addictive. People pay big money for these little pills, even in Incline Village."

"Especially here," Nick adds.

"What does that have to do with my Nibbles?"

"We watched you make your delivery," Nick replies. "Apparently, your Olympian client didn't want your cookies. After you left, the security guard polished one off. Then, he took something out of the bag and put it in his pocket. He threw the rest of the cookies in the trash."

Appalled, Natalie raises a hand to cover her open mouth. "He did *what*? That makes absolutely no sense. I can show you the email from my client. She said her friends devoured them all. That they were scrumptious. Gold-medal worthy."

"That's impossible," Hallie says. "The cookies are in the Nibbles pink bag in Nick's jeep. They're still packaged. Untouched. Exactly the way we found them when we pulled them out of the garbage bin."

Seeking sympathy, Natalie throws up her hands. "I don't get it. What are you saying?"

Gleeful, Logan turns to his sister and snickers. "I think they're calling you a drug dealer."

"We're not making any accusations," Nick insists. "Only telling you what we saw. Your cookies in the trashcan and an Oxy left behind in the delivery bag. It must've fallen out."

"You fished that bag out of the trash. Who can say how that pill got there? You two have some nerve accusing me of a crime when you're the ones under suspicion. For all I know, you put it in the bag yourselves to deflect attention."

Reminiscent of Elizabeth Sherman, Natalie's denials send Hallie over the edge. The complete failure to accept responsibility for any wrongdoing. The misdirection and manipulation. Stones cast, fingers pointed, often at Hallie's absent father. For too long, Hallie had believed her. And the worst part of it all, Natalie's side hustle feeds the addiction of people just like her mother.

"Just admit it, Nat. Your entire business is fake. You're not even trying. You're taking Robert's money and wasting it on Instagram followers. Who, by the way, aren't real either. You're a common criminal in designer clothing."

Natalie skirts around Nick, faster than Hallie anticipates, and winds up a punch. A viper ready to strike. While Nick restrains her sister, mid-tantrum, Hallie stands her ground, confident she can best Natalie in a fight. Only one of them has survived a head-on collision. Too many foster care and group homes to keep count. Only one of them has survived Elizabeth Sherman.

Natalie flails and kicks at the air, landing a strike to the vase on the end table. It topples to the hardwood and shatters.

"Natalie, get ahold of yourself!" Suddenly, Robert materializes on the landing with Shelly beside him.

His presence works like a shot of valium, immediately quieting Natalie's outburst. Nick releases his hold on her. Indignant, she shakes herself off and straightens her blouse.

"She started it."

"There's no excuse for that kind of behavior. She's your sister, and if you want to live under this roof, you will treat her with respect."

"Of course you would take the side of the stray." Pushing past her father and shrugging off her mother's pleading hand, Natalie stomps down the staircase. She puts an exclamation point on her tirade with a slam of her bedroom door.

"What was that all about?" Robert asks. "Why's she so upset?"

Hallie looks at Nick; Nick looks at Hallie. But it's Logan who answers with a smirk.

"Apparently, she lost a few Instagram followers."

FORTY

Hallie props a pillow behind her back and opens a weathered copy of *Treasure Island* that she borrowed from the Thompsons' bookcase. It was either that or Stephen King, and the last thing she needed was another reason to lie awake listening to the creak of the floorboards and the scuttle of raccoon claws on the deck.

Before she advances to the title page, the outside light flickers on, drawing her attention. She pads to the double doors and peers out the window to find Shelly seated below, a glass of wine in her hand and her feet propped on a wooden lounger. A photo album rests on her lap. As Hallie gazes down at her from the deck above, she hears the soft sound of Shelly's crying.

"Are you alright?" she asks.

Shelly startles and nearly spills her wine. Steadying her glass, she claps the album shut.

"Up here." Hallie leans over the railing. "I didn't mean to scare you."

"Oh, it's alright. My nerves are shot anyway. I haven't been sleeping all that well, especially since Jordan went missing. Not to mention the gun and my daughter losing her mind."

"Me either. Do you want company?"

After a brief hesitation, Shelly croaks, "Sure," and coats her throat with another drink.

Hallie doesn't wait for her to change her mind. She tosses on Nick's sweatshirt to protect against the chilly night air and hurries downstairs, hopeful that Shelly will finally spill those secrets Natalie mentioned.

It's the kind of night that would star in a photograph. The backyard glows, lit by a bright, white moon. Between the trees, slivers of velvet sky peek through. Hallie wishes she could enjoy it, but it only reminds her of the remoteness of this place. How easy it would be to disappear out here, to turn up mangled at the bottom of a cliff like Jordan.

Shelly glances at the nearly empty wine bottle, tucked beside the photo album at her feet. "You should've brought a glass. It takes a few to knock me out lately."

Hallie drops into the seat next to her, uncertain what to say. "I can imagine."

"I'm sorry that Natalie's been so difficult." Tilting her face skyward, Shelly sighs. "I hate to say it, but I feel responsible. After Robert's father died, he checked out for a while. So did I. We let them get away with too much."

"I'm sure you did the best you could. Robert mentioned that it was a hard time."

A tear rolls down Shelly's cheek. "When your father read that email to us, he was so happy, so excited. Family is everything to him. But I warned him to take it slow. With what happened with Jordan, it's been hard for me to trust outsiders. Then I found that burned photo, and my mind started running wild. It wasn't fair to you."

"It sounds like we have a lot in common. Trust doesn't come easily to me either."

Shelly sniffles, straightens herself, and guzzles the rest of her wine. "Rob told me about your mother's addiction to pills. That must've been so difficult, so confusing."

Now, it's Hallie who can't speak. Hallie who swallows the lump in her throat.

"Did she ever get help?" Shelly asks.

"She never believed she had a problem. She blamed everyone else. Nothing was ever her fault." In her mind's eye, Hallie sees herself on the morning of the accident. Her mother's precious stash of pharmaceuticals poised above the throat of the motel room toilet. Her best efforts were too little, too late. Twelve hours later, her mother was dead.

"Go easy on her. All mothers bear terrible guilt, even if they don't show it."

They sit for a while with only the sounds of the night birds between them. The sky grows darker; the moon remains white as a skull. When Shelly speaks again, her vowels thick with wine, Hallie stays statue-still, not wanting to break the spell.

"The other night, when Rob and I were late getting back... I feel horrible about it. You kids were here alone. God knows what would've happened if he'd been interrupted. If he'd had that gun I bought."

"Jordan, you mean?"

Shelly doesn't answer. Hallie wonders if she's even heard the question.

"The truth is, we never made it to the casino. Rob found me drinking in The Grotto after dinner service. Life's been so stressful lately. Too many sharp edges. But when I have a glass or three, it all goes a little fuzzy. I suppose it was that way for your mom as well. A mother bears such a burden. No matter who her child turns out to be, she keeps on loving. It's hard-wired."

"Is that a baby book?" Hallie points at the powder blue cover adorned with yellow ducks.

Shelly quickly snaps it up, holding it on her lap and stroking it like a cat.

"I hope you don't mind that I flipped through a couple of scrapbooks from the cabinet in the hutch. It was a relief to see that Nat had an awkward phase. But I would love to see her terrible twos."

"I keep their baby albums in the safe in our bedroom." Shelly gives a tight smile. "Do you have any childhood photos? I bet you looked like your father. He had the cutest little dimple in his chin."

"All our belongings were in a cheap motel room. By the time I got out of the hospital, everything was gone."

"Except your mother's pearls."

"She'd been wearing them."

Clutching her hand to her heart, Shelly frowns. "You poor child. Now they've shown up on a dead body. It's almost like they're cursed."

If Shelly knew how her mother ended up with them, she would be even more convinced that the pearls were bad luck. Maybe Hallie would be better off without them. She should've sold them when she had the chance.

"What about Logan? Who did he look like as a baby?"

Now that the album is within view, Hallie can tell it's Shelly's favorite. It's faded and worn on the edges. "Can I see?"

Shelly keeps it close, her fingers clasped around the fabric cover in a death grip. "This one is only for me."

EMAIL

To: Hallie Sherman <hsherman94@pacbell.com>

From: Robin Thompson <RThompson13@quickmail.com>

Subject: You've given me hope!

Hi Hallie,

I can't tell you how happy I was to receive your note. I don't recall dating a girl named Elizabeth, but then, my memory isn't what it used to be. Let me explain. About fifteen years ago, my daughter Samantha and I were hit by a drunk driver while bicycling near our home. Just a split second changed my life forever. I lost my only child and suffered a traumatic brain injury. My wife left a year or so later. It turns out that "for better or worse" didn't mean what I thought it did. Or maybe my worse was just too much for her. I don't blame her. Samantha was a daddy's girl. She was my best friend. To tell the truth, most days it's hard to go on without her. I feel like an empty shell. So, I submitted my DNA to Family Ties. What do I have to lose? It would be an unexpected blessing to have another child, even though no one can replace my Samantha. I must confess, I was so curious about you that I hired someone to investigate. But don't worry, I don't care about your past. You look just like my Sam, Hallie. You've given me hope.

Fingers crossed!

Rob

FORTY-ONE

Hallie awakens to rattling walls. *An earthquake.* The thought lasts until the pounding comes again from the front door. Fully awake now, she realizes it's far worse than a natural disaster. She should be so lucky that the earth beneath her would split into a chasm and swallow her whole.

"Incline Village Police! Open up!"

Imagining Andrew Sumner and his cop brother on the porch ready to lock her up, she lies there, stiff with fear. But her beating heart demands action, pounding furiously against her rib cage. She whips off the covers and flings open the double doors to the deck. The lake air rushes in, like a shot of cold water.

The pounding comes again. It sends a shiver through her, bone-deep.

"We have a search warrant."

Five horrible words that come as a relief. A search warrant, she can handle. Let them search all they want. She takes a breath to settle herself, then puts on a brave face and heads into the living room.

Already, she hears them clomping up the stairs in their heavy boots. When she peers down from the landing, the sight of Robert, helpless to stop them, takes her aback. It's unfamiliar to her, fear writ large across her father's pale face. Shelly cowers beside him as he points them upstairs. Logan and Natalie wait in the hallway, rumpled from sleep.

"Are you Hallie Sherman?" In the dim light, she can't make out the officer's features. Behind him, he commands a small army of identical troops.

"Yes."

"We need to confiscate your electronic devices. Cellphone, laptop, tablet. Transistor radio." He laughs at his joke, the hollow sound echoing in the empty space.

"I only have a cellphone." She forces a smile.

Hallie leads the officer to her bedroom and points to the charger on the nightstand. At least she'd been careful in deleting Maxine's voicemail days ago. After noting her passcode, he drops it into an evidence bag and rifles through the rest of her belongings, even rummaging through the drawers where she's stowed her underwear. Satisfied with his pillaging, he nods at her and turns to depart with her phone and her dignity. He offers a small consolation, assuring her that her phone will be returned to her possession soon.

But standing in her doorway, he delivers a final warning that leaves Hallie reeling. "You're a suspect now, Ms. Sherman. I expect you won't be leaving town. The entire Sheriff's Department will be watching you. And we've got eyes everywhere."

No sound comes out of her mouth. A silent bob of her head is all she's capable of.

"I'm sorry," Robert tells her, after the army of officers files out. "I tried to stop them, but I can't argue with a warrant."

"It's okay. I'm fine. No harm done." The Thompsons avoid her eyes. "You can all go back to bed."

"Right." Natalie's voice drips with her usual sarcasm. "Because there's nothing like cops banging on the door at 4 a.m. to put you back to sleep. It's just like a lullaby."

Too defeated to mount a comeback, Hallie simply turns and slinks back to her room, praying for daylight.

"If it's any consolation, it's probably only a matter of time before they interrogate the rest of us." Robert offers his words of comfort as he pilots the truck toward Cerulean to begin dinner preparations. "I feel horrible. This whole feud with Jordan put a target on your back. It has nothing to do with you."

"Was it really all about money?" The question leaks out now that she's too tired to censor herself.

"You know that adage that money is the root of all evil? It's true. Whether you have too much or not enough. And it's never enough. He made it clear he was willing to do just about anything to get the money we owed him. As you've probably noticed, I don't take kindly to folks threatening my family."

Hallie feels grateful for that, even as she accepts the bitter reality of her situation. The protector she'd wished so hard for as a girl might not be able to keep her safe. "I'm sorry about yesterday with Natalie. I don't think she'll ever trust me."

"She's too much like me," her father says. "Overprotective to a fault."

Hallie bites her tongue, nods. "Thank you again for inviting me here. For opening your home to me. For letting me help out in the restaurant and encouraging me to enter the contest. It's above and beyond what I ever expected."

"I have a lot to make up for." He pats her knee, then moves to open his door. "Oh, for God's sake. Not that busybody again."

Hallie follows his gaze to the restaurant entrance, where Julie Danbury of the *Daily Incline* waits, pacing like a wolf outside a henhouse.

"Do you think she knows about the search warrant?" she asks.

"I doubt it. Word travels fast around here, but not that fast."

"That's a relief." Truthfully, it's the least of her concerns. Though she buried most of her skeletons as deep as she could dig, a resourceful journalist with time on her hands would have no problem unearthing the bones.

"Why don't we go around the back, avoid her altogether?"

"No. She'll only try harder. I'm not scared of her." Hallie hops out of the truck, trying to convince herself while every cell in her body screams in terror.

"Good for you." In a whisper, he adds, "Rumor has it, she spent a few years in Club Fed for tax evasion. She lives on the Nevada side now. No taxes to worry about."

Hallie chuckles at the story. Still, she lets her father take the lead, uncertain whether it makes her feel better or worse that Ms. Danbury has her own secrets. Her own dark side.

"Just the young lady I was hoping to see." Julie flashes that same disarming smile that had tricked Hallie once before. This time she won't be so easily fooled. "Did you have a chance to think about the article? It would be the feel-good story of the year. With what's happened to that

Markum gentleman, we could use a little good news around here. I'm afraid we're a bit late for tomorrow's contest, but if we sit down today, I can have the story ready for the weekend edition."

"I hate to disappoint you, but I'm a very private person. It's not really something I'm interested in doing."

"I understand." There's a sharpness in her green eyes that unnerves Hallie. "It's just as well, since I had a hard time verifying your employment at El Mar. Was Natalie mistaken? That was the last restaurant where you worked, correct?"

Damn Natalie, opening her big mouth. "It was a while ago. Who did you speak to?"

While Ms. Danbury flips through her pocket notepad ready to identify her source, Hallie reminds herself not to panic. Panic will only out her as a liar.

Luckily, Robert puffs his chest and steps between them, ushering Hallie toward the front door of the restaurant before Ms. Danbury can mount a counterattack.

"Who gave you license to snoop around?" he asks.

Ms. Danbury shrugs, unbothered. "A reporter always has license, Mr. Thompson. Those who have nothing to hide, hide nothing."

Hallie heads inside, making it a point not to hurry. From the safety of Cerulean, she hears her father's reply.

"I'm sure we all have secrets we'd rather not air in public, Julie. Or am *I* mistaken?"

FORTY-TWO

Dinner service slogs by. No matter how Hallie tries to stay focused, her mind flits like a buzzing bee from one worry to another, and she nearly burns the branzino. She tells herself it does her no good to fret about Julie Danbury poking around in her business. Still, she can't help but feel like a wild animal cornered in a trap. Sooner or later, she'll have nowhere left to hide. She'll tell Robert the truth after the cookout. He'll understand. She's sure of it.

"Earth to Hallie."

Jerking her hand back from the hot pan, Hallie jumps at the sound of Natalie's voice. She's the very last person Hallie expected to see in the kitchen tonight. "You scared me," she says, trying to read her sister's face.

An uneasy tension builds between them until finally Natalie speaks.

"Dad wanted me to invite you to The Grotto tonight. We do a staff get-together after closing on the evening before the cookout. It's tradition."

Hallie nods and stirs. She can't manage a smile. Not after

Natalie's outburst, her staunch denials. Her fist aimed at Hallie's face.

"He asked me to extend the olive branch, so here I am."

"I'll be there." She lifts the pan from the burner and prepares the plate. "Now, if you'll excuse me, I have to get back to work."

Natalie huffs, obviously disgruntled by Hallie's lack of enthusiasm about her fake apology.

"What was that about?" Nick asks, after Natalie returns to the restaurant floor.

"The staff get-together."

"They're still doing it? I assumed it would be off this year with... well, you know."

Hallie does know. All too well. She shrugs.

"Alright. I suppose that's one way to deflect suspicion. Robert usually goes all-out for the staff. He breaks out the best bottles of wine, champagne. It's always a good time. I guess we can drink away our troubles."

"So, it's legit, then. Not some kind of awful prank. I was picturing Nat waiting for me in the woods in a bear costume."

They both chuckle until the reality of what they'd seen sinks in again. Hallie no longer considers Natalie a harmless annoyance.

Nick shakes his head. "Knowing Nat, she'd bring the real thing."

Two hours later, with dinner service complete, Hallie follows Nick and the rest of the kitchen crew down the familiar path, past the *No Trespassing* sign, to The Grotto. Outdoor lanterns illuminate the way, but beyond their glowing halos, the canopy of trees casts the woods in complete darkness. Laughter spills from the clearing, brightening the eerie surroundings. Still, Hallie can't stomach the idea of a celebration. Not with Jordan dead and her cellphone held hostage and the weight of her lies dragging her like an anchor.

Hallie gasps at the sight of The Grotto decorated in full splendor. Lights wrap around the trees and coil like snakes around their limbs. Robert sits at the head of one of the picnic tables, his tie undone. His face, already flushed from the fire flaring in the pit. Hallie spots Shelly on the periphery with her usual accessory, a wine glass in hand. Hallie squints into the slim dark spaces between the sugar pines, certain she sees a figure there. But then the light changes; the shadows move. Black on black. Nothing.

Nick nudges her with his shoulder and offers her a glass of red. "You okay?"

"It's a lot." She takes a sip, hoping the wine will settle her nerves. Now, she's seeing things. "The last couple of weeks I'm not sure whether I've stumbled into a dream or a nightmare."

"Yeah. I get it. I feel uneasy too."

"But you've been one of the bright spots."

His smile creeps up and surprises her. "That's good to know. Especially since I fully intend to beat you tomorrow."

Soon, she's smiling too, despite the knots in her gut. "We'll see about that."

"*If* you win, and that's a big if, what's your plan for the prize money?" he asks.

"A little independence." With Nick, she doesn't need to pretend. It's such a relief. "A cheap car would be nice. What about you?"

Nick twists his mouth until he finally spits it out. "Five

thousand will cover an in-home caregiver for my mom for a few months. It'll give me a chance to breathe."

Hallie's chest heaves at the thought of Sofia Morelli going it on her own. Nick, in a constant state of worry. It hurts to say it, but her heart gives her no choice. "What if we split the prize money?"

"You're assuming one of us will win."

She cocks her head at him. "Yeah. *Me*."

As the sky grows darker, the party gets louder. The neatly adorned tables devolve into messy crime scenes with spills and stains and crumbs scattered. Hallie spends most of her time in Nick's orbit where she feels the safest. She's not the only one. The rest of the crew, too, gravitate toward him, telling jokes and kitchen war stories.

After one especially funny story about a stray cat that ran through the kitchen and snagged three steaks in one dinner service, Nick pulls her aside, his laughter fading fast. "Hey, there's something I need to tell you. I should've mentioned it a long time—"

Robert stands and clears his throat. The staff quiets and fills in the long benches.

Nick whispers, "Later. You're being summoned."

Indeed, the Thompson family awaits her in front of the fire. Robert holds out his hands, welcoming her. Hallie freezes, suddenly terrified. She senses it. The impending doom. As if she's been invited to witness her own execution. Yet, she forces herself to take her position beside Logan and Natalie.

"Hallie doesn't know this yet. But usually, I give a speech. Sometimes, I talk about the legacy of this place. How we built it from the ground up eight years ago. Other times, I talk about Lake Tahoe and what it means to my family. But tonight, I want to talk about a special person. My oldest daughter, Hallie."

Behind Hallie, the fire burns hot, and sweat beads beneath her hair. She looks out into the crowd, searching for Nick, but she can't find him. In the soft light, faces melt. Mouths turn to caves, eyes to dark pits. Applause sound like the crack of a whip at her back.

"Hallie, I want you to know how much the last two weeks have meant to me. How much I've enjoyed having you here, in less than ideal circumstances." He retrieves a bag from the picnic table and thrusts it toward her with gusto. "This is for you as a token of our family's appreciation for all you've done for Cerulean. No matter what happens in the contest tomorrow night, I hope you'll stay on for the rest of the summer and work here in whatever capacity you choose."

Unable to speak, Hallie fumbles with the bag and withdraws a soft leather case. Inside it, a set of Masahiro chef's knives engraved with her initials. She knows these knives cost more than one month's salary at the diner. She's lusted after them.

"This is... I can't accept them. It's too much."

"I insist. A chef of your talent and experience should have the very best."

Hallie finally finds Nick, hovering on the periphery. He gives her an encouraging nod. It's the permission she needs to hold the leather case to her like a child. These knives belong to her now. She should feel grateful, relieved. But, her skin crawls with discomfort.

"This means so much to me."

From behind her, a pair of hands rip the case from her grasp. "Liar! Fraud! Impostor!"

The words ring out like gunshots, silencing the din.

Heads swivel from Natalie to Hallie and back again, awaiting the drama. It's the car wreck no one can look away from.

"I can't let her get away with this for one second longer. Hallie Sherman is not a chef. She never worked at El Mar. I spoke to Juan Antonio myself. He hasn't heard of her. You know where she last worked? A diner. A two-bit diner, Dad. She got herself fired for dumping dishwater on a customer. Not only that, she stole his wallet too. She maxed out his credit card and took his cash. There's a warrant out for her arrest in Sacramento for felony grand theft. She's a criminal. You invited a *criminal* into our home."

Reeling, Hallie wills herself to flee, but Robert's stare pins her in place. She waits for Andrew Sumner to step forward from the hazy crowd and point an accusing finger. Instead, it's her father's voice that indicts her.

"What is she talking about, Hallie? Is it true?"

The excuses, protestations, and pleas for forgiveness stick in her throat. There's nothing to say, only the roaring in her head. She can't even bring herself to call out Natalie's sins. What good would it do?

"That's not all," Natalie continues. "Your precious Hallie spent five years in California Youth Correctional Facility for larceny and the attempted murder of a sixty-year-old group home counselor. It makes me wonder what else she's lying about. It makes me wonder, did *she* kill Jordan?"

Hallie's entire world stops, hanging in the mid-air of Natalie's perfectly timed pause.

"Is she even your daughter?"

It feels as if there are a thousand eyes upon her, casting judgment. But she has to say something, even if it comes out in a squeak. "I submitted my DNA sample. I have the email from Family Ties. I clicked on the link, same as you." As if that's what Robert will be most concerned about. Not sweet Edna, who she'd never wanted to hurt. She liked Edna, but she loved Peter, the way-too-old-for-her counselor who led her on. She only pushed Edna to get away, never imagining the long fall down the staircase. The way the old woman's body thumped against the hardwood and lay crumpled like a rag doll at the bottom.

Natalie produces her cellphone with a number already cued, holds it up for everyone to see. It may as well be a loaded gun. "Let's call Family Ties right now, then. If you're so sure."

"Enough," Robert hisses. "Enough."

But the doubt on his face sends Hallie running down the trail, hurtling toward the restaurant and away from her sister. Away from all of them. Because she didn't lie about that. She *is* a Thompson. And if she isn't, then how in the hell did she end up here?

FORTY-THREE

Hallie takes refuge in Robert's office, flopping into his chair and dropping her head onto the desk. Her tears flow freely now that she's alone. She hears the outer door open and shut. If she had enough strength, she'd leave now. Except her bones have turned to straw. It's a struggle to pick up her head, especially when she realizes it's Robert in the hallway. He steps inside the room and closes the door behind him.

"You lied to me?"

At least it sounds like a question. But in a way, that breaks her heart. He still wants to trust her.

"About some things, I did. I'm so sorry. I can explain everything."

Robert lets out a shaky breath. "So, you were in prison?"

"The youth facility. From sixteen to twenty-one."

Hallie spent years forgetting it. But the memories return with vengeance, knocking the wind right out of her. Picking the lock on the group home office at Peter's encouragement. Rifling through the cash box after the yearly fundraiser.

Edna poking her head in, eyes wide behind her glasses. The strangled scream when she tumbled down the staircase.

"Not that it makes it any better, but one of the counselors took advantage of me. It was his idea to steal the money. He used me, and someone got hurt."

"Did somebody put you up to this too? Please tell me the truth."

"No. I was honest about who I am. I'm your daughter. I swear it."

"I want to believe you, Hallie." He pulls up a chair beside her.

Hope swells in her heart. Trepidation too. Because Natalie had seemed so certain that Hallie can only wonder what she knows.

"We need to call Family Ties," he says.

"But it's midnight."

"Their customer service line is open twenty-four hours. Nat checked."

Rage at her sister courses through her, but it won't do her any good to be angry. "Okay. If that's what you need to do, then let's do it."

Robert slips his cellphone from his pocket and positions it on the desk in front of them. After a few taps on the screen he locates the number and dials, placing the call on speaker.

Ringing. Ringing in her ears. Ringing on the phone. Every one of them shrill. A scrape to her brain.

"Family Ties DNA Testing and Ancestry Service, this is Felicia. How may I help you?" The woman's voice sounds unreasonably chipper for the late hour.

Hallie can hardly bear it.

"Uh, yes. This is Robert Thompson. I'm calling about an

email I received indicating that I had a match with, uh... a young lady who... well, she says she's my daughter. This may sound strange, but I'd like to verify that match."

"Certainly, Mr. Thompson. I'd be happy to assist you. Let me just take a look at the account corresponding with your phone number. May I place you on a brief hold?"

Elevator music fills the silence. Hallie digs her fingernails into her palms while Robert hunches over the cellphone and gazes into its face like a wise oracle.

Felicia comes back on. "Hmm... you said you received an email and it came from our service?"

Hallie starts to panic. Wine sloshes in her stomach, forcing its way back up. It burns at the back of her throat when she swallows.

"Yes." Robert tap, tap, taps on his screen again. "I'm looking at it right now. The address clearly says *family ties at family ties dot biz*."

"*Dot biz?* Oh, dear."

Hallie hates this woman, this Felicia. Pretending to care when Hallie's life hangs in the balance.

"When did you receive that email, sir?"

"It's been a few weeks now."

"I'm sorry to tell you this, Mr. Thompson, but it appears that you've been scammed. I can confirm that we received your DNA sample. As indicated in your welcome email, your results can take up to six weeks for processing. The latest information shows that your sample is still at the lab. I'm afraid we don't have any matches for you at the moment, pending completion of the testing. The email you received did not come from Family Ties."

Hallie reaches for the phone, planning to hurl it across

the room. Felicia must be mistaken. Hallie got the email herself.

"I see."

The coldness in Robert's reply makes Hallie reconsider. When she looks at his stony face, his eyes hard and unflinching as marbles, she sees a stranger. She's been living in his home, breaking bread at his table. Sleeping down the hall from him and his family. And now, she's caught up in their dark world. Where photos get burned and tires get slashed and a man ends up dead at the bottom of a ravine. She's the puppet at the center of it all, with a faceless master pulling the strings.

Still, she can't quite believe it. "That's not right. It can't be."

"I'm sorry, ma'am. I can transfer you to our privacy and security help desk. They aren't available after business hours, but you can leave a—"

With an accusatory stab of his finger, Robert disconnects the call. He's never looked less like her father.

"What do you want with my family?"

Hallie shrinks from him, suddenly terrified by her vulnerability. She confided in him. She cried on his shoulder. A realization zips through her like a lightning strike. "You're the one who invited me here. What do you want with *me*?"

"With you?" His scornful laugh cuts her with its sharp edge. "I've been a fool to let you into our lives. I don't even know you." He leans in so close she can feel the heat in his words. "The only thing I want is for you to get out of my house before the rest of my family gets back."

"Where am I supposed to go? The cops said I can't leave town."

"That's not my problem. You can't stay with us. Not anymore. Not with a warrant out for your arrest." He pauses, gathering himself. "And, Hallie—if that's even your name—I don't want to ever see you again."

FORTY-FOUR

Hallie feels empty, like the wind could blow her back to the Thompsons' house. She wishes it would, because the short, silent drive in Robert's truck takes a thousand years. The few words he'd uttered had managed to make her feel worse. *I'm only driving you because I don't trust you alone in our house.* Standing guard at the door to her bedroom, he waits for her while she stuffs her clothing into the suitcase she bought with Sumner's stolen credit card. The reality of it, that this stupid designer bag and its contents is all she has left, presses on her chest until she can hardly breathe.

She sits on the bed, trying to steady herself. When she glimpses her reflection in the mirror, all she sees is her old self. The stringy-haired brunette in the rundown apartment.

"Are you done packing?" Robert speaks the question to the doorframe.

She manages a nod and a strangled, "I think so."

"I still don't understand it. Is it money that you wanted?"

"I would never steal from you." Which she realizes sounds exactly like the sort of bald-faced lie uttered by a criminal. "I got that email, the same as you did. The link I clicked had all your information. If it wasn't real, then someone fooled us both. Someone who knows things about you. About me too. Personal things."

Hallie catches a flash of fear in his eyes that mirrors hers. Who would do this to them? And why? She tries to appeal to him again. "If I had my phone, I could show you."

Robert shakes his head, and his unease turns to frustration. "Can't you just be honest with me? Are you working with someone?"

That question again. "I *am* being honest. Yes, I was in a youth correctional facility. I lied about working at El Mar. But I just wanted you and your family to accept me."

"And you stole from a customer? Is that true as well?"

Hallie hangs her head. It's as much an answer as she can give right now without breaking down. He has no idea what it's been like for her. What she's done to survive. Besides, Andrew Sumner had it coming.

"After all the lies you told us, how can I trust a word that comes out of your mouth?"

Before she can answer, he cuts her off at the knees.

"Jordan put you up to this, didn't he? He sent you here to spy on us."

"What are you talking about? Until a week ago, I'd never even heard of Jordan Markum."

"Hallie, I have to ask you. Did you kill him?"

That accusation is the sudden stop at the end of the road. Hallie has never felt more alone. No mother. No father. No family. Surely, Nick hates her too. She's stuck in the middle of nowhere with no money, no cellphone, and no escape.

A sharp cry—half laugh, half sob—bursts out of her at the sheer absurdity of it all. That she'd come here to escape her troubles, to find a place to belong. Instead, she's ended up tangled in a web of secrets, set up for the murder of a man to whom she'd never spoken a single word.

"I can't believe I have to say it. *No*, I did not kill Jordan. But someone clearly wants to make it look like I did." Now that he's no longer her father, she doesn't hold back. Because he's put her in danger, bringing her here. "I could ask you the same question, Robert. You owed Jordan money that you couldn't pay. You two obviously didn't get along. And you believed it was him behind all those twisted pranks, threatening your family. The night he disappeared, you and Shelly were MIA, and you had access to my room. You knew what those pearls meant to me."

"How dare you?" When he shouts at her, teeth bared, she sees that he's just a man, a desperate and angry one. Not the hero she believed him to be. "I would never—"

"Neither would I."

All the bluster gone from them both, they stand there like two scarecrows. Finally, Robert reaches into his pocket and offers her a hundred-dollar bill. As if money can fix her problems. "This will get you a room for the night at that cheap little motel near Kings Beach."

"I don't want your money. I'll be fine on my own. I always am." Already she doubts herself. She has no plan. After taking a last look around the room, she retrieves the heart-shaped pebble from the nightstand and squeezes it in her palm.

"Well, then. Goodbye, Hallie." He steps aside, giving her the same wide berth he'd give a stranger.

As she wheels her suitcase past him, she extends her hand. "For you. It'll make a good skipping stone."

She wants more than anything to watch him curl his

fingers around the smooth stone. To see that he's hurting too. That he's frightened. That he isn't sure who he can trust. But she won't look back. She doesn't.

Hallie's suitcase rumbles against the asphalt as she heads down the road toward Lakeshore Drive. At least she'd thought to wear her warmest clothing. She tucks her hands into Nick's sweatshirt sleeves and presses on, dragging her only possessions behind her. When she reaches Lakeshore, she stops on the sidewalk outside one of the elaborate gates, with no clue which way to turn. She drops her suitcase to the ground and sits atop it. Damn, it would be nice to have her cellphone back. She doesn't even have the Masahiro knives, which she'd last seen in Natalie's grubby hands.

As she contemplates her fate, a strange sensation creeps up her spine to the back of her neck, raising the fine hairs there. She peers into the trees along the fence line. Only the trees peer back. Still, it's hard to convince herself that she's alone out here. That no one lurks in the shadows, relishing in her misery and waiting to strike the final, fatal blow.

From around the corner, a pair of headlights appears. The cops! She freezes like a small animal, caught in the blinding glare. The last time she saw lights this bright, it ended with a swerve and a crash. Her mother dead. Her life upended. She wills herself to move.

As fast as she can, she ducks behind a massive redwood, hoping not to be spotted. The Washoe County Sheriff SUV drives past in the direction of the restaurant. She can't stay out here, exposed, a moment longer, so she hurries toward the park near Ski Beach. Maybe Jay will be there. She could use some company right now. Worst case, she'll find a spot to sleep for the night.

Hallie wheels her bag toward the picnic tables and takes a seat on the grass. She scrounges through her suitcase, pulling out another long-sleeve top and a pair of jeans to use as a makeshift blanket and pillow. No matter how she and her mom had struggled it had never come to this.

Even with the light from the neighboring houses, it's too dark. So dark that she can't tell where the sky ends and the water begins. Her back aches against the ground. It's cold and hard as a slab of ice. No matter how she positions herself, she can't get comfortable. Her thoughts race in every direction, scattered and frenetic. But one keeps returning with striking clarity: Who sent that email? And why?

Hallie replays the last few weeks, starting with the message that arrived in her inbox on her birthday. How it felt like fate. That her twenty-eighth year might be the lucky one. The night she'd been fired from A La Mode. How easy it had been to pickpocket Andrew Sumner. The reel in her head speeds up, crashlanding tonight in front of the entire Cerulean staff when her whole life had been stripped bare by Natalie. It's a small comfort that she doesn't share DNA with that witch.

Hallie squeezes her eyes shut, glad that her tears have finally run dry. Now, she's pissed and not just at Natalie. At Robert, Shelly, and Logan too. They didn't give her a chance to explain. To tell her side of the story. After the last two weeks spent tolerating their whispered conversations, ferreting out their secrets, she'd deserved that much at least. She imagines them back at the house, tucked into their warm beds while she fends for herself alone out here.

Hallie adjusts her blue jean pillow, momentarily

confused by the solid object concealed inside the pocket. The spare key to the restaurant she'd forgotten to return. She considers hurling it into the lake. Instead, she returns it to its hiding place, content to hold on to a small piece of the Thompsons' legacy. A small piece of the life that could've been hers.

She rolls onto her back and gazes up at the starry sky, remembering her mother. Sometimes, when her mom wasn't zonked, they'd lie on the hood of the station wagon. Then, Hallie had always wished for the same thing. For her mom to get better. A lot of good that had done her. She's light years past wishing now.

FORTY-FIVE

Hallie knows it's a dream. Because her mother is still alive, and when she looks down at her leg, she finds only smooth, tan skin. No scar. Out the windshield, the highway stretches like a velvet ribbon into the translucent mist. Her mother slumps against the window, head knocking into the pane, and softly moans. It's not much farther to the school. Her mom can sleep it off in the car. But it's hard for Hallie to see above the steering wheel and keep her foot on the gas pedal at the same time, especially in this stupid costume with this stupid seatbelt latched across her chest. She hadn't figured on the technicalities of driving when she'd convinced her doped-up mother to climb into the passenger seat. The only other time she'd done, she'd only gone halfway around the block.

Blinding lights. A pair of headlights materialize on the horizon. So bright Hallie drops her eyes. She can't see a damn thing.

Intending to slam on the brake, the car jolts forward instead, and her stomach bottoms out as if she's on a roller coaster. The wheel spins out of her control. *Swerve.*

Finally, Hallie manages to find the right pedal. *Screech.* But it's too late. She's playing chicken with a tree, and the tree isn't moving. Just before impact, her mother reaches out to protect her. As Hallie catapults against her mother's arm, she hears the high-pitched wail of her own scream.

Blackness.

"Hallie." The man in the white coat says her name, shines a light in her eyes. "Wake up."

She blinks awake, expecting to see the gray walls of the hospital room. To smell the antiseptic odor. To be nine years old again, in the dream that isn't a dream at all but a memory of that final, fateful car ride with her mother. Instead, Jay leans over her with the thin beam of his cellphone flashlight aimed in her direction.

"The police are here looking for someone. You have to move."

A jolt of adrenaline courses through her. She springs up from the grass, tucks her clothing beneath her arm, and grabs her suitcase by the handle, ready to run. Through the trees, she hears the distant rumble of an idle engine.

"C'mon. I know a spot." Jay leads her through the dewy grass toward the snack bar, a small temporary hut that's been erected for the summer. He ducks behind the outer wall, pulling her along behind him. Hallie presses her back against the wooden planks, knees hugged to her chest. She makes herself as small as she can.

Holding a finger to his lips, Jay peers over the wall. "They're gone."

Relieved, Hallie reclines against her suitcase and stretches her legs in front of her. Now that she can breathe again, she spots Jay's red bike and backpack, hidden in the shadows.

"What happened?" he asks. "Why were you sleeping in the park?"

"Long story."

"Well, I'm a good listener. That's what a few years in lock-up will do to you."

More than anybody, Jay understands. After what he's done for her tonight, she owes him an explanation. She owes him the truth.

"The Thompsons found out I'm not exactly who they thought I was."

"Damn. How'd they take it?" He joins her on the ground, his head resting on his pack.

"I'm out here sleeping on the ground with my suitcase. So, I'll give you one guess. I'm not welcome there anymore. I'd planned to enter the cooking contest tomorrow night but now..." Hallie shudders at the death of her dream.

"So, who are you then?" Jay asks, looking her up and down with curiosity.

"A criminal. An ex-con like you." Saying it out loud comes easier than she'd thought. "I hurt someone. It was an accident, and it happened a long time ago, but..." She knows that's no excuse.

Jay sits bolt upright. "Are you serious? You certainly had me fooled. I guess my English teacher had it right when she said not to judge a book by its cover."

"Yeah. That seems to be the general consensus." She sighs at the realization of how far she's fallen.

"But to kick you out? In the middle of the night? That seems harsh. Families are supposed to love you unconditionally. To have your back no matter what. It seems like *they* weren't exactly who you thought they were either."

"I think it's mostly that I lied."

"And they haven't?" He grimaces at his fervor. "Sorry. It's none of my business. I just hate to see you treated unfairly. Talk around town is that the Thompsons had that Markum dude taken out, so maybe you're better off without them."

"People are actually saying that?"

"You know how word gets around in a small town. I heard Markum had some major dirt on them. Something about a fire and an insurance scam."

"At Last Glass?"

Jay shrugs, leaving Hallie desperate for more. Even now, when she should forget the Thompson family, she can't.

"Robert told me his dad died in that fire. But I couldn't find much about it online."

"A powerful guy like that can make a thing go away like it never happened. It sounds like he brought it on himself."

Hallie startles at this new side to Jay. Callous and unforgiving. It must be the side that landed him in prison. Her too, for that matter. "That's a horrible thing to say. What do you mean?"

"Well, if what I heard is true, Robert set the fire to collect the insurance money. He's a greedy pig. You play with fire, you get burned. But hey, I'm jaded. Don't listen to me. Parental drama is not exactly my strong suit."

Quietly reeling, Hallie clings to denial. It's her only lifeline. "Robert would never do that. He's not a horrible person."

"Yeah. Course he isn't. It's probably just a rumor." He pauses, mulling something over. "For what it's worth, I say enter the contest anyway. It's not like they can stop you. It's open to anyone, right?"

"I can't show my face. Not after last night." Hallie

grimaces. "I'm probably the person the cops are looking for out there tonight."

"Prove to the Thompsons you're not who they think you are. They're expecting you to run away with your tail between your legs. To cower in fear while they live it up, high on the hog."

"I'm good at running away." Truth be told, she's expert level. "That's sort of what I do."

Jay cocks his head at her, issuing a challenge. "Till now."

Hallie lets herself imagine it. Showing up at the cookout tomorrow. Presenting Norma Todd with her best effort. Collecting that prize money, and watching Natalie eat crow. She shakes her head, exploding her fantasy into a million little pieces. Knowing her luck, she'd leave the contest in a squad car under arrest for God-knows-which crime.

"What about *your* family?" Hallie asks. "Did you ever reach out?"

Instantly, Jay brightens, flashing a kid-in-the-candy-store smile. "Actually, I did."

"Well? Don't leave me in suspense."

"They agreed to meet up on Friday. I'm going to give them one last chance." He glances down at his watch. "I just realized. That's the day after tomorrow. And I look like this. Shit."

Watching Jay's face crumple reminds Hallie of her shame, of all the times she's felt less than. She remembers standing in the full-length mirror of her crappy apartment, what seems like a lifetime ago. The rip in the hem of her dress like a scarlet letter, reminding her she'd never be good enough.

"If I had a house, I'd invite you inside," she says. "I wish I could help."

They lie in silence, alone with their thoughts. But, somehow, Hallie doesn't feel lonely. Her eyes flutter. Grow heavy. Close.

Halfway to sleep, she hears Jay whisper, "Maybe you can."

EMAIL

To: Hallie Sherman <hsherman94@pacbell.com>

From: Robert Thompson <RTT@jsu.edu>

Subject: A Second Chance?

Hi Hallie,

Your message took me by surprise. To be honest, I thought about deleting it. I reread it a hundred times, maybe more. It took me a long while to realize I had no choice but to submit my DNA sample and write you back. I've blown it as a father... and not just once. I'm ashamed to say I have three children I've never met. In my early twenties, I was irresponsible, self-centered, reckless, impulsive. The list goes on. My children's mothers wanted nothing to do with me, and I can't blame them. I tried to see them a few times, not hard enough. I gave up too easily. Then, they grew up. So did I. Now, I'm a middle-aged man with a mile-high stack of regrets. Last year, I tracked down my oldest son with the help of a private investigator. He wanted nothing to do with me. Talk about a soul-crushing blow. If you are my daughter, I look forward to getting to know you on your terms. And if you aren't, I still want you to know that I'm sorry. I apologize to you—and to the three kids I may never know. They deserved better. You deserve better too.

R.T.

FORTY-SIX

Hallie awakens alone with no sign of Jay. She smiles when she spots his note—*Nothing says thank you like a dozen dumpster-dived cookies!*—scrawled on the outside of an unopened bag of Nat's Nibbles. Turns out, it's the breakfast of champions.

Munching on her third vegan chocolate chip, Hallie drags herself to the lakeshore to witness her final dawn in idyllic Incline Village. When the sun rises into the blood-red sky and lights the rippled clouds afire, it steals her breath and she sinks into the sand. As far as prisons go, it's beautiful. But she's confined here nonetheless. Without a penny to her name, her exit strategies are limited. She can't even afford a bus ticket.

Hallie gazes farther down the beach toward the wooden terrace that extends around the perimeter of Cerulean. Nearby, a small crew works to assemble the tables and cooking stations for tonight's event. Though she squints against the glare from the water, it's too far to make out their faces. But a brightly colored banner mocks her from the restaurant's deck: *Welcome to the Cerulean Anniversary Cookout Contest.*

Unable to fight her curiosity, Hallie approaches the restaurant just in time to watch Robert arrive. He stands at the periphery, surveying the beach set-up. He glides between the tables, pointing, organizing, directing, and the crew follows his commands without question until the layout takes shape. He wears his power as comfortably as an old coat, reminding her of the day they'd met in the Old Soul Café.

How had it come to this? All the letters she'd sent into the void. All the Robert Thompsons who'd replied. Somehow, *this* Robert never received her letter, a letter she confirmed that she sent weeks ago to the Eagle's Point Drive address. Yet someone sent an email to both of them, claiming to be from Family Ties. It doesn't add up.

Hallie checks her watch. The library won't open for another three hours. A good thing, since she'll need ample time to walk there.

At the library front desk, a gracious smile doesn't go as far as Hallie had hoped. Janice informs her that the computers are for use by library card holders only. No exceptions. Apparently, it would be easier to steal state secrets than to obtain a card from the Incline Village Public Library.

"I'm afraid you'll need two pieces of identification, dear, including a photo ID, and an item to verify your current mailing address, postmarked within the last thirty days."

Hallie sulks, cursing the police again for seizing her cellphone. As she wheels her suitcase toward the front door, Jay comes through it with his backpack slung over his shoulder. He peeks out from beneath the rumpled hood of his sweatshirt and gives Janice a wave. Hallie hadn't expected to see him again today. But she's relieved at the fortuitous timing of his reappearance.

"Are you following me?" he asks. When he holds up his hands in mock surrender, Hallie glimpses more of the scar on his wrist; it's worm-shaped and waxy. "I don't have any more cookies, I swear."

"What about a library card? I need to get online."

"Now that I can help you with. The trick is to show up in the evening around closing time. Janice's shift ends at 4 p.m. and Harry is a lot less militant about approving applications."

"Oh. Well, it's kind of urgent."

"Why didn't you say so? Step into my office." He motions for her to follow him, adding, "Sorry I turned tail this morning. I had to get an early start."

"You missed an incredible sunrise. It's a waste to be upset in a place like this."

"I know what you mean."

Hallie follows Jay to a computer terminal and pulls up a chair beside him. After logging in to the main screen, she directs him to her email, and he turns his head while she signs in.

Quickly, she navigates to the message from Family Ties. It's pinned at the top of her Robert Thompson folder. The email address matches the one Robert read aloud last night as her entire world crumbled at his feet.

"This address is bogus," she tells Jay. "I need to find out who really sent it."

He studies the header, highlighting and copying the address. "Simple enough. We do a reverse look-up. That will tell us any information that's associated with the account. Name, address, et cetera."

"How do you know all this?"

He opens another window, types in the web address for the site, and pastes the email address into the search bar. "Believe it or not, prison vocational training. I studied computer literacy, computer repair, even coding."

"That's impressive."

"Yeah, I'm a regular Bill Gates."

A sad smile crosses her face then disappears like a ripple in a pond. "Wanna know a secret? I had my first cooking job in prison. All five years of my sentence, I spent in the kitchen. Worked my way up to lead chef. But I can't exactly put that on my résumé."

"Don't I know it. If I tell anybody I studied computers in the clink, they assume I'm a black hat." Jay's finger hovers above the enter key. "Moment of truth."

An ellipsis bubbles across the screen while the website works its magic, reaching its fiberoptic tentacles into the void in its search for the truth.

"Well, we've got a name." Jay frowns at the computer, then at Hallie. "But..."

She leans in to look, hardly believing it herself. "Does that say...?"

"Natalie Thompson," he reads. "Isn't that your sister?"

A flame of pure rage burns white-hot at the heart of her. "Not anymore."

FORTY-SEVEN

Hallie doesn't need to hide. With the cookout in full swing, she moves unseen on the congested beach. She parks her suitcase in a shady spot with a view of the raised contest stage and the oversized clock, already set to fifteen minutes. In matching Hawaiian-style shirts, Robert and Shelly work the crowd like politicians, stopping to mingle, to share a joke, to kiss a baby or two.

Hallie focuses in on the cooking stations, counting ten in total. When Robert taps the mic, she becomes instantly aware of her heartbeat, hammering away in the base of her throat.

"Our annual cooking contest has been a crowd favorite since we started the anniversary cookout seven years ago. This year, our esteemed entrants include our very own head chef, Nick Morelli, and a bevy of local amateurs. The rules are simple. Make the most scrumptious summer dish you can whip up in less than fifteen minutes, as judged by Norma Todd, food writer and critic for *The Daily Incline*. The lucky winner will take home five thousand dollars and a Cerulean T-shirt, modeled by my lovely daughter, Natalie."

Natalie removes her Hawaiian shirt to reveal the Cerulean tee, tied like a crop top at her slim, tan midsection. Reveling in the spotlight, she saunters up to the stage and prances from one end to the other, tossing her hair like she's working the runway in Paris. She oozes the kind of attitude that makes Hallie wish for a spitball and a slingshot.

"Contestants, please take the stage."

Nick trails behind the rest of the group. He glances once over his shoulder before assuming his position and securing an apron around his waist.

"Contestants, ready?"

A single spot remains vacant. It belongs to Hallie. With the crowd hushed, she approaches the stage, towing her suitcase. "Wait for me!"

Robert gapes at her, hisses, "What are you doing here?"

"Cooking, obviously. I'm registered for the contest like everyone else."

His forced smile looks more like a grimace. "Alright then. A late arrival."

Shoulders back, head held high, Hallie nods and mounts the first step, then the second. No matter what she's done, she deserves to be here. She filled out the form and paid the ten-dollar entry fee like everybody else. Predictably, Natalie scowls down at her from the stage.

"You've got some nerve turning up here." To Robert, she adds, "Dad, you can't be serious. Why did you let them set up her station?"

"I didn't expect her to actually show up." He shrugs. "But fair is fair."

"She has just as much right to compete as anyone," Nick

says, gently guiding Natalie out of Hallie's path, allowing her to take the stage.

Already, Hallie's won. Nick's gesture, a clear victory. Beaming, she ties on her apron.

Robert clears his throat into the mic, sending echoes down the beach. "Contestants, get your ingredients ready. And cook!"

As the clock begins its inevitable countdown, Natalie stalks toward Hallie's cooking station and swipes her manicured hand at the bowl of fresh lobster. It flies off the table, landing face down in the sand.

"Oops." She covers her mouth in mock surprise.

Stunned, Hallie stares at the remaining ingredients. Stacked slices of Havarti and Gouda and a loaf of sourdough bread. How can she make an award-winning lobster grilled cheese with no lobster? She finds herself on the verge of tears, sinking again. No father. No family. No prize money. Nothing. Maybe it's what she deserves.

"Here. Take half of mine." Nick sets a bowl of lobster meat on her station and busies himself melting butter in his skillet.

"I can't do that. You need it."

"I'll manage. I've got enough for my dish." He pushes the bowl toward her. "C'mon, I want to beat you fair and square."

Hallie sighs. Glances at the clock. Fourteen minutes remain. "Don't you hate me? I'm not who you thought I was. I'm a criminal."

"Take the damn lobster."

She reaches, hesitates, pulls her hand back. From the crowd, Natalie shoots daggers. Another twenty seconds tick by.

"It's lobster, Hallie. Not a kidney."

"Alright, fine. I'm taking the *damn* lobster." She dollops out half the meat onto a plate and fires up her pan without a second thought. Only thirteen minutes remain, and she can't afford any more regrets.

Norma Todd takes a delicate bite of each dish plated before her, working her way down the line toward Hallie's entry. It's not her best attempt. The edges turned out slightly browner than she liked, and she layered on a little too much Gouda. But she's proud of herself. For showing up. For accepting Nick's help. For believing in herself.

Norma gives no sign that she prefers one dish to another. She simply sips from a glass of water and moves on to the next plate. Chew, swallow, sip, and advance. With the judging complete, she joins Robert centerstage at the microphone.

Hallie sneaks a glance at Nick to find him looking back at her. She drops her eyes and takes a breath.

"Bravo, to all the contestants! You've far exceeded my expectations. This year's entries were so delicious that it made my job nearly impossible. But very enjoyable, nonetheless."

"It's a tough job," Robert teases. "But somebody has to do it."

Excited laughter ripples through the crowd. Hallie finds Shelly at the periphery, whispering with Logan. About her, no doubt. Though she shouldn't think about it now, she finds herself wondering if Natalie is the only Thompson who betrayed her. Who had it out for her from the moment she arrived.

"Did you choose our winners?" Robert asks.

"Indeed. In third place, the watermelon salad with Cotija cheese and serrano chilis."

"That's the entry from Roman Yanez of Incline Village. He recently graduated from cooking school and plans to open a Mexican Asian fusion restaurant in South Lake Tahoe. Nicely done, Roman."

Hallie claps mindlessly like one of those wind-up monkeys. As badly as she wants to win, she fears it too. What will Robert say about her to all these people?

"In second place, the lobster roll with spicy avocado cream. A fresh take on a seafood classic."

"Ah, no surprise there. Our very own Nick Morelli, ladies and gentlemen!" Nick steps forward to a raucous cheer and waves to the crowd. From below, Natalie captures it through the lens of her cellphone, no doubt planning to inundate her fake followers with new content.

"And the grand prize?"

Hallie wonders if it's just her imagination that Robert's voice quakes. A projection of her anxieties. The onlookers begin to beat their hands against their thighs in a makeshift drumroll.

"The grand prize goes to the dish that was tailor-made for a Gouda lover like me. The extra cheesy lobster grilled cheese, the ultimate comfort food. A decadent treat for cheese lovers."

Robert nods, a thin smile pasted on his lips. "Congratulations to Hallie Sherman, amateur chef and former waitress at the A La Mode Diner in Sacramento."

Her face hot, Hallie steps forward. A riptide of emotions swirls at her feet and threatens to knock her off balance. She did it! But there's no one to celebrate with her. Only the applause of strangers and the knowledge that she's just been outed to the cops. To one particular cop and his brother from hell.

Robert manages to shake her hand without meeting her eyes. To hand her the T-shirt and the prize money, fifty one-hundred-dollar bills. They pose for a photo, side by side but never further apart. As the photographer snaps another few shots of the winning threesome, Robert drifts away. By the time Hallie's head finally stops spinning and she finds the courage to speak, she realizes he's gone. Exit stage left.

Hallie hops down and hurries after him, dodging high fives and congratulatory pats. She needs to clear her name, to tell him what she uncovered with Jay's help. "Robert, please, wait up."

He stalks down the beach toward the back entrance of the restaurant, practically running away from her. Finally, when she slips inside the door after him, he spins around and levels her with a look, worse than the frown of a disappointed father. It's the expression of indifference, and she knows it well. As a kid in the system, the cold detachment of her caregivers was a constant companion.

"We have nothing to talk about," he says.

But she talks anyway. Spits it out fast before he stops her. "I looked into that bogus email we received. It came from an address registered to Natalie."

He gives her a blank look.

"From your *daughter*, Natalie."

"I don't believe you. How can I after all the lies you told?"

"Let me show you on the office computer." She resists the urge to tug his arm. "It'll only take a few minutes. Please."

Robert shakes his head, unmoved by her pathetic display. "I won't play these games anymore, Hallie. I have enough to worry about with my real children. I can't take on a charity case."

Hallie staggers back. *My real children.* That sends her on a bad trip down memory lane, back to the front stoop of every home that had only been temporary. Garbage bag slung over one shoulder and a permanent chip on the other. This is why she never gets close, why she never lets anyone in. She understands now how it feels to be out of Robert's good graces. How the bitter cold sets in when he turns his back.

Robert vanishes into his office, leaving her there with her heart in her hands. She tells herself it's fine. She'll be fine. At least she won the contest. She got something for her trouble. By tomorrow morning, she'll be... well, who knows where? No matter Officer Sumner's warning, there's no way in hell she's sticking around.

Footsteps approach from the dining room. Hallie whirls around to see Nick push through the double doors and into the kitchen, wheeling her suitcase behind him.

"Forget something?" he asks.

Her mouth hangs open. This is what happens when she cares too much. She loses focus along with everything she has left. "I guess I got distracted." Relieved, she reaches for the case's handle and pulls it toward her.

"I wasn't talking about the bag."

He waits for her to fill the silence. She knows what he wants, but she won't give it to him. It's easier to make a clean break.

"A 'thank you' would have been nice. Thank you, Nick, for sticking up for me. Thank you, Nick, for having my back. Thank you, Nick, for—"

"You're right." She can't take any more of this torture. "Thank you, for all of that. And I'm sorry about everything. All the lies I told. I've made a real mess."

"Well, you're not wrong about that." He glances again at her suitcase. "I take it you're leaving town."

He says it like she has a choice.

"You're a suspect, Hallie. I assume the cops told you to stick around, same as me. It'll only make it worse. They'll think you're running for a reason."

He says it like she isn't.

"What else am I supposed to do?" She shrugs at him. "It turns out I'm not a Thompson after all."

"I heard."

"Nat?"

"Who else?"

"Who else," she repeats, with a rueful shake of her head. Natalie isn't her problem anymore. "I suppose she came out on top. She got rid of me like she wanted."

"You can stay with me, you know." A faint blush colors his cheeks, making him look like a schoolboy. He runs a nervous hand through his curls. "I mean, until you figure it out."

"I can't do that to you and your mother. You already have enough uncertainty in your life. Besides, it would only solidify the cops' theory that we're working together. It would put a target on both our backs."

"I wouldn't tell anyone, if that's what you're worried about."

Hallie sees that he's serious. He actually cares about what happens to her. That's why she has to tell him no. She can't drag him along on this ride. "I really have to go. Trust me, it's best for everyone this way."

"Okay, then." Nick reaches into a bin beneath the counter and places a familiar leather pouch atop it.

"My knives." The longing for what could have been thickens in her throat, and she struggles to swallow.

"I rescued them last night after Natalie tossed them in the firepit."

She slides the pouch toward her, fingering the edges, tinged black with soot. Blinking back tears, she lunges at Nick and wraps him in a tight hug. Slowly, his arms fold around her, and he rests his chin on her head.

"I tasted your dish. You deserved to win. Even if you did overdo the Gouda."

Hallie pulls back from his embrace and takes the prize money from her pocket. She counts out half and thrusts it at him. "A promise is a promise."

Gently, he pushes her hand back toward her. "No, you earned it fair and square. You're a talented chef, Hallie. And a scrappy fighter. I was wrong to underestimate you."

Through her tears, she smiles up at him. "Yeah, you were."

FORTY-EIGHT

Hallie stands alone on the quiet beach, shuffling from one foot to the other. In the moonlight, the empty stage looks lonely, haunted. Blown by the wind, a discarded streamer dances toward the lake. A gust sweeps it high into the air before depositing it at Hallie's feet. Just hours ago, it had been affixed to the restaurant deck, nothing more than a decoration. Now, it has a life of its own. It's going places. To Hallie, it feels like a sign.

She keeps an eye on the road. Her taxi should be here any minute. When the dispatcher had asked her destination, she told her Reno. It slipped off her tongue effortlessly. But the only thing she knows about Reno is the Great Balloon Race. Hundreds of hot air balloons dotting the sky like brightly colored birds to take her far away from the stark reality of her life. Her mother had promised once to take her to see it. But like all of Elizabeth Sherman's promises, it turned to fool's gold.

Hallie hears the rumbling approach of the taxi. Suitcase in hand, she trudges back up the beach toward the parking lot, where the lone vehicle belongs to Nick. Before they'd parted ways, he told her he'd be staying late to finish a cookie order for Natalie. Apparently his last, since he'd resigned his position as baker for Nat's Nibbles that morning.

The driver pokes his head out the open window. "Miss Sherman?"

She nods, lifting her bag into the waiting trunk. She keeps the knives with her, resting on her lap, where she can rub the soft leather like a touchstone.

Hallie shuts the door with finality. She gazes out at the blacktop, itching to get on the road. Soon, this place will be nothing but a bad memory.

"What the—?" The taxi driver pulls a face in the rearview mirror and mutters under his breath.

Hallie turns her head to look over her shoulder and spots the source of his frustration. The flashing red and blue lights behind them. At least it's not Officer Sumner strolling toward the taxi with his hand mere inches from his gun. But the scowling face that appears is no comfort. Because she's seen it before, two days ago, in the doorway of her bedroom, confiscating her belongings and assuring her that he would keep an eye on her.

"Good evening, sir. You mind rolling down your window?"

Though Hallie wills the driver to floor it, he complies with the order disguised as a request, offering a contrite, "What did I do wrong, Officer?"

"Pop the trunk."

Then, with eyes only for Hallie, the officer leans in the window. "Going somewhere?"

. . .

Helpless, Hallie kicks at her designer suitcase. She can only watch as the taxi cab's lights fade, then disappear around the bend. The driver won't be coming back for her. Not after that cop made it crystal clear that she was the prime suspect in the murder of Jordan Markum. That transporting her outside of county lines could be considered aiding and abetting. The officer had given her another firm warning before he too had vanished into the night.

Her shoulders slump with the weight of her new reality. She understands now the dangers of a sleepy town like Incline Village. She can't blend in. She can't disappear. The longer she stays, the smaller her world becomes. Until it's nothing more than a jail cell. She has no idea what to do now or where to go.

A flicker of movement draws her eyes to the wooded area surrounding The Grotto. She catches only a glimpse. A pair of shoulders. A shock of hair. The figure, disappearing down the trail before she can make an identification. She thinks of Jay, of the spare key that she gifted him last night. He promised her he'd wait until the wee hours to slip in unnoticed and clean himself up. Has he turned up early? Is he in trouble?

Hallie parks her luggage behind a tree and jogs down the dark path to investigate. Up ahead, a beam of light flickers between the sugar pines, drawing her in like a moth to a flame. When the path widens and the picnic tables come into view, she slows to a creep and follows its glow to the massive stones on the other side of the clearing.

She holds her breath now and pads softly around the perimeter of the stones. The figure kneels in the dirt, huffing with the effort of digging. A small spade, in one hand. A helmet light, illuminating a small grave.

Hallie ducks behind the rock. She presses her back into its cool, hard surface and grounds herself. She can't be spotted, so she scampers into the tree cover, treading lightly. Like mud in the hourglass, time slows. Her senses heighten until every chirp of a cricket, every snap of a twig echoes, and she's convinced she'll be caught.

Finally, when she's certain she can no longer bear it, the figure emerges from behind the stone, hands caked with dirt. At the sight of a familiar face, she clasps her hands over her mouth and watches from her hideout as the light grows fainter and disappears entirely.

Hallie moves with a sense of urgency toward the excavation site. The disturbed section of earth is clearly visible in the moonlight. She drops down and starts clawing at the soil, deeper and deeper until she strikes a solid object covered in plastic. Her hands ache, and even in the cold, sweat trickles down her forehead. Still, she can't stop now. More pulling and tugging and digging and then, it's free.

Exhausted, she sits back against the rock face and holds the bag in her hand. She peers inside and examines its contents, careful not to touch anything.

A button-down white shirt, stained with drops of spatter. She raises the bag up to her nose and inhales the unmistakable metallic scent of blood.

A wooden box that resembles a small casket. But not just any box. A box that once belonged to her mother and then belonged to her. It stored her mother's most precious items, until she sold them one by one, leaving only the lonely strand of pearls for her daughter.

Hallie returns the bag to its grave and covers it with dirt, staving off a shiver.

She knows who killed Jordan.

FORTY-NINE

Hallie runs back down the path toward the restaurant. Her thoughts spark like live wires, pitching and jumping across her mind. As she nears the parking lot, she pulls up short. The hairs on her neck raise in warning. She takes in a mouthful of lake air and wrinkles her nose at the unexpected acrid aroma. She walks a few more steps, and the smells grows stronger.

When she casts her eyes skyward, a tower of orange flames rises above the trees. Hallie can't yet see it, but she knows it as surely as her name. Cerulean has caught fire.

The realization punches a hole clean through her, stealing her breath. It reminds her of the moment of impact. The tree trunk, looming gray-white in the headlights like the eye of a monster. No one blamed her for driving. They'd run the tests on her mother at the morgue, seen what shape she'd been in. Only Hallie knew the ugly truth of the matter. How one selfish decision had changed the course of her life, like a felled tree redirecting a river.

Hallie runs as fast as her jelly-legs will carry her, dropping the leather pouch near her suitcase when she sprints past it. Horrified, she spots Nick's jeep still in the lot. And Jay? What about Jay? Her heart sinks.

Flames engulf the front of the restaurant. The closer she comes to the fire, the more labored her breathing. Her eyes tear up from the thick, black smoke pouring from the exploded windows. Another surge of panic courses through her when she spots an upturned gasoline can on the deck.

"Nick!"

Only the ominous crackling and popping of the fire answers her. Much louder and angrier than she'd imagined. She stretches her shirt to cover her mouth and heads for the side door that leads to the kitchen. The heat presses against her skin, heavy as a coat.

When she reaches it, she stares, horrified, at the open door. Her spare key is still in the lock. Nick's body lies slumped against the frame. One hand grips his flank. Blood oozes through his fingers. She falls to her knees beside him, trying to rouse him.

"What happened?"

Nick lifts his glassy eyes to her. His head lolls to one side, as he drifts in and out. "He shot me."

"Who?"

"Jesse."

"*Jesse?* Do you mean Jay?"

"Jesse," he says again, his voice weak and fading. The bloodstain on his shirt blooms like a rose. "Robert's son."

"But Robert doesn't have a son named Jesse."

"He's... dangerous... and..." Nick's eyes dim. "Hurt... my... dad..."

Hallie shakes Nick awake, but he only moans at her. He's losing too much blood. Not making any sense. Slipping her hands beneath his armpits, she drags him out of the doorway and toward The Grotto. When they're a safe distance from the fire, she collapses to the ground to catch her breath. She hears a far-off siren.

"It's going to be okay. Help is on the way."

Wincing, Nick pats his pocket and leaves a vivid handprint of blood on his jeans. "Keys," he rasps.

"What? I'm not leaving you."

"Robert... in... danger." He reaches for her, imploring.

Hallie lifts her eyes to the blaze that's consumed the front half of the restaurant. Its fury lights the night sky, and it shows no signs of stopping. Each time she looks, she fights the urge to scream. At least the sirens sound closer now, their hysterical keening echoing her state of mind.

Nick brings her back to him with his hand on hers. As he presses his jeep's keys into her palm, he strains to speak. "Be careful."

Armed with her brand new eight-inch chef's knife, Hallie fires up Nick's jeep and guns it toward the road, spraying out gravel behind the tires. She pauses at the parking lot exit and weighs her options. Turn right and make a run for it. This is her chance to blow out of town and never look back. Turn left and risk it all to save the wrong family. The family that never belonged to her. That doesn't want her. That lied to her so many times. *Another son?*

When the fire truck crests the hill, Hallie lays on the accelerator and peels out, surprising herself. Because when the rubber hits the road, it turns out it's not a decision at all.

FIFTY

Hallie zips down Lakeshore Drive. The palatial homes and their stony gates pass by in a blur. She cuts the headlights and stops the jeep before reaching the house, hoping for the advantage of surprise.

After slipping the chef's knife into her back pocket, she treks up the slanted drive. She shudders at the sight of the dark windows, matching the night sky. The open mouth of the front door. The red bicycle, tossed on the lawn.

As she creeps up the porch steps, a sinister voice reaches her from upstairs. It's all hard edges, meant to cut deep. Still, she recognizes it in an instant.

"You owe me. Every single one of you. You let me rot in that place. Do you know how slowly eight years goes by when you have no one?"

"What did you expect, Jesse?" Though Hallie has only known Robert for two weeks, she detects a tremor of fear in his voice. It's unusual, this uncertainty. "You killed Grandpa Wallace. You killed Albert Morelli. I love you. But even now, I can hardly look at you."

Albert Morelli? So, Nick had lied to her too. Hallie has no time to register the revelations. They just keep coming like hard-hitting waves, knocking her feet from beneath her and dragging her under. It's all she can do to keep her head above water.

"Seriously, Dad? Is that the story you're sticking with? What is it going to take for you to admit the truth? *This?*"

Shelly screams. "Honey, please put the gun down."

"And you? What kind of a mother are you? You abandoned me. You cut me loose. Not one visit. Not one phone call. You didn't answer any of my letters, my cards. None of you did. Did you think you could drown me in that bottle, Mom? I floated right back up, didn't I?"

Hallie inches across the threshold and into the shadowed foyer. A creak beneath her feet stops her cold. She holds her breath, waits. Listens.

"I'm sorry, son. Your father is right. You hurt so many people. Still, there wasn't a day I didn't think about you. A night I didn't look at your baby book and cry. But we had to move on for your brother and sister's sake."

A cackle sends another shiver up Hallie's back. "Of course, your little darlings. I hate to disappoint you, Mom, but Nat and Logan aren't as innocent as they seem. Guess the apple doesn't fall far. But we'll get to all that, won't we?"

Hallie reaches the first stair, then the second, taking each one with painstaking care until she can peek above the landing on tiptoe. The sight chills her. Jesse—the man who'd introduced himself to her as Jay—stands in the center of the room with his back to her, holding the Thompsons at gunpoint. For the first time since she'd met him, his arms aren't hidden under long sleeves. A burn scar snakes its way up toward his right bicep.

Barefoot and clad in their matching Hawaiian shirts, the Thompson family sits in four dining chairs arranged in a semicircle in front of the fireplace. A cellphone mounted on a tripod faces them to capture every move. The moon casts the scene in an eerie glow.

"First, let's catch up. Shoot the breeze. Chew the fat. I can't wait to tell you what I've been up to. You'll be so proud." He paces in front of them, waving the gun like an actor in a bad movie. "So, you know I got released from the youth facility months ago. Congratulations to me. That's what happens when you turn twenty-five. They have to let you go, especially if you've been a good little inmate like me. I hitchhiked my way to Lake Tahoe and started living right under your noses. I wanted to see what you've all been up to, so I started monitoring the mail. Imagine my surprise when I found Hallie's letter in the postbox just days after Mom and Dad mailed off their DNA samples to the same company. *Dear Mr. Thompson, blah, blah, blah.* What a sob story."

Hallie squirms at Jesse's cruelly mocking tone. So different from the Jay she'd come to know.

"From there, it was a cake walk. Set up a fake email account—in Nat's name, of course. That was a clever touch, don't ya think? I never thought you'd all fall for it. But once I sent out those *you-have-a-match* messages, it took on a life of its own. I just sat back and watched the shit hit the fan."

"You used my name to defraud her?" Natalie scoffs.

"Like you care. You didn't want her here from day one. You can't stand anybody blocking your spotlight." He leans in toward Natalie, expelling a puff of laughter in her face.

She rears back as if she's been bitten.

"Can you imagine if Dad *really* had another kid? The

bitterness. The bickering. The jealousy. Sisterhood really brings out the worst in you."

To Robert, he adds, "How'd you like it? To have the rug pulled out from under you. After we all turned out to be such disappointments, you thought Hallie was the golden child. The savior of the Thompson legacy. Now, she's gone. Guess what? So is your precious restaurant. You wanted a fire, Dad? You got one."

Robert begins weeping softly. "So, it was *you?*" he manages. "The rope bridge, the slashed painting, the tires, the stolen pearls? You were targeting us this whole time. You killed Jordan too, didn't you?"

Natalie turns to Logan. "I hate to say it, but I told you so. I knew it all along. Those pranks had Jesse written all over them. Classic big brother."

Jesse screws up his face at his father. "As much as I'd like to take credit for ruining your life, I didn't murder anyone. I'd only have been doing you a favor. And I certainly didn't steal any pearls. They're a little fancy for my tastes."

Hallie pulls the knife from her pocket. She holds it in a death grip, unsure what to do with it. She tries to imagine plunging the sleek blade into Jesse's flesh. The thought of it sickens her. For all that she's done, she's no assassin.

"You're probably wondering what I want from you. It's not your money, but I'll take it before I leave to survive. It's not your love. I've learned to do without it. All I want now is honesty." He points his free hand at the cellphone. "A simple confession from each of you, recorded on my cellphone, for me to use as I see fit. Or you pay a penance."

He paces in front of them, continuing his monologue. "What is your penance? Great question. If you choose not to confess, I kill the worst offender among you. Who is it? you ask. That's for me to know and you to find out."

Laughing like a petulant teenager, Jesse presses the barrel of the gun against his mother's head. From his pocket, he withdraws a notecard and places it on her lap. Then, he takes a step back. Hallie can hardly watch the tears stream down Shelly's face.

"It starts with you, Mom. Go on, read it," says Jesse.

"'On the day before...'" Shelly sputters and chokes.

"A little louder for the camera. I can't hear you."

"'On the day before the fire, your father and I had a huge argument about the Last Glass restaurant. It had turned into a money pit that we couldn't afford, and we were hemorrhaging cash. I was furious that Robert suggested we use the last of your college fund to pay the rent. I screamed at him that we should just burn the place down. That would solve all our problems.'

"But that's not what I meant!" Shelly breaks script, hiccupping out another sob. "It was just an expression. I was frustrated, scared. I never intended—oh, honey. How could you have thought... you were just a kid."

"Hurry up." Jesse punctuates his instructions with a flick of the gun. Quietly reeling, Hallie waits for the rest of it, feeling the shock of Shelly's words like a tremor through her core.

"'When you got caught, I came to see you in juvenile hall. I told you it wouldn't be a problem. That we'd take care of it. That you were only a juvenile. That if you confessed to accidentally starting the fire, you'd receive a slap on the wrist, at worst probation. I told you I would talk to your father and make him understand. But after he refused to hire an attorney to defend you, I gave up. I accepted the insurance payout and started a brand new life without you. I...'"

Hanging her head, Shelly rasps out the last of it. "'...I did nothing but drink away my guilt. Now, I'll stop at nothing to protect my reputation. When Jordan began making threats to expose us, to contact the insurance company and tell them it was a scam, I drove to Sofia Morelli's house and intimidated her not to tell anyone about the fire, even though she can't remember what she had for breakfast.'"

The puzzle pieces start to fit together for Hallie. She remembers how Sofia had feared the arrival of the truck, had wielded a bat and rambled about Hallie threatening her and Albert.

Robert can't look away from his wife. "You threatened Sofia? After everything she's been through?"

"I didn't know what else to do. You wanted to pretend it wasn't happening. That Jordan wasn't about to betray us and take us for everything we have left."

Jesse runs a hand across his throat. "Enough, both of you. It's confession time. Nat, you're up."

Studying the card on her lap, Natalie balks. "I'm not reading this."

"Yes, you are. Unless you want to see Mom's brains splattered on the fireplace."

"I don't believe you. A pathetic little wimp like you, you don't have the guts to do it."

Jesse stalks toward Shelly, aiming the gun at the center of her forehead. Shelly squeezes her eyes shut. Hallie does the same. She grips the knife tighter, willing herself to do something. Anything.

"Please, Nat, honey. Just listen to your brother. Do what he says," Shelly whispers.

"Screw that. I don't need your stupid script." Natalie tosses the card to the ground. "Yeah, I helped you set the grease fire at Last Glass while Grandpa and Logan were baking my cake. I knew you wouldn't have the courage to follow through. That you'd mess the whole thing up. That we were one month away from the poorhouse. It's not my fault you got caught. You should've run a little faster."

"C'mon, Nat. We both know why I got caught. I went back for Grandpa. The moment I heard him scream, I knew we'd messed up. That my life was over. I had to try to save him."

"Oh, whatever. I didn't realize he was still inside. Don't make it out like I'm a psychopath."

"What about a drug dealer? Would that be an accurate characterization?"

Shelly sucks a breath through her teeth. "What is he talking about?"

Before Natalie mounts her defense, Logan springs to his feet and steps between them. "I can't stand either one of you. Always sucking up the air in the room. Did you ever stop to think about me?"

"Boo-hoo." Natalie waves a hand at him dismissively. "Poor Logan didn't get enough attention. Maybe you should've tried harder, been better. Smarter."

"Where's *my* card?" Logan demands.

Jesse shrugs, grins. Turns his pockets inside out. "I must've forgotten about you, baby brother. The same way you forgot about me. But please, enlighten us. What very bad thing did little Logan do?"

Hallie gapes at the scene that unfolds before her.

Logan springs to his feet and charges at Jesse. Chest to

chest, they face off, the gun poised between them like a ticking bomb until Logan turns to his father instead.

"I did it for you, Dad. I did it for you."

Robert's face breaks into a mixture of confusion and pain. "What did you do? *For me?*"

Logan turns away from Jesse, seemingly unafraid of the weapon at his back. "I murdered Jordan."

FIFTY-ONE

In the pin-drop silence, Hallie's blood whooshes through her ears. Her heart, throbbing. The soft moonglow from the window reveals the dirt stains on Logan's shorts. Still, Hallie never expected a spontaneous confession.

"You what?" Robert raises up too, surprising Jesse.

"Sit down, both of you." He swings the barrel of the gun from father to son. "Don't make me say it again."

"That's what it took," Logan says. "For you to notice me at all. Think about it. The night I punched Jordan, you actually paid attention. You told me I did good, gave me a pat on the back. Otherwise, I might as well be invisible."

"So you ended someone's life? You tried to frame Hallie? Nick?"

"I didn't want to involve Nick, but I had to lure Jordan to the lookout somehow. He was all too happy to meet with Chef Morelli, thinking he could steal him from under your nose. And someone had to take the fall. Who better than your new favorite? Hallie's pearls were the perfect set-up. Not so bad for the son who can't do anything right." Logan's jaw hardens, as he barks back, "Now you see me, Dad. You see me. Finally."

Hallie feels Jesse's growing frustration. It radiates from him in waves. She creeps up another two stairs, staying low, and readies herself. She can't hide here forever.

"Alright, party's over. You all lose. You didn't play by the rules, so you know what happens next. I think we all realize who's most to blame here. Don't say I didn't warn you."

As Jesse raises the gun to his father's chest, Hallie rushes up to the landing and lunges forward, grazing Jesse's arm with the Masahiro. He cries out and drops the gun. It lands hard on the floor and skitters out of reach somewhere beneath the coffee table.

Hallie falls to her knees, scrambling to find it. A strong hand grabs at her ankle, drags her back. She kicks at Jesse, landing a heel against his shoulder, and he yelps.

"*This* is your family?" she yells. It's a question. A statement. A plea.

"It's certainly not yours."

Yanking his own knife from his boot, he dives back toward her, and they grapple for position. The serrated blade narrowly misses her hand and plunges into the coffee table. He tries desperately to free it, but when she swipes the Masahiro at him, he draws back. The butt of the gun, within her reach.

"The hell it isn't," she says.

One more inch, and she'll have it. But the sharp point of Jesse's elbow connects with her nose, momentarily stunning her. Water springs to her eyes and blurs her vision.

"Watch out!" Robert yells.

Through the haze, Jesse emerges, with the gun aimed straight for her.

Hallie braces for impact. She closes her eyes, listens to the sound of her breathing. The same way she had at nine years old, staring down that tree. At sixteen, watching Edna tumble head over feet. At twenty-one, feeling the grass between her toes for the first time in years.

He pulls the trigger. A single shot cracks through the air like a whip.

FIFTY-TWO

When Hallie opens her eyes, it's all wrong. Someone screams. But it's not her. Her vital parts remain intact. A few scrapes but no bullet holes. She's still breathing, not bleeding. Her heart, still beating hard.

Jesse bolts for the staircase, gun in hand.

No one follows him.

Instead, the Thompsons huddle together on their knees beside the coffee table, stunned. The knife's blade, still half-buried in its surface. As Hallie sits up, she locates the source of the wailing. Natalie lies on the floor, clutching her hip. Shelly presses a dishtowel to the wound with one hand while summoning an ambulance with the other.

"What happened?" Hallie asks.

Robert turns to look at her with haunted eyes. "I... I don't know."

"That was your son?"

He gazes off, nodding his head. "My oldest."

Hallie springs up and runs to the window to find Jesse in

the driver's seat of Nick's jeep. She pats her pockets, searching for the keys, but comes up empty. The screech of the tires confirms it.

"He's getting away."

Hallie spins from the window, preparing to give chase. Then, she spots Logan hovering over the tripod and Jesse's cellphone. With shaky hands, he stops the recording and holds the screen up to Hallie, rewinding the footage.

"Watch," he says.

Hallie wants only to hide. Not to witness how close she'd come to joining her mother on the other side. As the video plays out the final scene of Jesse's drama, he raises the gun to a terrified Hallie with the barrel aimed squarely at her chest. But as he pulls the trigger, Natalie lunges from her seat, throwing herself in the line of fire.

"She took a bullet for you, Hallie." Logan looks as shocked as her.

"Why?" It's a stupid question, an ungrateful one. Still, she asks it anyway.

He has no reply. Instead, his gaze drifts back to the screen. His finger hovers over the tiny trashcan at the bottom.

Hallie knows what's at stake. The fire at Last Glass. Natalie's illegal side hustle. Jordan's murder. Fewer than ten minutes of footage would be enough to mar the Thompson family's legacy forever. To put Logan behind bars. To destroy Natalie's online persona. To clear her name and Nick's.

"What're you doing?"

She grabs at the phone, but he jumps back, jerking it out of her reach.

"I'm taking control of the situation. Like I did with the search. For once, I get to be the hero of this family. The capable brother. The one calling the shots."

"No. You're just saving your own ass."

"Same as you would, right?"

Logan answers for her when he deletes it all.

FIFTY-THREE

When the sirens finally arrive on the front lawn, their wailing shatters the 1 a.m. stillness. An army of officers and emergency personnel descends on the Thompsons' compound, guns drawn. They swarm into the house, dispersing through the downstairs hallway and up the steps.

"Up here!" Robert directs them from the landing.

As the paramedics load Natalie onto a stretcher, Officer Sumner surveys the chaotic scene. Chairs upended. Blood pooling onto the hardwood. Hallie imagines the stain will take some scrubbing to get out.

"What happened here?" Officer Sumner directs the question to Robert. "Who did this?"

"Our son Jesse. He was recently released from California Youth Correctional Facility. It was him all along, breaking in, vandalizing the truck, the painting. He shot Natalie and took off in Nick Morelli's jeep." Robert glances at Logan. "It's possible he killed Jordan too. Who knows what he's capable of?"

Wordlessly, Shelly follows behind her daughter,

squeezing Natalie's hand as she's carted off down the staircase to the waiting ambulance. Despite it all, Hallie staves off a wave of jealousy. She wants someone to hold *her* hand. To comfort her. Her mother was no less, no more imperfect.

Officer Sumner nods at Robert. "We've already got a potential sighting on the jeep. A motorist reported a reckless driver near Sand Harbor Park. Officers are in pursuit."

Unable to stop herself, Hallie blurts out, "Is Nick alright?"

"Nick's been transported to the hospital with a superficial gunshot wound to the flank. He should be fine."

"Shot?" Robert looks like he might be sick. "By Jesse?"

Hallie nods at him. "I found him outside the kitchen door. Jesse had already left."

"And the restaurant?"

"It's hard to say. The fire spread quickly. They'll do the best they can." Officer Sumner meets Robert's eyes, even as Robert keeps his focus on Hallie.

"Why did you come back here?" he asks her. "I was so hateful to you. I said the worst things, kicked you out on the street. You must despise me."

"You were protecting your family."

He lets out a miserable laugh. "Some protector I turned out to be. If you hadn't shown up, I don't know what would've happened."

Officer Sumner clears his throat, a pointed interruption. "This may not be the time, Ms. Sherman, but it's my duty to advise you that I've become aware of your warrant and your connection to my brother. Word travels fast in a town like this."

At least he hadn't mentioned Jordan's murder. "Are you going to arrest me?"

"I can't. We're obviously well outside of Sacramento County, and your warrant isn't extraditable. But I'm giving you thirty days to take care of it. If you don't, I'll put you in the backseat of my patrol car and drive you across county lines myself. I'll be sure there's a deputy waiting for you."

"Now, wait just a minute, Jimmy." Robert steps in to defend her. "That's illegal, and you know it."

Hallie shakes her head. "It's okay, Robert. I'm ready to face the music." To Officer Sumner, she adds, "I'll take you up on that ride. You have my word. But there's something I have to do first."

Three hours later, Hallie reluctantly makes her way into the bowels of Incline Village Community Hospital, towing her suitcase behind her. Fortunately, the bag and the rest of her Masahiro knives had been rescued by a member of the fire department. When Robert had taken her to retrieve it, they'd both sat in his truck, speechless, staring at the charred remains of Cerulean. The front half of the restaurant was a total loss. The kitchen remained intact, saved by the sprinkler system.

Hallie hates hospitals. The antiseptic smell, the constant beeping and whirring. It conjures the past as surely as a séance, and she walks the hall with caution, averting her eyes from every open doorway for fear of seeing her mother half-dead with a machine breathing for her.

At the front desk, she's directed to room 322 where she finds Nick dozing. He blinks awake. Attempts a lopsided smile.

"How are you feeling?" she asks.

"Been better."

Steeling herself, Hallie pulls up a plastic chair and takes a seat. She quickly glances at the IV in his arm and the thick bandage affixed to his side and tells herself to keep her eyes on Nick's face, which looks no worse for wear. She smiles at him.

"My victory was a real blow, then?"

"That and the fire. The Thompsons' crazy son. The gunshot wound. My stolen jeep."

"Oh, yeah. *That.*" Hallie unzips the suitcase and reaches inside. Then, she sets a stack of bills on the bedside table. "This might ease the sting."

That gets Nick riled. He tries to sit up straighter, to talk louder, but he sputters out quick like a tired old engine. "I told you I won't accept half of your prize money. You deserve it, especially now."

"Well, it's not half. It's all for you and your mom. With the shape the restaurant is in, you might be out of work for a while. I don't want you to have to worry."

"But what are you going to do for money?"

She shrugs. "I'll make do. Same as ever. I'm sure there's a two-bit diner looking for an award-winning chef. Besides, I might have to spend a little time in jail for the thing in Sacramento, so..."

Nick doesn't argue. She's glad he doesn't press the issue of her impending arrest.

"There's something I need to tell you," he begins, wincing with the effort. "About my dad. I tried to tell you that night at The Grotto but..."

Hallie allows him to continue. She wants to hear it from him.

"I wasn't exactly truthful with you when you asked if my dad died in a fire. He was there that day at Last Glass, working as a handyman in the back office near the kitchen. Robert's father tried to get to him, to warn him, but it was too late. He suffered severe burns in the fire and contracted sepsis. Our lives were never the same after that."

"Why didn't you tell me?"

"I tried. I thought if I dropped a hint about the fire, you'd figure it out." On the monitor, the steady beep of Nick's heart quickens, then slows as he takes a breath. "Not telling was a condition of my employment. Robert asked me to sign a non-disclosure agreement. He was afraid that if word got out, it would tank the restaurant. I warned him that you'd learn the truth eventually, but he stubbornly refused to tell you. After what happened with your mom and how guilty he felt, I'm pretty sure he was hoping you'd think he was the perfect father."

"He was." Hallie reconsiders. "I wanted to believe he was."

After a brief knock, Logan appears in the doorway. Hallie searches his face for the traces of a killer. For the kind of coldness it takes to bludgeon a man with a rock and push him off a cliff. She finds only the cleft chin he inherited from his father and a smattering of stubble.

"Natalie is stable," he says. "Which basically means she's back to being herself. A spoiled brat. She's already uploaded a couple of videos about the shooting. Fair warning, Hallie, she's claiming online that you two were as thick as thieves. That she considers you a sister, even now, knowing the truth. That you aren't our biological relative."

"Of course she does." Hallie can only shake her head. A laugh spills out of her, unbidden, as she realizes that Natalie must fear her now that she knows all the Thompson family secrets. "And Jesse?" she asks gingerly, dreading the answer.

No matter what, he won't surrender willingly. He won't go back to prison. He'd told her as much.

"They found the jeep submerged in the lake. From what they could tell, he lost control near Sand Harbor and drove off the cliff. There's no sign of a body, but the police don't think he could've survived the fall."

"I'm sorry. I know the two of you were close as kids. He was the one in your story, right? About the Narrows hike?"

"Yeah. Growing up, Jesse was my hero. I was always tagging along behind him. We even won a few survival contests together, mostly in spite of me." He lowers his eyes.

Hallie almost feels sorry for him.

"In spite of everything he did, I would kill to have him back."

Hallie steps into the postcard blue of the morning. She wheels her suitcase toward the waiting patrol car and climbs inside. She rolls down her window and inhales the last breaths of lake air. Who knows if she'll ever be back this way again?

Once they pass the sign for Kings Beach, she summons her courage. "Am I still a suspect in the Markum murder?"

Officer Sumner shakes his head. "If you were, we wouldn't be making this drive."

"Then you know who did it? *How?*" She thinks of the unmarked grave in The Grotto. Of the confession Logan made to his family, then deleted.

"Forensics on the rock came back this morning." He meets her eyes in the rearview. "Fingerprints on the murder weapon don't lie."

EPILOGUE

TWO MONTHS LATER

Monday dinner service is packed. The dining room buzzes with laughter, the kitchen with the clatter of busy cooks. There's a line out the door that wraps around the block of Fern Street in downtown Sacramento. Word has gotten out about Hallie's menu. Tonight's special, beef stew. She prepares a taste from the industrial-sized pot and offers it to her sous chef, Ernie.

"That's mighty good, Hallie. The folks are gonna eat like kings tonight." It's no Michelin star but that's okay. She's cooking for the love of it. And she still needs twenty more hours of community service here at Midtown Homeless Shelter kitchen to be square with the law. A small price to pay for not looking over her shoulder.

Ernie wheels himself to the station beside her, where he'll dole out the fresh sourdough bread she prepared. The volunteer assembly line stretches the length of the kitchen and ends at desserts, where the chocolate chip cookies are certainly not vegan.

Hallie falls into a steady rhythm, serving her stew with a

smile and a side of friendly conversation. When she looks into the eyes of the next client, she drops the ladle into the pot. It sends up a splatter of gravy onto her apron.

"Hi, Hallie." Robert waits in front of her, offering his bowl to be filled.

She struggles to find the right words, any words, but comes up empty. It's been two months since the fire. In that time, all that she'd heard of the Thompsons came through her phone calls with Nick. Logan's arrest. The rebuilding of the restaurant. Shelly's attendance at Alcoholics Anonymous. And Natalie's sudden Internet fame. She'd finally gone viral, telling the world the story of her heroism. Of how she'd risked her life for the girl who wasn't even her flesh and blood. Showing off the jagged scar on her abdomen, she'd seamlessly transitioned to her new platform of body positivity. One night, Hallie had asked Nick, *Would Nat take a bullet so she could post about it on the Internet?* After a moment's pause, they'd both answered her question. *Definitely.*

"It's good to see you." Robert manages a sad smile. "Are you still looking for your dad?"

All the old feelings rise to the surface. "My Family Ties account is still active, and I've received a few more responses to my letters. But I realized that what I've been searching for isn't a person, it's a feeling. A feeling of belonging. I have to find that for myself."

"I get it. I'm looking for that too. I still have that pebble of yours, ya know." Teary-eyed, he glances back at the line of hungry patrons behind him. "Can you take a quick break?"

Hallie waves over her back-up server and skirts out from the kitchen. She follows Robert to an empty table on the periphery and takes the folding chair across from him.

"I know you're busy, so I'll make it quick. I wanted to say I'm sorry. Truly sorry. For all of it. I dragged you into our mess. I should've known how it would turn out. But I really believed you were mine."

"I believed it too," she admits. "I convinced myself, even when the details weren't adding up. My mom was no cook. Her idea of a gourmet meal was Rice-A-Roni. And she absolutely hated being called Lizzie. Sometimes I did it, just to tick her off."

They share a laugh until Robert's face turns serious again. "I suppose I thought taking you in could somehow make up for what happened with Jesse."

"Didn't you ever think of reaching out to him? Eight years is a long time."

"Every day. What can I say? I'm a stubborn fool. I couldn't see past what I lost. He was just sixteen when it happened. A kid. Too young to predict the consequences. He and Nat did exactly what I'd always asked of my children. Put the family first. And I threw him away. I'll always regret that. That's why I'm standing by Logan. I'll be there in his corner, no matter what he did. No matter the outcome or how it looks to everybody else. The same goes for Nat. My kids aren't perfect, but hell, neither am I. I don't want to have any more regrets."

Robert slips a folded paper from his pocket and lays it on the table. At the top, it reads: *Application: Executive Chef, Cerulean Restaurant.* "I hope you'll give me and the family a second chance. I know you're rebuilding a life here. And I realize I'm not your real father. But there's a place for you in Incline Village. We're planning to relaunch the restaurant in the spring and, with Nick opening his own spot, we'll need a head chef. I hoped you might know someone."

Hallie recalls the two weeks she spent in Incline Village. Of all the ways it went horribly wrong and still could. Even so, she can't disguise the hopefulness in her voice. "I'll think about it."

On wobbly legs, Hallie leaves Robert at the table and returns to her station. She ladles another heaping portion of stew and readies it for the next client.

Ernie sidles up to her. "You okay?"

"Yeah. I will be."

"Good. 'Cause somebody in line left somethin' for ya. He said to tell you that you can never be too careful when it comes to bears. Didn't make much sense to me, but... what do I know?"

Hallie looks down at the table. Next to the steaming pot sits a bright red can of bear spray.

Panic rises in her throat, and she clings to the edge of the table like a life raft. Heart racing, she scans the busy dining room. A slim figure in a hoodie cuts through the crowd and slips out the front door, leaving it open. She clutches her chest, feeling the quick push and pull of her lungs, and squeezes her eyes shut, trying to make sense of it all.

Ernie gives her a nudge. "Is everything alright?"

When she opens her eyes, it's easy to pretend nothing happened. But the pricked hairs on her neck tell her otherwise. "I think I just saw a ghost."

He frowns at her, then smacks his fist against his hand. "If you need me to knock some heads around, just say the word."

Hallie cocks her head at him, grateful for a friend who can make her smile in the face of sheer terror. *"Ernie."*

"Hey, don't underestimate a guy in a chair. I've got a

helluva strong upper body and two wheels that'll roll right over a fella."

"It's okay. Whoever he was, he was just checking things out. He wasn't gonna hurt me." As she measures out the words, they ring true.

"How do you know?"

Through the door, Hallie glimpses a section of the sky. Today, it's as crystal blue as Lake Tahoe. "Because he didn't."

With another successful dinner service on the books, Hallie finds herself back where she started, washing pots and pans in the shelter's kitchen. She'd sent Ernie and the other volunteers home, content to tackle the overflowing sink herself. As she scrubs, her mind wanders to the usual places. To Robert and the twisted family she'd stumbled into. To Nick and the possibilities slowly blossoming between them. To her mother and the pearls that had arrived in a padded envelope from the Washoe County Sheriff's evidence room. Hallie had immediately sold them, donating the proceeds to a local drug rehab. She'd like to think her mom would've wanted it that way.

When her phone buzzes in her pocket, notifying her of a new email, Hallie towels off her wet hands and studies the screen. Her heart takes off again with a life of its own. It all feels too familiar, too scary.

We are pleased to inform you that our ancestry team has identified a first-degree paternal match for your DNA sample.

She checks the email address to be certain this time. For a

moment, her finger toggles between the link and the delete icon, as she thinks of all the Dear Robert Thompson letters she sent and all the strange, tragic, angry, hopeful replies she received. Of all the stern warnings her mother had issued about the man who shares her DNA.

Her decision made, she returns to the sink to occupy her mind. Luckily, there are enough dishes here to last all night.

A LETTER FROM ELLERY KANE

Want to keep up to date with my latest releases? Sign up here! We promise never to share your email with anyone else, we'll only contact you when there's a new book available, and you can unsubscribe at any time.

www.bookouture.com/ellery-kane

Thank you for reading *The Wrong Family*! With so many amazing books out there, I am honored you chose to add mine to your library.

One of my favorite parts about being an author is connecting with readers like you. You can get in touch with me through any of the social media outlets below, including my website and Goodreads page. Also, if you wouldn't mind leaving a review or recommending *The Wrong Family* to your favorite readers, I would really appreciate it! Reviews and word-of-mouth recommendations are essential, because they help readers like you discover my books.

Thank you again for selecting *The Wrong Family*! I look forward to bringing you many more thrills, chills, and sleepless nights.

KEEP IN TOUCH WITH ELLERY KANE

www.ellerykane.com

facebook.com/TheLegacyBooks
twitter.com/ellerykane
goodreads.com/ellerykane

ACKNOWLEDGMENTS

Years ago, I spit into a small test tube and mailed off my sample to a DNA company very much like Family Ties. Weeks later, I learned that I am likely to have detached earlobes, few freckles, and a longer big toe. I am more likely to be afraid of heights; more likely to experience motion sickness; and more likely to be bitten by mosquitos. All true, by the way. Though my results did not reveal any long-lost relatives or end me up in the middle of a twisted family drama, the entire process left me wondering, *what if?* For an author, that dangerous little question usually leads to a story, and I hope you've enjoyed this one.

I owe a tremendous debt of gratitude to you, my avid readers, for joining me on my writing adventure. Hearing that my words have impacted you is a little bit of magic, and knowing that my stories have a special place in your heart makes it all worthwhile. A special thanks to Ellery's Entourage, whose members go above and beyond in supporting my work!

I am fortunate to have a fabulous team of family, friends, and work colleagues who have always been there to support and encourage me on this journey. Though my mom is no longer with me, she gifted me her love for writing, and I know she's cheering me on even though I can't see her. Thanks, too, to my dad, who's never been a reader but thinks I'm brilliant anyway.

To Gar, my special someone and partner in crime, thank you for patching all my plot holes without complaint; for cheering me on when I need it most; and for championing my dreams as much (and sometimes more) than I do. I know you don't believe me, but I couldn't do any of this without you.

I have been unbelievably fortunate to be matched with a fantastic new editor, Lucy Frederick, and a fantastic publisher, Bookouture, who truly value their authors and work tirelessly for our success. It's been a pleasure to team up with Lucy and the entire Bookouture family, including Kim, Noelle, Jess, and Sarah, who have worked so hard to spread the word about my books.

Lastly, I have always drawn inspiration for my writing from my day job as a forensic psychologist. We all have a space inside us that we keep hidden from the world, a space we protect at all costs. So many people have allowed me a glimpse inside theirs—dark deeds, memories best unrecalled, pain that cracks from the inside out—without expectation of anything in return. I couldn't have written a single word without them.

Printed in Great Britain
by Amazon